". . . I ate it up. I read the novel in a single sitting and enjoyed it entirely . . . Baker's characters are solid and believable, with real personalities and personal stories. The story is a compelling mystery with a hard edge. It's a fun, fast-paced adventure with interesting characters and setting, and enough grit and dark tone for me to take it seriously."

—*SF Site*

". . . Baker has a deft hand for teasing out the plot, wrapping up one story with blazing action while leaving other stories—and other conflicts—waiting for the sequel. *The City of Towers* is a great lead-in to The Dreaming Dark trilogy and to Eberron as a whole."

—*Black Gate Magazine*

The exciting saga of The Dreaming Dark begun in *The City of Towers* concludes.

To prevent a long-banished race from unleashing the ultimate horror upon the waking world, Daine and his companions will have to break through the boundaries of the world itself, to brave the fey realms of Twilight and Shadow. Their ultimate goal: the nightmare-haunted realm of Dal Quor. But first, they must cross a perilous realm where they are hunted, where every shadow holds the secrets of their past, where the only way out is through . . .

. . . The Gates of Night!

THE
DREAMING DARK

THE GATES OF NIGHT

THE DREAMING DARK
BOOK 3

KEITH BAKER

THE GATES OF NIGHT

©2006 Wizards of the Coast, Inc.

Cover art by Mark Zug
Map by Rob Lazzaretti
First Printing: November 2006
Library of Congress Catalog Card Number: 2005935542

9 8 7 6 5 4 3 2 1

ISBN-10: 0-7869-4013-1
ISBN-13: 978-0-7869-4013-4
620-95541740-001-EN

U.S., CANADA,	EUROPEAN HEADQUARTERS
ASIA, PACIFIC, & LATIN AMERICA	Hasbro UK Ltd
Wizards of the Coast, Inc.	Caswell Way
P.O. Box 707	Newport, Gwent NP9 0YH
Renton, WA 98057-0707	GREAT BRITAIN
+1-800-324-6496	Save this address for your records.

Visit our web site at www.wizards.com

DEDICATION

To Lee Moyer, a shaper of dreams.

•

Laraek ixen korth," the dwarf whispered, tracing his fingers along the edge of the metal disk. Runes etched into the steel burned with blue fire. The light faded, and as it did, the disk became blurry and indistinct, almost invisible against the stone floor. The dwarf took two careful steps back, slipping down the hall. He glanced up at Daine and gave a curt nod. If the disk were triggered, it would collapse the tunnel, which appeared to be the only entrance into this mysterious outpost.

Daine didn't relish the thought of being trapped below, but the odds of surviving the night had never been good. Whatever this facility was, it posed a clear threat to the people of Cyre. Daine intended to cripple the base. If he and his soldiers could complete this mission and escape, all the better. If not, collapsing the entrance would have to do. At least it would buy Daine's messenger time to warn the garrison at Casalon.

"It was a good plan, I'll give you that."

The sudden sound was a shock. No guards were in sight, but silence was clearly called for. Daine turned and glared at Jode.

1

"I ordered you to scout ahead," Daine whispered.

Jode shook his head. "Daine, it's time to wake up."

And with those words, memory returned—visions of another battle.

A kalashtar woman wreathed in shadows . . .

Lei stretched across a stone dais, surrounded by pieces of glowing crystal . . .

Betrayal . . .

And a rushing, hissing voice, demanding a vial of blue liquid . . .

Daine lowered his sword until the point was level with the halfling's heart. "Who are you? Lakashtai? Or Tashana?"

"You know who I am."

Cold fury gripped Daine's heart. *"Enough!* I've had enough of your games."

"I know what you've been through," Jode said. "I can imagine how hard this is for you. But it's over now. Let me show you."

Jode held out his hand, but Daine felt only anger. He was still piecing it together, but it was clear that Lakashtai had been manipulating him for weeks. Possibly months. She'd used his feelings for Lei against him, and now this. Daine slapped the halfling's hand aside with the flat of his sword.

The little man winced but held his ground. "Not exactly the joyous reunion I had hoped for." A drop of blood blossomed on one finger, and he sighed. "Daine, you know the truth, even if you don't want to see it. I need you to trust me. One more time."

Daine studied his old friend's eyes, searching for any signs of deception. More memories flashed through his mind.

Jode on the streets of Metrol, surrounded by tattooed men . . .

The halfling's body, lying in a charnel pit beneath Sharn . . .

Cursing himself, Daine reached out and took the halfling's hand.

For a moment Daine was blinded, overwhelmed by sensations. The world seemed to collapse, his vision rising up from the base to look out over Keldan Ridge. He could see every detail with crystal clarity. He knew the position of every shattered warforged, of every Cyran corpse. And he knew it was a dream. He could sense the boundaries of the battlefield, how it faded away just beyond the range of sight, a silver bubble, floating in darkness.

The darkness was alive, and it saw him.

Terror flowed through Daine. He couldn't even see the spirit that lurked in the shadows, but he could *feel* it—a cold giant reaching out to crush his tiny dreamscape. He felt icy tendrils clutch at his heart. But he could feel something else. A source of light and warmth. A force adding its strength to his.

Jode.

Daine felt his friend's laughter flow through him, along with a flow of memories.

Flying through the air astride a huge, birdlike reptile, a barren plain stretched out beneath him . . .

Daine and Jode's first meeting in Metrol, now seen from Jode's eyes . . .

And a ghastly purple face, with a ring of writhing tentacles reaching toward him. The mind flayer beneath Sharn, the last thing Jode had seen while alive . . .

There was no longer any doubt in Daine's mind. This was Jode, and the frigid darkness shattered against the two united minds.

Then he was back in the tunnel, staring at the face of his friend. Behind him, Krazhal and Kesht stood frozen. With his newfound senses, Daine could sense that they were empty, fragments drawn from his memory—as was the hall itself. But Jode . . .

Daine forgot about the darkness, about Lakashtai, about any of it. His sword slipped from his fingers as he moved forward and grabbed Jode around his shoulders, lifting him into the air.

"I know, I know," Jode said with a grin. "It's the miracle of me."

"How is this possible?"

"You think I know? Out of the two of us, who's been dead?"

"But you said you knew what I'd been through—"

Jode grinned. "And you've never known me to embellish the truth? After I was caught by Teral, everything sort of . . . fades. Every now and then I'd catch glimpses of the three of you or hear you talking to me. Occasionally your dreams—this place—would flash into view, and I could see the creature you were fighting, but I couldn't reach you. Then everything changed. I was here, and I could feel your thoughts."

Daine set the halfling down. "And how did you know what would happen when we touched?"

"It's a dream. Sometimes you just know things in dreams."

A chill ran down Daine's spine, the force watching in the darkness. He could still feel it out there, watching, probing his defenses. But even though they were no longer touching, he could still feel Jode's strength. He wasn't alone anymore. And whatever force had been fighting him before, it couldn't overcome them both.

"So tell me what I've missed!" Jode said. "I can see . . . an ocean voyage? A wall of fire? I want details. And how are Lei and Pierce?"

Lei! In the chaos of the dream, Daine had almost forgotten the battle he'd left behind. "There's no time. They're both in terrible danger. If this is a dream, we need to wake up. Now."

Jode shrugged. "It's your dream. That's your job."

Daine closed his eyes, then opened them quickly. Nothing.

"Dorn's teeth!" he swore, smashing his fist against the wall. Pain and numbness lanced across his nerves, but his surroundings never wavered. Helpless anger burned in Daine's heart. He glanced back down the tunnel, searching for the concealed blast disk.

"I wouldn't," Jode said, responding to Daine's unspoken thought. "I don't know what death would do to us, but if Lei's really in trouble, do you think that's the first thing you should try?"

"What else can I do?"

"Be calm," Jode said. "Remember this is a dream. *Your* dream. Close your eyes and take my hand."

Fighting against his raging emotions, Daine blew out his breath and reached out for the halfling's hand.

Wake up.

And he did.

⊛ ⊛ ⊛ ⊚ ⊛ ⊛ ⊛

Daine, Harmattan said, his voice a thunderous hiss, metal grinding in a great wind that seemed to come from all directions. *It's been a long time.*

Harmattan stood in the room's sole entrance. At first glance, he seemed a massive man in a flowing cloak—easily nine feet tall, with muscles to rival an ogre's. Metal glittered across his body, as if he were covered in chainmail. Even his cloak seemed forged from metal

5

links. Dark mist shrouded his head. Points of red light hinted at eyes within the shadow.

Pierce had seen Harmattan in action and knew that his appearance was deceiving. Harmattan was not wearing chainmail, and he was no man. As Pierce looked at Harmattan again, new thoughts flowed into his mind—

A web of magical force binds the metal fragments together. This energy is concentrated in Harmattan's head. The rest of his body is thus both malleable and expendable. A sufficient burst of abjurative energy could temporarily dispel the force holding his body together. However, this web is extremely powerful, and such an effort would be unlikely to succeed.

As an afterthought—

Your previous encounter suggests that Harmattan was once a warforged soldier and only discovered his full power after his original body was destroyed.

These seemed to be Pierce's own thoughts, a natural stream of consciousness in response to Harmattan's arrival. They weren't. Another force was sharing Pierce's body—an ancient intelligence named Shira that had been imprisoned for tens of thousands of years. Pierce wished to know much about the entity that called itself Shira, but this was not the time for questions. Daine had his blades drawn and strode toward Harmattan. Pierce had seen the strange warforged scour flesh from bone in a blur of razor-sharp shards, and he knew that Harmattan wouldn't hesitate to kill a human.

Pierce lunged forward, his flail spinning in a low arc. He had little experience with shame, but he felt a pang of guilt as he pulled back, dragging his surprised opponent to the ground.

"This fight cannot be won with a sword, Captain."

Pierce said. "Others need you. Do not throw away your life."

Daine glared up from the floor, fury burning in his eyes. A vibration ran through Harmattan's metal form—the rustling that served him as laughter—and Pierce saw drops of blood scatter to the ground. While he regretted having struck his friend, Pierce knew that it could easily have been Daine's blood on the floor.

If you think you can win my trust so easily, you are mistaken, little brother, Harmattan said.

"Indeed." It was a soft, feminine voice, all too familiar.

Warforged. The analysis came unbidden to Pierce's mind. *An unusual design, sacrificing durability for speed. Mithral plating with stealth glamer; improved visual acuity, allowing optimal accuracy even in conditions of darkness. Embedded . . .*

The mystical analysis continued, but it was drowned out by Pierce's own thoughts as the newcomer came into view. Slender, graceful, her mithral plates coated with deep blue enamel. Blades of dark metal extended from her forearms.

Indigo.

Pierce had felt a touch of guilt when he pulled Daine to the ground. Now it was a hammer, slamming against his spirit. He remembered the joy he'd felt fighting alongside her—mere moments before he tried to bury her and Harmattan by collapsing an unstable tunnel.

Indigo stood beside Harmattan, blocking any escape. Her face was a mask of blue metal, but Pierce could hear the anger in her words. "You made your choice, Pierce. You chose your masters. Now you will die with them."

Shame rose again, but Pierce countered it with the memory of Harmattan ordering his minions to torture

Lei. Pierce had indeed made his choice. Whatever bond he felt for Indigo, he had his own family to protect.

"You did not come this far to threaten me," Pierce said, helping Daine to his feet.

You are irrelevant, Harmattan said. *Despite Indigo's wishes, I think I shall let you live. Our family is small enough as it is. But you have already served your purpose. Your passage gave us entry. And as for why we are here . . . it seems I was mistaken, after all. Destiny is a strange thing.*

"What do you want?" Daine growled.

I came here in search of one thing alone. I knew that it was waiting for me in this ancient place, so I assumed it to be a relic of the distant past. But the one I serve leads me down paths I never considered. I want the vial.

Vial? This meant nothing to Pierce. "What are you talking about?"

He knows, Harmattan said, looking at Daine. *A vial filled with blue liquid, glowing slightly, with a familiar seal stamped on the top.* His cloak spread out around him, and at this distance it was easy to see it clearly—a rippling plane of metal shards. One thought, and this mass of razors would tear through them. *I have no desire to damage it, and I would rather let my brother live. But you will all die if we battle. Give me the vial, little fleshling, and I may even spare you and sister Lei.*

"Daine?" None of this made sense. But Pierce knew his captain. Daine was deep in thought. Clearly he knew what Harmattan was talking about.

Daine reached into his pouch and produced a tiny bottle—a sliver of crystal, pulsing with blue light. "Is this it?"

Yes.

"You came all the way to Xen'drik, you cut off Lei's finger, for *this?*"

Yes. Surrender it.

"No," Daine said, wrenching the stopper from the vial.

Harmattan hissed, and Indigo leaped forward in a blur of dark steel. Pierce was already in motion. A human might have been holding his breath or praying for a peaceful resolution, but Pierce had neither breath nor faith. While Daine was considering Harmattan's offer, Pierce was calculating Indigo's likely path of attack. He rammed into her, and she staggered back.

Indigo's gaze remained on Daine. "No! You must not!"

Pierce followed her gaze. Daine raised the vial and drank the liquid. Pierce leaped out of the path of Indigo's counterattack, half his attention still on Daine.

Daine collapsed.

NO! Harmattan's voice filled the chamber, a howl as terrible as any storm. *This cannot be!*

Pierce took a step back and stood over Daine. He could not defeat Harmattan. He knew that. But if he were to die, he would die with his captain.

This was DESTINED! Harmattan roared. His cloak dissolved into a whirling sheath of steel, a storm reflecting his inner fury. *This place. The vial. All has come to pass!*

"If our destiny is to leave with the liquid," Indigo said, her soft voice almost lost beneath Harmattan's rage, "then let us reclaim it from his body."

"No." Pierce held his ground, and Shira's thoughts converged with his own—

Harmattan is at a disadvantage here. He cannot unleash his full power without inflicting grievous injuries. If they seek to harvest Daine's bodily fluids, they will need to act with precision. And he has been reluctant to kill you.

It was the only weapon that might prove effective against Harmattan.

"Brother," he said, "this battle is over. Whatever

9

that liquid was, it is lost to you. I will not allow you to perform this ghoul's work. If you continue down this path, you will have to destroy me."

Harmattan said nothing. The storm of steel surrounding him slowed, drifting back into the shape of the billowing cloak. When he spoke again his voice was calm.

If that is what it takes.

Indigo lunged at Pierce.

It wasn't a battle but a dream. Pierce had spent hours contemplating her fighting style, considering her strengths and weaknesses, the tactics he'd seen her use. He knew exactly what she would do, and he was prepared for her.

But she was equally prepared for Pierce.

It was like fighting the wind. He tried to trip her, but she jumped over the blow. He had the advantage of reach, and he mirrored her motion. Blows that could split steel missed him by less than an inch. It was a deadly dance, yet Pierce had never felt so calm, so perfectly at peace. He didn't need to think. He *knew* what to do.

He knew that Indigo felt the same way. In the first blows of the battle, anger had driven her. She'd struck with less care. Perhaps, if he'd been more ruthless, Pierce could have brought her down in those first moments. But now she was as calm as he. The battle became a tapestry of motion and strategy, and just being part of it . . . it was what they were made for. Pierce could continue for days, and he could think of nothing that would be more satisfying. Indigo was his world. Every sense focused on their dance.

And that was his mistake.

Pierce leaped back a step, narrowly avoiding a fierce double blow that could have decapitated him. He was beginning his counterstroke when he felt a crushing pressure around his arms and chest.

Harmattan.

The strange warforged couldn't unleash his full might without shredding Daine, but even in his humanoid form his strength was astonishing. Pierce had been so focused on Indigo that he hadn't seen Harmattan move behind him. Now he was bound by metal and magic. For all that Harmattan's body comprised fragments of metal, the force that held them together was tougher than any steel. Harmattan's arms flowed together around Pierce's chest, creating an unbreakable band. Pierce's flail was half-caught in the metal mass, the chain dangling beyond. Indigo swept forward. Her adamantine blades flashed, and the flail fell apart, steel chain split as easily as rope. She took another step forward, a blade leveled at his eyes.

This ends, brother.

When Harmattan spoke, Pierce could feel the vibration. He struggled against his bonds, but his strength was no match for Harmattan's power.

"So it would appear."

"Why?" Indigo said. Pierce could no longer hear any anger in her voice. Just disappointment. "Why did you turn on us?"

"I did not want to."

"You destroyed Hydra. I could have died as well. And for what? These bags of flesh and blood? They will be dead in a handful of years, at best. We have eternity."

Yes. Think, little brother. You have nothing in common with these creatures.

"I have memories. I have friendship. Can you say the

11

same?" A thought occurred to him, as the spirit embedded in his chest passed along a piece of information.

"Is there nothing between us?" Indigo's blade hadn't wavered, the point an inch from his eyes.

Pierce searched for words. "In truth," he said, "I do not know what I feel. But I know I must protect my family."

We are your family, said Harmattan.

"Perhaps you are. But you are forgetting something."

And what is that?

"Our sister."

Indigo's gaze flickered to the side—

Too late.

Harmattan shattered into a thousand pieces, and Pierce lunged.

CHAPTER 2

Lei was cold. Every nerve numb. It took all her energy to open her eyes, and when she did, her surroundings were blurred and distorted. She could hear distant sounds, but she couldn't make sense of them or muster the strength to turn her head.

Memory trickled back through her mind. Crystals. Shards of crystal. A woman had given Lei a shattered object . . . pieces of a crystal sphere. When Lei touched it, a doorway had opened in her mind. She could *feel* the pattern within the sphere, *feel* its great age. The woman whispered to Lei, urging her to mend the broken pattern, and her voice was impossible to resist. Lei *knew* what had to be done. She felt as if she'd always known. She could see the proper pattern in her mind. She *knew* how to repair the damage. And at the urging of the voice, she had done just that. But it had taken so much energy— more than she had to give. She could see a network of light take shape as the crystal shards fused, the true shape emerging from the ruin. But as the pattern became clearer, her surroundings blurred. Thought became muddled. The only thing that mattered was repairing the damage. And as the last piece fell into place, everything else faded.

Sensation was returning. Lei flexed her fingers. Something felt wrong with her grip. Feeling returned to her arms, her legs. She was lying on a hard, cold platform. She heard metal scraping against stone. She turned her head to face the noise.

Pierce leaped into view. He was fighting another warforged—a smaller, slender figure who lashed at Pierce with twin blades. The two seemed well-matched, and their deadly dance distracted Lei. Then Harmattan bound Pierce with a coil of metal, and the battle came to an end.

The sight of Harmattan was a shock. Images flashed through her mind—

Harmattan ordering his minions to torture her.

Harmattan surviving a powerful blast of electricity, reforming after a hole was punched right through his torso.

Harmattan transforming into a storm of razor-edged steel, scouring the flesh from a pack of predators in the blink of an eye.

Lei blinked. The warforged were speaking, but there was no time to listen. Pierce needed her. There had to be an answer. Physical force was useless against Harmattan. He could reform from any injury. His body wasn't a body at all. It was a mass of shards held together by magical force.

Held together by magical force.

No time to waste. Lei visualized a pattern in her mind and traced it on the palm of her left glove. As exhausted as she was, she found a last ember of energy within her, just enough power to complete the ritual.

The warforged hadn't noticed her. The blue warrior had one of her blades leveled at Pierce's face, the threat unmistakable. Offering a prayer to Onatar, Lei clenched her fist and made a swift throwing motion.

Only the faintest ripple in the air marked the passage of the energy she'd released—until it struck Harmattan.

Agony tore through Lei. She'd woven a charm of abjuration into her gauntlet, a burst of power that could shatter other spells. During the War she'd used this technique to counter the arcane blasts of enemy sorcerers. But she'd never touched such a powerful force. It was as if she'd tried to snuff a candle with her fingers and found her hand in a bonfire. Dousing this flame seemed impossible, and every instant the pain grew. But she wouldn't let go. She remembered Harmattan's mocking words, the pain as his servant Hydra cut off her finger, and she clung to that rage, using it as a pillar against the pain.

Harmattan shattered, as if a figure formed of sand struck by a mighty gust of wind: His body dissolved, scattering mirror-bright shards across the floor.

Indigo responded instantly. As Lei struggled to her feet, the warforged assassin was already turning toward her. Under normal circumstances, Lei's powers might have proved a match for this foe; she had destroyed one of the warrior Hydra's bodies earlier in the day. But she was drained. The attack on Harmattan had used her last reserves, and she didn't have the energy to fuel any form of artifice. In her current state, a battle with Indigo would be brief and unpleasant.

But even as Indigo turned to face Lei, there was a flash of metal and the warforged tumbled to the ground.

Pierce!

Freed from Harmattan's grasp, Pierce brought Indigo down with a well-placed kick. Lei felt a wave of relief—but it soon turned to fear. Indigo regained her feet, and the warforged fought in earnest. Pierce lost his flail, and with Harmattan's fall Indigo fought more fiercely than before. Lei winced as a well-placed thrust sheared through Pierce's left shoulder. For a creature of flesh and blood the wound might have been mortal, but Pierce continued the fight. Nonetheless, the outcome wasn't in doubt. Weaponless, Pierce could slow Indigo but not stop her.

"Run, my lady!" he said as he dodged another blow. "Take Daine and go!"

Indigo hissed in fury, and her next blow shaved a layer of mithral from Pierce's chest.

I'm not leaving you to her, Lei thought. She reached into her satchel, the magical bag that held her gear. She was too weak to wield her staff, but there had to be something . . .

There. Her fingers found a long wand. She smiled, drawing the weapon. It might have proven useless against Harmattan, but Lei had a hunch that Indigo wasn't so durable.

Unfortunately, what Indigo lacked in armor, she made up for in speed. Indigo danced around Pierce, never staying in one place for more than a second, and the last thing Lei wanted to do was hit Pierce.

Now!

Pierce pulled back, and there was a boom of thunder as Lei released the lightning bound in the wand. The energy lit the chamber with a brilliant burst of light—but when Lei's vision cleared, Indigo still stood. The warforged had completely evaded the bolt of energy. She charged at Lei, her black blades spread like wings, ready to shear through flesh and bone. And Pierce was too far away to help her.

A chill ran through Lei's heart. Her instincts screamed *flee*, but the warforged was faster than she was—and there was nowhere to run. There was only one chance. As Indigo swept toward her, Lei steeled her nerves, raised her wand, and released the final charge of energy.

This time the bolt caught the warforged squarely in the chest. Indigo staggered backward, arcs of electricity crackling around her limbs. The blue enamel of her torso blackened and scorched, but she remained on her feet.

What is this going to take? Lei kept the wand pointed at Indigo. It was drained of power, but the warforged didn't know that. Lei struggled against exhaustion, fighting to keep her fear from showing on her face. Try me.

Indigo watched her warily. She was clearly hurt, but she'd managed to dodge the first blast. She might be able to dodge another.

"Enough." It was Pierce. "You can't win this. Don't make us destroy you."

Was that a note of sorrow Lei could hear in his voice? Or desperation?

"You already have," Indigo said, her eyes fixed on Lei, but her words were for Pierce. "I trusted you. I thought you were . . . my brother. But you choose this one over me. Not once but twice." Her armblades retracted half an inch, then extended again. A nervous tic? "Perhaps you will destroy me this day. But she will die with me."

Indigo spread her blades, leaping forward in a blur of blackened metal. But there was another flash of motion, another flare of light. A foot of steel burst through her abdomen. Perhaps it was a trick of the light, but it seemed to burn with an inner radiance.

17

Daine's sword.

Whether the lightning bolt had caused more damage than it appeared or some unknown magic was hidden in the gleaming sword, the blow brought the warforged to a halt. Indigo gazed down at the blade. Then she fell to her knees, the sound of metal on stone curiously muted. The light faded from her crystal eyes and she collapsed, deadly grace reduced to inert wood and metal. And there, behind her, stood Daine.

Lei fell into his arms, giving in to her exhaustion. She lay against him, her eyes closed, finding comfort in his warmth. She knew he was speaking, but the words just washed over her in a comforting wave. Then a thought penetrated her weary mind and jerked her back to the world.

Harmattan.

She pulled back from Daine. "We have to get out of here."

Daine frowned, laying his hands on her shoulders. "What's wrong?"

She looked over at the archway, at the shards of metal scattered across the floor. "He's not dead. I don't know how long the effect will last, but we may only have minutes to spare. Maybe less. If he recovers—I can't do it again. I can't."

Daine scowled at the remnants of the warforged leader. "Well, that's good news." He squeezed her shoulder and smiled, though she could see it was forced. "Pierce, let's go."

Pierce stood over Indigo's body, staring at the fallen warforged. After a moment he pulled the sword from her back. He joined Daine and Lei and presented the blade, handle first. He said nothing.

Daine sighed as he took the sword. He glanced around the room, searching for anything they might be leaving behind. His gaze passed over Tashana's corpse, the fallen Indigo, and the remnants of Harmattan. Was there a flicker of movement? A shift among the metal shards?

Lei pulled at his arm. "We need to leave. Now."

"I know. But . . ." He looked around again. "Where's Jode?"

CHAPTER 3

XEN'DRIK
KARUL'TASH
Lharvion 22, 997 YK

In their final battle, Tashana had torn into Daine's left arm. Her shadowy claws had cut through chainmail with ease, leaving deep gouges in the flesh below. Yet this wound wasn't bothering him; if anything, his arm was numb. Instead, he was troubled by a burning sensation across his back. He'd noticed it the instant he'd awakened: soreness and itching, as if he'd rolled in fireweed. But there was no time for back scratching.

"Where's Jode?" he said.

Lei and Pierce glanced at him, shock and concern painted across Lei's face.

"Jode is . . . dead, Daine."

"It's a long story. But I was just talking to him, and here I am, so I assume . . ." He glanced around the chamber. "Jode!" he called out. His voice echoed off of the walls.

"You were just *talking* to him?" Lei pulled her staff from her satchel and leaned heavily upon it. "Daine, he's *dead*."

"I know!" he snapped. His back itched, and he considered scraping off the skin with his dagger. "I was dreaming, and he was there, and he said—"

"You were *dreaming?* Are you even listening to yourself?"

"I'm not imagining this! It was *him*. The vial I was carrying, the liquid, it must have—"

A loud rattling interrupted him . . . a shiver running through the shards of metal scattered across the floor.

"We don't have time for this!" Lei said. "That thing could pull itself together at any moment. And I don't have the strength to bring it down again. We need to get out of here now!"

"She is correct." Pierce had abandoned the shattered remnants of his flail in favor of his longbow, and he had an arrow nocked to the string. "Whatever you may believe, Jode is not in this chamber. And we are in poor condition to fight any foe, least of all this one."

"You're right," Daine said. He knew his encounter with Jode had been more than just a dream, and he'd assumed that Jode would just . . . *appear* when he woke up. But Jode wasn't here, and this wasn't the time for analyzing dreams. He took a deep breath, clearing his thoughts and considering the situation. "If these two made it inside, perhaps their little friend with the spiked arms is here as well. Pierce, take point. Scout the path to the front gate, then return to the central chamber. We'll meet you there."

Pierce leapt across the shards and disappeared into the hallway. Following the motion, Daine's gaze was drawn to one of the pieces in the rubble. He plucked out an object battered and scorched, but quite recognizable. The head of a warforged soldier.

As he picked it up, two sensations swept over Daine. The first was a sense of familiarity: staring at the face and the sigil engraved into the forehead. He was certain he'd seen this soldier before. And now it occurred to him . . .

Greetings, Daine. It's been a long time.

The creature knew who he was. How?

At the same time, a wave of energy flowed out of the head . . . a faint, numbing tingle. As the sensation spread across his body, the links of his chainmail began shaking and pulling against him, as if caught in a powerful magnetic force. Daine tried to let go of the head, but he couldn't pry his fingers loose. The pressure on his armor grew greater, and the shards around him began to rustle.

"Lei!" he called.

Before he'd even completed the word, the stinging pain replaced the mystic tingle. Lei had smashed the head with her darkwood staff, catching Daine's fingers in the process. The head struck the nearest wall with a satisfying crash. The force pulling at Daine's armor disappeared, but as he rubbed his hand, he saw one of the metal shards skid across the floor toward the head, immediately followed by another.

"Are you hurt?" Lei asked.

Great, he thought. First I'm a madman, now I'm a fool.

He clenched his injured fist; the pain helped shield him from his embarrassment and the burning across his back. "Let's catch up with Pierce," he said. "I'm beginning to see why you want to get away from this thing."

The two sprinted out of the room. Behind them they could hear the sound of metal on stone, as an ever-increasing stream of shards flowed across the floor toward Harmattan's head.

Time was running out.

Daine was injured. He wanted to tear the skin off of his back. An unstoppable monster followed them. The mystery of Jode was heavy on his mind. And he was doing his best to prepare for whatever enemy might unexpectedly appear.

But the heart of the monolith still took his breath away.

Karul'tash was a hollow tower, an astonishing work of engineering. Daine could barely see across the central chamber, let alone spy the distant ceiling. He'd seen tall towers before. He'd spent much of the last year in Sharn, and the central spires of the city dwarfed the monolith. But it wasn't the size of the tower that was so impressive. It was what lay within. An obsidian column filled the center of the chamber, covered with glowing sigils and inlaid with a dozen metals and gemstones. The sheer mass of the cylinder was astonishing, making it all the more impressive that it hovered suspended in the air, a good ten feet off the chamber floor.

Dozens of rings floated around the central pillar, a myriad of metals and widths. The rings rose and fell, spinning in different directions and speeds.

And then there were the spheres: twelve crystal orbs drifted around the pillar. From the ground, it was easy to imagine them as a strange form of decoration. But Daine knew better. These were planar carriages, each one designed to carry passengers to another level of reality.

"One's missing," Lei said.

"Lakashtai," Daine said. "And somehow, I don't think she's going to come back on her own." He gestured at the tables scattered around the room, altars covered with glowing crystals. The magic exceeded his skills, but earlier Lei had used these to control one of the spheres. Daine could see her exhaustion, and he hated to make her exert herself, but there was no choice. "I need you to get this thing working again."

"You want to know where Lakashtai went?" Lei said.

"For a start."

Lei hobbled toward the bank of lights, leaning on her staff. Daine sprinted around the column, and what he saw made his heart sink. He'd brought two allies into the tower, and these warriors had helped them defeat the firebinders. One of these soldiers lay on the ground before Daine, the injuries so severe that it took Daine a moment to identify the corpse as that of the man, Shen'kar. Half of the dark elf's body had been sheared away, and the rest of corpse was covered with cuts, as if he'd been caught in a storm of razors—or Harmattan's whirling shards.

Damn it. Daine had spent more time fighting the savage dark elves than as their ally, but over the last hour he'd come to respect Shen'kar—and whatever their differences, no warrior deserved to die like that.

"Captain." Pierce had a body in his arms. A woman, limp, her pitch-black skin covered with cuts. The other dark elf. "She is seriously wounded, but her condition is stable."

Daine nodded. "Follow me. What did you find?"

"The gate remains open. The wards are in place. And the Sulatar elves are still camped at the perimeter of the magical defenses; I saw at least three of their flying sleds."

"Wonderful."

They found Lei working at the crystal consoles. "Status?" Daine said.

24

"I can't recover the sphere that Lakashtai used to escape," Lei said. "But she went to—"

"Dal Quor," Pierce said.

"That's right," Lei said, surprised. "How did you—"

"Later," Daine said. "Once we don't have that trash heap on our tails. I was hoping we'd be able to leave out the front door, but that's impossible."

"I can deactivate the wards—"

Daine shook his head. "There's an army camped out there, waiting for their high priest to return and lead them to the promised land. Even if we found some way to get past them we can't just leave this place in their hands. Who knows what we've already unleashed by helping Lakashtai? Besides, if your rusty friend can't lower the wards himself, we're doing the world a favor by keeping him here."

Lei frowned. "So you're saying we just give up?"

"You know me . . . I love to give up." Daine forced a grin. "Come on, Lei. You're our resident magical genius. You're the one who told me what these orbs are."

"Carriages to other planes. You want to leave in one of the orbs?"

"Want to? No." A vision of Shen'kar's ravaged corpse flashed through Daine's mind. "But it's better than the alternative. Can you do it?"

Lei looked down at the panel. "I . . . I think so. But where do you want to go?"

"Since when am I an expert on other planes? I want to go *home*, Lei. For now, I'll take anywhere that's not, say, a pit of endless fire."

"Even a plain of endless ice?"

Daine blinked. "That's the only other option?"

"Well, it's a possibility. I can't access all of the spheres. It must have something to do with the current conjunctions of the planes. And there's hardly any point to going to Dolurrh in an effort to avoid death."

Even Daine had heard of Dolurrh, the plane where the souls of the dead were drained of all memories of their former lives.

"Use your best judgment. But do it quickly!" Perhaps it was his imagination, but he thought he could hear the sound of metal on metal coming from the distant chamber where they'd left Harmattan.

"Perfect!" Lei said. Light flared around her hands, and one of the enormous orbs descended to the floor. "Well, not perfect, but given the alternatives . . ."

Now Daine was sure of it: a metallic roar came from the hallway. "Let's *go!*" he yelled, sprinting toward the orb.

A portal had opened in the side of the massive opalescent sphere, and Daine vaulted up and through it. The interior was a disappointment. Aside from a tall ledge running around the edge of the chamber, the room was completely featureless; Daine couldn't see any way to make the sphere move. But that wasn't his job. Lei was right behind him, and Daine pulled her up and inside.

Lei sat crosslegged at the exact center of the chamber, and the room lit up. A complex geometric pattern spread out around her, traced in lines of fire. Runes and sigils appeared on every surface. Each letter was as long as Daine's hand, a reminder that this was the work of giants. Lei studied the walls. She muttered a word in a harsh and unfamiliar tongue, and one of the glowing symbols on the wall flared brighter for an instant.

Pierce was at the portal. He handed the injured elf to Daine. Beneath her chitin armor, the woman was a waif and seemed like a feather in his arms. A moment later, the warforged was aboard.

"Lei! The door!" Daine cried.

"I'm working on it!"

Now the roar was growing louder, a hurricane howl combined with the gnashing of metal on metal.

"We're about to get another passenger!"

"I'm trying!" Lei said.

They saw him: a glittering cloud, steel death racing toward them.

"*Hul'kla'tesh!*" Lei cried.

It couldn't have been any closer; a handful of steel shards fell to the floor as the portal snapped shut. A terrible scraping sound came from the walls, metal gouging at crystal.

"He's all around us," Lei said.

"Then get us out of here!"

Lei closed her eyes, her hands set against the floor. Patterns of color danced over the floor, and they felt the orb rising.

Height alone didn't stop Harmattan. They could still hear the flurry of steel striking the walls of the sphere.

"Hang on!" Lei yelled. She sang a chain of harsh syllables, words flashing across the walls as she spoke.

And they fell out of the world.

CHAPTER 4

THE SPHERE
Lharvion 22, 997 YK

*T*his *vehicle has just transitioned through a planar barrier.
Your companions are suffering from vertigo and nausea as a result.*

As always, Pierce *knew* Shira's thoughts as much as he
heard them. When he looked at Lei, her discomfort was
a simple fact. Glancing at the dark elf warrior, Pierce
could sense the extent of her injuries, how she hovered on the edge of death. He carefully set the injured
woman down on the ledge that circled the chamber.

"Was that it?" Daine said. The scraping sound of
Harmattan's attack faded away, and the glowing lines
on the floor pulsed.

Lei opened her eyes. "Yes," she said. She lay back against
the floor, her legs still crossed. "We're safe now."

"Safe? We seem to have very different ideas of safe,"
Daine said, scratching his back. "Still . . . good work,
both of you. Where are we?"

"Nowhere."

"And how far is that from somewhere?" Daine said.

"About as far as can be. Until I complete the sequence
and open the door, we're caught between worlds. We're
. . . hypothetical, if you will."

Ethereal.

"Ethereal," Pierce said, echoing Shira's thought.

"That's right. We can stay here as long as we want." Lei spread her arms, stretching against the floor. "I'm completely exhausted. If I'm going to tend your wounds—or help our drow passenger—I'm going to need some sleep first. We should be safe here."

"*Should* be?" Daine said.

"Nothing's certain." Lei shrugged. "I'm not exactly a seasoned planar traveler. It's possible there are, I don't know, crystal orb-eating ethereal whales drifting about—"

There are no crystal orb-eating ethereal whales. Pierce refrained from sharing Shira's observation.

"—but if so, I've never heard of them. And if something does attack us, I could finish the transition with a word."

"And then we'll be somewhere," Daine said.

"Yes."

"And that will be?"

"Thelanis."

Daine sighed and sat down. "I hate to disappoint you, Lei, but I don't even know if that's a city, a country, or a plane of existence."

"Ignorant savage." Lei sat up. "It's a plane. Have you heard of the Faerie Court?"

"A magic realm filled with baby-stealing spirits, bottomless cauldrons of gold, and sinister hags who curse arrogant princesses?"

"You don't have to go to Thelanis to find a hag," Lei said. "But that's the one. According to the stories, it's much like the world we're used to. There's just more magic around. Spirits in the water and the trees, that sort of thing. What's important is that it's supposed to be one of the easiest realms to travel to or from. The reason we have so many faerie tales is because people accidentally fall into the realm, or because the spirits of Thelanis— the fey—make their way to Eberron. So not only is it not a lake of fire or endless tundra, but with luck we should be able to find a path home."

It's not quite that simple. Again, Pierce chose to ignore the alien thought.

"It's not quite that simple," Daine said. "Sovereign and Flame, what have we *done*? Tashana, Lakashtai . . . I don't know what to think."

"So don't," Lei said. "Sleep."

Daine sighed, but he finally nodded. "You're right, I suppose."

"Was there ever any doubt?" Lei pulled blankets and pillows from her pack; the magical satchel held an astonishing amount of supplies, and within moments Lei was laying out two bedrolls.

"Do you have enough for three?" Daine said. He'd made his way over to the wounded drow woman and was studying her wounds. He carefully lifted her off the ledge.

"I only packed for the two of us." Even Pierce could hear the slight chill in Lei's voice. It wasn't much of a surprise. Daine had had dealings with these dark-skinned elves, or drow as they appeared to be called. But Lei and Pierce had been captured by drow, Lei almost killed by them. This woman had helped to rescue them, and it was clear that she was of a different tribe from their enemies. But the half-drow Gerrion had also rescued them from one enemy, only to betray them at the end. This woman was a stranger, and after Gerrion and Lakashtai it was hardly surprising that Lei would be suspicious of strangers.

Then Pierce noticed something—an anomaly, a

trivial detail that had slipped by even his keen eyes in the excitement.

"My lady," he said. "Your hand."

She glanced over at him. "What?"

"You are no longer injured."

Lei dropped the blanket, and Daine almost dropped the woman he was carrying as he rushed to Lei's side. She held her hand out, as if it were a treasure. Earlier in the day, the warforged Hydra had severed the smallest finger on her left hand. Her glove was still damaged, but her finger was fully restored. She wiggled it in wonder.

"I . . . I didn't even notice," she said. "I think it's been back since I woke up. I knew something felt strange."

"How is this even possible?" Daine said.

"I don't know," Lei said, shaking her fist happily. "And you know what? I'm not going to think about it until I've slept for, oh, a few days."

"Well, I don't feel right about leaving an injured woman on the hard floor," Daine said, carefully laying the dark elf down on one of the blankets. "So I suppose you and I will just have to share."

"Or *you're* going to have to sleep on the hard floor," Lei said. But she was smiling, and she let Daine pull her down to the other blanket.

         ❂ ❂ ❂ ❂ ❂ ❂ ❂

Lei and Daine slept. The wounded elf still lay unconscious. Pierce studied the patterns on the walls. He always felt a vague discomfort when his companions were asleep. Even though he knew the experience was both harmless and necessary, it was completely foreign to him. The only time a warforged lost consciousness was if it was critically damaged, wounded so badly that it would need to be repaired before it could awaken. Early in his life, Pierce had assumed that sleeping humans were injured, and he'd been concerned that his companions might never awaken unless treated by a healer. He quickly learned better, but nonetheless, watching others sleep had always made him uncomfortable.

Now Pierce found there was another emotion at work. He knew Indigo would say that sleep was a weakness, one of the many flaws that made the so-called "breathers" inferior to the warforged. But watching Daine and Lei sleeping side by side, he felt a strange envy. The battle with Indigo, Lakashtai's betrayal . . . he wished that he could escape it, if only for a moment. He wondered what it would be like to dream.

You were not made for dreams.

How would you know? It was a strange sensation, trying to communicate with Shira. There was no sense of a separate presence, just thoughts that appeared in his mind as if they were his own.

Because you were made for me.

You are thousands of years older than I am, Pierce thought. *That makes no sense.*

It makes no sense. It felt as if he was agreeing with himself. *It is still true.*

Memory flooded through Pierce. A time of war. Shira's people were endangered on two fronts. They needed to escape their homeland before an impending cataclysm destroyed it, and they were fighting a fearsome enemy to claim a new home. He saw the creation of warforged . . . no, not warforged, but creatures much like them. These were soldiers, but they were also *vessels of hope*. Shira was the first of her kind to attempt the transition. Her essence had been fused to the sphere, where it could be bound to any vessel of hope. But only days after she had merged with her first vessel, she had been captured by the enemy. Her vessel was destroyed, and she was sealed away in the darkness of the vault.

That doesn't mean I was made for you, Pierce thought. *It sounds like any warforged would do.*

Would they? A new memory emerged, but this was one of his own. Harmattan speaking to him at the door to the vault—

This is a relic of this ancient land, a key of a most unusual nature. Only a warforged designed to interface with it can make use of it. Hydra, Indigo—it will not interface properly with their auras.

What makes you think I can use it? Pierce had asked.

Because I could, if I still had a body. And you are my brother.

The memory faded, and the next thought was Shira's. *It may make no sense. But it is true. You were not made for dreams. You were made to escape them.*

Pierce let this thought go. He still wasn't sure how he felt about Shira. Her knowledge and analytic powers were certainly useful. Even now, as he glanced around the chamber, Shira identified the symbols carved into the walls as one of the languages of giants, translating each word that he looked at. But as much as it was pleasant to have a companion, it wasn't the same as speaking with Lei or Pierce.

Or Indigo.

That was the heart of it. His mind still lingered on their last battle. He could remember every motion, and he walked through it in his mind, tracing the injuries she'd given him. The sight of Daine transfixing her with his blade, the surge of emotion he'd felt watching her fall, even as Shira whispered about the magical resonance of Daine's sword.

33

She would have won their fight. Without Lei, without Harmattan . . . Indigo would have defeated him. Somehow, it didn't seem fair that he should still be alive. He could see the battle in his mind, and he knew that he had lost . . . or would have. He couldn't even blame her for wanting to destroy him. He had betrayed her for Lei. He'd intended to imprison her in the ancient vault. Harmattan must have saved her, while Pierce had simply betrayed her again.

He remembered those final moments, looking down at her on the floor of Karul'tash, the gaping wound in her abdomen. Lying there as if she were asleep.

But warforged didn't sleep. Most people couldn't tell the difference between a warforged that had been destroyed and one that had simply been rendered inert.

Like Indigo had been.

Pierce knew that his friends would have wanted to finish the job if they'd known there was some chance of Indigo being restored. But Pierce couldn't bring himself to mention it. No artificer would ever find her in the depths of Karul'tash, and Harmattan's hands weren't nimble enough for such work. Surely the monolith would be her tomb. But somehow, he'd found that he couldn't betray her a third time.

In the end, she'd won their battle.

Pierce pushed the memory away. He studied the inscriptions on the walls, seeking to bury his guilt beneath this task. And once again, he wished he could sleep.

CHAPTER  5

THE SPHERE
Lharvion 23, 997 YK

"**Y**ou're all so gloomy," Jode said. "It's not the end of the world. Unless it is, I suppose."

Daine opened his eyes. He was alone in bed, in his room at the inn in Sharn. He'd fallen asleep nestled next to Lei, and without her the bed seemed doubly empty.

"It's a lot of space here for the three of you, don't you think?" Jode jumped up onto the mattress and glanced around the room. "Have you considered the life of an innkeeper? Your charm, Lei's gruel . . . that's gold for the taking, my friend."

Daine sat up. He noticed that his back wasn't itching anymore, which confirmed his suspicions.

"Yes, it's a dream," Jode said. "And since it's *your* dream, perhaps you could imagine something particularly delectable in the pantry."

"You know what I'm thinking?" Daine said.

Jode rolled his eyes. "I *am* what you're thinking, remember?"

"I thought you'd come back with me."

"It's hard to explain," Jode said. "I think I'm dreaming. But I don't have a body of my own anymore, so I'm dreaming your dream. When you woke up, I was still here. I feel things, hints of your emotions, flashes of events around you, but mostly I've been wandering in dreams."

"But you are real? I'm not just imagining this?"

"Daine, when you ask your imaginary friend if he's imaginary, what sort of answer do you expect to get?" Jode shook his head. "I don't know what I am. A ghost, maybe. Does it really matter? You've got more important things to worry about."

"Oh? Like what?"

"What are you planning to do next?"

"Get Lei and Pierce home." Daine rolled out of bed. The room seemed so *normal*. After weeks of night terrors and the journey through Xen'drik, he'd gotten used to horror.

"Of course. That's the noble captain. Just like when we fought our way out of Cyre to get Lei to Sharn. Smash every obstacle in your path until you reach your sanctuary."

Daine looked out the window. The sun shone down on the streets of High Walls, but they were empty, the district abandoned. "And what's wrong with that?"

"You're giving up."

Daine scowled. He felt anger and frustration building in his mind, and in that moment a bank of clouds passed over the sun. "And what should I be doing?"

"Finding Lakashtai."

A peal of thunder shook the room, and outside the window, rain began to fall. Daine turned to Jode, and now he felt real anger. "And how would I do that? I don't even know what she *is*."

"Or what she stole, or why she chose you. Or whether you're still in danger. Or if your little adventure has placed the entire world in jeopardy!" Jode gestured dramatically. "Just imagine, the fate of Khorvaire could hang in the balance."

"You think so?"

Jode grinned. "Well, no, but wouldn't it be something if it did?"

The fierce rain began to slow. "I suppose. I just . . ." Daine let the sentence trail off, looking away. Lakashtai had made a fool of him. He still didn't fully understand the chain of events that had led him to Xen'drik. When it came down to it, he was ashamed. His weakness had set all of these events in motion.

"Dorn's teeth!" Jode bounced off the bed and smacked him in the kneecap. "You didn't do this. *Lakashtai* did. Now you need to find out how and why."

"And how do you suggest I do that?"

"I think that's a job for the living," Jode said. "And now, if you're quite done with the rain, I think you owe me breakfast.

"What do you expect me to . . ." Daine paused in midspeech as the smell of cinnamon and fresh-baked bread rose up through the floor.

"That'll do," Jode said, pausing to savor the scents. "But first, let's have a look at that arm of yours."

❀ ❀ ❀ ❀ ❀ ❀ ❀

Daine's back itched.

Someone pulled at his left arm. He opened his eyes, reaching out with his right hand, grabbing hold of . . .

Lei.

"Sorry about that," she whispered. "I was trying not to wake you."

"That's fine," he muttered. He sat up, taking in his surroundings. He was back in the sphere. The air was chilly, and the only light came from the flickering sigils traced across walls and floor. Daine's thoughts were fogged with sleep, and he had no idea how much time had passed.

"Let's have a look at that arm of yours," Lei said.

Daine glanced over at her, and for a moment he wondered if he were still dreaming. The situation hardly seemed real. Then his stomach growled . . . and this time, there was no fresh-baked bread to appease him.

Lei heard the sound. "I've still got some rations in my pack," she said as she examined his tattered sleeve. "Not much, I'm afraid, but . . ." Her voice trailed off.

"What?" Daine said.

Pierce had been standing at the edge of the room, but hearing Lei's tone, the warforged turned to look at them.

"See for yourself," Lei said. Using both hands, she tore a hole in Daine's sleeve, widening the gap where Tashana's claws had torn into him.

"Hey!" Daine said, but he fell silent when he saw the skin below. The wounds Tashana had inflicted were gone, with no trace of bruise or scar. "That's good work. Can you do anything about—"

"I didn't do it." Lei said. "I worked on Pierce while you were sleeping, and prepared a healing charm for you. But I didn't use it."

"It may have been the same force that restored your hand, my lady." Pierce had moved closer, to better examine Daine's arm.

"I suppose," Lei said. "If her claws hadn't cut through the skin, I might think it was all some sort of illusion—"

"Jode did it," Daine said.

The others just stared at him.

The dream was coming back to him. Unlike his visions from the Keldan battlefield, this one was more like a true dream; the details were faint and fading. "I remember now. He healed me just before I woke up."

"Woke up," Lei repeated. "You're saying that Jode did this in a dream?"

Her tone irked him. "Do you have a better explanation? *Something* fixed your finger."

Lei sighed. "Daine, Jode couldn't have restored my hand even when he was alive. I don't know why you're fixated on this, but there has to be another explanation—"

"It was that bottle. The blue fluid."

"What are you talking about?"

She was unconscious when I drank it. "It's . . ." Daine scratched his back while he tried to put words together. "Last year, when we fought that thing in the sewers. Teral said that they were stealing dragonmarks. That they were going to steal *your* dragonmark."

Lei nodded. She shivered, no doubt remembering the chamber of horrors in the depths below Sharn.

"You remember how we recovered a few bottles of black liquid down there? And gave them to Alina? Well, one of them wasn't black . . . it was blue. And it had Jode's dragonmark engraved on the seal."

"You're saying . . . you *drank* his dragonmark?"

"You're the expert on magic here!" Daine said. "I don't know what it was. But even the Jorasco healers couldn't explain what happened to Jode, remember? I drank the potion, and then I saw Jode in my dreams. And now . . . I think he healed me."

"That's impossible," Lei said.

"Tell it to your fingers," Daine replied. "All ten of them."

Lei glanced down at her hand. "But he wasn't in *my* dreams. And I told you, Jode couldn't do that."

"If you say so," Daine said. "Me, I'm not complaining." He glanced at the other bedroll; the drow woman was still wrapped up in the blanket. "Have you checked to see . . ."

"I wanted to help you first," Lei said, glancing to the side.

"Well, let's see if the mystery healer paid our friend a visit." Daine carefully drew back the blanket.

Whatever force healed Daine and Lei hadn't touched the dark elf. Her ebon skin bore dozens of cuts, and the blanket was covered with crusted blood. None of the wounds were deep, but the sheer number was appalling. Daine had seen far worse sights, but he still felt a deep weight on his heart. That warforged . . . thing . . . was looking for me. She just got in the way.

"Heal her," he said.

"What?" Lei didn't sound pleased.

"You said you made a healing charm. I don't need it. So heal her."

Lei hesitated, and Daine put his hands on her shoulders. "I'm not asking you to like her, Lei. But the woman helped save you from the firebinders. She risked her life for us—less than a day after I beat her bloody myself. She was guarding our back when this happened."

Lei said nothing, and they stood in silence. Daine wondered what was going through her mind. Gerrion's betrayal? "Lei," he said at last. "Please."

She nodded and broke away from him, kneeling next to the drow woman. Lei took a silver coin from her purse and passed it over the injured woman, starting at her feet and slowly moving toward her head. A faint, resonant chime filled the chamber, and the multitude of cuts began to fade. The power of the charm was limited, and only a few of the injuries were completely healed. But deep gashes became shallow wounds, and signs of infection disappeared.

The chime came to an end. The drow woman appeared to be sleeping, and Daine studied her. She was unquestionably elven, with fine features, large almond-shaped eyes, and long, pointed ears. Like most of the other elves Daine had encountered, she was short and slender—athletic, but built for speed instead of strength. Where most elves had light complexions, this woman's skin was pitch black, a shade far darker than he'd ever seen on a human. This darkness was broken up by a web of pale white tattoos, abstract but almost hypnotic in their complexity. Her long hair was the color of moonlight, silvery-white and shimmering in the reflected flame. This cloak of hair covered more than her actual clothing. Vambraces made from some opalescent shell covered her forearms, and she wore shin-guards made from the same material. Aside from this armor, she wore a short, dark loincloth and a few bands of leather wrapped across her torso. Two short scabbards dangled from this makeshift harness, but her knives must have been left behind at the monolith.

The worst of her wounds were healed, and her breathing was slow and even. But her eyes remained closed, and she did not move.

"Lei?" Daine said.

"The charm's exhausted. If she's still unconscious,

there's nothing more I can do." Lei bent to look more closely at her patient.

"She is conscious," Pierce said.

"And angry." The voice was rough, the accent strange, the words blending together . . . *anangry.* The woman's eyes opened, pure silver-white with no trace of iris or pupil.

And then everything went black.

CHAPTER 6

THE SPHERE
Lharvion 23, 997 YK

The unnatural darkness was deep, but not complete. Daine could still see the vague shapes of Pierce and Lei in the shadows. But the drow woman had vanished, disappearing the instant the darkness fell.

"Draw your weapons." The dark elf spoke with a low, lyrical cadence, but an occasional pause suggested that she was not entirely comfortable with the common tongue. "You should not die unarmed."

Lei's never going to let me hear the end of this, Daine thought. He could see motion in the shadows—Pierce raising his bow. But Daine wasn't going to play this game. "No," he said. "Lei. Pierce. Stand down. We're not fighting."

"No?" The voice was all around them, seeming to emerge from the shadows. "Am I unworthy of your blade? Change your mind swiftly."

The blow was a hammer in his back, a solid kick that landed directly on his spine, forcing him forward. He turned around, but the woman faded back into the shadows. Pain pulsed through his nerves, and he was tempted to give into his growing anger, to draw his sword and give this woman the battle she sought.

Then the battlefield at Keldan Ridge flashed through his mind. This woman might be a stranger, but they'd fought the same foe. He'd lost too many of his comrades-in-arms over the last two years to give up on one now—even one who considered him an enemy.

"Why are you doing this? We saved your life."

"You *gave* me life?" Her voice reminded Daine of the buzzing of hornets . . . musical, but full of deadly fury. "*You?*"

There! Daine ducked to the side, and this time the kick brushed past him. He reached out, trying to touch her, but his hand fell on empty air.

"*Enough!*" Lei cried, and light flooded the room. She had her hand raised above her head, and her glove glowed with brilliant illumination, a magical radiance that shattered the shadows. "Enough of this! I don't know what's wrong with you, woman, but I brought you back from the edge of Dolurrh. If you want to return, I can show you the way!"

Even as the light revealed the presence of the drow woman, she was moving, a blur of shadow. She leapt into the air, spinning up and over Lei in an incredible display of agility; Lei had barely finished speaking when a dark-skinned hand appeared around her throat.

"Light the path, then, spellweaver," the drow said. "I am ready."

The dark elf was holding Lei's neck with three fingers, but the effect was dramatic. Lei's face went pale; she was struggling to keep from choking, and her arms were hanging limp at her side. The dark elf's other arm was curved back, fingers and thumb drawn together to form a point, reminding Daine of the tail of a scorpion.

Daine's sword was in his hand; he didn't remember

drawing it. Next to him, Pierce had an arrow to his bowstring and a second between his fingers, ready to loose in the blink of an eye. Daine felt fury building within, and if anything happened to Lei, it really would be his fault. He opened his mouth, but before he could speak another voice filled the chamber.

"Your anger is misplaced," said Pierce. The words were sibilant and swift, spoken in the language of the dark elves. Lakashtai had granted Daine the power to understand the speech of the drow, but even he could not speak it. "We fear your fury, but know not why we face it."

While the woman's pale eyes widened a fraction, her hands never wavered. "I tire of this mockery, man of metal," she said, answering Pierce in the drow tongue. "You have broken my path, and the last of my blood is lost to me. And you boast of your deeds!"

The point of Pierce's arrow never wavered, but his voice was soft and steady. "We know nothing of your customs," he said. "We sought only to save the life of a valued ally, and we would have done the same for your companion if it had been possible. If death is what you wish for, it is a gift easily given. But do not make Lei pay the price for our ignorance."

"*Kkk*." The drow made a sharp noise with her tongue. "Your gift of death is as flawed as your gift of life. Do you know nothing of the world that lies beyond? You have shattered my path to the final land, and now I must begin anew."

"This was never our intent," Pierce said.

The woman narrowed her eyes. "How can you not know these things? You are warriors. Why follow this path if you do not look to its end?"

Pierce was distracting the woman, but her fingers

were still wrapped around Lei's throat. Daine could see the pain and anger in Lei's eyes, and it burned like fire. He still didn't know what power the woman was holding in reserve, but if he moved swiftly, he might be able to push the distracted dark elf away from Lei before she could move. He tightened his grip on his sword, and a rush of adrenaline flowed through him. He prepared to move . . .

. . . and the sphere shook.

Previously, the floor had been perfectly stable—none of the motion of a ship, and it was easy to forget that it was a vehicle at all, and not simply some sort of windowless building. This was false security. A second tremor struck, and Daine staggered a few steps, struggling to keep his footing. Lei stumbled and fell to her knees, but the drow woman kept her balance and her grip on Lei's throat. This was no storm. The second quake was accompanied by a heavy thud, a massive impact against the outer shell.

"What is this?" hissed the drow.

"Harmattan?" Daine shouted to Pierce.

"I think not," Pierce called back. The room still rang with the sound of the impact, and sigils and lines were glowing with shifting patterns of colored flame. Pierce turned his attention back to the dark elf, speaking in the drow tongue. "We are all in equal danger, and the one you threaten is the only one who can save us. Is this truly the death you seek?"

The room shook under a third impact, and a passage of glowing words etched into the wall flared and then faded with an eerie fluting. The drow woman remained perfectly poised in the chaos, her right hand coiled back and ready to strike, her eyes narrowed in thought.

"No." She released Lei, and the artificer dropped to

the ground, choking and rubbing her throat. Daine rushed to her side, while Pierce continued to cover the dark elf with his bow.

Lei had pushed herself up on one arm by the time Daine reached her, and was struggling to catch her breath. "Center . . . of the floor . . ." she gasped.

Glowing lines and symbols covered the floor of the chamber, reminding Daine of the pictures he'd seen of wizards constructing prisons for demons or wayward spirits. He remembered Lei sitting in the middle of this vast seal when they'd left Karul'tash, and he helped her reach the center of the pattern. Another impact shook the chamber, and this time there was a fearsome *crack* of shattering glass. Lei sat down, and the cold fire of the mystic pattern grew brighter. Daine could feel a cold tingle against his skin as the magical forces grew.

"Helkad thelora!" Lei's eyes were closed, her skin sheened with sweat. Another *crack*, and fragments of crystal fell from the ceiling. A terrible sense of vertigo swept through Daine, and suddenly he felt *solid* . . . it was if he had been floating for the last day and never noticed it, and gravity had suddenly returned. The light from the glowing inscriptions faded, and Lei let out a deep breath. Her breathing was still a little ragged, but her expression remained calm. It appeared their journey was over.

He turned back to the drow woman. "You!" he said. Daine's sword was still in his hand, and as his anger swelled within him he could swear that the hilt grew warmer in his hand. "So, you still want to die?"

Though unarmed and outnumbered, the dark elf showed no signs of fear. She met his gaze; he kept his blade level, ready to strike at the first motion. At last, she spoke. "This man of metal speaks truth," she said. "This is not the death I seek. Where is the storm of razors?"

Harmattan? "We left him behind when we fled the monolith, and he's not getting out."

"Then let us return!" she said. "If it is your enemy as well, let us fight together once more. Let us face our destiny together!"

"Or we could not return, leave him trapped in the monolith, and go on to live long and fruitful lives," Daine said.

The woman hissed. "You are a warrior. You fought the firebinders. And yet you would walk away from this enemy?"

"For now," Pierce said. "Only a fool fights a foe he knows he cannot defeat, and we have found no flaw in his armor. This one is our prey, and in time he will fall, but this hunt will be a long one."

"Then I will join you," the woman said. "I must defeat this creature if I am to find my way to the final land. Let me fight by your side, and I may forgive the wrong you have done me."

We saved your life, ungrateful wretch, Daine thought. But they were in an unknown land, and whatever her flaws, this woman was a skilled warrior. "We accept your gracious offer," he said. "What was your name again?"

"Xu'sasar," she replied. "A child of the scorpion, blessed by three moons."

"How do you feel about 'Xu'?"

The woman hissed again. "You outlanders despoil all that you touch. I suppose that it is only natural you should destroy the beauty of my name."

"Xu it is, then. I'm Daine. This is Pierce."

"And I'm Lei." The darkwood staff flashed in the dim light. The thrust caught Xu'sasar directly in the throat, and the staff struck with tremendous force. The dark elf flew back against the wall. Lei had pulled her staff from her pack while the others were talking, and now she stood next to Daine, the point of the weapon leveled at the drow. Daine could swear he heard faint *singing*, a beautiful voice just on the edge of hearing. "If you change your mind about dying, let me know."

Xu'sasar was crouching against the wall, ready to spring, and Daine thought the battle would begin all over. Then the dark elf relaxed.

"Well met, weaver Lei," she said. "When we next do battle, let us fight on equal terms." She turned back to Pierce. "So, man of metal, where does our hunt begin?"

"Right here," said Lei. "Welcome to Thelanis."

CHAPTER 7
NIGHT: THE HUNTER'S MOON THELANIS

*T*he planar transition was completed successfully, but *this vessel has suffered considerable damage.* In this instance, Shira's insight was unnecessary. A web of fine fractures spread across the ceiling, and powdered glass and crystal shards littered the floor. The lines etched into the floor still burned with mystic light, but that radiance was faint and flickering, and many of the sigils scattered around the chamber had faded completely.

What is the impact of the damage? Pierce thought.

Any attempt at further travel would likely result in the destruction of the vessel and all aboard.

Lei had apparently come to the same conclusion. "Let's hope we're in the right place, because I don't think this hunk of crystal's going anywhere soon."

"What was that?" Daine said, running a finger along the crack on one of the walls.

An attack by some form of predator native to the ethereal plane.

I thought there were no ethereal orb-eating—

It wasn't a whale.

It was the first time Shira had actually interrupted his train of thought, and it was a disturbing sensation. But even as he considered this, he could feel the spirit's remorse.

It has been a considerable time since I have been able to share my thoughts. I do not intend to interfere with your actions.

But could you?

There was no response. Shira was not an active presence in Pierce's mind. He could only feel her when she "spoke," and when she chose to retreat there was no way for him to sense her thoughts or emotions.

Was he concerned?

A moment ago, he had allowed Shira to take control of his voice. It was Shira who had concluded that beneath her bravado, the drow woman was confused and afraid, and it was Shira who spoke the language of the dark elves. While Pierce focused his attention on his bow, remaining ready to loose an arrow the instant danger threatened Lei, Shira spoke through him and tried to calm the drow warrior. She had asked his permission, and Pierce *felt* as if he'd been in control of the situation, but could she have taken his voice against his wishes?

We were designed to work together. The thought blossomed in his mind. *I have no desire to take away your freedom.*

But could you?

"Pierce?"

Lei's voice pulled Pierce from his reverie. Both Daine and Lei were staring at him. Usually he could listen to Shira and another conversation at the same time, but this time he'd been so distracted by the inner voice that he'd lost track of the outside world.

Daine asked if you were prepared to explore.

"Yes, captain, I am ready," Pierce said. "I apologize, my lady. There is much on my mind of late."

Daine nodded, but Pierce could see concern—or

was it suspicion?—in his eyes.

"Well, Lei," said Daine, "open it up."

Lei laid her hand on the center of the floor. *"Doreshk tul'kas,"* she murmured, invoking the powers of the sphere. Light pooled around her hand and surged toward the wall. A moment later the glass fell away from the light, opening a portal to the outside world.

And the night flowed in.

There was only a whisper of wind, but the change in the atmosphere was remarkable. The air of Thelanis was moist and rich, heavy with the scent of grass and fresh rain. Both Karul'tash and the crystal capsule had been dry and sterile, and his three companions paused to enjoy the cool breeze and fresh air. Pierce didn't breathe. Though he felt the change in temperature and humidity, there was no pleasure in it; the sensations were simply information, warning of what might lie beyond the portal. He glanced at Daine and received a confirming nod. Bow in hand, Pierce slipped through the opening and into the world.

The ground was cool beneath his feet: soft soil, sedge grass sheened with evening dew. Pierce took a step to the left, his back against the crystal shell of the sphere, and surveyed his surroundings. They appeared to be in the middle of a vast, rolling plain. A few small shrubs scattered across the landscape, but no trees could be seen. What stood out were the stones. These outcroppings of gray rock varied tremendously in size, ranging from boulders barely the size of Pierce's head to massive tors that dwarfed the planar carriage. Faint patches of light glistened on the stones—some form of phosphorescence, which gave the impression of ghosts clinging to the granite shards. The sky was the pure black of deep night, clear of all clouds. A multitude of stars filled the heavens, surrounding a single moon: a full orb larger than any of the twelve moons of Eberron. Pale gold, its dim radiance spread across the moors below.

Pierce circled the sphere. The plains stretched out in all directions. While the stone outcroppings offered easy cover for enemies, Pierce could see no motion. Returning to the portal of the orb, he gestured to Daine—*Clear passage.*

Daine emerged from the orb, both blades drawn and ready. Lei followed him; she held her staff, and Pierce clearly heard a faint moan as the artificer passed him.

As Pierce's gaze passed over the darkwood staff, a thought occurred to him. *The powers of the object are masked and cannot be determined.* He felt a faint hint of frustration, and he was certain that this was an echo of Shira's injured pride. At first he'd thought that the spirit had no emotions, that it was a purely analytical entity; but the more they communicated, the more he felt that he was gaining deeper insight into the personality of the construct. He glanced at Lei's staff again. The head was carved to resemble the face of a woman with delicate, fey features, whose long hair wound down around the shaft of the staff. This face was turned toward him, and Pierce had the distinct sense that the staff watched him.

"Onatar's hammer," Lei breathed. She had turned away from the field and was gazing up at the sphere itself. Pierce followed her gaze. He had never acquired the habit of swearing, but it was easy to see what drew the words from Lei. There was a crater in the shell so wide that Pierce could crouch inside it; cracks spread out around the deep wound.

"Can you explain that?" Daine said.

Lei shook her head, eyes wide. "My first ethereal jaunt, I'm afraid."

"And hopefully our last, if they're always this much fun."

"Well, we're not using this sphere again," Lei said. She ran a finger along the hull. "Honestly, I'm surprised it didn't shatter when we struck the planar barrier."

"The stars are wrong." None of them had seen the drow woman emerge from the sphere, but somehow she had slipped past the trio. Now she stood a dozen feet from the sphere, gazing at the sky. The wind ruffled her long, silver hair.

"That's right, princess," Daine said. "We're not in Xen'drik anymore."

Xu'sasar studied the stars with a fierce intensity. Finally she turned to face them. "Let us kill something," she said.

Daine and Lei exchanged glances. "Why would we do that?" Lei said.

Xu frowned, clearly confused by the question. "It is the simplest way to learn the nature of this place."

"Have you ever heard of maps?" Daine shook his head. "Pierce, I don't know where we're going, but I want more information. Give me a circle, one league around our current position. Swift and silent, and . . ." He glanced at Xu'sasar. " . . . don't kill anything you don't have to."

"Understood," Pierce said.

"Be careful if you see any lights," Lei put in. "The stories of Thelanis often mention floating lanterns that try to lead mortals astray."

"Understood."

"And I will accompany you, in case there is anything to kill," Xu'sasar said.

"Or you'll stay here," Daine said. "All I want is information."

"Which is why—"

"—you'll let Pierce do his job," Daine said. "You want to kill the walking junkpile we left in Xen'drik? Then we need to work together. And when I say 'work together,' I mean you'll do what I say."

Xu'sasar said nothing; she turned her attention back to the stars.

"Pierce, you know what to do."

"Yes," Pierce took a moment to study the stones around the crystal sphere, imprinting the shapes and patterns in his memory; he wanted to make sure he could find his way back. Then he set off into the darkness, another shadow in the night.

● ● ● ◉ ● ● ●

Pierce had already seen that the smallest of the stones scattered across the field were the size of his head. It was only when he drew closer to one of these boulders that Pierce saw that it *was* a head . . . a sculpted face, staring up at the sky. The first one Pierce found was the face of a male elf, with delicate features and long tapering ears; the eyes of this stone eidolon were covered with phosphorescent moss, gleaming in the darkness. The head was half-buried in the soil, and Pierce wondered if it might just be the face of a complete statue, its body buried beneath the earth.

Anything to add?

Stay out of sight. Shira's thought seemed curt, and she did not respond to further queries.

The granite elf was just the first of the visages Pierce encountered as he made his way across the plain. A human child, a wrinkled gnome, a dwarf with a luminescent beard—Pierce could see no pattern to their placement, no common theme save for the fact that they all gazed up at the moon. Only when he reached the crest of a small hill was he able to gaze down on one of the larger tors, and then he realized: They were *all* faces. The features of large outcroppings were rough and grainy, and seemed to be the work of wind and weather as opposed to hammer and chisel, but they were still recognizable as humanoid heads, patterns of hair traced out in strands of glowing moss. Silence ruled the valley. There was an utter absence of insect sounds, no calls of night birds. Just Pierce, making his way across the valley of faces.

The faces weren't the only thing Pierce found as he surveyed the plains. The region might be still and silent, but it wasn't empty. The trails in the damp grass were almost invisible, but Pierce had tracked Valenar commandoes through the forests of Cyre, and he could see the patterns of passage. Large, canine tracks—wolves, most likely, though easily the size of ponies. Occasionally Pierce caught traces of a horse's passage, but these tracks were old and faint, fading in and out as if the stallion were leaping hundreds of feet at a time.

He'd been walking for nearly a quarter hour when he heard the howls.

The calls were deep, the full-throated baying of hounds as opposed to the cries of wolves. The sound was closer than Pierce had expected from the faint trails. After a moment of silence, the calls began again, even closer. Pierce already had his back to one of the stone buttes; he made his way up the barren edge of the tor, finding a narrow ledge a good distance from the ground. Pierce set an arrow to his bowstring and waited.

The hounds arrived. There were two of them, both larger than any wolfhound Pierce had ever seen. Their coats were thick and glossy—and the color of fresh, wet blood. Muzzles, ears, and paws were darker and dull, as if this blood had dried and clotted. The eyes of the beasts were pale rubies, shimmering in the moonlight, and steam poured from the nostrils of the lead hound as he tasted the air.

Pierce remained perfectly still. Both hounds lowered their snouts to the ground, snuffling through the grass. Certain that they had found his scent, Pierce considered the best angles of attack. He was confident the beasts couldn't reach him on his ledge, but he had no idea what sort of help they could summon if they escaped. One of the hounds raised its head. Its gaze fixed on Pierce, and as it opened its mouth to howl, Pierce loosed an arrow.

Xu'sasar struck before the arrow reached its target.

She seemed to materialize out of the night, shadows trailing from her skin like mist. She carried no weapons, but it made no difference. Her elbow slammed into the mastiff's throat with tremendous force, cutting off the howl before it began. Her rigid fingers darted toward the beast's eyes, striking with a scorpion's speed, but Pierce looked away before the blows landed; the second hound was still on the loose. He needn't have been concerned. This beast wasn't as alert as its companion, and it was still turning toward the drow when one of Pierce's arrows passed through its throat. Pierce's second arrow sent the creature tumbling to the earth, but to his surprise, it didn't remain there long. It was as if the creature was in fact made of blood. It *melted*, flowing out across the grass. A glance confirmed that the same fate had befallen Xu'sasar's prey.

Pierce leapt down from his perch, kneeling to study the grass. Traces of blood were already evaporating. Even the trail left by the beasts was faint, as if their feet had barely touched the ground. The blood on his arrows quickly faded. Within moments, there was no sign of the battle.

"Daine told you to remain behind," he said, not looking at Xu'sasar.

"He is not of my family," she replied, moving up beside him. Her bare feet were silent against the grass, and her voice was a quiet song. "I wished to hunt, and to find information. And I have done both."

"What have you learned?" Pierce was truly curious. The drow woman seemed extremely pleased with herself.

"We are all dead," she said, beaming.

CHAPTER 8

NIGHT: THE
HUNTER'S MOON
THELANIS

Lei's satchel was far larger than it appeared. During her time in the army, Lei had carried the supplies for her squad in her bag. These days she made sure that she always had an array of mystical tools on hand. She spread these supplies out on a blanket— short lengths of carved wood, polished semi-precious stones, envelopes of rare herbs, preserved body parts of strange creatures, scraps of parchment covered with intricate glyphs, and other odds and ends. She plucked a small piece of quartz out of a bag and began pulverizing it with a mortar and pestle.

"Thrice-damned drow!"

It had taken Daine a few minutes to realize that Xu'sasar had disappeared. Wherever she had gone, she'd left no trail that he could find. He had circled the sphere a dozen times, searching for any signs of movement or life. The plain was empty and silent; the only motion came from the slight breeze that ruffled the grass. At last he sat down next to Lei.

"I told you not to pick up strays," Lei said.

"I know it's not easy to sympathize with someone who's just tried to kill you," Daine said. "But things aren't always simple. When we first met, I held her at knifepoint, tried to use her as a hostage. And she still fought to free you from the firebinders."

"Well, if she gets herself killed, all we've lost is a healing charm," Lei said. "If she comes back, I think *you* should be the next hostage."

"At least I've got something to look forward to." Daine studied Lei's makeshift magical workshop. "Is this going to get us home?"

"It's not that simple."

"Try me."

"I know it's possible to walk from Thelanis to Khorvaire," Lei said. She added a few verynx whiskers to the mortar and continued her work. "There are soft places between the worlds, and all we need to do is find one. But . . . that's like saying that there's a tree in Breland with golden roots. Thelanis is another *world*, Daine. It's another level of reality, and time and distance may not even work the way we're used to. If we wander around blind, it could take us years to find our way home."

"But you've got an idea."

"Well . . . it's the Traveler's own odds, but yes, I have an idea."

Daine set his dagger on the ground, reaching over his shoulder to scratch his back. "I'm listening."

"We need an oracular vision."

"And?"

"Augury and divination are forms of magic. The priests who practice true divination call on the gods for guidance."

Daine frowned. "So you're telling me our only hope rests in the hands of the Sovereigns?"

Daine's voice was cold. Religion was a subject he preferred to avoid. Daine had been a devoted follower of the Silver Flame when he and Lei had first met, but over the course of the war, he'd slowly turned away from the Flame and belief in the higher powers. Lei still remembered the day in the ruins of Cyre when he'd broken his bow; she'd never seen him touch an arrow since then. She understood this bitterness. In the wake of the war she'd met many people who felt that no just god would allow such horror to occur. But Lei still believed in the Sovereigns. The Last War was the work of human hands. Lei didn't believe in predestination. She didn't accept the idea that divine hands shaped every event on Eberron. The Sovereigns were ideals, and they were a source of inspiration. Onatar might guide the hands of the craftsman, but it was still the craftsman who chose to make a sword instead of a shovel. Right now, however, inspiration might be all they needed.

"Not at all. But divination works, Daine. Whether it's guidance from Aureon, the Silver Flame, or some pure force of knowledge, there is a power out there that we can call on for guidance."

"If we were priests." Daine said, his voice still full of bitterness.

"Power is power." Lei found a small vial of pure water and added it to the mixture. "If this works . . . well, it should send the question into the ether. I don't know what will respond, if anything. But it's the only idea I've got."

"And if it works?"

"We get a push in the right direction, which is more than we have now."

"And then?"

Lei was used to Daine's sarcasm. This calm, serious tone was unlike him. "What do you mean?"

Daine scratched his back again. "I had another talk with Jode last night."

"It was a dream—"

"Perhaps it was. But he had a point. What happened on Xen'drik, Lei? What did we do?"

Lei suddenly felt cold. "It's over now."

"Is it? Lakashtai went to a lot of trouble to get us out to Xen'drik, Lei. We don't know why, and I don't like it. We've lost a battle, and we didn't even know we were at war. At the least, I want to understand what we're fighting for."

Lei's heart was pounding. Somehow, just thinking about the events of the previous day drove her into a sweat. She reached down for an empty wand, but her hands shook and she knocked over a vial of preserved lizard eyes, which spilled across the blanket.

Daine took her hand. "What's wrong?"

"I . . . I don't know," she said. "I just . . ." She tried to gather her thoughts, to focus on that final encounter with Lakashtai, but she couldn't. There was a wall in her mind, and even trying to approach the subject filled her with dread. Vertigo washed over her, and she reached out for the ground. Her hand found the darkwood staff, which lay next to the blanket.

She stiffened in shock the instant her fingers touched the wood. A wave of pure anger flowed from the staff, smashing into the wall within her. Time fell away. She could hear Daine's concerned voice and the faint sound of song, but all outer sensation was overwhelmed by the war in her mind. The staff was a bottomless well of rage and pain, and this emotion poured into Lei. The pressure built, driving out all conscious thought—and then she felt something break within her. Fear and rage drained away, leaving her weak and empty.

Slowly, she became aware of her surroundings. She was clutching the darkwood staff, both hands white-knuckled around the shaft. Daine had his arms around her, holding her steady while he murmured reassuring sounds in her ears. Many of the objects she'd arranged on her blanket were scattered or even broken; it seemed that Daine's embrace served a purpose beyond simple comfort.

"I'm . . . fine now," she said. Her voice sounded strange to her, rough. She looked at the staff. Perhaps it was a trick of the moonlight, but the sculpted face seemed especially lifelike, its eyes filled with sorrow.

"Are you sure?" Daine kept his arms around her, and now Lei relaxed and leaned back against him. "What happened?"

As Lei searched her soul for answers, memories began to return of a voice whispering in her mind in the depths of Karul'tash, a voice that was impossible to resist. "I think it was Lakashtai." She could feel Daine stiffen at the sound of the name. "Back at Karul'tash . . . she did something to my mind, forced me to follow her instructions. She must have implanted some sort of defense, a mental compulsion to prevent me from remembering what I'd done."

"*Flame!*" Daine swore. "If she's in your dreams, now . . ."

"I don't think she is," Lei said. Reluctantly, she broke free of Daine's embrace. As comforting as his arms were, she needed to stand, to regain her balance. She used her staff to push herself to her feet. Despite its strange performance earlier, at the moment it seemed to be a simple length of wood.

This wasn't the first time the staff had displayed hidden abilities. When they had faced a mind flayer deep below Sharn, the staff's song had shielded her and Daine from the monster's mental powers. Lei had spent days trying to unlock its secrets, studying it with every mystical technique at her disposal, but all to no avail. There was magic within it, but she could not identify its nature or what events were required to trigger its release. The staff had been given to her by her Uncle Jura, a man who had been driven from the house after marrying a dryad. She'd never been close to Jura, but she'd heard her share of disturbing stories. The final story was that Jura's wife had died under mysterious circumstances—and she'd been a dryad bound to a darkwood tree.

Lei stared at the staff, at the carved face. *Do you have a story to tell?*

No response. No song or motion. Just a sorrowful face carved in darkwood.

"Are you sure you're not hurt?" Daine was standing behind her, his breath warm against her neck.

She nodded and took a step forward, moving out of his reach. "I'm fine. Whatever Lakashtai did to me, it's gone."

"And your memory?"

Lei tightened her grip on the staff, but there was no need. The unnatural fear had been fully wiped away. She let her mind drift back to the chaos of Karul'tash.

Crystals. Shards of crystal. Pieces of a sphere. But there was more. When she'd held the shards, she'd *seen* into them. Just as she could sense the magical energies of a warforged when she used her gifts to repair it, she could feel the pattern of the sphere, what it had once been, the state it yearned to return to.

"A moon," she whispered. "They broke the moon."

"What are you talking about?"

Lei tried to force the image out of her mind. The pattern was painfully complex, more intricate than anything Lei had ever tried to create. For a moment, she feared it would swallow her thoughts. She pushed back, trying to ground herself in familiar concepts—words, numbers, stories. "Legends say that once, there were thirteen moons above Eberron," she said.

"And we just lost one somewhere along the way?"

"Yes," Lei said, still struggling to control her thoughts. "Some say that the planes are tied to the moons. Lakashtai said that the monolith was a place where the giants built weapons for their war. I think she was telling the truth. The central pillar was designed to allow travel between the planes. The orb I restored was supposed to prevent it."

Daine frowned. Magical theory was hardly his greatest strength. "How? Smaller words."

"The orb . . . it was designed to represent both the moon and the plane of Dal Quor. It's called sympathetic magic, though I've never heard of it being used on such a scale. I think that by destroying the sphere, they severed the connection to Dal Quor and drove the invading spirits away."

"And the moon?"

"Vanished? Shifted to another plane? I'm just guessing."

Daine nodded. "And Lakashtai somehow controlled your mind and made you put it back together?"

"Yes. But there's more to it. It was so complex. I could never repair something like that. But I just *knew* what to do. It was as if the knowledge was hidden within me, and Lakashtai somehow pushed all other thought away and forced it to the surface." She remembered that moment, that utter focus on *fixing the damage* . . . and a second revelation pushed its way forward. "Daine . . . *I* healed my hand."

"What?"

"I don't know how. But whatever Lakashtai did to me . . . when I repaired that orb, I healed myself as well."

"How is that even possible?" Daine said. "You said that not even *Jode* could heal that level of damage."

"He couldn't. I can't. I don't know!"

Daine threw up his hands. "One mystery at a time. This orb. You're saying that those dead giants used it to stop an invasion."

"I think so."

"And Lakashtai . . . *is* one of these invaders?"

"I don't know. We need to talk to a kalashtar!"

Daine shook his head. "After all we've been through? That's the last thing I'm going to do. Still, this is starting to make sense. When Gerrion separated us, Lakashtai was furious. She almost killed him. What if this whole thing—the entire trip to Xen'drik—was staged to get you to Xen'drik?"

"What?" Lei shook her head. "You were sick—"

"What if she *made* me sick to begin with? Back at Karul'tash, she said this was never about me. She said, 'Sometimes the best way to achieve your goals is to threaten another piece.' She couldn't get you to go to Xen'drik on your own. But she knew you'd do it—"

"To save you," Lei breathed. "And we played along. But why didn't she just drive *me* mad? And why me, in any case? I'm hardly the best artificer in Sharn, let alone in the world."

"Perhaps—"

A new sound cut off Daine's speculation. It was faint, distant, but set against the silence of the night, it might as well have been a thunderous explosion.

It came again. The baying of a distant hound.

"It seems like we'd best prepare for company," Daine said. "How quickly can you finish this oracle of yours?"

Lei studied her scattered tools, searching for the mixture she'd been working on. Luck was with her. In the midst of the chaos, the mortar remained undisturbed. "It's ready for use. And if we may have a fight ahead, I'd rather use it now."

Daine nodded. "Get back inside the sphere. I'll watch the door. Hopefully Pierce and our wayward drow will return before anyone reaches us. All the same . . . as soon as you're done, I want you to prepare a blinding charm, and to toughen your armor. We've been running hard for days now. This time, let's be *ready* for a battle."

Lei gave a quick salute. "Yes, Captain Daine." She made her way into the carriage, and Daine moved to block the portal. Glancing back, she caught sight of something strange. Daine was facing away from her, watching the plains, and she saw a strange mark at the base of his neck. It was only the briefest glimpse, a flash of black and red rising up from his chainmail byrnie, the edge of a bloody bruise.

But this was no time to look into injuries. She set the mortar in front of her and sat on the floor. Searching through the pockets of her pack, she found a long match and lit the contents of the mortar, producing a stream of aromatic smoke. Lei closed her eyes and breathed in the vapors, trying to set her thoughts adrift, to release the stress of the last few days and hours. Perhaps it was only her imagination, but as moments passed she felt that there was a *presence* surrounding her, a force that was watching, listening. Lei tried to speak, to open her eyes, but her body seemed distant and unresponsive.

What should we do? she thought.

The answer was immediate. The thoughts seemed to fill the world—

Your answers lie in the evening twilight beyond the Gates of Night. Darkheart must taste the blood of the Huntsman. She knows the path, and she is the key.

With those words, the presence faded, and Lei's eyes snapped open. The last traces of the smoke were fading, drifting out the portal. She felt lightheaded, and the word *Darkheart* hung in her thoughts. But there would be time to consider this riddle in the future: Daine had given her orders, and she had to prepare for battle.

CHAPTER 9

NIGHT: THE
HUNTER'S MOON
THELANIS

Daine kept his eyes on the plains, searching for any sign of movement. Since they'd last heard the distant baying of the hounds, he'd seen nothing. But now it was clear that they weren't alone . . . and the cries had sounded like hunting hounds to his ears. Trouble was coming, he was sure of it. Just a matter of time.

If anything, the possibility of battle was a relief. Being alone with Lei was both joy and torture. In the brief moment of Lei's seizure, Daine had felt a terrible helplessness. He was a man with a sword, and there was little he could do when the battle was purely magical. And Lei . . . Daine knew that she cared for him. There were times when she relaxed her guard, when she allowed herself to let her emotions show. But then she would push him away, force distance between them. He knew what the problem was: blood. Lei was an heir of House Cannith, and she bore the magical Mark of Making. Daine was born into House Deneith, and while he did not carry the Mark of Sentinel, the blood of the house was in his veins. It was said that mingling the blood of two houses was a sure way to produce a child with an aberrant dragonmark. Daine had never placed much stock in these stories or the tales of the malign consequences of carrying an aberrant mark—until he'd settled in Sharn. Last year he'd fought members of a guild formed by people with aberrant marks, a group that called itself House Tarkanan. Beyond the powers granted by their marks, many of these people were disturbing or disturbed. Daine could still remember the halfling girl sitting under a table talking to her rats, and the rotting flesh of the Tarkanan warrior who'd almost killed Daine with a touch.

Lei had been driven from her house, while Daine had turned his back on his family. But their blood remained, and it was one barrier Daine couldn't break through.

A sound cut through the silence—the call of a Cyran dusksinger. It was a signal. Pierce had returned. Daine gave an answering call, signaling a clear path, and the warforged soldier emerged from the shadows of a massive tor. As Pierce approached, Daine saw that Xu'sasar was with him, the dark elf almost invisible in the night.

"Report," he said, keeping his voice low.

"We encountered two hostile beasts," Pierce said. Speaking quickly and concisely, he described the encounter with the strange hounds and how the battle had come to an end. "We struck swiftly and with the advantage of surprise," he concluded. "But the tracks I found suggest that there are other creatures out there."

"And you," Daine said, turning on Xu'sasar. "Was I unclear? 'Stay here. Don't kill anything.' "

The woman was a full foot shorter than Daine, but she stared up at him with no trace of embarrassment.

"You are not of my family. You sought information, and I have obtained it."

"I'm listening."

"You foolishly sought to save my life," Xu'sasar said. "And yet you failed. This is the first of the final lands, the hunting ground, where the spirits of the worthy dead come in search of judgment."

"What could possibly make you say that?"

"Among the Qaltiar, life is a preparation for death and that which lies beyond. I have been taught the ways of the final lands since I was first marked as a hunter. The moon has not moved since we have arrived. You can see the faces of the failed buried in the soil, and the watchful spirits burning in the sky."

Daine glanced up. "We call those stars."

"Then you are a fool," Xu'sasar said. "Have you ever seen stars of such size and such color, shining so bright in the light of the moon?"

Daine frowned. She had a point. The moon was full and brilliant; the light should have made the stars seem faint. But each star in the sky was a blazing brand, brighter than any he'd seen on Eberron.

"Go on," he said.

"Can you not feel the energy that surrounds us?" Xu'sasar raised her hand, her eyes shining in the moonlight. "Can you not sense the truth of this place? We have seen the hounds of blood. This is the hunting ground. Here we must prove our worth in battle, earn our passage or spend an eternity to contemplate our failure."

Lei emerged from the sphere and stood behind Daine. "That's preposterous," she said. "The souls of the dead go to Dolurrh. There's no testing. No punishment. You go to Dolurrh, and the memories of your life fade away."

Xu'sasar seemed baffled. "Why?"

"There is no why," Lei said. "It's just what happens. You might as well ask why people die to begin with."

The drow blew out her breath, which Daine took to be a dismissive gesture. "Death is only the beginning. If you do not know this, small wonder that your people go to this . . . place of fading. You are blessed. Surely it is your death at my side that has granted you passage to the hunting ground."

A new sound filled the air: a distant horn, rising up against the darkness.

A hunting horn.

The bay of hounds began anew. And this time there were clearly more than two hounds. This was a full pack.

"You see?" Xu'sasar folded her arms. "The Huntsman comes. My deeds have brought you here, but only you can earn your final passage."

Daine glanced at Lei, who rolled her eyes.

"We're not dead," she said. "I told you, there are portals to Thelanis across Eberron. Some of her people must have found one, stumbled through it, and come up with this story."

"Fine," Daine said. "Right now, I don't care if we're alive or dead. I just don't want to be any deader."

"There are fates far worse than death," Xu'sasar said as the hunting horn sounded again, nearer still. "Worse even than your feeble death-of-fading. Fight fiercely and well."

"We don't know what we're dealing with!" Lei said. "We don't know if this is your 'huntsman.' We don't know if he means us any harm."

"*You* may not," Xu'sasar said. "I do. And the time for talking is at an end." She turned and walked around

72

the sphere, and as she slipped away, the shadows seemed to rise up and engulf her.

Daine grabbed Lei's shoulder before she could charge after the dark elf. "Enough," he said. "You're right. We don't know the situation, and I don't want to be the first to strike. Pierce, I want you in high cover."

Pierce glanced up at the crater sunk into the shell of the crystal sphere. Daine nodded, and the warforged slung his bow and scaled the edge of the carriage, crouching in the gaping wound.

Daine turned to Lei. "Did you make the blinder?"

Lei took her left hand off the shaft of her staff, revealing the golden glyph painted on the palm of her glove.

"Good. We're strangers here, and whatever Princess Xu may think, we're not going to attack unless they make the first move. But if we are beset by a pack of ravenous hounds—"

"Agreed," Lei said.

"Otherwise, best to keep it simple, I think." He drew his sword and dagger. "Back against the wall. If either of you are seriously injured, get inside the sphere. Lei, can you still close the portal?"

"I think so, yes."

"Than that's our redoubt. Be ready to fall back if needed. That goes for you too, Xu!" he called. The drow woman was nowhere to be seen.

"I told you not to—" said Lei.

"You're just jealous because she knows more about the afterlife than you do," Daine said.

"We're not dead!"

"And let's keep it that way." The baying of the hounds drew ever closer. "Stand ready."

The pack came into view.

Seven hounds loped forward in a perfect wedge formation. They moved in eerie unison, every motion precisely aligned. Despite their apparent bulk, each dog moved with a fluid grace. Remembering Pierce's tale, Daine wondered if the beasts were made of flesh at all, or if they were simply pure blood bound in canine form.

A single rider emerged from the cover of the tor, close on the heels of his hounds. Tall and lean, the man rode a sleek black stallion, whose coat shimmered in the moonlight. The hunter carried a short spear in his right hand, and on his left arm . . . Daine had to glance up to be certain his eyes weren't deceiving him, for he first thought the man had pulled the moon from the sky and was using it as a shield. The moon still shone above, but the disk on the Huntsman's arm was a perfect mirror of it, golden and glowing.

The shield seemed to draw all light away from the rider himself; even as he drew closer, all Daine could see was a silhouette, occasionally sparkling with a flash of silver or gold. "Pierce," he called. "If there's trouble, I want the horse down first."

"Understood."

The rider passed the last tor, and now Daine could see that the Huntsman wore a flowing black cloak studded with gleaming stars. A coat of mail covered his chest, dark steel glittering in the light from his shield. A deep hood hid his face.

Even as Daine braced for an attack, he saw that it wasn't coming. The rider gave no signal, but horse and hounds slowed their advance. The dogs spread out in a crescent, three to each side, coming to a halt dozens of feet from the sphere. The seventh hound, the largest, strode proudly along beside the dark horseman.

The Huntsman stopped a half-dozen paces away from Daine, lowering his spear. The rider wore a mask sculpted from stone, depicting the face of a man with a well-trimmed beard. His lip was curled in a sneer, his frozen features suggesting arrogance and cruelty, but a streak of luminescent lichen traced down from one eye, forming a single tear.

"I have come for the Lady Darkheart," the Huntsman said. His mouth was hidden behind his stone mask, but his voice was rolling thunder echoing across the plains. "Surrender her, and I shall make this hunt a sporting one."

CHAPTER 10

NIGHT: THE
HUNTER'S MOON
THELANIS

Darkheart?

Lei's thoughts were racing. When her uncle Jura was driven from House Cannith, he took the name Darkhart, and called his home Darkhart Woods. Was his wife this Lady Darkheart? If so . . . *Darkheart must taste the Huntsman's blood.*

"Generous of you," Daine said. "But you'll find no hunt here. And I don't know any Lady Dark Heart, unless you mean the drow girl who's lurking in the shadows and thinking of ways to kill you."

The stranger laughed behind his sneering mask. His glowing shield should have illuminated his face, but instead it seemed to draw the light away from him. "You do not know the one who stands beside you? Come, my lady. Your betrothed awaits."

He was talking to Lei.

Betrothed? Does he mean Hadrian? A year ago, Lei had been promised to Lord Hadrian d'Cannith, a wealthy artificer of Sharn. He'd been killed before Lei had even reached Sharn . . . they'd been led to believe Tashana was responsible, but now everything seemed to be in doubt. Could there be some mad truth to Xu'sasar's tales? Could this be the land of the dead?

Daine's gaze flickered to Lei, but he wasn't going to let the enemy distract him. "Who are you, exactly?" he said. "And what makes you think we'll let you walk off with the lady?"

The Huntsman laughed again. "My name is not for you, mortal man. I am the ninth brother of night, and I ride beneath the Hunter's Moon. I come on behalf of the Woodsman, to secure his bride."

Lei felt a growing sense of anger—resentment building in the staff and spreading out through her nerves. She took a step forward, ignoring Daine's sharp gesture. She wanted to attack, to drive the tip of her staff into the soft flesh beneath the stone mask, but she pushed down the alien emotions. "How do you know me?"

The effect was dramatic. The Huntsman's horse recoiled, and every hound took a step back, whining. The rider's stone face concealed his true expression, but his spear twisted to cover her.

"Truly, it is ghastly what has become of you," he said, and his deep voice was filled with sorrow. "But the Woodsman will still accept you, I think."

Lei didn't remember closing the distance to the rider. The staff filled with rage, and this fury drowned out all rational thought. One moment Lei was standing by Daine. The next, she was lashing out at the dark rider, throwing all her strength into a swift thrust.

Driven by anger, she moved with uncanny speed. But the Huntsman was quick to react. Man and horse moved as one. The stallion stepped to the side and the rider raised his lunar shield.

The impact was stunning. Thunder rolled across the valley, as if the sky itself were outraged.

The staff howled.

It was a terrible sound, a keening filled with agony and grief. The cry tore away hope, leaving a horrible void and sense of doom. As painful as it was, Lei could sense that she was only feeling the barest edge of the despair it channeled at the Huntsman and his hounds. The rider fell back before her, wilting against the force of the wail. Then the moment passed, and the blood-hounds charged.

"I hoped to escort you, my lady," the hunter cried over the continued keening of the staff. "But I will bring you by force if I must."

Lei let the fury guide her. The first hound to reach her leapt into the air, intending to tackle. Lei's thrust caught the beast directly in the chest, sinking deep into the flesh as if the staff was a spear. Even as Lei staggered back against the impact, the hound seemed to *boil*, lines of heat rippling around it. An instant later it exploded, and Lei felt warm blood splatter across her face.

Lei reached up to wipe the blood from her eyes, but the distraction came at a crucial moment. A second hound smashed into her, throwing her to the ground and pouncing on her chest. It knocked the staff from her hands. The wail came to a sudden end, and Lei's strength and anger drained away. The hound moved with blinding speed, striking at her throat with blood-stained teeth. Powerful jaws closed, straining to snap her neck . . . and failing.

Before the battle, Daine had ordered Lei to weave a protective enchantment into her vest, and this magic dispersed the brunt of the attack. The pain was great, and Lei gasped for breath, but the hound couldn't pierce her armor. There was a breath of wind, and the creature jerked back as it was struck by Pierce's arrows. It dissolved, pressure vanishing as blood flowed over Lei's chest.

Xu'sasar danced among the hounds, lashing out with knee and elbow. Lei heard the *thrum* of Pierce's bow as arrows cut through the air around her. Then she saw the dark stallion charging her.

At one point in her life, Lei might have been terrified. But after all she'd been through over the last few days, a man on a horse just couldn't frighten her. She saw the stone mask of the Huntsman, the single tear gleaming in the moonlight, the silver tip of his spear leveled at her heart, and the stallion's hooves, tearing the ground as it thundered toward her. Her staff had been knocked from her grasp, and there was no time to reach it. She was empty-handed.

But there was a golden glyph painted on the palm of her left hand.

Raising her hand, she reached out with her thoughts to touch the power she'd bound into the glove. The symbol exploded outward in a burst of light, catching horse and rider in a brilliant spray. Thousands of golden motes filled the air, then the light condensed around the Huntsman and his mount, covering both with a layer of glittering dust. The stallion staggered to a halt, stumbling blindly and pawing at the earth. Two of Pierce's arrows sang through the air—one was aimed at the stallion's eye, while the second caught the rider in the throat. Both shafts shattered on impact. The hunter didn't even seem to notice the blow.

"*Fie!*" the Huntsman cried, his voice thundering

across the plains. He shook his head, but the magical dust could not be removed that easily. "Such trickery will not keep me from my lady!"

"Then let's try a new trick." Daine vaulted up behind the hunter and wrapped his arm around the man's throat. The blinded stallion bucked and leapt, but Daine clung to the hunter with grim determination. The two struggled, and Daine pulled the rider from the saddle, sending them both tumbling to the ground. The Huntsman roared with rage. He spun, catching Daine with a wild, backhanded stroke of his shield; the man was far stronger than his slender frame suggested, and the blow sent Daine flying.

"Your weapons cannot hurt me!" The Huntsman brandished his spear, and his voice seemed to roll down from the sky itself. "I am a lord of the night! I—"

"Talk too much," Lei said. Daine had bought her time, and she'd risen to her feet and recovered the darkwood staff. As the outraged knight howled his fury, she drove her staff into his back. Once again, wood parted metal and flesh with the ease of the sharpest spear. The harrowing cry of the darkwood staff mingled with the Huntsman's howl of pain. The hunter fell to his knees, reaching down to grasp the wooden head protruding from his chest. Though his voice was a whisper, Lei could hear him perfectly.

"My lady," he rasped. "It seems you deserved your fate."

Then he was gone.

Horse, rider, hounds . . . the entire pack vanished. Even the traces of blood were quickly fading. Only one thing remained: a stone face staring up from the ground where the Huntsman had stood, a single glowing tear traced down its cheek. At first Lei thought it was the hunter's mask, but when she prodded it with her foot she found it was firmly embedded in the soil.

The staff had fallen silent, but Lei could feel its emotions. There was a certain satisfaction, a sense of victory. But this was overshadowed by deep pain and lingering anger.

"Hello?" Lei whispered. She felt a vague flicker of emotion, the faintest acknowledgment . . . but no words in response. Could it actually speak? She turned the staff so she could look directly into the eyes of the carved face. Before she could say anything, a hand closed on her arm and spun her around.

"You want to tell me what that was about?" Daine had a gash across his scalp, and blood was streaked across his forehead. "By now, I thought I could rely on you to follow orders." While he was angry, concern was the stronger emotion.

"I . . . can't explain it."

"Try. *Betrothed?* Hadrian's dead."

"So are we," Xu'sasar pointed out. The drow woman was helping Pierce recover the arrows scattered across the battlefield. Most were intact, and given the circumstances they couldn't afford to waste a single one.

Lei shook her head. "I still don't believe that."

"But he knew you."

"I don't think he did," Lei said. "I think he knew this." She pushed the staff between them.

"Go on."

"Remember my Uncle Jura? Jura . . . Darkhart?"

Daine nodded slowly. "You said his wife died."

"And that she was a dryad," Lei said, turning the face on the staff toward Daine. "I think some part of her still lingers within."

"So it's a *haunted* staff?"

Lei shrugged. "Dryads are bound to trees. If this is

from the heart of her tree . . . I don't know. But perhaps we should save this discussion for another time."

"And why's that?"

"She doesn't want to talk about it." Since the Huntsman had fallen, the presence within the staff seemed much stronger—and throughout the conversation, Lei could feel the spirit's discomfort growing.

Daine shot a glance at Pierce. "Am I the only one without an imaginary friend?"

"Perhaps you should ask Jode."

"Good point." Daine sighed. "So now what?"

"Surely we have another battle to fight," Xu'sasar said, sticking her head into the conversation. "I do not think that we truly defeated the Huntsman, and we must still earn our passage. More blood must be spilled."

I've had quite enough for one day, Lei thought. The gore from the hounds had largely evaporated, but the memory of warm blood flowing across her skin was all too fresh. "No," she said. "The vision I had said the answers lie in twilight. Beyond the Gates of Night."

To Lei's exasperation, Daine glanced over at Xu'sasar.

"She doesn't know anything about this place—" Lei began, but the drow cut her off.

"The spirits told you this?" Her musical voice was low and serious. Xu'sasar was a head shorter than Lei, and she pushed closer and stared up into Lei's eyes.

"I suppose you could say that . . ."

The drow girl reached up and placed her hand on Lei's forehead. Her skin was smooth and cool to the touch. Lei wondered if the blood of the dark elves was colder than that of humans. Then Xu reached out with her other hand, touching the face of the carved dryad.

"Ask her," she said.

"What do you mean?"

"Ask her. This tortured one, whose spirit has been bound in wood. She is of this world. She can show us the path to Dusk."

Lei frowned. She didn't like the drow girl. Lei had learned planar theory in the Towers of the Twelve, and she didn't want to debate with a jungle savage. The problem was, this time Xu was right. *Darkheart knows the path.*

She looked at the staff. "Can you lead us to the Gates of Night?" she said.

And the spirit showed her the way.

Chapter II

Night: The Hunter's Moon
Thelanis

Daine caught the moonlight on the edge of his sword, watching the light shimmer across the steel. In the chaos of recent events he hadn't had the time to study it, but he knew that something had changed. It wasn't that he felt a living presence in the weapon, and thank the Sovereigns for that; between Lei's sobbing staff and Pierce's unusual behavior, the last thing Daine wanted to deal with was another strange spirit. Still, he could feel some force stirring within the weapon, a power he couldn't quite touch with his conscious mind, which he could draw out in moments of anger. Just days ago the traitor Gerrion had been stunned when he'd tried to sunder the sword with Daine's own dagger—a blade of Cannith-forged adamantine, which should have sliced through the steel with ease. In Karul'tash, Daine had been filled with rage and fear at the sight of Lei in peril. Somehow, that emotion flowed into the sword. He'd brought the warforged assassin to the ground with a single blow. He should have been pleased; it seemed he had a powerful weapon at his disposal. Still, he didn't like mysteries. What were the limits of this power? How could he control it? And what was its origin? Daine had inherited the sword from his grandfather, and if it had a fabled history, Daine had never heard it. But it seemed there was much Daine didn't know.

One more thought nagged at the back of his mind, the faintest fear. When Daine and his companions had first arrived in Sharn, Jode had pawned Daine's sword. Some time later, the blade had been returned to by Daine by Alina Lorridan Lyrris, a gnome with considerable magical talents. Daine had scored the House Deneith sigil off the pommel when he had left the house, but Alina had restored it and refurbished the blade. Today, the sword was in better condition than it had been when Daine had first received it. Alina was a manipulator by nature. While she worked to increase her own wealth and power, her favorite pastime was toying with the lives of others—and she certainly wasn't known for her altruism. Alina did nothing without a reason.

So why had she gone to the trouble of finding and returning Daine's sword?

For that matter, how did he know that it *was* his sword? The balance was perfect. Refurbished as it was, it was the very image of the blade he'd seen his grandfather wield in battle. Still, could it be that Alina had given him a *different* weapon?

Daine sighed.

Lei led the way across the rocky plains, her staff held before her like a torch. Occasionally the staff would murmur, a fluting sob that sent a chill down Daine's spine. After their experience with the Huntsman, he found himself studying each stone face buried in the ground with suspicion, wondering if a new warrior would rise out of the soil.

"How much farther?" Daine called.

"I don't know," Lei said. "It doesn't talk. I just sense emotions, I guess. I don't know what we're looking for, or how far we have to go. Just that it's . . ." She paused and changed direction. "This way."

"There's nothing out there!" Daine gestured ahead of them. The light of the full moon spilled across the plains, illuminating a seemingly endless expanse of grass and stone. "What are we looking for?"

"Dusk." Xu'sasar and Pierce had been bringing up the rear. The two seemed well matched in the arts of stealth and stalking. Daine hadn't noticed the drow girl's approach, but now she stood between him and Lei. "The spirits say we must find our way to twilight. We wander through the deepest night, and head toward the day."

"Lei?"

Lei shrugged. "I wish I knew more, but that is what I heard in the vision. The answers lie in twilight."

"So why don't we just set camp and wait for a day?"

Xu'sasar blew out her breath. "Do you truly know so little of the way of the world?"

Daine bit back an angry remark. Most of his experience was on the battlefield, but in dealing with enemy officers, he had learned a little about reading his opponents, and he could sense something Xu'sasar didn't want to share. She was afraid. The drow woman had lost her companions, been thrust in among a band of strangers, and torn from her world. She didn't want to admit it, but Daine could read the fear behind her carefree mask. Xu's aggression, her search for conflict, was her way of pushing back the terror. Daine had to respect her skills. While Xu was at least a foot shorter than Daine, a fraction of his weight, unarmed, and barely armored, she'd taken on three of the Huntsman's hounds and brought two of them down with her bare hands. It was hard to reconcile such deadly prowess with her youthful appearance.

"No, Xu'sasar, I know nothing of the world," he said at last. "Enlighten me."

"This is the night," Xu'sasan said. "Even if it was dawn that we sought, it would not come to us. Dawn must be found. It is the way of the final lands. In life, we pass through all times, the world always changing around us. Not so in the final lands. The deep of night is a place, as is the dawn and the dusk. We must move through the night, and we must pay for our passage in blood."

"The Huntsman?"

"He may return. He is a spirit of the land and not easily destroyed. Despite the silence all around us, the Huntsman and his hounds are not the only creatures that walk beneath this moon. The spirits of the wild and the spirits of the past both watch us, and either may send deadly challenges to test our worth."

"Wonderful," Daine said. "With that in mind, why don't you keep a watch on our left flank?"

"Flank?" the girl replied, puzzled. Her knowledge of the Common tongue was remarkable but apparently not perfect.

"Follow. Watch. That way?"

The dark elf clicked her tongue. "I understand." She slipped away, leaving Daine alone with Lei.

"What do you think?" Daine said. "She does seem to know quite a bit, but I have a little trouble taking the word of a woman who wishes we were all dead."

"I still think it's a coincidence," Lei replied, shifting direction again. "The sulatar elves thought the realm of fire was some sort of paradise. Thelanis touches Eberron in many places. I know dozens of stories tied to the fey realm. That's all this is—stories her people have developed through planar travel, twisted with the passage of time. She's not lying. She's just seeing things through a lens of superstition."

"And this whole business of finding dawn?"

"I think she's right about that. Look at the moon. We've been walking for hours, and it hasn't moved at all. Nothing's changed. I don't know about buying passage with blood, or where my staff is leading us. But it knows where we need to go, so I say follow."

Daine looked up to study the moon. He watched the sky, then frowned and grabbed Lei's shoulder, pulling her to a halt.

"What?" she said crossly.

"Didn't you say that we should watch out for floating lanterns earlier?"

"Yes?"

"Look up."

A handful of lights drifted across the firmament, a careful, controlled flight unlike the swift motion of a shooting star. These lights were set against the darkness of the sky, and it was impossible to judge size, whether they were enormous orbs coasting miles above the ground or tiny sparks floating just out of reach. Whatever they were, they were moving toward the group.

"Cover!" Daine yelled. He threw himself against a massive chunk of stone, pulling Lei with him.

A trio of stars streaked past them. Now the lights were moving closer to the ground, and Daine could see them more clearly. The brilliant glow made it difficult to focus directly on the orbs, but Daine could see that they were balls of energy, approximately the size of his head. Each orb moved with the speed of a hunting owl, flying with eerie precision. Daine held his ground, keeping his back to the stone and his blade before him. Next to him, the darkwood staff sang quietly; Daine couldn't understand the whispered words, but he knew a warning when he heard one.

The orbs swept past Daine's position. They rose in the air, and he thought these fallen stars were going to return to the sky. Then they changed direction, shifting velocity and course to streak toward Daine and Lei.

The orbs were fast—but Daine's allies were faster. Before the spheres could close the distance, Xu'sasar appeared, loping across the plain and leaping into the air in an astonishing arc that seemed to defy gravity. Shadows writhed around her fists as she struck at one of the fallen stars. As Xu'sasar's momentum carried her back to earth, three arrows cut through the night. All of Pierce's shafts struck the same globe Xu'sasar had attacked. The arrows passed directly through the globe, and for an instant it seemed as if there was no effect. Then the sphere shattered in a brilliant burst of light. A shower of golden sparks drifted to the ground, swiftly fading.

The orbs could be hurt. But whatever these spirits were, they were far from helpless. The two remaining lights orbited Xu, then in the blink of an eye they dashed forward, passing *through* the dark elf. Light flared and electricity crackled. The smell of storm and burnt flesh filled the air, and while Xu'sasar did not cry out in pain, the stagger in her step was proof enough of her agony. While one of the spirits continued to circle the wounded girl, the second darted at

Daine. It was a streak of pure energy, and between the speed and brilliance it was almost impossible to see. Daine held his ground. He still had his hand on Lei's shoulder, and without thinking he tightened his grip. Her presence filled him with comforting warmth, and that strength seemed to flow into his blade.

He made his attack at the same instant as Lei, launching into a long lunge just as she lashed out with the darkwood staff. Both blows struck home, and the orb shattered into a thousand golden shadows. He felt a burst of joy and glanced at Lei. Her staff had fallen silent, and her smile lit a fire in his heart. But there was no time to bask in such emotion.

Turning his attention back to the struggle, he caught a brief glimpse of the third orb as it circled the rock Daine and Lei were using as a shield. Xu'sasar was already in pursuit, and while he had misgivings—*could it be leading us into an ambush?*—Daine darted after her, drawing his dagger and hurling himself forward. He turned the corner as swiftly as possible, both blades at the ready, poised to strike against the foe.

He immediately regretted the decision.

Daine had expected to battle the floating light. He'd considered that there could be a number of the ghostly orbs, a squadron of spirits lying in wait. For all that the lights had hurt Xu'sasar, they seemed fragile enough, and Daine was ready to deal with more of them.

The scorpion was a surprise.

Daine couldn't understand how the creature had come so close without their seeing it. It was the size of a wagon. Its massive pincers looked strong enough to cut a man in two, and its stinger was a long spear glistening with crimson venom. Pale opalescent plates that seemed to capture the moonlight covered its body, thicker than any armor Daine had ever worn. Its tail was raised high above its head, and raw panic filled Daine's heart—sheer, primal terror at the sight of this arachnid monstrosity. He staggered back a few steps before he managed to force down the fear, mastering his emotions and raising his blades. His mind was already racing, trying to come up with tactics that might let them overcome this monster.

And then it spoke.

"You have done well, warriors," it said. "But your trials have just begun."

CHAPTER 12

NIGHT: THE HUNTER'S MOON THELANIS

The night whispered to Xu'sasar, the barest wind stirring the dew-flecked sedge. The humans she followed paid it no heed. They continued to mutter in their barbarous tongue, oblivious to the wonders that surrounded them. She felt the breeze, and she knew it for what it was—the breath of the higher spirits, and a warning. She listened, trying to discern the words of the wind, but all she found was a vague sense of unease, of danger ahead.

This pleased her.

Xu'sasar's memories were a patchwork of strife and struggle. Her people were always on the path of new prey, and there was never a shortage of enemies. She was still riding her mother's back when she'd seen her first giant. The brute's strength was no match for the speed and skill of Xu'sasar's kin, and she'd felt only joy as her mother danced through the motions of battle. She learned the dance herself as soon as she could walk. She'd chased tilxin birds through the jungle canopy, leaping from bough to bough to keep pace with the tiny creatures. She'd fought giants on her own and faced firebinders, dream serpents, and creatures who walked like men but fought as insects. And she'd hunted outlanders who sought to plunder the ancient ruins. Sometimes her tribe fought these foreigners, as they had battled this Daine when he had first appeared. Other times, they simply followed the strangers, shadowing them and striking only if the spirits demanded it. Though the humans were rarely worthy prey, Xu'sasar enjoyed these long hunts, and over many cycles she had even come to understand their common tongue, though she found it painfully slow and clumsy.

Xu'sasar did not know what she would find under this moon. Nonetheless . . . this was the hunting ground, first of the final lands. Here she would prove herself. Here she would earn her passage to the next realm, and the next, until she joined her kin on the fields of endless struggle. She was the last of her tribe, and with her death the Jalaq Qaltiar left Eberron behind. Now it was her duty to honor her tribe in death and make her way to the last battle. As she moved through the night, she studied the stone faces buried in the earth, and she took pride in the fact that none were Qaltiar.

The wind whispered again, and Xu'sasar saw motion in the sky. A trio of glittering sparks had come loose from the firmament and were streaking toward the ground.

Wandering wisps. Even as she took cover against the stone face of the closest tor, she recalled the words of the Teller of Tales as he spoke of the many dangers of the final lands. *Remnants of the fallen, bound in the sky as others are buried in earth. They are deceivers who will lead you into bog or battle. Do not underestimate them; they burn with jealousy, and this fire is as deadly as any blade.*

These wisps had no interest in deception. They overshot Daine and Lei, then shifted trajectory, darting back toward the humans.

Xu'sasar never thought of leaving the outlanders to their fate. Whatever she thought of their graceless motions and foolish ideas, these were her companions on her final hunt. *A hunter who leaves her comrades to die is no worthy warrior.*

From that moment forward, all of her thoughts were focused on her prey. Distance was irrelevant. Xu'sasar was one with the wind, and she leaped into the air with no concern for height; her passion for her prey *pulled* her forward. Reaching within, Xu'sasar summoned the darkness that was the birthright of the drow, the cold night that consumed light and life. Shadows wreathed her fist, and she struck at the heart of the glowing sphere.

This was no creature of flesh and blood. Xu'sasar felt the barest resistance as her hand passed through her prey, as if she had struck a ball of water. Flesh or not, she could feel a pulse of agony radiate from the spirit as the darkness passed through the light. Xu'sasar twisted in the air and fell, spinning to face the wisps as she braced for her landing.

Three arrows sang through the air, reducing the weakened wisp to a shower of burning dust. Surely this archer thought he was doing her a favor, but Xu'sasar was not expecting the blow. She had yet to learn the tactics used by these three, and one of her own kin would not have stolen Xu'sasar's prey in this way. For an instant she lost her focus, and that was all the wisps needed. There was a flash of light, swift as the lightning itself, and a wisp crashed into Xu'sasar, passing through her chest.

Agony lashed through every muscle. The pain redoubled as the second wisp passed through her. She could feel the raw fury of the spirit, and this anger seared her thoughts even as its blazing light scorched her flesh. The torture might have forced a scream from the throat of a soft outlander, but Xu'sasar was a war-wraith of the Qaltiar, a hunter hardened by ritual. She had undergone countless trials, and the elders had burned the spirit-wards into her skin with the sacred venom of Vulkoor himself. Xu'sasar called on the memories embedded in these pale tattoos, and the strength of her triumphs dulled the pain of her current wounds. Her vision cleared, and she turned to face her foes.

The spirits split, one darting toward the humans while the other circled Xu'sasar. It was as swift as lightning, but Xu'sasar had fought giants who could call storms from the sky, and she had dodged lightning in the past.

She let her mind go blank, until her foe was the world. The wisp flashed before her, but it seemed to crawl through the air; the slightest motion was all it took to move out of its path, and she slashed her palm through the gleaming globe as it passed by. For an instant she wished that she had her knives, the long daggers that had belonged to her mother and to her grandmother before her, but it was no surprise that one should be forced to face the trials of the final lands with only hand and foot. Here she needed to prove the strength of her spirit and her knowledge of Vulkoor's teachings. It was strange that the outlanders were allowed to keep their tools, but they were soft and weak, and it was hardly surprising that they were not pressed as hard as the children of the night.

The metal hunter still sought to aid Xu'sasar. An arrow passed through the heart of the wisp, but this second attack was insufficient to shatter the orb. She caught a flash of light in her peripheral vision as the humans brought down their prey. The last wisp had no desire to share the fate of its fellows, and it sped away across the field. Xu'sasar sprinted after the wisp, letting the panther's speed flow through her limbs. She heard a warning in the back of her mind—*they are deceivers*—but the thrill of the hunt was upon her, and her prey would not escape her now. With every step she closed the distance between them. The wisp darted behind a tor and she raced after it, spinning around the corner.

The scorpion was waiting for her.

The Jalaq Qaltiar revered many spirits, but the greatest among them was the scorpion, known as *vulkoor* in the tongue of her people. Many lessons could be learned from Vulkoor, and the scorpion shared its armor and its venom with the drow. Many tribes refused to listen to any spirit but the scorpion, and her father had been killed in battle with drow who saw the pantheistic beliefs of the Qaltiar as heretical. For an instant Xu'sasar was paralyzed with fear. *He has come to punish me.*

Then he spoke. At first she thought he was speaking in the tongue of her people, then she realized that she couldn't hear the actual words; she simply *knew* their meaning, as if his language was so primal that it bypassed all mortal knowledge.

"You have done well, warriors," he said. His voice was deep and strong, and the mere sound of it seemed to push the lingering echoes of pain from Xu'sasar's breast. "But your trials have just begun."

The humans had come around the edge of the tor, the metal hunter behind them. Xu needed to act quickly; the outlanders were fools when it came to matters of the spirit, and the man was likely to raise his sword and doom them all. She fell to her knees, raising her palms before her.

"Forgive these people their ignorance, great Vulkoor," she said. "You in your wisdom have let them walk this path. Tell us what we must do to find our way to the endless struggle."

"What endless strug—" Daine said, but the mighty spirit cut him off.

"You honor me, Xu'sasar of the Broken Oath, but you are mistaken in many things. I am but a servant of Vulkoor. The highest spirits cannot be known in this life, even to those such as I. The path you walk does not lead to the endless struggle. Though you pass through the final lands, you still have a duty in the lands of the living."

Xu'sasar reeled. How could she be so close to her destiny—so close to her reunion with her fallen kin—and have it torn away? Was she to be reborn in a lesser form? A thousand cries echoed through her mind, but one did not challenge the words of so great a spirit.

Apparently, no one had told Daine. "So we're *not* dead?" he said.

Xu'sasar almost struck the rash human. If he angered the spirit, rebirth would be the least of the punishments it could inflict upon them. But the scorpion did not move, and when it spoke there was no trace of malice in its voice.

"You are not dead, traveler, though many perils still lie before you, and I make no promises that you will survive to see the light of evening."

Daine considered this. "And you're not planning to . . . eat us, tear us apart, marry us, or anything like that?"

"I am only a messenger, sent to offer guidance and advice."

"Sent by who, exactly?" Lei said. Far from being grateful, she sounded suspicious. She still held her staff at the ready, as if she could fight the great scorpion with her little piece of wood.

"I heard your call earlier, child of Cannith. Have you forgotten the message you were given? Your answers lie in the twilight."

"Beyond the Gates of Night," Lei said. "And what does that mean, exactly?"

"You have already learned what you need to know. You stand beneath the Hunter's Moon. The Gates of Night lie beneath the Deepwood Moon, in the domain of the Woodsman. You hold the key to the gates in your hand. Open the gates, and pass into Dusk and the domain of the one I serve."

"And the danger?" Daine said.

"These are the realms of the Nine Brothers of Night. The Woodsman is the mightiest among them, and he has been waiting long for the return of the Lady Dark-heart. He guards the Gates of Night, and he will kill you if he can."

"Look," Daine said. "Gates, woodsmen . . . I don't pretend to understand any of this. I don't care about the mystery. All I want is to get home."

"Your answers lie in Dusk, traveler, as do passages to your world. Open the Gates of Night, and you will find the path to your future."

"And what is my fate?" Xu'sasar said, finding her voice at last.

"For now, you must protect this one," the scorpion replied, indicating Daine with the slightest twist of its mighty stinger. "Set aside your questions and place your trust in our guidance. Your kindred watch you with pride and await the night when you will fight alongside them once more. But you have yet to earn your way. For now your path leads back to the world of the living. Honor your ancestors, heed the spirits, and let no harm befall this man."

The words burned in her ears. Protect this outlander? She had spent decades hunting his kind! But it was not her place to question the commands of the spirits or the wishes of the fallen. She bowed her head.

"Do I get any sort of say in this?" Daine said.

"No." The voice of the scorpion grew cold, and the slightest shift of its stance served as a subtle reminder of its power. "You will need her aid if you are to survive the dangers that await you. Now you must make your way to the realm of the Woodsman."

"And where's that? We haven't seen a lot of woods lately."

"Xu'sasar is correct. You will have to pay for your passage in blood. Seek Colchyn, the Great Boar of the Hunter's Moon. Lady Darkheart will guide you. Defeat Colchyn, and the path will be clear."

Lei considered this. "If you want us to do this, how come *you* don't beat this boar for us?"

"*We* must earn passage," Xu'sasar said. "Another cannot earn it for us."

"It is as she says," the scorpion replied. "I can only advise. Were I to fight your battles, you could never leave."

Lei nodded but still looked unconvinced. Xu'sasar blew out her breath. *Humans!*

99

"Your trial awaits," The scorpion said. "Heed the voice of Lady Darkheart, child of Cannith. Beware and be wary. Many a hero has fallen to Colchyn's tusks, and you will find him a formidable foe."

With that, he was gone. There was no sound, no burst of light. One moment the scorpion towered over them, and the next they were alone. Even the grass was undisturbed.

Daine broke the silence. "Lei?"

The woman ran a hand along the shaft of her dark staff, which murmured slightly. "I can feel the direction she wants us to go. Beyond that, your guess is as good as mine. At least we're not dead."

Xu'sasar blew out her breath. To be so close and have eternity stripped away—this was nothing to celebrate. Still, she had been entrusted with a task by one of the mighty spirits. This was the stuff of tales—were there any other Jalaq left to tell them.

She watched the human she had been ordered to protect, and wondered what interest the spirits could have in such a man.

CHAPTER 13

NIGHT: THE
HUNTER'S MOON
THELANIS

Chaos. That's what troubled Daine.

"We're following a haunted stick, which is going to help us to hunt a boar," Daine said, "because a scorpion says that's the only way we can get through the night. And why do we think this makes sense?"

"It's not about sense," Lei replied. "This is Thelanis. This is the source of faerie tales and superstitions. Remember the story of the Tower of Thorns, where Kellan kills the ogre and its ribcage becomes a ladder? That's what we're dealing with. This is a world of magic, not logic."

"So you're saying that we should believe it *because* it doesn't make sense?"

"No. I'm saying that it doesn't matter." Lei raised her staff. "The spirit in the wood wants to lead us *somewhere*. We can choose to follow. We can look for a boar. Or we can wander aimlessly around this wasteland waiting for more stars to fall from the sky and kill us."

Daine glanced at Pierce, who had remained silent throughout the exchange with the scorpion. "Pierce, anything to add? Any insight from your mysterious friend?"

"No," Pierce said. "My companion is disturbed by

this realm. It is sensitive to the flow of mystical energies, and the ambient level of magic in this place is causing it pain. I agree with Lei. We have nothing to lose from hunting this beast, and I would rather pursue a goal than act without guidance."

"Why do you question this?" Xu'sasar said. The drow girl was just behind Daine, having slipped closer while he talked to the others. "We have a goal now, a path to follow."

"I don't like other people choosing my path," Daine said. "Still, we don't have much of a choice. But let's not go into this blind. Lei, I want you to charge Pierce's bow. Make it more effective against animals. I want this to be as quick as we can make it."

"Be without fear," Xu'sasar said, even as Lei took Pierce's bow and began whispering over it. "Mine is the speed of the shifting panther, and I strike with the skill of the scorpion. This beast shall not escape us."

"I'm not worried about it escaping," Daine said. "Let me explain something to you. If you're going to stay with us, you need to do what *I* say. When I come up with a plan, you follow it. If you can't do that, go looking for your own boar. I don't care how fast you are. We work as a unit, or not at all."

Daine expected a hostile response. Instead Xu'sasar glanced down at the ground. "I meant no harm with my actions. I am the last of my tribe. Now my place is with you, and I will do as you say."

Her voice was low, her words slower than usual. For a moment, the mask of the deadly warrior seemed to fall. Since the fight in the planar sphere, Xu'sasar had been arrogant, overconfident, grating. But . . . *last of my tribe.* Daine had expected her to be grateful to be saved, but he'd never considered what she'd lost. He didn't know her relationship to Shen'kar or the other drow that had died at Karul'tash. But she was alone, just as far from home as the rest of them were, without even the comfort of familiar faces. It was impossible to tell her age—had she been human he might have guessed eighteen or twenty years, but an elf could reach a century with few signs to show for it. Still, in this moment she seemed like a child, embarrassed, lonely, and confused. She wanted to help, to impress him with her skills, and he'd snarled at her.

"I know you're skilled. I'm sure we'll need your help if we're going to get through this. I just need you to follow my orders. I need to know what my people are going to do. Strike out on your own and you place us all in jeopardy. Understood?"

Xu'sasar didn't look at him, but she clicked her tongue. Daine remembered the drow captain Shen'kar doing the same thing as a sign of affirmation. He reached out to put a hand on her shoulder, and found only empty air; dejected as she was, Xu'sasar apparently had no need of physical comfort.

"Done," Lei called.

"Good. Now, make a tangler. We let your staff lead the way, and hope that it has a taste for boar. Xu, Pierce, I want you flanking, searching for spoor. If the staff doesn't do its job, we'll have to do this the hard way. When we find the boar, Lei uses the tangler to root it to the ground. Pierce brings it down from a distance. Xu, you and I stay by Lei, and we engage the creature only if it breaks loose. Is that clear?"

Xu'sasar clicked her tongue again, and the others nodded.

Daine scratched his back and allowed himself to

smile. "Good. Now stay alert. We've dealt with blood-hounds, falling stars, and scorpions. Surely we can handle one little boar."

❀ ❀ ❀ ❀ ❀ ❀ ❀

"That's no little boar," Daine said. "You're sure about this?"

Lei nodded, and her staff murmured in acquiescence.

They were clustered at the base of one of the massive stone faces, looking down into a valley. A minute ago, Pierce had seen what they'd first taken to be a torch, moving through the night. It was no torch. It was Col-chyn, the Great Boar of the Hunter's Moon. The beast was easily the size of a full team of horses. Black bristles covered its body, and a ridge of flame ran down its back; the same fire burned in its eyes, and sparks flew from its nostrils as it snorted and smelled the air. Pierce racked his brains, trying to come up with some sort of plan that would keep them from going toe-to-hoof with this monstrosity, but nothing came to mind. He studied the sheltering tor, wondering if they could climb it, but another glance at the beast dispelled that notion. He was sure the boar could reach them even if they did climb atop the sculpted face.

"This cannot be avoided." Once again, Xu'sasar had slipped just behind Daine. "This is our trial. Let us face it with courage."

"We'll need more than courage. Lei, how about some haste?"

She nodded, reaching into her pack and producing her mystical tools.

Daine peered around the edge, studying the approaching monster. "Try the tangler. I doubt it'll hold this thing, but we've got nothing to lose. Pierce, keep your distance and just hit it as hard as you can. With Lei's enchantment, your arrows are still our best weapon."

"Understood," Pierce said.

"Xu," Daine said. "I know you held your own against those bloodhounds, but do you really plan to *punch* this thing?"

"I do not fight with only my fists. I strike with the scorpion's sting and the chill night. I have no fear of this creature."

Daine was tempted to tell her to stay back. Kicking a beast the size of a barn was madness. Still, Xu'sasar was swift even without Lei's magics, and distraction was what he wanted. "If it breaks free, do what you can to keep it off-balance. If we stay on opposite sides and keep hitting it . . . we need to buy Pierce as much time as we can."

"What about me?" Lei said. She'd just finished painting a silver symbol on a quartz disk.

"Stay out of the way." Daine said.

"What? Are you—?"

"This isn't a discussion. I know you can take care of yourself. But *look* at that thing. One kick and I'm bleeding out in the dirt. You're the only one of us who can heal, and I need you to stay out of harm's way. Stay back, and use that lightning rod of yours. Surely a blast from that will be more effective than a poke with your stick."

He could feel her frustration, but he was right and she knew it. It made sense . . . and the fact that it kept her away from this monster was a fortunate coincidence.

"Let's hope that scorpion wasn't lying.," Daine said. "Lei? Let's have that speed."

Lei closed her hand around the shard of stone and

whispered an indistinct word. Daine felt only the faintest tingle through his muscles, but he knew what to expect. "*Go!*" he said, darting around the edge of the tor.

The boar was at the base of the hill, trotting toward them. Thanks to Lei's magic, the beast seemed to be moving in slow motion, barely crawling up the slope. Still, at this distance Daine could see just how huge the boar was, and the thought of charging such a creature seemed ludicrous. Its tusks were as long as Daine's arms, and flames licked around its massive hooves, searing the grass as it lumbered forward. It was a creature of nightmares.

But they'd fought nightmares before.

Lei was first to act. She'd woven the entangling charm into a curled root, and she flicked the makeshift wand toward the great beast. Vines and roots flowed up from the ground around the boar, twining around its legs and holding it fast. Pierce's first volley of arrows flew through the air, blazing with eldritch fire. The beast howled as the missiles struck home, and Daine felt a glimmer of hope. Perhaps the beast wasn't as fearsome as it appeared.

Those hopes were soon dashed. The beast roared, its vitality undimmed by the arrows in its neck. Massive muscles flexed as it tore free from the binding roots, striding slowly across the treacherous ground. Pierce loosed a second volley as the boar emerged from the tangle, and lightning flared as Lei brought her wand into play. If the beast felt anything but anger, Daine couldn't see it. It bounded forward, quickly closing the distance. It was time to move.

Grandfather, guide my arm, he prayed as he charged down the hill.

The beast snorted as it caught sight of Daine and Xu'sasar, dousing the warriors in a shower of sparks. Daine howled as he broke to the left, lashing out at a massive leg; he wasn't sure if the monster noticed the blow.

Moments passed in a blur of sensation. Blazing hooves gouged great holes in the ground. Foul breath washed over him, long tusks sweeping down at his chest. Daine didn't stop to think or plan; he just *moved*, instinct and supernatural speed keeping him ahead of the deadly blows. He slashed at its ankles, thrust at its nose, taking any opening he could find.

It was a masterful performance—but even a master could fall to such a monster. With each passing moment the blows came closer and closer, and Daine's own strokes grew weaker. His back burned as a tusk tore through chainmail and flesh. The blow knocked him to the ground. He turned in time to see tusks descending—

And a dark shape flashed forward, diving into the jaws of the beast.

Xu'sasar.

Daine saw her for only an instant, but the image was burned into his mind. The web of silver-white lines tattooed across her inky skin gleamed in the faint light, but what truly struck him was her expression . . . a combination of grim determination and joy. There was no doubt, no fear. For a moment she was silhouetted, struggling to hold the creature's jaws apart as it thrashed and gurgled. Then its mouth snapped shut, and Xu'sasar disappeared within.

There was no thought: only fury, a raw howl of *not again!* Daine cast his entire body into one final thrust, both hands wrapped around a blade blazing like the sun. As the sword sunk into the creature's throat,

Daine heard the roar of an army, the clash of a thousand weapons.

And the boar exploded.

There was no fire, no heat. The flesh of the boar seemed to *expand*, flowing outward and *around* Daine, and the world changed as it did. The boar was gone, and so was the barren moor.

CHAPTER 14

NIGHT: THE
HUNTER'S MOON
THELANIS

Lei had watched many battles during her time with the Cyran Guard. In those days her first loyalty was to her house, not to Cyre. She was paid to repair warforged soldiers and to perform other supporting tasks, but she wasn't expected to risk her life on the front lines. Once that had seemed normal. Breland, Cyre—why should she care who won the battle? All that mattered was her house.

Now she was an outcast, banished from her house for reasons she didn't understand. Pierce and Daine were all she had left in the world. And once again, she was watching as they fought.

He needs me, she thought. Daine's swordplay was flawless; he slipped between the legs of the mighty boar, slashing at an ankle and rolling to the side before the beast could find him. It was an amazing display, but how long could it last? Arrows studded the creature's hide. Blood dripped from a dozen small wounds, the work of Daine's swords. Xu'sasar had managed to leap on top of the boar, and she struck at its spine with elbow and fist. Yet the boar fought on, its fury burning hot as the fires in its jaws.

Frustration warred with despair. There had to be something she could do, some magic she could weave that could help turn the tide of battle. But what? She could produce a burst of fire or a blast of cold, but she'd already loosed two bolts of lightning at the boar and aside from two patches of scorched skin the creature had hardly seemed to notice. Watching the battle, she tried to reduce it to an equation, seeking shelter in her formulas. What could she do to even the odds?

The boar laid a mighty blow across Daine's back, tearing through his armor and slamming him to the ground. Time shattered, and images flashed through Lei's mind—blood dripping from the beast's tusks; Daine on the ground, struggling to rise; Xu'sasar leaping into the creature's gaping maw. And then Lei found herself beside the beast, its rank odor washing over her as she darted around a massive hoof. She didn't remember moving. Rage, fear, and the howling song of her staff drowned out all thought as she lashed out again and again.

Her staff struck empty air. Flesh and blood transformed into black smoke, boiling out and over her. Warm wind and dark fog blotted out moonlight and moor.

When Lei's vision cleared, everything had changed. The moonlight outlined the lean shapes of a dozen giants, reaching for her with emaciated limbs. She spun around, fighting back panic. The creatures were all around her, and her companions were nowhere to be seen. Even her staff had fallen silent. She was alone. Mastering her fear, she raised her staff and waited for her enemies to strike.

No one moved. Lei's eyes adjusted to the darkness, and things became clear.

Trees surrounded her.

The moor had become a forest, and the trees weren't the only change. Moist, warm air flowed around her, rich with the smell of moss and sweet flowers. Calls of night birds merged with the sounds of insects and frogs.

Lei cursed her stupidity. *Teleportation, I suppose.* At the same time, something about her surroundings was deeply disturbing, beyond the sudden change. The gnarled hulks of the trees seemed to move in the shadows, in ways that couldn't be justified by the slight wind. At the edge of her vision the trees were twisted into contorted human shapes, and she could almost see screaming faces pressing out from the trunks . . . but when she turned to look, the shadowy images fell away, leaving plain wood and bark.

"My lady?"

Shock and relief rushed over Lei as the war-forged stepped out from behind a tree. "Pierce! What happened?"

"I do not know. I had one arrow left, which I intended to use in close combat. I saw Daine rise to his feet and strike the beast. Then I found myself in this place."

"Daine!" A chill ran through her heart. She'd thought she was alone, but if Pierce was here . . . Lei charged through the trees, ignoring clawing branches and leaping over roots as she tried to remember exactly which direction Daine had been in.

Lei found him sprawled across the ground, his sword a few inches from his outstretched hand. Blood glittered on the grass.

Xu'sasar knelt over him, and she glared at Lei like a challenged cat. Lei felt her fury grow . . . then she saw what Xu'sasar was doing. The dark elf had removed Daine's cloak and cut it into strips. She had bound the

smaller wounds and was applying pressure to the deep
cut on Daine's back.

Lei stepped forward. "Let me—"

The drow's hostile gaze stopped her short.

"I protect him," Xu'sasar snapped. There was something in her hand, a curved rod of ivory.

"Then you'll let me work," Lei said.

"You know nothing," Xu'sasar said. "You would send
him to your cold and empty place of death."

"Daine's on the brink of death, and you're argu-
ing *cosmology?* Get back, girl. I know you mean well,
but he needs my help. Out of my way, or we'll all die
together."

Lei could feel Pierce behind her; he might only have
one arrow, but his strength and speed could make all
the difference if it came to a fight.

Xu'sasar held Lei's gaze, her silver eyes glowing in the
light of the moon. Then she vaulted backward, a swift
flip that brought her down a few feet away.

"Save him, or we *will* all die together," she said.

Lei barely heard the threat. She knelt by Daine, taking
stock of the situation. Xu'sasar knew her work. Daine's
injuries were grave, but the dark elf had stanched the
bleeding and done as much as could be expected with the
limited tools at her disposal. Lei drew a small wand from
her pouch, falling into the meditative state required
to weave her magic. Reaching out with her mind, she
grasped the magical energies that lay just beyond the
everyday world and *pulled*, forming strands of mystical
power. Working as quickly as she could, she spun these
threads together, completing the familiar pattern of
healing and tying it to the rod in her hand.

Lei opened her eyes. Her nerves were sore; using
magic was always a trial, and she'd stretched herself

near to her limits. But there was no other choice. Daine could take days to heal on his own, assuming that natural healing was even possible in this place where the moon stood still. Taking a deep breath, Lei drew the wadded cloak away from Daine's back.

She winced at the sight, holding back bile. Though Lei had seen terrible things over the last four years, she'd never gotten used to the stench of blood or the sight of wet bone. She was trained to repair warforged, to work with stone and wood, not unlike snapping the pieces of a puzzle into the proper shape. The body of a warforged made sense to her. Humans were blood and meat bound within thin skin. She hated the idea that her friends—that *Daine*—could be so fragile.

It's a weakness of the medium. Who had told her that? She shook away the thought; this was no time for reminiscing. The gouges across Daine's back were deep. Links of torn chainmail were crusted in dried blood. Lei picked up the rod and passed it over the wounds, slowly releasing the power held within. Muscle and flesh flowed before her eyes, knitting together. New skin formed over the injury, without even leaving a scab.

But something was wrong.

Daine began coughing as he returned to his senses. True to form, his first action was to reach out and grasp the hilt of his sword. "Where . . . Lei?"

He tried rise up, to turn and face her, but she pressed him back down against the ground. "Shh," she said. "I'm here. Pierce is watching over us. Just lie still. I'm working."

"I feel fine." He started to stand, and again she pushed him down. Despite his words, he was far from his full strength.

"Please," Lei said. "Be still. Just a moment more."

"Will you at least tell me what's going on?"

"Quiet. I need to concentrate." Working as swiftly as she could, she wove two new enchantments. She studied Daine closely as she unleashed the first spell, a second charge of healing. She could feel the strength flowing into his limbs . . . but what she saw on his back didn't change.

Clotted blood covered Daine's torso. Two lines arched across his back, where Lei had healed the deep wounds. The skin *should* have been clean and unblemished. It wasn't. There were mottled patterns of red and black, bright blemishes or bruises. Holding her breath, Lei activated the other charm she'd just woven . . . a simple domestic spell, used for cleaning houses and clothes. Daine's chainmail was polished to a mirror sheen. Blood and dirt were forced from his clothes. And the dried blood around his wound vanished.

Lei staggered backward, stumbling away from Daine. Her foot caught on a root and she thought she was falling, but Pierce was there at her side, to catch her and hold her steady.

"What is it?" Daine said. He rose to his feet, and Lei could see the fear in his eyes—concern for *her*, she realized. But she couldn't keep from flinching as Daine reached out for her, and she pressed back against Pierce's reassuring bulk.

"Take off your shirt," she whispered.

Daine took a step back, his brow furrowed. "This is a dream, isn't it?" He glanced around. "Jode?"

"Your back," Lei said. "I need to see it. Now."

Daine nodded and began removing his armor. "Sure. I've actually been meaning to ask you about that."

"You *knew?*"

"Knew what? I think I've got a rash of some kind. It itches like the Flame." He pulled off his shirt and turned around. "How bad is it?"

Lei didn't know what to say.

"What's going on?" Daine said, trying to peer over his shoulder.

In the end, it was Xu'sasar who spoke. "You have red and black lines spread across your back, much like the wards of the warrior that grace my skin. Did you not earn this honor?"

"Lei?" Daine said. "What's she talking about?"

"It's a dragonmark," Lei said, her voice little more than a whisper. "An aberrant dragonmark."

CHAPTER 15   NIGHT: THE DEEPWOOD MOON THELANIS

You carry the greatest treasure of the house in your veins. Your blood is our power. This is a glorious gift, and a fearsome responsibility.

Daine had abandoned House Deneith many years ago. Even as a child, he hadn't paid much heed to his father's lessons. At the time, it had seemed like so much arrogant propaganda, designed to preserve the power of the dragonmarked bloodlines. Daine had dismissed the warnings against mixing the blood of two houses, and the tales of the bitter war fought to purge this tainted blood. That was before Sharn. Now Daine remembered the wild eyes of the little girl who spoke to rats, and the chilling touch of the rotting man.

As our blood can produce champions, so can it produce monsters.

Rage and fear warred within him. Daine wanted to shout, to deny it, but even as he drew in his breath he knew it was the truth. Now that he knew it for what it was, Daine could feel the mark on his back. It was as if three living serpents had been fused to his flesh. He could sense the pattern they formed, their coils intertwined and woven together in an intricate pattern. Worse than that, he could feel them writhing.

The terrible itching was no rash: it was the mark, *moving* against his skin.

"How?" he asked.

Lei shook her head. Fear rimmed her eyes, and Daine couldn't decide if she was afraid for him or afraid of him. Lei had taken the lessons of her house to heart, and Daine remembered her horror when they encountered the aberrants of Sharn.

Daine took a step toward her, and Lei shrank away from him. Pierce moved between them, and a chill settled over Daine's heart. He was certain that Pierce knew he wasn't a threat, that the warforged was simply acting to reassure Lei. Nonetheless, the two were the only anchors he had left in the world, and to have both desert him at once . . .

Vertigo swept over him. The world spun around Daine, the ground rushed toward him, and his head slammed into the soil. Then he felt Lei's hand wrap around his. Drawing strength from that contact, Daine pushed back the nausea. He made a cage of his thoughts and wrapped it around the writhing vipers, crushing them into a ball of energy and forcing it into the darkness.

Daine opened his eyes. His face was still pressed against wet grass, and his skin was clammy with sweat. The woman holding his hand braced herself and helped pull Daine to his feet.

"Thanks," he said. He reached out to embrace his benefactor, and then stopped short in surprise. A woman had come to his aid, but it wasn't Lei holding his hand . . . it was Xu'sasar. The drow's silver eyes were locked on his, twin moons gleaming in the dark woods. In the past her pale gaze had always been unnerving; now it seemed softer. Still, it was not the face Daine had expected to see, and he pulled away.

Now Pierce was there, towering over him. "Can you stand, Captain?"

"I think I'm fine now," he said. And it was true. The crawling, itching sensation was gone. He could feel the spark of energy burning within him, but it wasn't entirely painful. He found that he felt sharper, more alert. Even the smell of fresh grass seemed strong and clear. For a moment he wondered . . . "Is it still there?"

"Yes," Lei said. "I—" Her voice caught in her throat as Daine turned to face her.

"Fernia's flames!" he swore. "We're in the middle of the thrice-damned forest of eternal night. I didn't ask for this to happen, and there's no time for us to turn on each other. Lei, I don't care how scared you are, I need you to tell me what's going on!"

"Perhaps you did." Pierce's voice was steady and calm, slow flowing water.

"What?"

"Perhaps you did ask for it to happen."

"What are you talking about?" Daine said.

"The blue fluid you consumed last night. You said that it held the essence of Jode's dragonmark."

"Yes," Lei said. "The blood of two dragonmarked lines . . . he's right, Daine." There was still fear in her voice, but now her curiosity was getting the better of it. She moved next to him. "Let me look."

"Pierce, Xu, watch the forest," Daine said. "See if you can find any signs of tracks. Sovereigns know what's out there." He turned his back to Lei.

"What does it feel like?" she said, searching through her satchel for tools. "You said it feels like a rash?"

"Yeah, sort of . . . itching, faint burning. I was trying to ignore it. It's faded, though."

"When did this begin?"

"Pierce is right," Daine said. "I don't remember noticing it until we were in the planar sphere . . . after I drank the blue liquid."

"Let's avoid any speculation right now," Lei said. She produced a slender wand and chunk of crystal from one of the pockets of her bag. "At a glance, the pattern is reminiscent of a dragonmark. However, the pattern and color are inconsistent with any of the twelve true dragonmarks . . . which is, of course, the defining element of an aberrant dragonmark."

Her voice gained strength as she spoke. Clearly describing it helped her feel more in control of the situation. Even Daine found himself feeling slightly better. This was what Lei did. Surely she'd find an explanation.

"What's especially unusual is the size of the mark," she continued. "I've never heard of an aberrant dragonmark larger than the least true dragonmark. They are invariably small enough to fit on the palm of the bearer's hand. But this . . ." She walked around Daine, studying his skin. "I've only seen its like once before. In Metrol, one of my cousins was said to be marked by Siberys. He's a legend in our house; he can create objects from pure thought, bringing imagination into reality."

Daine twisted around, trying to look at his back, but he could only see a few vivid red stripes along his shoulder blade. Still, he remembered the pattern he had *felt* only moments ago, traced across his entire back. Lei was right. Daine had seen only one person with such a mark in his own house. And the size of the mark was always an indication of its power. "So what does this thing *do*?"

"I don't know," Lei said. Daine felt slight warmth against his skin as she passed the wand over it. "There's no aura of magic, but that's not unusual. Sometimes it's possible to draw conclusions from the pattern, but I can't make sense of it. Have you had any sort of unusual visions, emotions, anything like that?"

"I don't know. Something like talking to a dead half-ling in my sleep and having injuries disappear?"

Lei chewed on her lower lip. "Yes . . . that would qualify."

"That hardly seems like a terrible thing," Daine said. "If that's the worst—"

"What makes you think that's the worst thing you'll have to deal with?" Lei said, her voice rising. "It's an aberrant mark. You know the stories as well as I do! Madness. Sickness. You think talking to our *dead* friend is a good sign?"

Daine's frustration grew. "I know the stories. And what if that's all they are? You've never seen anything like this before. So why do you still believe something just because your parents told it to you? After all the lies—"

The world dissolved in a flash of agony, and Daine cried out in pain.

Lei had brushed her hand along the path of the mark. In that moment of contact, the spark that had been burning at the base of his spine flared into fire, burning a twisted path across his skin. Lei jerked back, and the pain subsided. Daine gasped for breath.

"Daine," Lei said. "I didn't . . . I don't know what that was. The red lines along your skin glowed, and there was a burst of heat. Are you hurt?"

"I don't think so." The spark had flowed back into his bones, and he slumped against the cool grass. "I guess talking to Jode isn't the worst thing I'll have to deal with."

"Hold still."

Daine felt a spot of warmth, growing stronger and sharper. "Just bringing my finger close to the mark is enough to cause a reaction," Lei said. "I've never seen anything like this."

"So if you touch me, it causes excruciating pain? Well, that's just wonderful."

"We'll get to the bottom of this, Daine. There's got to be something we can do about it."

"Not right now," he said, pushing himself up and grabbing his shirt. "We've wasted enough time on this. As long as you don't touch me, I seem to be fine; it's not even itching anymore. So if you think you can keep your hands off me, let's find our way out of these wretched woods."

"I don't think that's—"

"Lei, the mark has most likely been there for at least a day. I'm not dead yet. But we could all be dead in a few hours if we don't find a way out of these Flame-forsaken woods. So let's get moving!"

Daine whistled a call to Pierce as he pulled his chain shirt over his padded vest. The answering call came quickly, and the warforged emerged into the grove.

"No sign of anything I would consider a threat, captain. No humanoid tracks beyond our own, no creatures larger than a fox."

"You overlook the dangers, man of wood and metal." Xu'sasar appeared next to Pierce, sliding out of the shadows. "There are birds in the trees, owls and other night hunters. There are eyes in the darkness. In the land of the living, such a creature may not threaten you. But this is the realm of the spirits, and size alone means nothing."

"Well, Xu," Daine said, "why don't you tell us what we're

supposed to do, since you seem to be the expert here?"

"Nothing has changed."

"*Everything* has changed! We're in a *forest!*"

"Yes. We have bought our passage further into night. It is as the great scorpion told us. The gates to Dusk lie in the domain of the Woodsman. We have come to this spirit's demesne. Now we must find our way to the gates themselves." She turned to Lei. "You still hold the key, shaper."

"The staff," Lei said. She'd dropped the darkwood staff to tend to Daine, and even as she knelt down she paused before taking hold of it.

"Lei?" Daine said.

There was doubt in her eyes, but she finally shook her head. "She's right. The staff does know the path, and we haven't reached the end of it. There's just . . . such anger and pain within the wood." She placed her hand on the shaft, and stiffened slightly. A faint moan rose through the air, the whisper of an elven voice. "She knows where we must go," Lei said, rising to her feet. "And she knows that danger awaits."

"And it's been so peaceful so far," Daine said. But his smile was forced. Traces of pain lingered in his memory, and he could still feel the spark burning at the base of his spine, a reminder of the mystery etched across his back. *This is no time for fear,* he thought. *Accomplish the mission. Keep moving forward.* "Lead on," he told Lei.

❀ ❀ ❀ ❀ ❀ ❀ ❀

Khorvaire had its share of vast forests and jungles, and this wasn't Daine's first journey through deep woodlands. Yet there was something disturbing about it, something that lent credence to Xu'sasar's tales of spirits and ghosts.

None of the trees stood straight. They were gnarled and bent, their outspread limbs suggesting giants contorted in pain. Daine would swear that he could see faces in the wood, distorting the bark—but when he turned to look, trunks and boughs were unblemished.

Trees or no, eyes were all around them. Rodents rustled in the low shrubs, creating just enough motion to keep Daine's nerves on edge. He caught sight of an owl the size of his head, a beautiful bird with black plumage and golden eyes. The creature sat in a high branch, watching the travelers below with proud indifference. Daine considered having Pierce shoot the bird, but it seemed pointless; he felt as if the entire forest was arrayed against them, and it was hard to imagine the death of one owl doing anything more than annoying whatever spirits might be present in the trees and the beasts. Besides, Pierce only had one arrow, and it seemed unlikely that a bird would be the greatest threat the forest had to offer.

Lei forged a path, pushing aside vines and shrubs with her whispering staff. She had enchanted one of her gloves, and pale white light illuminated the area around her. She pressed at a nest of vines—and jerked back as the web of interwoven boughs came to life.

"Balinor's bow!" She jerked backward, nearly dropping her staff.

Daine pressed past her, his sword gleaming in the eldritch light. He saw three writhing tendrils disappear into the shadows, oily black and glittering silver. He poked at the underbrush and caught a glimpse of a pair of pale eyes, before it disappeared into the undergrowth.

Lei seized his arm. Daine flinched, waiting for the excruciating pain that had accompanied their last moment of contact, but all he felt was the pressure of her hand.

"I'm sorry," she said, breathing deeply. "I just . . . I wasn't expecting that."

"Only a few snakes," Daine said. "It's nothing to worry about. Let me take the lead. You just tell me which way to go."

Lei nodded and Daine pushed forward. A few more serpents slid away into the shadows as Lei's light fell upon them. Lei shuddered whenever she saw sinuous motion. Daine was certain there was something behind this strange fear. She'd seen far worse in the Mournland and the sewers of Sharn, and never reacted in this way. But he knew to leave it alone if she didn't want to talk about it. They could survive a few snakes.

Then he looked up.

The trees were covered with serpents.

Black and silver scales were almost invisible against nightshadowed bark and the light of the moon, but now he saw the motion in the branches, the heavy coils hanging from the boughs. The viper that darted away from the light was barely as thick as his thumb; looking up, Daine found himself gazing into the eyes of a scaled beast whose head was larger than his own. Dozens of cold eyes were watching them, and looking at the silhouette against the moonlight, it seemed as if the trees themselves were moving.

Daine said nothing, glancing at Pierce. The warforged had his eyes on the canopy, his last arrow nocked to his bow. Should a serpent strike, Daine was certain it would fall with that arrow through its skull. Xu'sasar was nowhere to be seen, but Daine was beginning to expect that.

"I'm sorry, Daine," Lei said, right behind him. "I

know this is stupid, especially with everything you've gone through. It's just . . . when I saw those snakes moving, I remembered that *thing* below Sharn. The mind flayer."

She was talking about a horror they'd fought when they'd first arrived in Sharn, the squid-faced monstrosity that had murdered Jode and almost killed Lei. Daine could only imagine the trauma of seeing such a creature looming over him, tentacles reaching down to grip his skull . . . he could certainly understand her fear.

The ground was uneven, and a maze of treacherous roots hid beneath the carpet of moss. In the gloom of night, vines and roots were all too easily mistaken for snakes, the shadows creating monsters at every turn. But it was a different sort of serpent that brought their progress to a halt. Pressing forward, Daine saw a glittering, sinuous shape stretched across their path. It was no snake, nor even a living creature.

It was a river.

The river formed a canyon through the dense forest, a rift in the dense canopy of foliage. Looking up, Daine could see the sky. As on the moor, there was only one moon in the sky, but this moon was larger than the last had been, and silvery-white. The stars formed unfamiliar patterns, and Daine was comforted by how faint they seemed to be. The water of the river was eerily silent, and to his eyes it seemed perfectly still . . . as if it were frozen.

Daine knelt on the shore. He wasn't much of a swimmer, but with water this calm, perhaps they could make it across. He could just see the far side of the river, another wall of trees rising in the darkness. As Daine knelt by the water, a sibilant whisper filled the air—the eerie song of Lei's staff.

"*Stop!*" Lei's voice was low and urgent. Her hand gripped his cloak, pulling with surprising strength; Daine stumbled, his left hand sinking into the moist earth as he flailed to keep from falling.

"What?"

"Don't touch the water. I don't exactly understand what she's saying, but there's great danger there."

"Ah." Daine looked out at the river. "So . . . this *isn't* the way we want to go?"

Lei ran a hand along the staff, which moaned softly. "We need to cross the river," she said, "but . . . we can't touch the water."

"What then? Do you have the energy to teleport us?"

Lei shook her head. "It took all I had left just to create the light. Perhaps we should rest here."

Daine glanced over Lei's shoulder and saw a twenty-foot snake slip up into the canopy. "I don't think this is the best place to set up camp."

"There is a bridge," Xu'sasar said. The shadows seemed reluctant to release the drow woman as she stepped out from the forest and into the moonlight. "I can show you the way. It has a fearsome aspect, but it can provide the passage you seek."

"Fearsome aspect?" Daine said.

"Yes," Xu'sasar said. "The bridge is alive."

CHAPTER 16

NIGHT: THE
DEEPWOOD MOON
THELANIS

Pierce had said little over the course of the
last day. Even as he had grown closer to his friends,
he had never developed a knack for idle chatter. He
preferred not to speculate. If he was uncertain about
a subject, he held his peace unless he was ordered
to give his opinion. And so he had been silent for
much of this journey, doing his best to watch Lei
and to make sense of the things around him. So far
he'd had little luck. The memory of Indigo lying
on the floor of the Monolith lingered in the back
of his mind, and his thoughts kept drifting back to
that battle. The conflict with the Huntsman and the
boar had been welcome distractions, but he seemed
to be losing something with every battle. Indigo
had shattered his flail, a weapon that had served
him well for many years. And now he had but one
arrow left for his bow. Pierce was far from helpless.
His fists and feet were made of steel, and he could
crush bone if he landed a solid blow. But he had
minimal training in unarmed combat, and he felt
curiously impotent, as if he were a sword that had
lost its edge.

The mark on Daine's back was another threat he could not battle. He could sense Lei's distress, but he had no power to help either of his companions.

The mark resembles an archaic form of the Draconic language but matches no known character, Shira told him. *This unusual coloration and atypical design indicates that this is an aberrant dragonmark. Such things appeared tens of thousands of years after my imprisonment, and all that I know, I know from your mind.*

Pierce could feel her ghostly touch sifting through his memories. Traces of thought rose to the surface—

A history of House Cannith he'd read while studying the origins of the warforged.

His battle with an aberrant half-orc who fought with a blade of fire.

And Lei, expressing her fears at finding these aberrants in Sharn. When Daine expressed ignorance about the mark, it was Shira who suggested its possible origin, the blending of Daine's Deneith blood and the concentrated dragonmark he had consumed. But she could provide no insights into its power or what threat it might pose to Daine himself.

The magic in this place is too strong, she thought. *It is painful for me even to look through your eyes.*

We are blunted blades, Pierce replied. *I have lost my weapons, and you have lost your eyes.*

You are my eyes, even when I cannot share your vision. We are one.

Even as he found some faint comfort in this thought, Pierce was frustrated by the mark. Daine was angry, Lei was afraid, and Pierce found himself stepping between them. For all that he respected Daine, he had to protect Lei from any threat. Pierce was relieved when they began moving again, but the tension remained. Pierce did his best to set it aside, to focus on his surroundings and on moving with silence and grace. He kept his last arrow nocked, listened to the sounds of the night, and tried not to think of Indigo.

❀ ❀ ❀ ◉ ❀ ❀ ❀

"That's your idea of a bridge?" Daine said.

"You seek a path across the water, and the spirits provide," Xu'sasar replied.

"Not very well," Daine said. "How is that a path, exactly?"

Following the dark elf along the shore, the companions came to a slight rise. Peering over, they could see the path she spoke of.

It was a snake.

A pillar of dark stone stood on the shore, and a serpent was wrapped around it. It was the largest reptile Pierce had ever seen, with jaws that could swallow a wolf—or a man. Its coils were deep black banded with uneven crimson stripes, and the sight reminded Pierce of the disturbing mark on Daine's back. It took only a moment to evaluate its potential as a threat. Lei had pushed herself to her limits. Pierce had only one arrow. To fight such a monster in their current condition was an invitation for disaster.

"You still do not understand the ways of this world," Xu'sasar said to Daine. The wind caught her silver-white hair, and she seemed to be shrouded in a cloak of moonlight. "Just as the great boar provided passage to this place, surely this serpent is the key to our next challenge."

The drow warrior was still a mystery to Pierce. Her talents were impressive and somewhat disturbing. Pierce placed great faith in his senses, and it was troubling to deal with someone who could so easily elude him. And while Pierce might have fists of steel, Xu'sasar's skills at unarmed combat clearly exceeded his own.

She is no longer unarmed.

Pierce could *feel* Shira indicating a point in space, and he let her guide his eyes. Xu'sasar held her right hand low and close to her side, and had casually placed her body between the others and the object she held . . . but Pierce caught a glimpse of a curved point of ivory.

"What is it that you hold?" he said.

Guilt was not an emotion Xu'sasar seemed to feel. Her expression was utterly innocent as she raised her hand. The object appeared to be a primitive double-bladed dagger. It might have been carved from the claws of some great beast, two curved spurs sharpened to hold an edge and joined.

"Where were you hiding that?" Daine said, surprised.

"I hide nothing," Xu'sasar said. "The spirits gave me this gift as a reward for my courage, and to meet the challenges of the path that lies ahead."

"The *spirits* did this," Lei said. "And when was that?"

The dark elf turned to fully face Daine, ignoring Lei's question. "I have shown you the way. The bridge awaits."

"I know you fought a giant boar with your fists," Daine said. "But do you really want to attack that serpent with a little knife?"

"That would be an act of a fool," Xu'sasar said. "To fight such a creature, I should want a longer weapon, one with which to hold the creature at bay and force open its jaws."

"Right, which means—*Flame!*" Daine swore.

The double dagger expanded in Xu'sasar's hand, a

leather-wrapped shaft of bone extending even as the claws on each end stretched into long, flat blades. Xu'sasar shifted her grip, and now she was holding a double-bladed halberd. The claw-like blades merged seamlessly into the haft.

There is great power in that object. Shira's thought came before Pierce had even formed a query. *I cannot see it fully at this time, but be certain—it has strength beyond the bones of any mortal creature. It may be impervious to physical harm.*

"Yet this is meaningless," Xu'sasar said. The pole-arm twisted and melted in her grasp, and an instant later she held a three-pronged wheel of bone in her hand—a bone variation of the wooden throwing weapons they had seen the drow use before. "I would no more fight this creature than great Vulkoor. Do you know nothing of the spirits? This is surely Ko'molaq, the Keeper of Secrets. We must buy our passage with our words."

"So you want to *talk* to the serpent?" Daine said. "I—"

Lei grabbed Daine's shoulder and pulled. "She may be right, Daine."

This surprised even Pierce. Since their arrival in Thelanis, Lei had seemed unwilling to accept anything the drow girl said. It was clearly difficult, but she pushed the words out.

"Xu'sasar, your people have a tale of this? The serpent by the river?"

The dark elf clicked her tongue.

"That's what this *is*," Lei said. "The realm of stories. I don't know if some force is shaping the realm to match her expectations, or if one of her people journeyed through Thelanis and returned to tell of it, but after that scorpion, I think we need to take her tales seriously."

Daine looked down at the massive snake. "Fine. Xu, it's your story. How do we do this?" He glanced around. "Xu'sasar?"

"Captain?" Pierce pointed.

The drow was already halfway to the serpent.

Cursing Sovereigns and snakes, Daine rushed after her.

● ● ● ◉ ● ●

Pierce remained at Lei's side as they approached the serpent. He shouldered his bow, returning his last arrow to the quiver. He knew this beast could not be felled with one blow, and if he needed to protect Lei it seemed best to have both hands free.

Daine caught up with Xu'sasar, and the two approached the pillar together. As they drew near, the massive snake loosened its coils, turning its head to fix Daine with gleaming golden eyes. Then a second serpentine head peered around from the other side of the pillar, a great wedge covered with crimson scales. *Two of them!*

"I give you greetings, traveler." The voice was the hiss of a thousand serpents, woven into words. Both mouths spoke as one, moving in perfect unison, and Pierce realized they were the opposite ends of the single serpent. "What is it you seek?"

Xu'sasar knelt, dwarfed by the immense snake. "I give you greetings, great Ko'molaq. My companions and I seek to cross the river you guard."

"And will you pay my price and abide by my rule?" The serpent watched from each side of the pillar. Pierce studied it, considering how long it might take the creature to uncoil should they choose to retreat.

"What price is that?" Daine said, at the same moment Xu'sasar said, "We shall."

The crimson head rose to regard Daine, while the black-scaled serpent kept its gaze on Xu'sasar. "Knowledge, traveler. Truth. Answer my question, and you may cross the river unharmed. But once you cross you may never return. Be certain in your choice."

"And what's so terrifying about this river, anyway?"

"Knowledge," the serpent said. "Truth. It is a stream of consciousness, but no mortal mind can survive the pure knowledge that lies within.

Daine took a step back, turning to Lei and Pierce. "Thoughts?"

"I don't see that we have a choice," Lei said. "I don't exactly understand what this thing is talking about, but we need to cross and we can't touch the water. It may seem insane, but I think that's fairly normal for this place."

Daine glanced at Pierce.

"I will follow your lead," the warforged said. Shira was silent, and he had seen nothing to suggest another course of action.

"Very well." Daine turned back and walked up to the serpent, staring into the golden eyes of the crimson head. "Ask your question."

"Questions," the serpent said. "One for each who would walk my path. Answer, then cross, leaving all else behind."

As it spoke, one end of the serpent entered the river, slowly making its way across. It seemed impossible for the beast to reach across the river, yet somehow it did. A few coils remained tightly wrapped around the dark pillar, and slowly it rose up above the water, apparently anchored on the far shore.

The serpent spoke only through the head with the blood-red scales, but its voice was just as strong.

"You will be first," it said to Daine. "You have led in battle. You have left many things behind. So shall it be here."

Daine frowned, and Pierce could almost hear his thoughts—his reluctance to abandon the others, set against the need to evaluate the dangers of the other side. "Very well," he said at last.

The serpent reared up, towering over Daine. "Tell me, traveler, and tell me truly. Where does your journey end?"

Daine opened his mouth, and then closed it. He looked at the others. "Is this some sort of riddle?" he said to Lei. "You know that's not my—"

"This is your question, and yours alone." The voice of the serpent drowned out Daine's objection. "Think of what has brought you to this place, traveler. And tell me where your journey ends."

Daine was silent for a moment and stood staring into the serpent's eyes. Then he said, "My journey ends beyond the Gates of Night, at the end of my dreams. My journey ends when Lakashtai falls by my hand."

"Then cross the river, and do not return." The serpent lowered its flat head, and Daine gingerly stepped atop it. The creature raised him up, and a moment later he was walking cautiously along the snake's length, struggling to keep his balance. Soon he was on the opposite shore. Pierce could just see him leaping down from the serpentine bridge.

Now the beast fixed Xu'sasar with its stare. "Child of the scorpion, tell me truly, what has your journey cost?"

Xu'sasar didn't pause. "The lives of my family, the lives of my foes, and my place in Final Lands."

The serpent lowered its head and Xu'sasar raced up

and across its back, seeming as comfortable on the scaled bridge as she was on the ground. Now only Pierce and Lei remained, and the snake looked at Lei.

"Tell me, shaper, and tell me truly, where did your journey begin?"

Lei's brow furrowed in thought. Pierce tried to imagine what answer he would give. Did the beast mean this recent journey, which began in the Monolith of Karul'tash . . . or perhaps in Sharn, depending how far back one went? Or was it speaking of a longer journey?

"My journey began in my mother's womb," Lei said. There was a slight tremor of uncertainty in her voice, but the snake lowered its head for her. Lei slid her staff into her bag, freeing both hands, and made her way up onto the creature's back. Slowly, carefully, she made her way out across the river.

"You have much to learn," the serpent hissed.

And it bucked.

The movement hurled Lei up into the air, and Pierce could see that she would come down in the water. He charged into the river. He'd forded rivers in the past; he had little skill when it came to swimming, but he didn't need to breathe, and the water was calm and still. He wondered what dangers might wait in the water, but he had no intention of allowing Lei to face them alone.

The water barely reached his hips. This was no river; it was little more than a wide stream. There was a massive splash as Lei struck the water, followed by a disturbing stillness. She did not thrash about, or even rise to break the surface of the river. Pierce pressed forward, struggling against the mass of water.

She is alive. Shira's thought brought a flood of relief, and even as he moved forward he *knew* Lei's approximate location. He shifted his course and reached down, pulling a soaking Lei up from the riverbed. She lay limp in his arms. Her eyes were closed, her skin pale.

She is alive.

CHAPTER 17

NIGHT: THE
DEEPWOOD MOON
THELANIS

"Tell me, shaper, and tell me truly, where did
your journey begin?"

Daine could barely see Pierce and Lei in the shadows across the river. But the snake was still speaking
through both its mouths. Daine and Xu'sasar stood
on the far shore, where the serpent was wrapped
around another pillar of dark stone. The creature
was ignoring them, and its golden gaze was fixed on
the opposite shore.

Shaper, Daine thought. That has to be Lei. Sure
enough, a slender shape rose up onto the serpent's
back and began the crossing. Daine remembered just
how treacherous that passage had been. The scales of
the snake were smooth and slippery, its flesh yielding
beneath his boots. His heart leaped every time he saw
Lei miss a step, but she always managed to recover.

"You have much to learn," the serpent hissed.

Daine saw Lei thrown into the air. He felt his feet
pounding across the soil, breath filling his lungs as a
shout built inside him. But the shout never came, and
he never reached the water. A moment of pain, a swift
blow against the back of his legs, and Daine tumbled

down against dirt and grass.

Xu'sasar was upon him. She gripped his neck with one hand and pressed three fingers against the base of his spine. A surge ran through his nerves, a flash of adrenaline and pain, and every muscle in his body went rigid. Fury and fear for Lei flooded his mind, and he struggled against the treacherous drow, but to no avail. She held herself steady as a statue, and as long as she remained still, he found he was powerless.

"You have crossed the river," Xu'sasar said. "You cannot return!"

Daine wanted to scream at her, to strike her down. Only when Pierce had risen from the river with Lei's dripping body in his arms did Xu'sasar release him. A moment later he was by Lei's side, driving the water from her lungs. She breathed, but her skin was pale and cool, her body limp and unresponsive. He was vaguely aware that he was shouting at her, ordering her to wake up, slamming his fist into the dirt.

Pierce was holding him, pulling him away. "She is alive, captain. You cannot help her."

"Why won't she wake up?"

"I do not know. But her condition is stable. Nothing has changed since I removed her from the water."

Glancing back at Lei, Daine saw a dark shadow kneeling over her . . . Xu'sasar. Pulling free from Pierce, Daine smashed into the drow girl, striking her full on with his shoulder. She was caught completely off guard. She fell over Lei and barely kept from slipping into the water herself.

Daine's sword was in his hand, blazing with the fire of his fury. *"What have you done?"* he said.

Xu'sasar rolled to her feet, crouching on the narrow strip of shore. The bone wheel was in her hand, and even in his frenzy Daine noticed the drops of greenish fluid coating the tips of the tooth-like prongs. "I have saved you," she said. "Had you entered the river, you would have suffered a fate far worse."

"What are you talking about?"

"Did you not listen to the Keeper of Secrets? The river is knowledge. The river is truth. It chose to bathe her in the waters, and ordered you to remain on the shore."

"And what were you doing just now?"

"The dangers of the land are many, and my people must learn to heal as well as kill. It was I who tended you after our battle with Colchyn. I simply wished to study your companion, and make certain I knew what afflicted her."

The rage that burned within Daine was dying now, the furious energy fading even as the gleaming blade of his sword became mere metal. "Tell me."

"I have," Xu'sasar said. "This battle is within her. Only she can fight it."

"There's got to be something we can do!"

"You can protect her body, but this battle is in her mind. It is an honor to be chosen in this way. If she survives, she will be the stronger for it."

Daine's anger grew at *if she survives*, but he fought back the fire. Xu'sasar wasn't to blame for this.

Pierce stood next to Daine. His deep, familiar voice was an emotional anchor. "We have few alternatives, Captain. Her lifeforce is stable. I believe that our best course of action would be to find sustenance and shelter. It has been a long journey, and you must rest as well."

Pierce was correct, of course. Even aside from Lei's predicament, Daine knew his limits, and he was struggling with them. "We're not staying here. I want her away from that snake and this water. There's got to be something defensible around here."

"Look." Pierce pointed at the stone pillar the serpent had used as its anchor. It took Daine a moment to realize what Pierce was talking about, and then he saw it.

A path.

To this point they had wandered through untamed land. The pillars of the serpent were the first signs of civilization they had seen. But there was no question about it. Traces of a trail could be seen at the base of the pillar, growing wider and clearer as it went deeper into the woods.

Daine stood over Lei, his sword still in his hand. "See what you can find," he told Pierce.

He turned to the drow woman. There was no guile in her eyes, and he found that he believed her—that she had done what she thought was best for him. But his anger still needed an outlet, and at the moment, he felt a fire burn within him whenever he looked at the dark elf. Lei, Pierce . . . he knew what to expect from them. He knew what they would do. Which was far more than he could say for Xu'sasar. "You," he said, perhaps more gruffly that he had to. "You don't leave my sight, is that understood?"

Xu'sasar looked away and blew out her breath. "I am swifter than the man of metal, my steps are just as silent," she said. "My eyes are sharper when the moon is high, and this land is bathed by moonlight. It is foolish to send that one in my place."

"I don't care how fast you are, princess. Pierce follows orders, and right now trust is more important than anything else. You were told to protect me, weren't you? Why don't you start by doing what you're told?"

THE GATES OF NIGHT

"I saved your life," she said. Her words flowed together, but Daine didn't know if the speed of her speech was a sign of shame or anger.

"There were better ways to do it," he said. "We work together or not at all, is that understood?"

A moment passed, but Xu'sasar finally clicked her tongue. "As you will," she said.

Daine knelt next to Lei and placed a hand on her cheek. Her skin was cold. He felt a stirring within him, a physical sensation more tangible than his concern or anger. It was the ball of energy at the base of his spine, the presence he'd felt when Lei had first uncovered the mark. At first he'd thought it was all in his mind, but he could *feel* it, a raw burn just beneath the skin—and this pain grew worse when he touched Lei. Looking back on the last few minutes, he couldn't help but wonder about the frenzy that had taken hold of him. Was it just frayed nerves and the sight of Lei in danger? Or was it something more?

Kneeling over Lei, Daine watched the serpent coiled on the distant shore, fighting back the fury he felt and struggling to forget every story he'd been taught about aberrant marks.

❋ ❋ ❋ ❋ ❋ ❋ ❋

The only sound was the faint flow of the water. Lei lay still, her chest barely rising and falling. For all that her stillness struck a chord of terror in Daine's heart, she had never seemed so perfect, so beautiful as she did in the moonlight of Thelanis.

"Do you wish the watchers to be killed or taken alive?"

These were the first words Xu'sasar had spoken since Daine had rebuked her, and the sound pulled him from his reverie. Even as he tried to make sense of this statement, there was a flurry of motion in the branches of a nearby tree. It seemed that Daine wasn't the only one listening, and the interloper wasn't waiting for an answer. Daine caught a glimpse of dark feathers as a bird took to the air, but the creature wasn't fast enough. Xu'sasar's bone wheel *whirred* through the air, and—*THACK!* A dark shape fell to the ground. The throwing wheel didn't fall with it. The weapon retraced its path through the air, returning to Xu'sasar's hand.

Daine sprinted over to examine the fallen creature. It was a crow, about the size of Daine's head. It seemed that Xu'sasar had opted against killing, as Daine saw no blood . . . but the impact of the blow might have broken bones, and the crow was staying on the ground.

"What makes you so sure it's a spy?" Daine said.

"It's a fair catch, I'll give you that." Though masculine, the voice was high-pitched, not unlike some male gnomes Daine had met. It was cracked and wheezy, forced through pain. It was the voice of the crow. The bird stayed on its side, tilting its head to stare up at Daine. "Your girl's got a good eye. She could almost be an owl, that one."

Xu'sasar said nothing. She held the bone wheel in her hand, with a reversed grip; a strike from the weapon would drive one of the three curved spikes through the crow's flesh.

"First scorpions," Daine said, "then snakes. And now you. Did all of the snakes on the other side of the river talk, or just the big one?"

"The snakes?" The crow gave a faint chuckle, a little blood bubbling from its beak. "Don't be stupid. They're cold-blooded, you know. Bastards don't like anyone outside their little clan. Me? I'm a bird who likes to talk. Don't have to go breaking my wing to get my attention."

"You were spying on us, and you tried to flee when Xu spotted you."

"Oh, that. Well. Yes. She didn't exactly offer a good option for me there, did she? 'Catch or kill?' Not, 'Have a nice bit of talk.' Someone says, 'Shall we beat the man or kill him?' What are you going to do?"

"Perhaps I'd avoid the situation by not spying to begin with," Daine said. He drew his dagger and knelt next to the crow. "And I still haven't answered her question."

"Threatening the bird with the broken wing. Very nice. What's next then? Torture? Plucking out the feathers one by one?"

"Nothing so slow," Daine said. Another man might have found it difficult to see the bird as a threat. But even beyond Thelanis, this wasn't the first time Daine had encountered a talking animal—or even an intelligent bird; the war-wizards of the Valenar often used avian familiars as scouts. "I'm in no mood for games." He raised his dagger.

"Wait!" The crow twisted its head back and forth. "I can help you. I can help the lady."

Daine kept his dagger hanging over the bird. "I'm listening."

"You're looking for shelter, yes? You're wise not to rest in the open. That one may have seen me, but many powers walk these woods. Thanks to you lot, I need healing myself. I don't want to die out here, under your blade or in the jaws of the night. You take me with you, I can lead you to a safe haven."

"What sort of haven?"

"An inn," the bird said. "The Crooked Tree."

"An *inn?*"

"That's right," the crow said. "You know, bit of brew, bit of bread, roof over your head? What, you thought that was a human idea?"

"I don't think of crows as needing any of those things," Daine said.

"Well, it's not always about need, is it? You people don't give beasts many options now. Besides which, we've got your kind here as well. Ferric, who runs the Moon's Rest, he's handy."

"Handy?"

"Has hands, see where I'm going? Not like me. And he'll find someone who can take care of me, sure enough. He likes to make a deal, Ferric does."

Daine considered this. "And you claim this inn is safe?"

"I did no such thing," the crow said. "Ferric, he likes to make a deal. But he has no love for the Woodsman, and I think you have that in common, yes?"

Daine tightened his grip on his dagger. "What do you know about that?"

"Your killer there had it right. I'm a watcher. I look and I listen, and information is what I trade in. The news of Darkheart's return has spread across the night, and the Woodsman wants her back. But what's that to me? I may make a deal now and again, but I'm not one of his creatures. You get me out of this, I'll keep mum about what I've seen. And Ferric, he'll be right pleased to spit in the Woodsman's eye."

"Xu'sasar. Opinions?" Daine kept his eyes on the crow as he spoke. For all that the creature appeared to be injured, Daine wasn't taking anything for granted anymore.

"Kill the bird," the dark elf said. "And find our own shelter. This is not one of the great spirits. It is a spy and a trickster, seeking to buy its life with words."

"All I have except feathers," the crow chimed in. "But come now, what have I ever done to you?"

"Nothing yet," said Xu'sasar. "And if you die in this place, nothing ever."

Daine stared down at the wounded bird. He had no reason to trust anything the creature said. They were in hostile territory, and the crow could easily be lying. But he'd never liked killing human prisoners, and somehow there was little difference here. And if the bird spoke the truth, perhaps this was an opportunity to make a few allies in this strange place. And he knew what Lei would say if she were awake.

The call of the Cyran dusksinger came through the woods—Pierce's signal. The warforged had heard voices and was calling for instructions. Daine gave an answering call—*safe to return.*

Pierce emerged from the woods. "The path is well traveled," he said. "Both hooves and boots have passed this way, and not long ago. Far in the distance, there is a strong, flickering light . . . a lantern, or a fire."

"That would be the Tree," the crow said. "Not much of a walk for the likes of you. Bring me along, then, and I'll put in a good word. That's the least you can do, isn't it? The Moon only knows when I'll be flying on this again."

"Well," Daine said, "we'll take you with us. Pierce, you carry Lei. I'll bring this one . . . and I warn you, little bird, that if we encounter any trouble between here and your inn, you'll be the first to die."

"Fair, that is," said the crow. "And if it's friends we are, it's Huwen to you, right?"

"Let's get to your inn before we settle our friendship, bird."

Daine took one last glance across the river, where he could see the shadow of the great serpent twined around the pillar, then he scooped up the injured crow and made his way into the forest.

CHAPTER 18

NIGHT: THE
DEEPWOOD MOON
THELANIS

Xu'sasar lived in a world without shadows. According to Qaltiar tales, the first drow had been imbued with the essence of night itself, which accounted for the jet-black skin of Xu'sasar's people and the magical powers of her race. One of those mystical gifts was the ability to see in darkness with the ease that outlanders saw during the day. She was just as comfortable in the utter gloom of a deep cavern as she was in the dappled light of a moonlit forest. As a child she learned to recognize the spectrum of gray shades that reflected the light others saw. When hunting, she needed to know when she was standing in shadow and stepping into the light. Nonetheless, the only true darkness she had ever known was the magical shadows that were part of her own blood—the mystical darkness a drow could project into the world.

For Xu'sasar, the night held no fear. Outlanders feared the darkness, but Xu'sasar had to be taught to recognize the shadows. The night was her dominion, her time to stalk and hunt. Given the choice, she would be dancing through the deepest, darkest woods of the final lands, searching for the most fearsome threats that the realm had to offer.

But the choice wasn't hers.

"Not my place to say, I'm sure," Huwen had said. "But if I was a creature what walked on my legs, I'd take the path, you see? You might be running into something coming the other way, yes, but there's far worse in the deep woods. You've crossed the river now, and you've come to the heart of the night. Even I don't know all of what's out there, and I know enough."

Xu'sasar should have killed the creature with her first blow. She wanted to show her respect for Daine, to give the outlander the chance to make a decision. She hadn't expected him to make the wrong one. Did the outlanders know nothing of the final lands? This was a bird of ill omen, surely sent to test and trick them.

And now they were following the path it had suggested for them.

Xu'sasar led the way, searching the trees for any sign of motion. The others followed close behind. This road was cobbled with disks of densewood, irregular circles of many sizes, likely harvested from fallen boughs. The path was wide enough for two giants to stand side by side, and it reminded Xu'sasar of the ancient roads in her homelands of Xen'drik. She tried to remember how many times she had used such roads as the foundations for ambushes, leaping out from the sheltering jungle and scattering unwary explorers with a swift and furious assault.

"She's got some colorful ideas, that one," said the crow. "If I had friends in wait, you think I'd do something as obvious as this? I'm so clever I'm stupid, is that it?"

Daine was just behind Xu'sasar, his black-feathered burden in his hands. Xu'sasar turned swiftly. "Stay out of my mind," she said. "There is still time for you to suffer. You might even live long enough to reach your shelter."

"So you're making the decisions now, are you?" Huwen said. "Here I thought you were this one's hou— Oww!"

Daine prodded the bird's injured wing, silencing the creature. "Stay out of your mind?" he asked.

"It feeds on secrets," Xu'sasar replied. "How do you suppose it learned the things it knows? There is still time to kill it and let the knowledge die with it."

The crow managed a chuckle. "You don't know nearly as much as you think, girl. You have a few dozen threads, and you think you've seen a tapestry. For every two things you know, you've got a vast gap in between. Me? I'm no deceiver, no servant of some great evil. I just live here. Everyone's got to live somewhere, don't they? This is my patch."

Daine tightened his grip on the black bird. "And the mind reading? Is that a thread of truth?"

"Oh, well, that," Huwen said. "I suppose it is. I like the taste of thought, a bit of sorrow, a colorful secret. That's just what I am. So I have a few memories when I'm feeling peckish. No harm in it, no more than you having a spot of stew now and again. You do me a good turn here, and I'll be in your debt, won't I? So why would I let on what I know?"

"I've done you a good turn already, bird," Daine said. "Don't push me further. If you betray us . . . well, why don't you just take a look at my thoughts and see what I have in mind?"

Huwen shivered, ruffling his feathers. "That's quite . . . colorful. I'm not sure it's even possible, but truly, I have no intention of testing it out. As I see it, we're all on fair ground here. I was doing a bit of snooping. I'm the first to admit that. You caught me, laid hurt on me good. You help me get fixed up, I help you find some shelter for our lady friend here, and everyone comes out even. No need to go thinking things like that."

"But I still am," Daine said. "Remember that."

Daine turned to Xu'sasar. "Your instincts are good, Xu. I understand what you're thinking. But I've made a choice, and I need you to back me on it."

She was surprised, less by what was said than by the way in which he spoke. Xu'sasar was a child of the wilds, trained to hear the voice of the spirit, and she could sense a growing strength within Daine—something he might not even be aware of himself. She still knew very little about the outlander. She gathered that he'd been suffering from some sort of illness in Xen'drik and that he'd earned the warrior's marks on his back at the same time that he'd overcome this affliction. She wondered if this predatory spirit had always been within him, or if it was a seed that had taken root in the final lands.

He was waiting for a response. She clicked her tongue and inclined her head, a gesture she'd learned from watching him.

"Good. I need Pierce to carry Lei. If Huwen is telling the truth, that spark of light is the inn. Scout ahead. Take to the woods, whatever you think best. You know how you'd plan an ambush, so use that knowledge."

She clicked her tongue again.

"Do *not* engage strangers. I can't afford to lose anyone else. If you see anything threatening, return and report. If that's impossible, we'll need a warning signal. Can you match this?"

Daine whistled, mimicking the call of an outlander

bird. It took Xu'sasar two tries to match the call. He taught her two more calls, one for "all clear" and another for "response requested." At last he was satisfied.

"You may be as sharp as Pierce," he said. "You may be as quick in the night. Now show me you can be reliable. Good hunting."

Xu'sasar clicked her tongue and stepped off the path. The bird watched her go but didn't say a word.

❊ ❊ ❊ ◉ ❊ ❊ ❊

As soon as she stepped off the path, Xu'sasar could feel the presence of the trees. A human might have dismissed this, shaken it off as general paranoia. Xu'sasar knew better. The trees were alive. They were more aware than the moon-dappled oaks on the other side of the river. With every step she took toward Dusk, the forest grew more aware and more hostile. Every step brought them deeper into the domain of the Woodsman. Xu'sasar wondered what shape this spirit preferred, what powers he possessed. She knew nothing of a Woodsman from the tales, and part of her took pleasure in this. She had the chance to carve out new legends. But now she had a task, a duty to protect this outlander. And she found herself feeling the first touches of fear. A noble death was no longer sufficient. She needed to live, to find a way to overcome her foes. What if she couldn't? What if it was beyond her powers?

She pushed away these fears, pushed away all thought. A slight breeze blew through the trees, and Xu'sasar moved with this wind, slipping through the woods with such silent grace that not even the trees felt her presence.

There was no traffic on the path and little motion in the forest. Xu'sasar saw an owl swoop down on its prey,

151

taking to the air with a tiny man in its talons. A silver fox crossed her path, slipping between bushes. But neither owl nor fox saw Xu'sasar.

Only once did she come upon true danger, and she never even learned what it was. As she drew closer to the light, Xu'sasar felt a swift drop in air pressure. She froze in place, remaining perfectly silent and still. Even her keen eyes could see nothing in the forest, but she *felt* a presence ahead of her, moving through the woods. At first she thought it was a spirit of pure air, much like the spirits of fire bound by the hated Sulatar. Then it drew closer. The chill she felt was not due to icy air. Once in her life, Xu'sasar had encountered a true ghost, a restless spirit torn from the path of existence. That tormented soul gave off the same chill, but if that had been a light breeze, this was the heart of winter. *Even I don't know all of what's out there,* the bird had said, *and I know enough.* Now Xu'sasar knew what he meant. She didn't want to know what this being was. She just wanted it to pass her by.

And it did.

The sensation lasted only a moment, and then it was gone. Xu'sasar held her breath a little longer, but the spirit had moved away, deeper into the woods. It was traveling away from Daine, and it hadn't touched the path, so perhaps the bird had spoken truly after all. Perhaps the road was safe. The memory of the chilling presence lingered long after the spirit had passed, and Xu'sasar moved closer to the path for the remainder of the journey.

She didn't have far to go. The point of light grew larger, and soon she could see that it was a lick of cold fire contained in a crystal cage, hanging from the bough of a tree. She had reached their destination.

It was easy to see how the Inn of the Crooked Tree had come by its name. The building itself was made of thatched straw and black mud, but it was built around a graywood oak, a twisted tree with a dozen crooked boughs stretching out over the long roof. Windows were made of a dark stained glass, but Xu'sasar could see the flicker of fire within, and she could smell smoke in the air. Shadows shifted against the windows, and Xu'sasar could hear laughter and conversation. She circled the building, listening to the faint sounds until she could distinguish the voices. Then she sprinted back through the night, skirting the edge of the road. The cold spirit that had brushed against her had moved on, and she encountered no significant threats on her return.

"The path is clear," she said, when she reached Daine.

He nodded, and she fell into step alongside him as they moved down the road.

"Well, someone said it was, didn't they?" Huwen said. "Oh, right, that was me. Seems like I know a thing or two after all."

"There are two levels to the building," Xu'sasar said, ignoring the bird. "I believe there are only four people inside—at least, four who are awake. I saw no guards or sentries. The surface of the walls is easy to climb. I would suggest that I enter the second floor, kill any who sleep, and wait for you by the stairs. When you enter the front, we can converge on the four below, taking them off-guard."

Daine and Huwen stared at her.

"What?" Daine said at last.

"We are outnumbered, but we will have the element of surprise. Our enemies may not be fully armed, though in this land we must obviously be wary of magic."

"Did you . . ." Daine shook his head. "Just tell me when these people became our enemies."

Now it was Xu'sasar's turn to be puzzled. "We seek to claim their shelter, do we not?"

"It's an inn," Daine said. "You know . . . inn? Where people give you shelter in exchange for gold?"

"Gold?" Xu'sasar considered this. In Xen'drik, shelter was a precious thing. Her people did not build. Once they traveled to a new area, securing a ruin or a cavern was always the first order of business. You might share shelter with a tribe bound to you by blood, but when strangers held that which you desired, violence was simply the way of things. Unless . . .

Had she misunderstood Daine? Did he mean a place where people exchanged shelter for flesh? Certainly, that would make more sense than a gift of soft metal.

"Who are you planning to give to these strangers?" she said. The scorpion had ordered her to protect Daine. It said nothing about allowing him to sell her.

Daine frowned. "I'm not giving them anyone. It's an inn." He sighed. "I guess you've never seen one. They make a living providing shelter to strangers. In exchange for valuable goods. Not people." He glanced down at Huwen, who had kept his beak shut throughout the exchange. "Since she's brought it up, what sort of coin do you trade in here?"

"That's all down to Ferric," Huwen said. "Whatever he deems fair. He'll make you a deal. I'm sure of that."

"It would be far simpler to kill those inside," Xu'sasar said. "We could make a beginning with the bird."

Daine held the crow's beak shut with his thumb and forefinger, silencing the bird before it could respond. "Enough, Xu. There's no need for killing here. If I have to drop an enemy, I'll do it. But I'm not killing a man just to get a roof over my head for one night. Understood?"

Xu'sasar clicked her tongue, and they moved forward once more.

Daine was a mystery to her. Xu'sasar would follow his orders, but she would be ready for whatever treachery awaited them. Clutching the bone wheel in her hand, she concentrated, remembering the lessons she'd learned as a child and envisioning a new shape. The wheel flexed and contorted in her grip, ivory melting and stretching. Xu'sasar reached down with her left hand to grip the second hilt. A moment later she held a bone dagger in each hand, with an ivory chain connecting the hilts. She tested the blades. Their balance was a thing of beauty, and she felt as if they were her own claws. She showed her teeth to the moon above and hoped the people at this "inn" would give her a reason to shed blood.

❀ ❀ ❀ ❀ ❀ ❀ ❀

"You're certain of this?" Xu'sasar said. They stood outside the Crooked Tree.

"I'm certain," Daine said. "Now open the door for us. And put the knives away. We don't want these people thinking we're killers."

"That would be a ludicrous misunderstanding," Huwen said. "I'd laugh at the very idea of it, if I weren't distracted by the agonizing pain of a broken limb."

Xu'sasar tucked the blades into the straps of her harness, shortening the chain with a thought. She felt a slight emotional tremor as she approached the door, and once more she realized the touch of fear. It was the chaos, the uncertainty. In Xen'drik, life had always been simple. Strangers were enemies. Life was conflict. She was always ready for a battle,

155

prepared to die with a weapon in her hand. But to enter a stranger's lair with empty hands, to trust the unknown, was terrifying.

Xu'sasar forced down the fear, struggling to keep her emotions hidden from the outlanders. She was a war-wraith of the Qaltiar, and there was nothing this human could do that she could not. She threw open the door and stepped inside.

The room was warm, the air smoky and slightly sweet. Fires were set in stone hearths to each side of Xu'sasar, and the low and steady flames seemed the only source of light in the wide room. It was likely a dark chamber, little better than the moonlit night, but shadows meant nothing to Xu'sasar, and she scanned the room, taking in every detail. Packed earth floor. No tables or chairs, only large cushions scattered across the floor. A short man watching from behind a long counter, sorting through piles of leather water-skins. The wide trunk of a gnarled tree rose up in the center of the room and extended through the roof. A spiral staircase coiled around the trunk. And a man and a woman danced, moving slowly to the soft and somber music.

"Welcome!" The innkeeper made his way out from behind the counter and strode toward Xu'sasar. He was a soft man, bones hidden beneath rolls of fat, and he wore a coat of gray velvet and a comforting close-lipped smile. He seemed in good health and good spirits, yet his voice was that of a dead thing, as if his lungs were rotting within him. Xu'sasar stepped to the side, setting her back against the wall, and her left hand slid to the hilt of a dagger.

"Welcome to the Inn of the Crooked Tree!" the man continued, pleasant words at odds with his ghastly tone. "Always a pleasure to see one from the quiet lands under our humble roof. It has been so long, and even longer since I've seen one of your kind."

Xu'sasar evaded the innkeeper's embrace, but his smile didn't falter. He indicated the cushions on the floor.

"Please make yourself comfortable. May I get you some food, something to drink, perhaps?"

"We need a room for the night." Daine had followed Xu'sasar into the building.

"And just wait until you see who's with them, Ferric!" Huwen crowed.

"Huwen!" The innkeeper said, beaming. "It has been far too long since you graced us with your presence. Now, what's this ab—"

The innkeeper fell silent, and the music came to an abrupt halt. The dancers stopped where they stood.

Pierce entered the common room with Lei in his arms.

"Lady . . . Darkheart?" The innkeeper said, his face paling.

"In a manner of speaking," Huwen replied.

"I don't know what this is about," Daine said, "and I don't care. Huwen says that you're no friend to this Woodsman. Is that the truth?"

"Oh, yes," the innkeeper said. "Have no fear, good sir. We won't be telling the woods of your wounded lady."

"Good," Daine said. "Then you'll give us a room?"

"Of course. But there is the matter of price. This is a business, not a sanctuary."

Daine nodded. "I have gold."

"Gold? We have no use for coin beneath the Deepwood Moon. It will take more than metal to earn your

board beneath the Crooked Tree. What else do you
have to offer?"

"The life of a wounded bird," Daine said, placing his
free hand around Huwen's neck.

Xu'sasar was impressed. She'd thought Daine a fool
for sparing the creature. It never occurred to her that
he might use it as a hostage. Still, she was not convinced
that he would stand by his hard words.

Neither was Ferric. The innkeeper laughed, a gasp-
ing, wheezing sound. "Good sir, Huwen is a customer,
and if he seeks my shelter, he too will need to pay a
price. You cannot trade on his life. No, if you wish the
protection of our walls, you will need to give of yourself. Say . . . your fine voice."

Xu'sasar glanced at Daine. She could draw and strike
in the blink of an eye. Surely now he would see the
wisdom of buying their shelter with blood.

Perhaps the innkeeper could read her thoughts;
perhaps he simply saw her hands slip to the hilts of
her knives. "I do advise against it, miss," he said.
"I'm sure you could kill me, but I assure you that the
Crooked Tree would be no safe haven after my death."
His smile widened, and now she could see his needle-
sharp teeth.

"Tell me your terms," Daine said.

"Oh, I'm a fair man, sir," Ferric said. "I do not
expect you to be silent forever. I will simply take
custody of your voice during your stay. I have this time
to enjoy it, and you have our hospitality."

"Do not do this," Xu'sasar said. She needed no tale
to tell her that this was unwise, but the stories of her
people were filled with legends of those led astray by
cunning spirits.

"Shelter for myself *and* my companions," he said.

"One price for all."

"That sets such a bad precedent," Ferric sighed. "Nonetheless, you travel in august company, and it pleases me to place a thorn in the foot of the Woodsman. How is this: As only you will pay the price, I will give you but one room. How you use that space is your concern. You will be silent for the duration of the stay, until I give you a voice when you leave our company. A fair deal, yes?"

"And you guarantee our safety?"

"For as long as you remain beneath the Tree, yes, sir."

"Do not do this," Xu'sasar said again.

"I must agree with Xu'sasar." It was the first time Pierce had spoken since they had left the banks of the river. "There are strange forces at work in this place, Captain. Surely we can find other shelter."

Daine released his grip on Huwen's neck, and the bird chuckled. "Not likely, tin man. The closer you get to the Woodsman, the worse things will be for you. This is one of the few free houses in this hour of night, and Ferric speaks truth. If you want true shelter, you'll be needing to meet his price."

"Enough!" Daine said. "Lei needs the rest, and we don't know what's out there. If I can buy us safe haven with one silent night, that's a worthy exchange." He turned to the innkeeper. "How do we do this?"

"It won't take a moment, sir. Not a moment. Just open your mouth and we'll be about it." The pudgy man reached up, placing one soft hand on Daine's throat.

Daine screamed.

Xu'sasar drew knives and set the points against each side of the innkeeper's neck. Daine had dropped the wounded crow, and his face was a mask of pain. His scream seemed to hang in the air, and then Xu'sasar realized that it *was* hanging in the air—that a wisp of silvery smoke had emerged from Daine's mouth, and that the agonized sound was emerging from this floating mist. The smoke flashed through the air and into Ferric's mouth, and the room fell silent again.

"If you don't mind, miss, that's rather uncomfortable." It was Daine's voice, steady and firm—but the words came from Ferric's mouth.

Xu'sasar's knives still pressed against Ferric's throat. She looked at Daine. His face was pale and covered with cold sweat, but it seemed that the pain had passed. He opened his mouth, closed it, opened it again. Finally he stepped forward and pushed her blades from the innkeeper's throat.

"Thank you, sir," Ferric said with Daine's voice. "I do appreciate a man who keeps his word, even when he sells his words. Now let me show you to your quarters. Afterward, you and your companions are more than welcome to enjoy the hospitality of our common room."

Daine shook his head.

"As you will, sir. Follow me."

The innkeeper led them to the staircase that wound around the gray tree. As they crossed the room, Xu'sasar noticed a detail that had escaped her, and despite the many terrors she had seen, she felt a slight chill. The fires in each hearth burned merrily, but they were fueled, not with wooden logs, but with human bones, intact but blackened and charred. As they ascended the staircase, Xu'sasar saw that the bones bore the marks of tiny, needlelike teeth.

❖ ❖ ❖ ❖ ❖ ❖ ❖

The room on the second floor was gray. The gray mattress was stuffed with withered hay and covered with a blanket of gray wool. A small, scratchy woolen carpet covered the floor, and the rug was as gray as the wood beneath it. The window was covered with dust, and the moon beyond cast a faint gray light across the floor.

Pierce set Lei down on the bed. "Her condition is unchanged," he said. "Is there anything we can do for her?"

Daine opened his mouth. He blinked, then shut it again, lips twisted into a scowl. He looked at Xu'sasar.

"There is nothing to be done," Xu'sasar said. She thought of the tales she had heard of the Keeper of Secrets. "We can only watch and protect her body. The struggle is within, and nothing we do can affect it. Nor can we see what she faces. The battle may already be over, and she may have lost. If this is the case, she will never wake, and we will know only when she starves to death." She met Daine's gaze. "It may be a mercy to end her misery."

Daine shook his head, his gaze was hard. Xu'sasar could see his anger at the very suggestion, and she felt a strange pang of guilt. She did not know this Lei, and she barely knew Daine. With each passing hour, she felt ever more alone. She was the last of the Jalaq Qaltiar, and the voice of Vulkoor had forbidden her from following her kin along the paths of death. Her destiny had been bound to this Daine. These three were the only family she had left, and while she did not know Lei, she meant her no harm. She would have offered the same swift mercy to any member of her tribe suffering from a lingering ailment.

"That would be unwise," Pierce said. "You may not care for Lei as we do, Xu'sasar, but she is our guide in this place. Without her, our odds of survival are slim."

"I meant no disrespect," Xu'sasar said. "Starvation is a slow death, and if her soul is already lost, I should not wish to watch her body suffer."

Daine's scowl deepened.

"Let us hope it does not come to that," Pierce said. "My lady has a strong spirit, and I am certain she will rise again."

Xu'sasar cast about her mind, searching for words of apology. In the end, she simply clicked her tongue and bowed her head, breaking contact with Daine's accusing gaze.

She felt his hand on her shoulder. She flinched slightly at the unfamiliar touch but raised her eyes. His expression had softened, and he pointed at the bed.

"I do not understand," she said. Was this some sort of sexual overture? Despite the growing bond she felt with the trio, they were still outlanders.

"I believe that the captain is offering you the remaining space on the bed, so you may rest in comfort," Pierce said. He paused, then continued. "I believe that he is unaware that your race does not sleep."

Daine's eyes widened slightly, and he glanced at Pierce. *Not sleep?* he mouthed.

"Indeed," Xu'sasar said. "This weakness was purged from our kind in the time of horror, when darkness struck at the dreams of the mighty." She looked at Daine. "Take this comfort for your own. I shall watch over you."

Daine shrugged. He glanced at Pierce.

"I will guard the door, captain. Do you wish to obtain food before you sleep?"

Music had begun anew in the common room, and

the sound of laughter rose through the floor—Daine's laughter. Daine frowned as he heard, and he shook his head. He sat down on the bed, and for a time he stared at Lei. Then he removed his armor and settled onto the bed next to her. Moments later, he was fast asleep.

Xu'sasar looked at Pierce. The warforged towered over her, and he watched her with glowing eyes. Moments passed in silence, neither one moving. She wondered if he was evaluating her potential as a threat, considering the ways he would defeat her if they faced one another in battle. That's what she was doing as she studied him. She knew that this man of metal was an ally, and she respected his skills as a hunter and fellow traveler in the night. But he was still a strange and unnatural creature. As she looked at him, the memory rose of the being who had transformed into a storm of razors—the creature who had killed her father and left her for dead. The desire for vengeance against this Harmattan still burned within her, and when she looked at Pierce it was difficult not to see the shadow of that monster.

"I will stand outside the door and guard the hall," Pierce said. "From that position, I will be able to hear the events in the common room below, and any sounds of alarm from this room. You will defend my companions?"

"With my blood," she replied.

Soon Xu'sasar was alone with the sleeping humans. She knelt in a corner of the little room, setting her back against the wall. She drew her bone knives and let her thoughts drift across the linked weapons, watching them ripple and shift in response. *The Tooth of the Wanderer*, the man had called it. *A weapon of destiny, the blade you were born to carry.*

And what destiny do we share? she'd said.

What would have happened if she hadn't asked? Now, there was no way to know. She could only sit in the gray room, watching the humans dream and preparing for the battles tomorrow would bring.

CHAPTER 19

NIGHT: THE DEEPWOOD MOON
THELANIS

Tell me, shaper, and tell me truly, where did your journey begin?"

Lei's thoughts whirled. The others had crossed without incident, and part of her wondered if this was all simply a formality, if a wrong answer existed.

The staff whispered in her hand. The words slipped away before she could grasp their meaning, but she felt fear. There was power here, and danger.

Where did my journey begin? Which journey?

She sifted through a dozen answers, thinking of riddles she'd learned as a child, of tales told of trickster spirits. Finally, she chose her answer.

"My journey began in my mother's womb," she said.

Her heart skipped a beat as she spoke, then the serpent lowered its massive head. Lei slid her staff into her bag. She wanted both her hands for this, and the last thing she needed to worry about was dropping the staff into the deadly water. She made her way up onto the creature's back and stepped out onto the scaled span. She was halfway across when it spoke again.

"You have much to learn," the serpent hissed.

Though she was far from either head, the voice seemed to echo around her.

The bridge rose up beneath her, flinging her into the air. She reached out with her thoughts, trying to weave an enchantment that would slow her fall, but it was all too sudden and sharp. The wind roared, blood rushed through her—

And then she hit the water.

❂ ❂ ❂ ❂ ❂ ❂ ❂

The light was blinding. Lei's eyes had grown accustomed to the dim moonlight of the forest, and now brilliant light flooded the world.

Sunlight.

The air was warm, moist, but it was *air*. Where was the water? Lei reached down, or tried to. She could feel the warm breeze, she could smell the rich soil. But she couldn't move. No, she simply wasn't *there*. She could see the world around her, but she was trapped, a disembodied presence.

Where am I? she thought.

Wait. It was a woman's voice, low and liquid, filled with deep sorrow. Lei had never heard the voice before, and yet it was immediately familiar to her. Despite the mournful tone, Lei found she was comforted, as if she'd just seen an old friend.

Who are you?

Wait, the voice said, and now Lei realized that it was a thought, more like a memory than a voice. *Watch. Learn.*

Lei's vision cleared, and she knew where she was.

Xen'drik.

She didn't recognize her exact surrounding. She hadn't been in this particular clearing, she was sure of it. But there was no mistaking the land. The foliage around her was painted in vivid orange and yellow, colors so sharp that the trees and shrubs appeared to be on fire. This was the jungle where they had first encountered the drow, the region surrounding Karul'tash and the obsidian city Daine had spoken of. As she studied the ground, she saw a patch of darkness, a circle of smooth, black glass half-hidden beneath fiery orange moss. She heard sounds coming from behind her, people moving through the undergrowth, but try as she might, she couldn't turn toward the sound.

Wait. Watch and learn.

The sounds drew nearer, closer with every moment. A figure stepped into her field of view.

It was Lei.

She was wearing her green and gold jerkin, and holding a wand of white wood in her hand—a wand Lei herself had never seen. Her eyes were hidden behind goggles, a complex array of crystal lenses bound to leather straps, and she was studying the ground. She stopped when she spotted the patch of black glass, and pointed her wand at the earth. The moss shriveled away, turning to dust, and a wide patch of black glass was revealed. "Here!" she cried out. Something was wrong. Her voice wasn't Lei's voice.

Another figure came forward from the jungle. It was a man, a tall young man armored in deep blue chainmail. He held a long gray staff in one hand. His skin was pale, his short, wavy hair brilliant red. Lei knew this man. She had seen him in a dream only days earlier. It was her father.

"Excellent, Aleisa," he said, pausing as he reached the edge of the glass.

Aleisa! This wasn't Lei at all. It was her mother. The sahuagin guide, Thaask, had told Lei that he had met her parents decades earlier, that they had come to Xen'drik in search of knowledge. Was this a vision of the past? It made no sense. House Cannith certainly had an interest in the secrets of the shattered land, but why would her parents have come alone? Surely Cannith would have sent a full expedition if there were knowledge to be claimed. Xen'drik was a land of many dangers, and if this could benefit the house, it would look after its own.

Watch and learn, came the voice.

"There's immense power in the glass," the woman said, and now Lei recognized that voice. "Are you sure of this?"

"Beloved, are you questioning my faith?" The man's voice was cold, accusatory, but Lei could see the hint of a smile playing around his lips. Lei remembered her father as an intense, driven man, utterly dedicated to his work. He rarely smiled. "Do you distrust the gifts of our lord?"

"Of course," Aleisa said.

The man—Talin d'Cannith—nodded, and now he truly smiled. "You are as wise as you are beautiful, my dear," he said. "But I do trust in the grand design. I won't die today."

He reached into a pouch on his belt and produced a massive gauntlet, longer than the pouch was deep; clearly this was an extradimensional pocket, like Lei's own bag. As he drew the object into the light, Lei could see that it wasn't simply a glove but the hand of a warforged soldier. The design was unusual. Sharp points rose from each joint, and the tips of the long fingers ended in vicious claws. The wrist had been hollowed out, and Talin placed his own left hand into the socket. He began tracing patterns along the metal, whispering to himself. Lei couldn't hear the words, but she could tell that he was calling on his skills as an artificer, weaving a magical pattern into the metal.

There was a *hiss*, and her father clenched his teeth. Aleisa rushed to his side, her hand on his arm. "Talin!"

His face twisted in pain, but intense concentration soon pushed away the agony. He opened his eyes, staring down at the hand, and the fingers flexed. He was controlling the hand as if it were his own. "Success," he said. "Now give me the key."

Aleisa rummaged through her own pouch and produced a flat metal disk. "I just hope you can remove it when this is done," she said. "Luck has been with us this far, but I think Merrix would notice that."

"It would be just the way of our guide to leave me bound to this thing," Talin said. He pressed the disk against the palm of the warforged claw; when Talin removed his hand, the disk remained fused to the gauntlet. "But it is too early in the game, beloved. We will not be sacrificed so soon."

Talin turned and embraced Aleisa. Lei wasn't sure she could remember ever having seen them kiss, and the sight was both heartwarming and disturbing. For all his calm words, she could sense her father's fear, something else she had never seen. Finally Talin pulled away from his wife and knelt next to the patch of glass. He looked up at her and smiled once more, then he pressed the warforged hand against the glass.

The air above the glass *rippled* with energy. The

glass grew red with heat, collapsed in upon itself, and cooled. Now, in place of the obsidian circle, a set of glass stairs descended down into darkness.

Talin raised his hand, and cold fire wrapped his staff. In silence, the two began the descent into the passage, and Lei found herself drifting forward to follow them. The enormous steps and the height of the ceiling left no question as to the origin of this place. This was a compound of the ancient giants.

The air was still and silent. Aleisa took the lead, and she drew a different wand, darkwood bound with strips of red gold. Her goggles shimmered in the shadows as she studied the floor, and she flinched. "There," she said, pointing at the floor ahead. "I've never seen a glyph with such power. Ah! It's blinding!"

Talin came forward, the warforged fist held out like a shield. He stretched out his hand, palm first, as if pressing against a physical force. Once again, there was a *ripple* in the air. "Clear?" he said.

Aleisa nodded, and they continued through the hall. Soon the corridor came to an end, a tall archway opening into a vast chamber. Aleisa walked through the doorway, glancing.

The blade missed her by inches.

Watching from the hallway, all Lei saw was a section of the obsidian sword. Her mother saw her attacker just in time, and threw herself to the side as the blade came crashing down. As the sword rose again, Talin charged into the room, and Lei's vision followed with him.

A giant, a tall warrior with jet-black skin and glistening ebon armor, towered over Talin. The giant held a glass sword in two hands. The blade flashed toward Talin, breaking the man's staff and scattering glowing shards of wood across the chamber. Talin didn't hesitate. Stepping forward and under the sword, he placed his human hand against the giant's leg. A crackling filled the air, and Lei saw fissures run across the giant's armor and skin. That was when she realized that the giant was a statue—an animated warrior. Her father struck at the magic that empowered the creature, as Lei had when she had fought warforged.

The giant emitted no cry of pain, just as it had given no warning when it launched its attack. It simply struck at its foe, and this time Talin couldn't get out of the way. The force of the blow sent him flying through the air, into the shadows and out of Lei's sight.

Aleisa howled as she threw herself forward, catching the giant's leg in a lethal embrace. The creature shattered in her grasp, and chunks of obsidian rained down around and upon her. "*Talin!*" she howled into the darkness.

"I am here." Pain filled Talin's voice, but he kept his composure. Cold fire filled the room, surrounding Talin's fist. His left arm hung limp at his side and blood flowed from a corner of his mouth. His armor was unbroken; clearly there was magic at work, and it had likely saved his life. "And behold, my love. We have found the treasure that was promised." The glow surrounding his fist grew even more intense, filling the room with the light of day.

Corpses were scattered around the chamber, armored bodies affixed to the walls and spread across the floor. There were bodies of all sizes, from halflings to a few that must be ogres. Some were intact, while others had been dismembered. Lei drew closer to one of the corpses, her vision adjusted to the light, and she realized that these weren't the corpses of men.

They were warforged.

She could see the fibrous roots emerging from the stump of a wounded soldier, the cold fire reflected in crystal eyes. There could be no question what these were, but the designs were unfamiliar. As Lei tried to examine the bodies, a terrible vertigo swept through her. Her vision blurred, and the light faded to darkness.

Mother! Lei tried to speak, but she had no body and no voice. She tried to resist the force that was pulling her into the shadows, but she couldn't. As the world dissolved around her, her father's words echoed in her ears.

"Our work can begin at last."

⚫ ⚫ ⚫ ⚫ ⚫ ⚫ ⚫

Darkness.

No. Stone. Black marble. She was staring at a stone wall. The air was cool, but far fresher than that of the giant tomb. She was in a hallway, and she could see the cold fire lanterns embedded along the walls. There was no dust in this place, no cobwebs. This was no ruin.

What is this place?

Disembodied as she was, Lei couldn't judge the scale. She didn't know if the hall was built for giants, gnomes, or humans. She studied the bare walls, searching for any clue, some hint as to the purpose or inhabitants of the building. There was something very familiar about the barren hallway, something she just couldn't quite grasp. Then she looked at the lantern, and a shock ran through her. The ball of cold fire was held with a cage of mirrored glass and steel, designed to intensify the magical light. It was a common Cannith design, and such lanterns could be found anywhere in the Five Nations. What caught her eye was the decorative point of the lantern—a lion cast in black steel.

Blacklion!

Lei spent her childhood in the Cannith forgehold of Blacklion, a center for warforged research and production hidden in the wilderness of Cyre. It was a lonely place for her. The Cannith artificers stationed at Blacklion, Lei's parents among them, were absorbed in their duties and had little time for a child. Lei spent most of her time among the warforged. When the soldiers emerged from the creation forges, they underwent training before being sent out to the battlefield. Warforged learned quickly. Much of the knowledge they needed to perform their functions was carried on an instinctive level, and within a few months of training a warforged might prove a match for a veteran human soldier. During this time of instruction the warforged were much like children themselves, and Lei enjoyed the company of her metal companions. She even came to envy them. The warforged had a purpose, a place in the world, while Lei was just the little girl lost in the shadows of Blacklion.

A door opened, and a figure came into view. She was small and slender, a pale girl with coppery hair and wearing a long, blue dress. Her feet were bare, and she made no sound against the stone floor. Lei hadn't seen this girl's face in almost twenty years, but there was no doubt in her mind. She was looking at herself.

Watch and learn. It was the woman's voice again, maddeningly familiar.

Lei drifted behind the silent child. She had forgotten how somber she had been. Lei studied her young counterpart. Nine years old, perhaps?

The girl moved cautiously down the hall. She might

173

be silent by nature, but Lei could see that she was taking extra care to be stealthy. When a pair of magewrights entered the hallway, the child slipped into an open door, hiding until the researchers passed by. Where was she going? Lei tried to remember the layout of the building, but the passage of years had worn down her memories.

As the girl moved deeper into the forgehold, Lei heard noises ahead, the clash of steel on steel. *Battle!* For a moment, she thought that the building was under attack, but then she remembered the work that went on at the forgehold. *Combat training.* Blacklion had a virtual arena, where the warforged fought one another to draw their latent combat skills to the surface.

Lei knew what day this was.

Many levels of the forgehold were off-limits to her, but Lei's thirst for knowledge prodded her to see all of the forbidden zones, to learn everything that went on in the forgehold. She had memorized the patterns of the guards and magewrights, finding hiding places that would let her slip past patrols. She was usually caught, but every so often she managed to reach one of the restricted regions. As she had today.

She watched her younger self move closer to the source of the sounds. She entered an armory filled with racks of weapons and shields, and she slipped past a man who was checking the inventory. Creeping across the room, she walked through a large archway.

And onto a battlefield.

The war chamber mimicked conditions of battle. Physical props were combined with magical illusions to create scenarios for the soldiers in training. The girl was unaware of this; she knew only that this was a place that was forbidden to her. And so she was unprepared for the chaotic scene. She found herself in the ruins of a city, in the foundations of a building broken by a mighty siege engine. She was surrounded by rubble and dirt. The clash of steel grew louder. Lei's curiosity drew her forward, treading lightly over the ruined ground. Soon she crouched behind a shattered wall. The sounds of violence were just beyond, and had she ever known battle, fear might have driven her back. Instead she peered over the wall, desperate to see what lay beyond.

Two warforged were locked in battle. One was a shock trooper, a heavily armored warrior built to drive deep into enemy forces. He bore a massive tower shield on his left arm, and held a morningstar studded with vicious spikes. As Lei looked on, he landed a solid blow on his opponent, denting his enemy's armor and sending the smaller warforged staggering backward.

This opponent, a lighter model of warrior designed for stealth, was surely faster than his foe and should never have let his enemy close the distance between them, but he lacked experience, and he hadn't realized how seriously outmatched he was in close combat. The young Lei gasped as the dark warforged landed another blow, a powerful stroke that sent his opponent crashing to the ground. The victor looked down on his foe, searching for any signs of motion; when his victim remained still, he strode off into the ruins, in search of a new enemy.

The girl scrambled over the wall and rushed to the side of the stricken scout. The morningstar had punched a hole through his chestplate, revealing a mass of metal and stone surrounded by torn tendrils. Watching as a ghost, the elder Lei could see that the scout was simply inert. While he was unconscious, his condition was stable and he was in no real danger. But the child didn't know this. She only saw the wound, and she was certain the creature was dying. She reached out, desperate to comfort him, to save him. She laid a hand on the warforged, and she stiffened in shock. Lei remembered that moment, the very first time she had seen the web of energy that comprised the life and consciousness of the warforged . . . the day her dragonmark had appeared. It was strange to see it from the outside, to watch mystic energy ripple around the child's hands and to see warforged's damage fade. Within seconds torn tendrils had regrown, and gouged metal straightened itself and fused over the wound. Light flared in the warforged's crystal eyes, and the child beamed as the soldier sat up and stared at her.

"Halt!" The voice echoed around her, louder than any thunder. "All units disengage!"

The child's eyes widened as her surroundings changed. Much of the cityscape was an illusion, which faded to reveal the true arena of Blacklion. The walls and rubble were obstacles fixed to the ground, and the ground itself was a carpet, designed to feel like soil but clearly artificial in nature. Before she could move, she was caught in a brilliant pool of light.

"Don't move!"

A man in a blue doublet stepped out of the darkness. The girl didn't know that these events were closely monitored, or that magewrights were standing ready to repair the damaged warforged. The man stepped back in surprise as the warforged soldier rose to his feet.

"What have you done, girl?" he said.

Young Lei had no response. She didn't know the

answer. She was overwhelmed by the experience, and even the elder Lei found that she had no memory of what had happened next. She had passed out, awakening much later to find that she was the youngest Cannith heir to develop a dragonmark.

"Out of my way, Banon." It was Lei's father, older now than when she'd seen him in Xen'drik. Age had made him harder, and his voice carried cold authority. The magewright stepped away from the warforged without question. Talin bent down and picked up his daughter. "Lei," he said. "Are you hurt, Lei?"

The girl went limp in his arms.

"She's sick!" he said. "Banon, examine this unit. I'll take care of my daughter. And don't breathe a word of this until I speak to you, is that understood?"

"Yes, master," the magewright said.

Talin carried his daughter across the arena, and Lei found herself following him. Her thoughts raced. She'd passed out. She knew that. It was stress, the unprecedented manifestation of her dragonmark. That was what she'd been told, what she knew to be true.

But when her father touched the girl, when he picked her up . . . Lei had seen the moment of concentration, and she'd seen the mystic glow around his hands, out of Banon's view. She hadn't collapsed on her own. Her father had done something to her. But what? And why?

Talin made his way out of the war chamber and into a storeroom. This room was filled with props used in the arena, objects that could be hauled out and cloaked with illusion to become trees, walls, and other obstacles. Lei's father walked to the back of the chamber. He glanced around, making sure he was alone, and then shifted his grip on his daughter and placed his right palm against the wall. He paused, and then he stepped *through* the wall. *An illusion!* Lei was drawn after him, passing through the seemingly solid wall and into the chamber that lay beyond.

It was an arcane workshop, as well equipped as anything Lei ever seen in a Cannith facility. One wall was devoted to alchemy, with a vast assortment of herbs and fluids spread around bubbling beakers, alembics, and other tools. Ahead of her, a pylon rose from the floor, a stone pillar encrusted with glowing dragonshards and mithral inscriptions; while Lei could not divine its purpose, there was no question that this was an eldritch machine designed to channel vast amounts of magical energy.

Talin laid the little girl down on a long stone slab set into the floor, a table covered with runes of divination and conjuration. He adjusted a flexible cold fire lantern, focusing a beam of light directly on the child. Five other identical slabs were spread around this operating theater, and Lei felt a terrible chill. She couldn't remember having seen this place in waking hours, but she had been here in her dreams. When she'd passed out in the sewers of Sharn, when she'd nearly died in the vault beneath Stormreach, she'd found herself here, lying on that same table where her father was now examining her younger self.

"What is it?" A woman stepped out of the shadows and rushed to the table. Lei's mother. Older now, just like her father, but unmistakable. "What's happened to her?"

"I've disabled her," Talin said, his voice cold. "We have problems. She just repaired an inert scout in the battle room, and there were witnesses."

"Repaired?"

"Repaired. Restored a critically damaged soldier to peak condition with a touch."

"So soon? But this is more than we could have hoped for!" Aleisa's voice was filled with amazed joy, but Lei's father was still cold.

"Don't you see? *There were witnesses.* They won't rest until they have an explanation. And we can't risk exposure so soon." He looked down at the unconscious girl and shook his head. "We'll have to destroy her. A freakish accident, a dragonmark arising before the body is ready—"

"Are you *mad?*" Aleisa shoved her husband away from the child. "This is our *daughter!*"

"I knew you'd be emotional about this," Talin said. "But think of the greater goal!"

"Lei's always been my greater goal," her mother said. "I thought you understood that."

"Aleisa." Talin looked down at the child. "I love her too. You know that. And even I am amazed at what she has done today, and what it says of her potential. But we have *always* known this day could come. She is the most dangerous thing we have ever created, and if our designs are revealed, excoriation is the least of the horrors awaiting us. All that is flesh and blood must die, Aleisa, and she dies today."

"No!" Aleisa said. "What of our faith? This is a challenge. And you would surrender? There must be another path, a way to emerge from this stronger than before."

"There's no time—"

"Hold." Aleisa's eyes narrowed, and now Lei could see the more familiar face of her mother, the calculating artificer. "You said that we can explain her death as the early manifestation of a dragonmark."

"Yes."

"What if she manifests the mark—and lives?"

"Explain," Talin said.

"If we *give* her a mark, that explains what she has done. It gives us reason to begin her training at this unprecedented early age. Should she flare again, it will be dismissed as the talent of a prodigy, which is essentially the truth."

"Yes," Talin said. "For her to manifest the mark at this age . . . a historic event, but hardly one requiring a thorough investigation. I am humbled by your wisdom, my love."

"It will take time to synthesize a mark that will meet all tests, but for now the outline will do," Aleisa said. She sorted through a rack of arcane tools, twisted rods, and strange blades. "This should be sufficient," she said, holding up a rod of ebony bound with brass and tipped with a dark dragonshard. "Where shall our daughter have her dragonmark, my husband?"

"Why, I think she should take after her lovely mother," Talin said.

Aleisa smiled at that. "Prepare her, then."

Talin turned the child onto her stomach, brushing her hair to the side. "*Verentis ierjyx!*" he said, and the power in these syllables tore at the air. The column in the center of the chamber burst into brilliant light, and runes covering the table were traced in lines of fire. The girl herself *glowed*, as if power were flowing through her.

Aleisa cut her palm with a silver blade. Blood dripped onto the floor as she gripped the ebony rod. "Now, my daughter," she said. "Let my blood flow into you once more. Take this gift, and may it save us all."

She pressed the rod against the child's neck, and as

she did so, Lei felt an agonizing pain as if her dragon-mark were acid against her skin. She tried to scream, but she had no voice. The pain consumed her, and the chamber burned away in a burst of white light.

✸ ✸ ✸ ✸ ✸ ✸ ✸

Consciousness returned. She was floating, falling.

She opened her eyes. *She opened her eyes.* After so much time as a bodiless presence, she was herself again! But where *was* she? There was pressure all around her, and she felt as if she were falling, slipping down through a still pool of water. But this water wasn't pressing into her nose, mouth, or eyes. She breathed with no difficulty at all. And all around her, there was . . . nothing. White light.

Someone held her hand.

"You are in yourself," a voice said. It was musical, inhumanly beautiful yet filled with terrible misery. The woman's voice, the one she'd heard earlier. "You've seen the past. This is the now. Only you can decide what happens next."

The air was like water, and Lei found she could push against it. She turned in place, and a woman came into view.

A woman made from wood.

The stranger's skin was polished bark, dark as any night. Black leaves enshrouded her head, this inky foliage taking the place of hair, and cascading down to cover back and breasts. Even her eyes were wood, though they glittered with bright dew. She was beautiful, and though Lei have never seen her before, she was achingly familiar.

A woman of wood . . . a woman of *dark* wood . . .

"You're the staff," Lei breathed.

"Once I was much more," the dryad said. "But now, the staff is all that remains of me."

"Why haven't you spoken to me before?"

"I have done all that I could. My spirit is bound deep within the wood, and song and whisper are all I have left. Yours is the only mind I can touch, and I can speak to you like this only because you have fallen so far within yourself."

"Why me?" Lei said. "Why can you only speak to me?"

"I have no answers for you, but you drift through the river of knowledge. Have you learned nothing from what you have seen?"

The memories rushed back. Xen'drik. Blacklion. The blazing pain of the brand. "That wasn't real," she said. *It couldn't have been.* "I don't know what you're trying to do, but this is a trick. You—you're probably Lakashtai, trying to manipulate me the same way you did Daine."

"This is no dream," the dryad said. "And it is not my doing. I am here only because of the bond between us. The serpent is the Keeper of Secrets, and these are your secrets revealed."

Lei's head pounded. No ground lay beneath her feet, and she was still falling into the endless white. No escape from these terrible thoughts. "No. This can't be real."

"Of course it is. This is the answer to the questions growing within you. Why could you hear the voices trapped in the dream-chamber of Karul'tash? How did you escape death beneath Stormreach? How did you repair the shattered orb? And how can you speak to me? In any other hand, I would be cold wood. But you can reach within."

"What am I?" Lei whispered.

"I do not know what you are," the dryad said. "But you are not human."

"No!" Lei reached back, placing her hand across her dragonmark. Memories tore at her mind.

She spoke of her desire for a daughter, whispered the sahuagin Thaask. *It was a subject of sorrow for her, one of great difficulty.*

Everything is an experiment, her father said. *All that is flesh must perish. We knew that from the start.*

Just remember, I always loved you, her mother said, then her voice grew cold. *Do what you must.*

Lei's dragonmark burned beneath her hand. *It will take time to synthesize a mark that will meet all tests, but for now the outline will do.* The pain grew sharper, brighter, until she tore her hand away from the mark.

"What am I?" she cried, howling her pain into the white void.

"You are Lei." The dryad still held her left hand. "You are what you have always been. Nothing has changed but your knowledge."

Tears seared in Lei's eyes. "No. Everything. Everything I thought . . . my mark . . . do I even have parents? Am I even *alive*?"

The dryad slapped her.

It was a gentle blow, cushioned by the thick air or liquid that surrounded them. But it still came as a shock.

"You think you know loss? I have lost more than you can imagine. My world was torn from me. And when I thought I was at my lowest point, when I thought I had nothing more to lose, I was bound to this staff, a prisoner in the last fragment of my beautiful tree. Once my voice shaped the night, and now I am but a whisper. So your illusions have been stripped from you. *You have life.* You have love, if you have the courage to seize it. You have been given the gift of truth, and the truth is a burden. So tell me, girl. Do you have the strength to rise, to pull yourself up? Or will you surrender and drift down into the darkness at the bottom of your mind?"

Lei gaped. "Who are you?"

The dryad smiled, but it was a grimace of pain. "I am the Heart of the Darkwood Grove, the last of the Darkwood Daughters. You stand in my hour of night, in a realm that once echoed with my song. I sought to escape my destiny, and I paid for that folly with all that I had."

Curiosity warred with Lei's self-pity. "What destiny?"

"I was to wed Torenas the Woodsman, youngest of the Nine Brothers of Night. The land beneath the Deepwood Moon was his as much as mine, and only in our union would he gain his true dominion. But I sought to escape this destiny. I wished to be more than a wood-wife, bound to live beneath a single moon. She promised to help me, and I, fool that I was, believed her words."

"Who?" Lei said.

"She has many names, almost as many as she has faces. Thelania, the Queen of Dusk and Shadows. She is one of the mightiest spirits of this plane. I knew she would not act out of kindness, that she would help me only if it served her own goals. But I was impatient. She promised an escape, and I thought she might free me from my tree, give me the freedom my kind cannot have."

"But she betrayed you."

"She tore my tree from Thelanis, taking me from my beautiful night and binding me to your dry and color-less world. Worse yet, she gave me to Jura d'Cannith. I don't know what dealings she had with him." She looked away. "And that is where I failed. Perhaps I could have found some way to escape my prison, some way to redeem myself. But I gave in to despair. I surrendered to anger, and I turned that hatred against Jura. Perhaps, if I'd done things differently, I could have found the light within him. Instead, I drew out the worst within him, his own dark heart. And it cost me all I had left. I underestimated him. I pushed too far. He felled my tree and bound me within the staff, with magic I still don't understand. And I cannot help but wonder if this was Dusk's plan all along."

"I . . . I don't know what to say," Lei said.

"Say nothing. It is my folly, and I brought it upon myself. But now you must make your own decision. Look down."

The white void was no longer eternal. A black spot grew beneath them.

"The decision is upon you," Darkheart said. "Fight for the sky above. Fight to rise through the waters and break the surface. Or surrender and fall forever into the darkness below."

"And you?"

"This is your battle, and I have done what I can. You must make your decision alone, and you will need both hands to swim. Farewell, Lei. I hope that one day I will hold your hand in truth, and we will gaze together on the moon above."

The dryad released Lei's hand, and the instant wood left flesh she was gone. Lei was alone, falling toward the spreading shadows. The visions flashed through her mind once more, and she felt a sick sense of loss and betrayal. But there were other memories.

Jode's laughter.

Daine giving orders in the camp at Keldan Ridge.

Pierce carrying her through the streets of Sharn after she'd been driven from Hadran's house.

Daine holding her as their boat was tossed about on the waters of the Thunder Sea.

Whatever she was, whatever these awful visions meant, her life lay above her. Daine. Pierce. She would not let them go.

Struggling at first, then with increasing strength, she began to swim upward, away from the darkness and moving up through the light.

CHAPTER 20

NIGHT: THE
DEEPWOOD MOON
THELANIS

Daine was growing used to his nightmares. Ever since Lakashtai entered his life, sleep had become a battleground. Monan the changeling. Lakashtai and her trickery. The horrible visions of Kelden Ridge. He had come to expect terror in the night. It was strange to have normal dreams . . . a night where his visions drifted from place to place.

Daine was at a party. A masquerade, at the Metrol manor of Alina Lorridan Lyrris. Dressed as a bodyguard, he watched the revelers, trying to guess what lay under each mask. Huge windows of stained glass lined the hall. Beautiful work, but Daine knew that all was not as it seemed. The Karrns had launched a mystical assault on Metrol yesterday, and fire had destroyed a few of the windows. Now they were covered by wooden boards, but Alina couldn't abide such an eyesore; she concealed the damage beneath illusion.

The Karrnarthi attacks were designed to cause terror. Karrnath couldn't bring serious firepower to bear so far within Cyre's borders, but the firestrikes sent ripples of fear and uncertainty throughout the populace. And the damage was done. This morning, Daine had stepped over the charred body of a child on the way to the market. It wasn't his concern. He had a duty to his family. He—

"Living in the past?"

For a moment the speaker was a child wearing a blue mask shaped like a dragon's head, one of the many revelers around him. Then the party was gone the mask with it.

Jode smiled. "Don't you think it's time to put it behind you?"

They were on an airship, one of the largest Daine had seen. The ocean below was a sea of clouds. "Where are we going?" he said.

"Do we need to go anywhere?"

"I suppose not."

They watched in silence, Daine simply basking in his friend's company. The setting sun painted the clouds orange and gold, and as it slipped beneath the surface, three moons claimed possession of the sky.

Jode took Daine's hand. No . . . this hand was too large to be Jode, too small for Pierce.

"Daine," a voice whispered. It was Lei.

He turned to her, and now he was on a tiny gray bed in a tiny gray room. She was stretched out before him, and she was the most beautiful thing he had ever seen. Her skin seemed to glow in the moonlight, and her hair was aflame.

"Daine," she said.

He tried to speak and found that he had no voice. But the emotion demanded release. There was no time for thought as he kissed her. Her hand traced patterns of fire across the back of his neck, but she fell into his arms, warm and yielding.

"Do you wish privacy for this act?"

Xu'sasar stood at the foot of the bed, watching them. Lei stiffened, pulled away, and Daine realized that he wasn't dreaming at all. Lei pulled the gray blanket up and around her, her pale skin flushed.

Daine sat up and snapped at Xu'sasar, anger mingling with his own embarrassment. At least, he tried to. No sound came from his mouth. Slowly the events of the night came back to him.

"Daine?" Lei said, clearly wondering why he hadn't answered.

"He cannot speak," Xu'sasar said. If she was uncomfortable, she didn't show it. "I do understand your head motions. Do you wish me to leave?"

As angry as Daine was, he knew this wasn't Xu'sasar's fault. She'd been in the room to begin with, and he had no idea what the customs of her people were. *Damn it, she can see in the dark!* Then it occurred to him. It was still dark. How long had he been asleep?

The door opened, and Pierce entered. Lei leapt out of bed, a sound between laugh and sob escaping her lips. She wrapped her arms around the warforged, and he returned the embrace.

"It is good to see you well again, my lady," he said, his low voice filling the room.

The darkness beyond the window, the curse of silence, the mysterious journey that still lay ahead—these things would sort themselves out in time. For now, they were together again, and that was all that mattered. Daine smiled like a fool, and he couldn't have stopped if he'd wanted to. Xu'sasar watched him, waiting for an answer, and he looked at her and shook his head.

"What happened?" Lei said when she finally released Pierce. "Where *are* we?"

"Not far from the river where you had your accident, my lady. We were able to find shelter in this inn, so that you could rest. By the bell in the common room, eight hours have passed since our arrival."

Eight hours? The faint moonlight beyond the dusty window was just as it had been when they arrived. The room looked just the same as it had when he had fallen asleep. *Thrice-damned world of darkness.*

But none of it mattered now that Lei was awake. Pulling on his shirt, he rose out of bed and took her arm.

"Daine," she said, gazing into his eyes.

For a moment he was lost again, and Pierce and Xu'sasar were forgotten. He tried to speak, to tell her his feelings, but his throat was empty and his tongue could not shape the air.

Lei could see that something was wrong. Xu'sasar's words must have finally registered. "What's happened to you?" she said, joy turning to concern.

Daine shook his head and made a dismissive gesture with his free hand.

"He loaned his voice to the innkeeper in exchange for our lodging," Pierce said.

"What do you mean, loaned his voice?" Lei said, eyes widening.

"Just that," Pierce replied. "I do not understand the magic involved, my lady. The innkeeper employed necromantic energies to remove Daine's voice from his body. I have heard him making use of it downstairs, while you have been sleeping. He vowed to return it to Daine when we left. Hopefully we can trust his word."

Lei turned and slapped Daine, leaving an angry red mark across his cheek. *What?* He tried to say, with no success.

"What did you think you were doing?" Lei said. As surprised as Daine was, he now saw that fear, not anger, drove her. "Making *deals* with these people? Haven't you listened to anything I've said about this place? Haven't you read a damned *story* in your life?"

"I told him the same," Xu'sasar said, but Lei wasn't listening.

I did it for you, Daine thought, and I'd do it again.

Lei pulled her hand away from him. "We're leaving. Now." She strode across the room and grabbed her satchel. "Pierce, I want to see this innkeeper."

"My lady, you have been ill. We do not even know what you have been through. Perhaps this is not the time for a conv—"

Lei reached into her satchel and pulled out the darkwood staff. The staff *moaned,* a clear note of warning and woe. "Pierce, take me to this innkeeper or get out of my way so I can find him myself."

"As you wish," Pierce said. Daine had just finished pulling on his chainmail byrnie. Buckling his belt, he grabbed his boots and rushed after them.

❋ ❋ ❋ ❋ ❋ ❋ ❋

The fire still burned in the common room, and the fiddler was playing a merry tune. Huwen the crow chuckled and cawed as Daine entered the room. The bird's wild gestures proved that his wings had been healed, and he was chattering to Ferric, pecking at a crust of bread and occasionally dipping his beak in a wide cup. The portly innkeeper guffawed at one of Huwen's jokes, and Daine winced at the sound of his own laughter. He glanced around the room, but it seemed that the two other patrons had taken their leave.

"You," said Lei, striding across the room.

Ferric turned with a smile, but his face froze when he saw the darkwood staff leveled at his throat. There was a moment of fear, but Daine saw something else in his eyes, as if he had just recognized a stranger behind a mask.

"Lady . . . Lei," Ferric said, and it was Daine's voice, full of emotion, the voice he would have used when he saw her in the dim light of the gray room.

"You don't know me," Lei said coolly. "You made a deal with my friend. We're here to settle the bill."

As she spoke, the unseen fiddler changed his tune, increasing the tempo to a jolly jig. The music wormed its way into Daine's mind, pushing away thoughts, encouraging him to forget his troubles and dance. Even Pierce began tapping his foot. Then the darkwood staff answered the tune. Her song was one of loss and sorrow, and Daine didn't need to hear the words to be affected by the dirge. The voice of the staff shattered the cheery tune, and Daine could gather his thoughts again.

"Try that again and I'll feed you your fiddle," Lei said. She glared across the room, and following her stare Daine finally saw the source of the music. The fiddler was a tiny man, and only magic could account for the volume of his music; his instrument was little more than a toy. The musician's head might have reached the top of Daine's knee if he stood as straight as he could. His jacket was soft brown velvet, buttoned with gemstone shards, and he had the lower body of a grasshopper. He paused in his song, looking at Lei with great reproach.

"All is well, Zimi," Ferric said. "It seems we have a guest musician under our roof."

The fiddler tossed his head and tucked his fiddle under his arm. One leap took him halfway up the stairs, and he disappeared onto the second floor.

"Now," Lei said. "I believe you were going to give my companion his voice back."

Daine watched in wonder. Lei seemed to have the situation well in hand.

"You're feisty when you're awake, aren't you now?" Huwen chuckled, then squawked as a swift stroke of the staff sent him tumbling off the table. "Should have left that one asleep, you ask me," he muttered from the floor.

"*Lady* Lei," Ferric said. He still had Daine's voice, but now his tone was formal, respectful. He took a step back and looked her in the eye. "Do stop abusing my guests and the help. I made a simple business arrangement with your companion. I fully intend to honor the terms of our agreement. And trust me, you'd rather have me as an ally than an enemy. So why don't you calm down and have a little dinner? I think you'll find we have much to discuss."

"I think we'll be leaving now," Lei said. "And I don't see what help you could offer us."

"Don't be so quick to judge, my dear," Ferric said. "You don't know what you're dealing with. The Crooked Tree is the only free house under this moon, and the path leads ever deeper into the domain of the Woodsman. I don't know what you know of him"—his eyes flickered down to the darkwood staff—"but given your companions, I can assure you that he is your enemy. Sit at my table. Eat my bread. Tell me your business in this land. And perhaps I can help you with your problems."

"Not interested," Lei said. "Just give Daine his voice back, and we'll be on our way."

Ferric sighed, raising his hands in surrender. "As you wish." He walked out around the counter, stopping in front of Daine. "You know how this works. Just open your mouth."

Smoke flowed from Ferric's throat, and an awful scream filled the air. The vapors flowed into Daine's mouth, pressing against his skin like a writhing serpent, and Daine fought to push away the images of the snakes he'd seen hanging from the trees. He struggled to keep from gagging—and then it was over.

"Thank the Flame," he said, for the first time in a year.

It felt as if the words were rotting in his throat. He knew that sound. It was the voice the innkeeper had greeted them with when they'd first arrived.

Ferric opened his mouth, and it was Daine's laugh that came from his lips.

"Honor the terms of your agreement?" Lei said, and the staff was raised again.

"I have, my dear," Ferric said, "and not even your companion can challenge me on that."

"You said you'd give me my voice back," Daine said, every word a new horror.

"That I did, at first. Than you said you wanted the price to cover your companions as well. I told you that in that case, I'd give you *a* voice back, and you agreed. I've upheld my end of our bargain."

Huwen chuckled from the floor. "Likes a deal, he does. I did tell you that."

"This will not stand," Lei said.

"Oh, it will," Ferric said. "Don't you think to threaten me beneath the Crooked Tree. But if you want your lad's fine voice back, I think we can come to an understanding."

Sword and dagger were in Daine's hands, but the darkwood staff whispered and Lei waved him back. "No, Daine. You know the stories. I think he's right." She turned back to Ferric. "What do you want?"

"Her," Ferric said, pointing at the staff. "You have quite a bond, I can see. But I have . . . a way with the spirits of the wood. I don't know how you came by her, but I can't imagine she means more to you than young Daine does. Give her to me, and I return Daine's true voice to him."

"I can't," Lei said. "We need her."

Ferric nodded. "Oh, I think you'll find that once I've taken her away, the Woodsman will no longer have an interest in you. What more do you need? A path home? I'm sure I can help you with that, as well."

Lei looked at Daine, and he could see the uncertainty in her eyes. The staff began to sing, a low and mournful song.

"Don't worry, Darkheart," Ferric said. "You'll find my home a fair one . . . once we've established the order of things."

Lei's face paled, and she took a step toward Daine. Her hand tightened around the staff. Daine reached out, taking her arm. "I can't," she whispered. "I can't do that to her."

Daine didn't know what Lei was talking about, but it didn't matter. This was his mess. "Well," he said, and the sound of his ghastly voice brought tears to her eyes. "There's no deal."

Ferric smiled, his pointed teeth gleaming in the firelight. "As you wish. I come out ahead either way. I will enjoy your fine—"

The innkeeper's eyes widened as the point of an ivory blade burst through his throat. No blood flowed from mouth and wound. Instead there were wisps of smoke and the faintest whispers.

"Open your mouth!" It was Xu'sasar. The drow girl pulled her blade from the innkeeper's neck, and shoved the wounded man. Ferric staggered a few steps and collapsed at Daine's feet. Now smoke was pouring from the dying man's neck, and a terrible scream filled the air—Daine's scream.

Daine opened his mouth without thinking. The nebulous smoke converged into a tight column and flowed down his throat, and now *he* was screaming as it burned within him. He was screaming. With his own voice. "Flame!" he said, marveling at how wonderful it sounded.

"What have you done, girl?" Huwen flew across the

room and landed next to Ferric's twisted form. "You can't kill the likes of him. Not here!"

Lei seemed just as shocked. The staff had fallen silent, and Lei knelt over the corpse. Ferric's body seemed to be collapsing in on itself. "He's right. The tales—"

"It seems our people tell different tales," Xu'sasar said. "I suggest we leave."

"You would kill my husband, and leave me his corpse? You would break an honorable vow?" It was the voice of an old woman, cold and penetrating. For all that it was a rasp and a whisper, it carried over the chaos and brought silence in its wake. A woman stood in the corner of the room, and despite her stooped posture she stood almost as tall as Pierce. She stepped into the light, and Daine saw that she had withered vines in place of hair, and her skin was rough gray bark. Her limbs were long and twisted. Daine knew little of magic, but he was no fool. The Inn of the Crooked Tree, the gray trunk rising up through the center. And Ferric's warning . . . *the Crooked Tree will be no safe haven after my death.*

"I would," Xu'sasar said. She raised a bone blade. "Behold the Wanderer's Tooth, withered old tree. Husband and vow, both fall to its edge."

"Aye," the dryad said. "A foul thing indeed. I pity you, child." She looked at the others. Daine's sword was still in his hand, Pierce had his last arrow nocked and ready, and the darkwood staff was steady in Lei's hand. "With your vile claw and dear Lady Darkheart, you might even bring me down." She shook her head. "Ferric should have known better. And I hardly approve of his interest in you, Darkheart. I suppose he deserved his fate."

"So what happens now?" Daine said, still crouched

and ready to strike. The sound of his voice was music to his ears.

"You take what food you require and leave," the dryad said. "And never seek shelter beneath my boughs again."

Daine nodded. He took a step back and slowly sheathed his weapon. "You are gracious, lady. I am sorry to have brought sorrow to your door."

"Just take it with you, child. And never return."

Daine turned to the others. "You heard her. Grab some grub and let's be on our way." He wasn't thrilled with the thought of eating Ferric's food, but his stomach was rumbling, so he took a loaf of bread and a wineskin. He looked back at the old dryad. Huwen was perched on her arm, and she was talking quietly with the bird.

"Let's go," Daine called out to the others. As he made his way to the door, something caught his eye: Ferric's corpse. At first it seemed that the body had disintegrated. All that was left was an empty set of clothes. Then Daine saw the withered body of a weasel, poking out from the collar, a ghastly wound in the animal's neck.

Daine took one last glance at Huwen, wondering what the next innkeeper of the Crooked Tree would look like.

•

CHAPTER 21
NIGHT: THE
DEEPWOOD MOON
THELANIS

"Don't even think about eating that," Lei said.
Daine paused, a chunk of bread halfway to his
mouth. "What?"

"By the Sovereigns, you're lucky your voice was all
that you lost. *Don't eat the food.* Did you *have* a mother?"

"She was a swordsmith," Daine said. "My bedtime
stories taught me the dangers of battle, not traveling
through other planes."

"Just trust me. Leave it alone. I'll make you a bowl of
gruel when we find a place to stop."

"Oh, *gruel*," Daine said, regretfully tossing the bread
into the bushes. "Now there's an appealing offer.
Aren't *you* hungry?"

"I've got other things on my mind right now. You," she
said to Xu'sasar. "That weapon of yours. What is it?" Her
voice was hard, her anger still searching for an outlet.

"It is nothing of your world," Xu'sasar replied. "I said
before, our people tell different tales."

"Then tell me a story," Lei said. "Because we're not
going anywhere until I choose our path."

Pierce looked to Daine, but it seemed that the captain had chosen to leave this in Lei's hands. Pierce

himself was curious. While Xu'sasar seemed to be an ally, there was much they didn't know about the drow girl. Where had this weapon come from, and what was it capable of?

Xu'sasar stared at Lei, silver eyes gleaming with the light of the moon. But Lei wasn't backing down. Xu'sasar brought the bone blades together, and the two weapons *merged*, twisting into a longer sword with a blade made from a giant tooth.

The total mass of the weapon has increased, Shira observed. *I am still unable to ascertain its true nature, but it holds great power, such that I can sense its energy, even over the ebb and flow of the realm.*

"Behold the Tooth of the Wanderer." Xu'sasar said. "The world is filled with spirits. You outlanders do not see them and do not heed their calls. Tree, scorpion, wind. Vulkoor the scorpion is predator and provider, and there is power and wisdom in his lessons." She ran a finger along the opalescent vambrace covering her right forearm.

Scorpion chitin, Shira observed. *Alchemically treated. Flexible but strong.*

"The scorpion of our world is a symbol of Vulkoor, a lesson we must learn. So it is with all things in the first land, from the shifting panther to the foul giant."

"I asked about the blade," Lei said.

"Then listen," Xu'sasar replied. "The great spirits are known by name. Hul'drac. Vulkoor. Kura'tra. Each one is a lesson, and each guides us down a particular path. But there is one who bears no name, who cannot be bound by a single form, a wanderer who follows every path, and none."

Lei's eyes narrowed. "And this Wanderer . . . does he give gifts, perhaps?"

The drow girl clicked his tongue. "Dangerous gifts, traps for the weak and unwary. The Wanderer is the lesson that remains unknown until the end, and those who survive will be stronger for it."

"And you're carrying his *tooth?* How is that even possible, and who would be fool enough to do such a thing?"

"The Wanderer is not bound to mortal flesh." As Xu'sasar spoke, the blade in her hands shifted, transforming into the three-pronged throwing wheel she had used before. "The blade is an idea, just as the Wanderer is . . . chaos and change, bound together as tooth and bone. It is my destiny to bear it, and if I am strong, I will survive this task. Already, my blade restored the voice of Daine when you lacked the courage to act. Who are you to question it?"

Lei took a step forward, but Pierce put a hand on her shoulder.

"I understand your frustration, my lady," Pierce said. "But perhaps it would be best to continue this conversation when we are no longer standing in the shadow of an enemy."

Lei took a deep breath, then released it. "It's not that easy, Pierce." Lei looked at the forest around them, and a mournful whisper filled the air, the voice of the darkwood staff. "As long as we remain in this wood, the enemy is all around us."

"The Woodsman," Daine said. "In Aureon's name, who *is* this Woodsman? The demon prince of lumberjacks?"

"No," Lei said. "He's not a woodsman. He's *the* Woodsman. He's the lord of this forest, a being of fey magic." She raised her staff. "This is what he seeks. This is why he's hunting us. He wants the spirit of the woman who was to be his wife."

"Why does everyone want that thing?" Daine said. "And if it's the source of all our troubles, then why in Aureon's name don't we get rid of it?"

"Do you not remember the words of the scorpion?" Xu'sasar said. "Only the spirit bound within can open the gate that lies at the end of our path. It is the key that will open the Gates of Night."

"My vision said the same thing, Daine." Lei stared into the carved eyes of the staff. "And she wants to be free. I won't let her go."

Pierce had come to expect sarcasm from Daine. *So I can't have a bite of bread, but you can keep the haunted staff?*

Not this time. There was no twinkle in Daine's eyes, no sardonic note in his voice. Daine had been just as worried about Lei as Pierce had, and surely Daine could sense her distress as well. He nodded. "So what do we do? How powerful is this Woodsman?"

"I don't know," Lei said. "I think . . . I hope . . . the staff can shield us. He's lord of this forest, but the spirit in the staff was once lady of the woods. Her power is diminished, but I think that if we stay close together—*very* close together—she can hide us from his eyes until we can reach these gates."

"And your magic stick can show us the path?"

"Yes," Lei said, as the staff whispered again. "Yes, she can."

"And what's the range of this protection?"

Lei walked to the edge of the clearing, about twelve paces. "About this far, I think."

Daine nodded. Steel gleamed in the moonlight as Daine drew his sword, and he tossed his dagger to the warforged soldier. "Pierce, you stay with her. Xu'sasar, you're with me. Eyes sharp. Bird, weasel, anything you see . . . I want it dead."

Xu'sasar smiled, and her twin blades merged together to form the bone throwing wheel she'd used against Huwen.

"Very well, Lei," Daine said. "Lead the way."

❦ ❦ ❦ ❦ ❦ ❦ ❦

Lei led them off the path and into the forest. The staff was singing a song without words, a soft and mournful tune. The wood responded to the song. Vines rose up and out of their way, while roots that could catch underfoot sank into the soil. A new path opened before them, closing after they passed. Glancing back, Pierce could see that the ground held no trace of their passage; plant and soil shifted to cover their trail. Pierce wondered why Lei hadn't called upon these powers earlier, and Shira responded to the thought.

The power of the staff grows as we move deeper into these woods. If these woods were once the stronghold of this spirit, her strength should be greater in this place, just as the power of your enemy is. She paused, considering. *Or perhaps Lei has changed since rising from her sleep.*

Pierce had wondered this himself. He was pleased that Lei was functional once more, and the mere sound of her voice brought a sense of satisfaction, of a mission completed successfully. Yet he could hear the tension in her words. Human emotions were often difficult for Pierce to recognize, but he had a bond with Lei; he felt her sorrow and her joy as if they were echoes, faint but clear. She was angry, but Pierce could feel the fear and confusion beneath that mask of anger. At first he thought it was merely the aftermath of the battle in the Crooked Tree. But as time passed, the tension remained, growing stronger with each passing hour.

"My lady," he said at last. He moved closer to her, so he could speak quietly. "What troubles you?" He didn't touch her. For all that he felt concern, Pierce was warforged, and he'd never taken comfort in physical contact. He could feel pressure against the metal plates covering his body, and it was painful when a blade tore through his rootlike muscles. But these were tactical indicators, not nearly as sharp as human senses. Pierce knew when he'd been injured, but he took little pleasure in touch.

Lei glanced at him. Pierce thought she was going to snarl, but when she finally spoke, he heard the fear and not the fury.

"Where do I begin?" she said. "I almost died in Xen'drik, Pierce. I *should* have died in Xen'drik. Instead, I repaired that shattered orb for Lakashtai. How did I do that?"

"Do you not repair me when I have suffered damage?"

"It's not the same," she said. "The power in that orb, the skill and energy that must have gone into making it . . . I wouldn't know where to begin. I don't know of a Cannith artificer alive who could make such a thing. And that's just it. Why me? Why would Lakashtai go to all that trouble, all that trickery with Daine, to lure *me* to Xen'drik? Sovereign and Flame, she was in *Sharn!* Some of the finest minds of the house are in that city. Why me? And why go through that charade with Daine instead of striking at *my* mind?"

"At this point we know nothing about Lakashtai, my lady. Everything she told us may have been untrue. This makes it difficult to analyze her motives."

"That final battle," Lei said. "The other one—Tashana—why were they even fighting?"

They were beings of two different orders. Shira's thought was a calm statement of fact. *The one you knew as Tashana possessed a bond to a spirit of Dal Quor, the plane of dreams. This bond was a weak and vestigial thing; the spirit barely touched her soul.* Pierce felt the faint touch of Shira sifting through his memories. *This is in keeping with the beings you think of as kalashtar. The other served as a mortal vessel for a quori spirit, which was likely in full control of her actions. I suspect this spirit was truly Lakashtai—and the flesh you dealt with was a simple shell.*

While this was intriguing, Pierce was more concerned with Lei. As upset as she was, he could sense something held back. "What happened to you, my lady? What happened while you slept?"

Lei stopped moving. She turned, looking into Pierce's eyes, and he could see the fear within.

"What is it?" Daine said, as he and Xu'sasar caught up with them. "What's wrong?"

Lei closed her eyes, massaging her temples with one hand. "I don't know how to say this. When I fell, I had a vision. And—"

The staff screamed.

Lei convulsed, clutching at the staff and gritting her teeth to fight through the pain. "He knows," she said. "He knows we're here."

A chill filled the air, and the wind rose around them. The growing gale howled in the distance, and the wind whipped branch and leaf. The darkwood staff moaned with the gale, singing an eerie counterpart to the rising storm.

"Stay close," Lei said. "He knows we're near, but we still might escape the eyes of his minions. And the gate . . . we're almost there. I can feel it."

"So do we run?" Daine said.

"No." Lei's voice was almost lost beneath the howling

wind. Her eyes were distant as she listened to the song of the staff. "Wait. Wait to see if they pass us by."

"Then fight back to back," Daine said. "Pierce, cover Lei on the other side. And Xu, you heard her. If we're attacked, we defend ourselves. But you strike the first blow and I swear I'll kill you myself. Is that understood?"

The drow blew out her breath, but the sound was lost beneath the gale.

Pierce watched the woods. The storm shook the trees and drowned out all sound, but Pierce's eyes were sharp. His flail was destroyed. He had one arrow for his bow, and then he'd have to rely on Daine's dagger. Nonetheless, he felt warmth spread through him, the pleasing calm that always came before battle. Any doubts and uncertainty in his mind faded as every thought turned to the coming conflict.

There.

A flicker of motion, a shadow slipping behind a tree, darting out, moving forward to the next line of cover, passing across dense undergrowth as if it were open grass. And there—another, and another. There were at least six of them, no larger than halflings or goblins, features hidden by storm and shadow. No glint of metal on moonlight, but Pierce could see the silhouettes of swords and bows.

Thorns, Shira observed. *Soldiers of the wood. Tough and sharp, resistant to mortal steel. But they can be fought.*

Pierce touched Lei's shoulder and pointed at the oncoming strangers. She nodded and flashed two signals with Cyran fingerplay. *Hold position. Do not engage.*

The thorns advanced through the forest, moving slowly and carefully. Now one stepped into the moonlight. The little man had rough green skin, and a layer of pine needles in place of hair. Its torso was covered by a jerkin made from large, leatherlike leaves. Pierce idly wondered if this was clothing, or if the leaves were a part of the creature's skin. Its weapon was a thorn, a long thorn from some enormous plant, which the creature held as if it was a rapier. The little man's eyes were dark and shiny, like little beetles—and they fixed directly on Pierce.

Calculations flashed through Pierce's mind.

Distance to the foe.

The capabilities of Daine's dagger.

Could Pierce reach the thorn and cut its throat before the creature could alert its allies? No.

Pierce wasn't even certain that his weapon could hurt the thorn, or what its weaknesses were. Though human in appearance, its anatomy could be very different. More important, if Pierce abandoned his position he was both disobeying orders and leaving Lei vulnerable. He faced the creature, dagger ready, waiting for the thorn to close.

The green man moved forward, thorn-sword lowered. Then, just before it came within Pierce's reach, it shifted its path and slipped past the group. Now there were thorns all around them, at least a dozen of the little creatures, but not one paid any mind to Pierce or his companions. The thorns kept moving through the forest. The storm lashed the trees, the wind howled, but within moments the thorns had moved on.

Lei caught his attention with a gesture. *Follow.* Her fingers flickered, using more complex signals difficult to catch in the dim light of night, but Pierce's eyes were keen. *Objective close.*

Lei walked slowly through the storm-torn forest, bracing herself against the wind, and the trees moved out of her way once more. Moments became minutes as they moved farther through the wood. The storm raged, thorns scuttled through the shadows, but these lesser forces could not match the power of the staff.

Another thorn caught Pierce's eye. This was the fifth of these creatures he'd had a good look at; the little man was only a few feet away. He was looking at Pierce and the others, but Pierce could tell that the green man couldn't see him. Still, something was different about this thorn. While the man wasn't looking directly at him, there was a look of intense concentration on his face. As if he were . . . listening.

Pierce reached out to grab Lei, but it was too late. The thorn raised a hand, and lightning flared in the sky. The ground exploded behind Pierce, forcing him away from his companions.

The staff stopped singing.

Your protection has fallen. The enemy is aware of your presence.

Movement all around him, thorns emerging from the woods and darting forward. Through his link to Shira, Pierce could *feel* the positions of his allies, *feel* them spreading to engage the foes. The thorn beside him kneaded the air with its hands, and as Shira's knowledge flowed through him Pierce knew that the creature was gathering the power of the storm. Another instant and the lightning would strike again.

Pierce didn't hesitate. He slammed into the thorn, knocking him to the ground and disrupting the complex spell the creature had been weaving. Before the thorn could react, Pierce drove his dagger into its throat.

A thin trickle of sap oozed from the wound, and the thorn jerked in pain. But it was not so easily felled. Pierce felt its empty hand strike his chestplate. Warmth spread over him, emanating from the point of contact.

Magic! Shira said.

The heat grew with each passing second, and Pierce could smell the rootlike tendrils below his armor starting to burn. No time for mercy or careful consideration. Pierce smashed the thorn to the ground and slashed with his dagger. The heat was overwhelming his senses. Bubbling sap, the feel of green wood beneath his dagger, and the all-consuming heat. It was a horrible blur of pain and pure force. He could feel his mithral plates beginning to melt . . . and then it stopped. The thorn's head had come free in Pierce's hand, and his armor was cooling in the storm-torn air.

There was motion all around him. Light flashed in the darkness—Daine's sword, glowing like the moon itself. Xu'sasar spun through the motions of a deadly dance, lashing out with twin blades attached to a long haft. His friends were holding their own, but not without cost. The thorns were hardy and did not fall easily. Shira told him of the wounds of his allies, of the thorn-blade that had pierced Daine's thigh and the arrow in Xu'sasar's shoulder. And while a thrust of Daine's sword brought down the last thorn of the first wave, there were others in the darkness, racing toward the sounds of battle.

"We're almost there!" Lei cried. "Follow me!"

Pierce followed right on her heels. Movement brought new signals of pain as Pierce's body warned him of the damage he had suffered, but he fought past the agony and kept moving.

The power is growing. Even without Shira's thoughts, Pierce would have known. He could feel it in the air, a presence pressing in on him. It seemed that the trees were *fighting* him, roots reaching for his feet as branches flew against his face and arms. Lei forced her way through the treacherous undergrowth. They burst out from the trees and into a clearing, into . . .

The Gates. Nine archways, towering portals even larger than the doors in Karul'tash . . . doors built for giants. Each arch was made from a different material. One was rough stone, with traces of luminescent moss; it could have been carved from one of the tors they'd seen in the realm of the Huntsman. Another was formed from dark ice. Eight spread in a circle around the clearing, while the ninth stood in the center—a mighty arch of twisted black briars, each barb the length of Pierce's forearm.

But all were empty. They were open archways. There were no doors to open, and they didn't appear to go anywhere. Looking through an arch, all Pierce could see was the other side of the meadow.

Look at the sky, Shira thought. *Look to the moon.*

Pierce looked at the gates again, and then he saw what she meant. When he looked through the different arches, the clearing was the same, but the sky was slightly different. Darker in some, lighter in others. And the moon varied—color, size, and position shifting in each arch.

These are the Gates of Night, Shira thought, *the passage to the hours of darkness.*

"What do we do?" Pierce said.

"I'm working on it!" Lei said. The staff was singing again, its voice faint, unsteady.

"Work fast," Daine said, emerging from the treeline with Xu'sasar at his heels. Blood and sap covered his armor.

"Thanks for the advice." Lei walked forward, approaching the central arch—

And the trees attacked.

No time to react. Roots rose from the ground, gripping Pierce's legs and pinning him in place. His dagger was out, but before he could cut the tendrils he felt a crushing force around his chest—a tree branch, acting with the fluid motion of a snake and the strength of thick oak. Pierce struggled, but to no avail. The tree was far stronger than he was.

The trees clustered around the clearing, holding just beyond the ring of eight gates. Their limbs flexed and twisted in the darkness, a sea of motion in the shadows. Daine was helpless in the grip of an old pine, while Xu'sasar was nowhere to be seen.

Lei stood in the center of the ring, watching but taking no action. Before Pierce could speak, a passage opened in the wall of writhing wood, and a tall man stepped into the clearing. Both his height and his bearing were reminiscent of the Huntsman they had faced earlier, but where the hunter had been lean, the Woodsman was broad and muscular. He was dressed in loose trousers and a hooded vest woven from dark leaves, and thick vines twined around his powerful arms.

The Woodsman strode slowly into the ring, moving with the confidence of a predator in his lair. A huge axe balanced across one shoulder; he gripped the haft with his left hand, and the polished blade gleamed in the moonlight. Pierce saw that the Woodsman wore a mask beneath his hood, depicting the face of a bearded, smiling man with long mustaches. As Pierce watched, the wooden smile widened.

"So, beloved," the Woodsman said. "You have returned to me at last."

CHAPTER 22

NIGHT: THE
DEEPWOOD MOON
THELANIS

The songs of the darkwood staff had no words, only the music of an inhuman voice. It did not speak, but Lei could *feel* the emotions of the spirit trapped within the staff as if they were echoes of her own thoughts. She could sense Darkheart reaching through her to touch the forest, to shield Lei and her companions from the eyes of the enemy. When the storm rose around them, Lei didn't need the staff to tell her what was going on. She *knew* the Woodsman had found them. She could sense his presence, fearsome and terribly familiar, as if this man had haunted her dreams all her life.

At first the staff gave her courage. Darkheart had no fear of the thorns, and as these soldiers of the forest moved around them, this confidence had helped Lei keep her silence and hold her position. The Woodsman had sensed their presence and dispatched these minions, but that was to be expected. Lei and her companions were entering the very heart of his dominion. They simply needed to wait out the storm, until the Woodsman's attention moved elsewhere.

Then lightning struck. The flare wiped away the night, and a giant's hand slammed into her. Lei kept her hands locked around the shaft of the staff even as the shockwave threw her to the ground. Somehow she maintained her grip through the pain and through the fall. Her body ached, but something was wrong on a deeper, more fundamental level. The song had stopped, and so had the stream of emotions flowing from the staff. She felt strangely empty. The only sound was the wind and tiny feet moving through the forest.

Thorns!

A little man emerged from behind the nearest tree, a long thorn-blade in its hand. There was no time for pain, no time to worry about her wounds. Lei could move, and she could fight. The darkwood staff flashed in the night, and the thorn staggered backward. Lei lunged, driving the end of the staff into her tiny foe. She was fighting on pure instinct, spinning, thrusting, turning to face new enemies. And through it all, Lei felt numb, almost detached. It was like another dream, watching another Lei do battle.

Am I?

Lei had received combat training in preparation for her military duties, but she'd never been expected to fight on the front lines. Her task was to repair the injured warforged, not to join them on the battlefield. Despite this simple training, she'd accomplished remarkable things. Less than a year ago, she'd fought a minotaur with her bare hands. She'd battled monsters in the Mournland and horrors beneath the streets of Sharn. Lei had never questioned her abilities before. She'd been taught the basic principles of battle, and usually she was caught up in the moment, letting anger carry her through combat. Surely anyone else would do as well in her place.

Or would they?

The thorns focused on her companions. Three tried to encircle Daine, and Lei brought one down with a perfect blow to the back of the knees. How did I know where to strike? she thought. Was it training? Common sense?

Or had the knowledge been placed within her?

Pain. Triumph. They were Darkheart's emotions, faint but growing stronger with each passing second. She could see the path to their destination.

"We're almost there!" Lei cried. "Follow me!"

The forest fought her. Briars tore at her skin, while vines and roots sought to trip and entangle. She could feel the malevolent attention of the Woodsman, a presence watching from every tree. She kept moving, forcing her way free of branches and brambles. With every step, she found a new strength flowing into her.

Darkheart.

Once she had shared this forest with the Woodsman, and her power grew as they moved toward the center. Lei could feel the anger within the staff. Exile, imprisonment, and a deep hatred for the fey prince who had driven her to it; these joined to form a wave of fury that drove back treacherous vegetation and pursuing thorns. Lei let the rage carry her through the woods, driving her forward.

And then they reached the clearing. Nine towering arches formed of stone and wood, earth and water. The Gates of Night. Eight spread in a ring around the largest of the gates, an arch of black briars. Looking at them, Lei knew this was the very center of the realm, the heart of the Deepwood Moon . . . and the seat of the Woodsman.

"What do we do?" Pierce said.

The staff sang once more. Emotion raged within it, fear mingled with fury. Its anger still burned, but its song was faint and unsteady; it had used much of its energy in the passage through he forest.

"I'm working on it!" Lei said. *What do I do?* Her vision had said *Darkheart is the key*, and the dryad had led them to the gates. *What happens now?*

"Work fast," Daine said, emerging from the treeline with Xu'sasar at his heels. Blood and sap covered his armor.

"Thanks for the advice," Lei said. She walked toward the arch of thorns.

She *felt* the surge around her. Roots rose from the ground, branches lashed out like striking serpents, and a wall of wood rose around the clearing. She turned toward Daine, intending to rush to his aid.

No!

It wasn't a word. It was a burst of pure emotion, an order so strong that it stopped Lei in her tracks. Even as her fury grew, Lei saw that it was too late. Pierce and Daine were helpless in wooden bonds, while Xu'sasar had vanished; if she'd fallen into the sea of writhing trees, there was no telling what might have become of her. Lei couldn't fight that force. If she moved in, she'd simply be trapped herself. She took a step back toward the arch and waited.

Lei felt a surge of recognition as the Woodsman strode out of the forest—recognition and anger. He smiled when he saw her, and shifted the long axe that lay across his shoulder.

"So, beloved," the Woodsman said. "You have returned to me at last."

"*Beloved?*" Daine said. "Lei, wha—"

His words cut off as a branch wrapped around his head, gagging him.

"I knew you would return some day, my Lady Dark-heart." The Woodsman's voice was deep and soft, wind rustling through a field of pine, and his smiling lips did not move as he spoke. "I thought you would travel in better company."

"And I owe my friends an apology," Lei said. "I told them you weren't an idiot with an axe."

"My axe is for flesh and blood. For your kind, vessel."

"Show me."

Lei lunged, remembering how deadly her staff had been in her battle with the Huntsman. In her mind, this fight was already over. She could hear the Woods-man scream as the staff pierced his body, see his mask falling to the ground.

Wood struck wood, the powerful blow shattering her dream. The Woodsman parried her thrust with his axe. His strength was incredible; the force of his stroke almost knocked her to the ground. Lightning flashed in the sky above, and the laughter of the Woodsman echoed in the thunder. "You threaten me, creature of flesh? Do you even know whom you address?"

"Torenas," Lei said, speaking with all the confidence she could muster. "*Youngest* of the Nine Brothers of Night. An overweening youth, a preening pine-lord held in contempt by the true powers of this plane."

Thunder rolled again, but the Woodsman wasn't laughing. Lei saw his sculpted smile waver, and in that moment she lunged. The darkwood staff howled, and the Woodsman leapt away from her, barely avoiding the blow. He brought his axe down in an arc of silver and polished wood, and Lei raised the staff to block the stroke—but he checked the blow. *He doesn't want to hit the staff,* Lei realized.

"Halt!" the Woodsman said, and Lei was gratified to hear a little concern in his voice. "I have no wish to hurt you, vessel, nor to harm my beloved Darkheart. Your companions are another matter."

Daine's mouth was gagged, but Lei heard the muffled cry of pain as the tree limbs twisted flesh and bone. While Pierce made no sound, Lei could see his wooden bonds flexing, and she recognize the terrible stress this was putting on his joints.

"Stop!" she cried, lowering the staff. "Stop. Don't hurt them. Damn you, what do you *want* from us?"

The Woodsman lowered his axe, his smile cold and triumphant. "What do I want? I want justice, seedling. I want what is mine. I want the Lady Darkheart. For now that means I must have you as well. Fear not, my lady. I will find a way to untangle your roots from this creature. I do not know who worked this foul magic, but once we are bound as one, I will find a way to restore your true beauty. And together we shall take vengeance on those who wronged you so."

There was curiosity in the staff, but fury was the stronger emotion. "Don't you see?" Lei said. "*You* drove her to this. *You* drove her away." Her own anger began to grow, as she felt herself warming to the dryad's tale. Throughout her life, she had let others tell her what to do. House schooling. Service in the war. Betrothal to Hadran. All the way to Lakashtai's deception. Had she ever been more than a tool? A useful pawn?

"You lie," the Woodsman said, and a gust of wind forced Lei back a few steps. "Our paths were twined from the moment of creation. Lord and lady, male and female. We were made to rule this moon, to shape this hour of night, and I cannot reach the pinnacle of my power until we are joined. It is destiny."

"*Your* destiny. *Your* desire. Maybe she wanted more." The staff was singing now, its voice clear and beautiful, a piercing lament echoing Lei's words.

"More? At my side she would rule over this dominion! What more could she want?"

"Freedom," Lei said.

"*Bah!*" the Woodsman roared, raising his axe once more. "You fill her mind with madness, mortal! I had hoped to use you as a bridge, to join with Darkheart through your frail body, but I will not allow you to poison her any further. Cast aside my mate and you will die swiftly. Fight me and I will grow a garden of agonies within your flesh!"

He leapt forward, his axe flashing with the speed of a falling star. Lei brought the staff up, directly into the path of the descending blade, and once again he pulled back. It was a deadly game of cat and mouse, as the Woodsman sought to evade her guard and land a blow on her soft flesh. His speed and strength were astonishing, and he handled his axe as if it were the lightest rapier. Lei staggered backward, seeking respite in retreat, and barely escaped disaster as a tree root grasped at her foot. The living trees massed just beyond the gates. She had to stay within the ring or the battle was over.

Lei redoubled her efforts. She wasn't even trying to hit the Woodsman anymore. It was all she could do to defend herself. Yet as she fought, she found herself falling into a rhythm. It was Darkheart. The dryad knew the Woodsman, knew how he fought, and she was guiding Lei's motions. He was still too swift, and even the dryad couldn't help Lei launch an attack of her own. But with the dryad directing her actions, Lei's thoughts were free.

How is this possible? she thought. Is it all some power of the staff? Or is there something more? Something in me?

I will find a way to untangle your roots from this creature, the Woodsman had said.

Darkheart's words in the clear white water: *In any other hand, I would be cold wood. But you can reach within.*

And one memory rose above all others—the time she had fought Pierce in the sewers beneath Sharn, when she'd seen a vision of his lifeweb and had first thought of him as a brother. She'd seen four patterns, all connected, and now she was sure that one of those was her own.

It made no sense. She was flesh and blood, and a point made all too clear by her scorched skin and aching muscles. Yet in the heat of battle, there was no time to question.

She let go of all thought. Her body was moving under Darkheart's guidance, but Lei fell within, searching for that thread she'd seen once before.

There. A trace of energy, a beam of light stretching off into darkness. Lei seized it and *pulled,* and there it was: the web of light and life she knew as Pierce, that pattern she'd adjusted so many times before. In the past, she'd had to touch Pierce to bring up his lifeweb. Now she could feel it her mind. But could she affect it? Drawing on her talents as an artificer, she tried to pull at the threads, to weave a new, temporary pattern into the web.

And it responded. Though Pierce was across the clearing, held high in the air, she could feel the changes taking place. *Strength. Take strength from me, my brother.*

The images dissolved in a burst of pain. She was staggering across the clearing, and fell just before she reached a writhing mass of foliage. Wet numbness spread across her right leg, and fierce pain told her that the handle of the Woodsman's axe had cracked a rib. She tried to collect her thoughts, but the pain was too great. The Woodsman came forward, his bloody axe held high.

Pierce crashed into him, leaving a trail of torn vines and scraps of roots in his path. Grabbing the Woodsman's wrists, Pierce forced the masked man away from Lei. Though the Woodsman had the strength of an ogre, Pierce was stronger still, and he forced the Woodsman to his knees.

The Woodsman screamed.

The cry came as a surprise to Lei; Pierce was fighting with magically enhanced strength, but he had no weapon, and was doing little more than holding the Woodsman at bay. Then she saw a flash of white bone, as Xu'sasar's throwing wheel spun back across the clearing. The drow girl stood next to an arch of dark stone, and she caught the boomerang and prepared for another throw.

"No!" Lei said, hobbling across the clearing. "No. Don't kill him."

"*Unhand me!*" the Woodsman roared, still struggling in Pierce's grip. "You will *pay* for this indignity! I will see you buried in the earth and devoured by insects, alive and aware until your bones are shards in the—"

His words dissolved into a howl of agony as Lei pressed the end of the staff into the wound on his back, where blood and sap were flowing freely.

The staff shivered in Lei's hands as power flowed through the shaft. The Woodsman stiffened and screamed again as his body *stretched* upward. Pierce let go before he was lifted into the sky, and they watched in wonder as the being that had once been the Woodsman completed his transformation. He towered over them, forty feet tall, his limbs stretching out across the ring of gates.

He had become a tree.

His bark was as pale as the skin of his arms, his leaves dark as the clothes he'd worn, and Lei thought she could see a face faintly traced into his trunk, the vague image of the mask he had worn. But the storm winds were gone, and his limbs did not move.

"Can someone help me down?" The trees around the clearing had fallen still, but Daine was still hanging in the air, branches wrapped around his torso.

As Xu'sasar and Pierce ran to assist Daine, Lei turned to the great gate at the center of the clearing. She could still feel the power churning within the staff. There was a sense of satisfaction, but the sorrow remained.

"What happens to you?" Lei whispered.

In answer, Darkheart reached into Lei. Her power and presence were stronger than ever, and Lei moved without a thought. She struggled with the force controlling her body, but Darkheart was too powerful. Against her will, Lei stepped forward . . . and drove the staff into the ground before the briar gate.

Thunder shook the world. Lei's hands locked around the staff, and she could *feel* the power the staff had drawn from the Woodsman fading away, being forced down into the earth itself. And the gate before her changed. Threads of gold ran up from the ground, twining along the black briars. And then she saw the light. Sunlight, faint but clear, the first pure light she'd seen since she'd entered Karul'tash so long ago. The dark forest was all around her, but through the arch she could see the setting sun of dusk.

Free me.

The thought was clear and vivid, the voice of the woman Lei had seen in her coma. And then it was gone. Lei swayed, and almost fell. She felt as if every ounce of energy had been drained from her bones. The staff was utterly silent, physically and emotionally.

"Lei!"

Daine ran to her, Xu'sasar and Pierce behind him. She turned toward him, but before she could speak she felt a sharp pain in her shoulder, pain followed by a chilling numbness. It was an arrow, a thin arrow made from a long, sharp thorn, with leaves in place of feathers.

"*Lei!*" Daine cried. He caught her as she pitched forward, catching her before she hit the ground. A volley of arrows came flying out from the dark trees. Pierce dove forward, shielding Lei with his body.

"Gate . . ." she whispered to Daine. "Dusk . . ."

"Get to the gate!" Daine cried.

And the thorns charged.

The creatures came at them from all from all sides, and Lei couldn't begin to count them. The night was full of thornblades and beady eyes, and the sound of tiny feet against the grass. Lei's head span as Daine swept her off her feet, holding her in both arms. Xu'sasar scattered their enemies with a long chain formed from links of razor-sharp bone, carving a sap-drenched path to the central arch.

"Go!" Xu'sasar said as they approached the gate. There was an arrow in the girl's thigh, dark blood almost invisible against her skin. She whirled her chain, ripping the links across a thorn and pulling the creature to the ground. Daine hesitated, and then he ran through the arch . . .

And into the light.

In the distance, the setting sun made a silhouette of a range of mountains, but after the long night, the fading sun was the most beautiful thing Lei had seen. The sounds of battle were gone; all she heard were crickets and songbirds, and Daine's labored breathing.

"Welcome to Dusk," a voice said. Male, young. "It certainly took you long enough."

CHAPTER 23

Adrenaline surged through Daine's body. He was still battered and bloody from the battle with the thorns, and while Lei was his greatest concern, Pierce and Xu'sasar were still on the other side of the gate. He'd hoped for a moment of peace, yet a new threat awaited them. Dropping into a crouch, he lowered Lei to the ground as gently as he could. As soon as he'd released her, Daine drew his sword and turned to face the speaker.

"Please, no need for *that*." The stranger was leaning against the gate. On this side, the arch was formed of polished mahogany inlaid with gold sigils that gleamed in the light of the setting sun. The archway was empty, and Daine could look through to see waves of grass and wildflowers rippling in the meadow on the other side. No sign of the realm of Night. *Pierce!* Daine thought.

The stranger was human, on the edge between man and boy. Wavy golden hair fell to his shoulders, and his flawless skin was slightly tanned. His clothes were black velvet and orange silk. A fine sword hung from his baldric, and he wore an amulet depicting a golden sun setting behind a mountain. He was a prince pulled from a storybook, an ideal image of charm and grace. His voice was just one more piece of perfection, melodic while still firm and masculine. "I assure you, Daine, I mean you no harm."

Before Daine could respond, Xu'sasar appeared in the gate, rippling into existence in the blink of an eye. Blood and sap covered the drow girl. She vaulted up and over Daine, turning in mid-air to face the stranger, but she landed on her injured leg and almost fell. An instant later a thorn came through the gate—and not under its own power. The green man flew backward and struck the ground hard, and Pierce appeared behind him. The warforged held Daine's dagger in one hand and the darkwood staff in the other, and like Xu'sasar he was covered with sap and torn foliage.

"Well, that's everyone then," the stranger said. Xu'sasar spun her gory chain and Pierce leveled his dagger at the portal, but the young man raised his hands disarmingly. "Please, warriors. You're safe now. You're under the protection of my queen, and no mere thorn would challenge her power."

Daine kept his sword steady. "And what does she want with us?"

"I am only an envoy, Master Daine, but I assure you that my mistress means you no harm. Please. Let me to take you to her home, where your wounds will be tended and all questions answered." Concern colored his voice, but Daine wasn't fooled. There was something about this boy . . . he was *too* perfect, *too* charming.

"And what do you get in exchange? My voice? My heart? My—"

"My mistress only wishes to help you. She has watched you for some time, Daine with no family name."

"And you expect—" Daine paused. "What did you just call me?"

"The words of my mistress, Master Daine. I'm certain that she will explain."

"Do . . . do it." Lei had raised herself up on one arm. Her face was pale, her eyes unfocused, but her voice was steady. "The Queen of . . . Dusk."

"Well," Daine said, helping Lei to her feet, "show us the way."

* * * * * * *

As bruised and battle-worn as Daine was, he found his spirits rising as they followed the young man. It must be the sun, he concluded. Beyond the gloomy nature of the environment—the bleak moor studded with faces, and the dark forest with its serpents and its thorns—the realms of night were cold and empty. Not so the twilight land. A vast meadow stretched across rolling hills. Wildflowers filled fields with color and unleashed a symphony of scents into the air. The sky was a tapestry of light, clouds painted brilliant rose and orange by the setting sun. Bright birds sang songs of the evening, fluttering among scattered trees. Despite the beauty, Daine couldn't help but wonder how many of the birds could talk.

Other things were troubling Daine, and with no enemy in sight, he turned his attention to the events in the ring. "What happened back there? Pierce, how did you get free?"

"I have no explanation," Pierce said. "My own strength was insufficient to the task, but as I strained against my bonds I felt a rush of strength, power that remained with me throughout the battle."

"Could this be the work of your little friend?"

"No, captain. Shira identified it as an augmentation of my abilities, clearly derived from an exterior source, but she cannot identify that source."

Daine didn't like mysteries. "Lei, can you explain this?"

"Hmm?" Lei had recovered from the thorn venom, and reclaimed her staff from Pierce. Her eyes were distant, focused on the horizon.

"Pierce. Aren't you worried? And what did *you* do back there? Did you kill that man?"

Lei shook away the cobwebs. "No . . . no. He's not dead. He's trapped in that tree. Powerless, at least for the moment. That's what Darkheart wanted."

"Your staff. That's what it wanted. So now we're doing the bidding of a piece of wood?"

"She saved us, Daine."

"We wouldn't have been in danger if we'd just given it to the Huntsman!"

Lei's eyes flashed, and she backed away from Daine. "You don't know what you're talking about. She gave everything she had left to open that gate. We wouldn't be here without Darkheart."

"She speaks the truth, Master Daine." It was the first time the guide had spoken since they had left the arch. He was looking back over his shoulder, and now Daine saw that the youth's eyes were multicolored . . . rose and orange, just like the sky above.

"Who are you?" Lei said to their guide.

"Call me Kin," the young man said with a brilliant smile. "I run errands for her majesty." Ahead of them, a fox peered up out of the grass and then disappeared again; in the brief moment, its fur looked like fire. "Let me assure you once more, your troubles in this realm are at an end. You need fear no treachery in my lady's house. I swear it by twelve and one."

Daine glanced at Lei. "You're the expert here, Lei. Do

we get to eat the bread?" Despite his misgivings, he realized that he was starving. In the chaos of the forest, Lei had never found time to make her promised gruel.

"I'll want to hear our hostess swear to our safety," Lei said. "And this time, I'll be listening for tricks. From what I've heard, this queen is no stranger to subterfuge. But vows have power in this place."

"Then I think you'd better do the talking," Daine said. "Now, about Pierce—"

"Please, my companions, stay your speech," Kin said, interrupting.

They crested a hill, and the guide swept his arm to encompass the valley below. The rays of the setting sun played on the waters of a small lake, and a castle rose up from the center of the water, with no path or bridge. It was a beautiful thing, with walls of deep green marble topped with spires of rose and gold. As Daine looked down on the castle, a stream of color emerged from the tallest tower—a host of brilliant butterflies that flew overhead and dispersed into the skies.

"Our journey is over," Kin said. "Thelania awaits."

❀ ❀ ❀ ❀ ❀ ❀ ❀

"You must address the queen as her majesty, unless she gives you permission to do otherwise."

"This isn't the first time I've met a queen, boy." In truth, Daine had met the young queen of Cyre only once and hadn't been allowed to speak on that occasion, but he was confident in his ability to handle the situation.

"Perhaps, so, Master Daine. But your companions . . ."

"Good point. Xu'sasar, don't say anything. Starting now."

"You know nothing of the spirits," the drow girl said. "I—"

"You'll keep quiet unless I say otherwise, and that's an order."

Truth be told, Daine was beginning to warm to the dark elf. Despite her strange habits and unpredictable behavior, there was no faulting her courage. She'd put her life on the line time and again since their arrival in Xen'drik, and she hadn't hesitated to engage the thorns when Daine needed time to get through the gate. Even now, covered with blood and sap and limping from a leg wound, she refused to acknowledge her pain. He could have used a few like her in Cyre.

"—bath," Kin was saying.

"What?"

"You cannot see the Queen of Dusk and Shadow in your current state. Upon our arrival, you will be bathed and your wounds tended. Then you will be conducted to the feasting hall."

Daine looked to Lei.

"And do you give your word that no harm will come to us within these walls, at your hands or any other?" Lei said. "Do you swear that you know of no plots against us?"

"The queen keeps her own council," Kin replied, "and I cannot promise things beyond my power. But I swear by moon and blood, if any within the castle intend to do you harm I have no knowledge of it. And whatever it is that her majesty wants with you, she is a gracious host. Abide by the laws of hospitality, and she will do the same. If you face danger, it will be beyond the castle walls."

"Very well." Lei looked at Daine. "That's good enough for me."

They were approaching the shore of the lake. A golden portcullis faced them across the water, but

Daine still couldn't see any signs of a bridge. However, two creatures waited for them by the shore. Horses. A beautiful white destrier with a golden mane and a sleek black stallion with silver. And horns. Each horse had a single horn rising from his forehead. The horn of the white horse was brilliant gold, while the horse with the stars on his back had a horn that glowed like the moon. While Daine had heard of unicorns, he'd never seen one, and he was impressed by the aura of majesty that surrounded these creatures.

"Hail, traveler," called out the white unicorn, in a voice like a lion's roar.

"You are expected," said the black unicorn, its words like velvet wind. "Let the way be opened."

The unicorns turned and touched their horns to the water. There was motion in the lake, a bar of water rippling from the shore to the castle, and then a pathway rose to the surface, a span of iridescent stone that gleamed in the twilight.

The unicorns stepped back. "Go, honored guests. Destiny awaits."

Daine glanced at his companions. Pierce was as impassive as always, and Xu'sasar seemed just as calm; of course, having lived all her life in Xen'drik, perhaps this sort of thing was an everyday occurrence for her. Then he looked at Lei, and her smile was brighter than the sun itself. He offered her his arm. "Shall we cross, my lady?"

"Of course, Lord Daine," Lei said, twining her arm in his. "We shouldn't keep the queen waiting."

❀ ❀ ❀ ❀ ❀ ❀ ❀

"There's something I need to tell you," Lei said. She took a deep breath, savoring the sweet steam that filled the air. "I'm never leaving this bath."

Daine sympathized. He hadn't seen such luxury since his days working for Alina Lorridan Lyrris. The last hour was a blur. He remembered a pair of nymphs massaging his sore muscles and rubbing cool salve into his wounds; this ointment had magically wiped away his injuries, and he felt truly healthy for the first time in weeks. He could still feel the warped dragonmark across his back, but even that felt more like the presence of a warming fire than the aggravating itch that had tormented him before. What does it do? he wondered. Even he knew that the size of a dragonmark reflected its power. He closed his eyes, sinking into the water and concentrating on that sensation of heat. He tried to remember everything he'd heard about controlling dragonmarks. He tried to trace the pattern with his thoughts, following the sensation on his skin.

Nothing.

"I offer my apologies."

"What's that, Xu?" Daine opened his eyes—and snapped them shut again. Xu'sasar had moved next to him. Both Lei and Daine had found a few scraps of cloth to preserve their modesty in the water, but it seemed that Xu'sasar's people had little use for modesty. Considering how little she wore in battle, it was hardly surprising that she would shed it all to bathe. Taking a deep breath, Daine opened his eyes again, carefully looking straight ahead. "There's no need."

"When you took me from my death, I thought you a fool, and weak," Xu'sasar said. Even looking away, Daine could see her reflection in the water, her pale eyes and silver hair shining in the faint light that permeated the room. "Yet I have learned that it was not my time to die, and I have watched you in battle. You fight bravely and well, and you risk your lives for others, even making a fool's bargain to buy us shelter. I still do not know your ways, and I am sorry for the difficulty that I have caused, but you have my gratitude."

"Yes," Daine said. He glanced over at Lei, praying for an interruption, but her eyes were closed in blissful enoyment of the bath. "Well, don't worry. We'll find a way to return you to your people."

"My people?" Xu'sasar always spoke swiftly, mimicking her fluid native tongue. But now her words caught in her throat. "My people are dead. I am the last of my family, and the burning jungle is no home to me. You heard the voice of Vulkoor. My path lies with you. You are my people now, and I will follow you until death takes us both."

She leaned against his arm, resting her head against his shoulder. Daine could hear the sorrow and loneliness in her voice, and he couldn't bring himself to push her away.

"Honored guests, your presence is requested!"

At the sound of Kin's voice, Lei's eyes snapped open—and widened as she saw the drow girl leaning on Daine's shoulder. Daine leapt to his feet, sending Xu'sasar tumbling into the water. He felt Lei's icy glare as he helped Xu'sasar up. He turned to give Lei a hand, but she had already climbed out of the pool.

"We took the liberty of cleaning and mending your clothes and armor," Kin said. "Have no fear, Master Daine, for your companion Pierce maintained the vigil of a hawk throughout our work, and you will find your goods intact. You will also find gifts from her majesty. I will leave you to decide what would be most suitable to wear to the feast."

"How kind of you," Daine said. "If there's one thing

I've learned over our long night, it's not to trust strangers with gifts."

Then he saw the gifts.

"Lei?" he said, looking down at the marble table. "Can we keep them?"

Two items had been set next to Daine's clothes. The first was a coat of mithral chainmail painted in black enamel. Despite the density of the chain links, the shirt was almost weightless, one of the finest pieces of smithwork he'd seen. The second gift was a hooded cloak of shifting black glamerweave, clasped with a dragonshard brooch.

"The magic in these items is benign," Pierce said. The warforged had been waiting for them in the antechamber, and Daine couldn't remember ever seeing Pierce in such good condition. All signs of damage had been repaired, his metal plates polished.

"I have had time to study these objects while you cleansed yourselves," Pierce continued. "The armor is mystically reinforced, the mithral strengthened by magic. The cloak will help you move unseen in conditions of darkness. The locket presented to Xu'sasar toughens the skin, giving it strength to resist physical blows. And Lady Lei, those lenses—"

"I know what they are," Lei said. She was holding an unusual pair of goggles, with an assortment of adjustable lenses bound to leather straps. Her voice was quiet, and she seemed slightly pale.

"Lei?" Daine said, taking a step toward her. She stopped him with a raised hand.

"Get dressed," she said quietly. "If Pierce says these things are safe, I'm sure they must be. Now let's find out what the Dusk Queen serves for dinner."

CHAPTER 24

DUSK
THELANIS

The great hall of Dusk was an imposing sight. Pillars of green marble rose up on each side, wrapped in delicate ivy strands formed from pure gold. Narrow streams flowed along both sides of the hallway, and the air resounded with the sounds of water and spectral music. Cricket fiddlers played in the shadows, and tiny men with butterfly wings played flutes and pipes from high in the air. The arched ceiling was painted with the image of the rosy sky of Dusk, and while it was static, it glowed with an inner light.

Pierce had rarely seen such spectacle. He had spent his life on the battlefield, with little time in the towers of lords or dragonmarked barons. Despite his best efforts, he still had trouble seeing the purpose in such things as golden ivy or painted walls. Many said that the warforged lacked the ability to appreciate art, but it wasn't so simple. For Pierce, there was beauty in function. A well-made bow, a sturdy shield; these things inspired awe and respect in Pierce. The purpose of a building was to provide shelter and defense. The extravagant decorations were unnecessary.

They passed through a feasting hall with a table long enough to seat a hundred. It seemed their hostess intended a more personal experience, for the immense table was bare. They entered a far smaller chamber. An oval table dominated the center of the room, laid out with crystal goblets and large plates hidden beneath silver covers. A vast chandelier hung over the table, or so it seemed at first. As they approached the table, Pierce saw that it was a complex array of hundreds of points of light, suspended in the air with no visible means of support. The lights reflecting in the dark surface of the polished ebony table created the illusion of a starry sky.

"Please be seated!" Kin cried.

Xu'sasar sat next to Daine, while Lei chose the seat across from him. Pierce stood behind Lei and folded his arms.

"Master Pierce, do sit down!" Kin said. The fey courtier pointed to the place next to Lei, and Pierce realized that the chair was considerably larger than the others around the table—as if it had been specially prepared for someone of his height and mass.

"I do not eat or drink," he said. "And my limbs do not tire."

"Perhaps you've never eaten in the past," Kin said, "but you would be wise to try our fare. And it would be an insult to her majesty if you were to stand at her table. Please indulge me."

"Come, Pierce," Lei said, pushing out the chair. "You don't want to make a bad impression."

"As you wish, my lady." Pierce settled into the proffered seat. As he had thought, it seemed to be the perfect size. He found himself wondering about Kin's words. *Try our fare?* Pierce didn't have a stomach. He couldn't consume food if he wanted to.

"Please, help yourselves to food and drink," Kin said. "I give you my promise that neither will harm you in any way. My mistress only wishes to strengthen you for the journey that lies ahead."

"Lei?" Daine said.

Pierce could sense discomfort in the interactions between these two. Lei had not met Daine's eyes since they had emerged from the bathhouse. There was anger in her, but there were still many conflicting emotions, things she was holding in. For now she studied Kin, weighing his words. "I believe him," she said at last. "Go ahead and eat."

Daine uncovered his plate. "Is this *gorgon?*" he said in surprise. "I haven't had this since I was nine years old! And this sauce—red wine and selas. This was my grandfather's favorite dish."

Lei filled her glass from the flagon by her plate, and blinked at the rising steam. "Blackroot tal," she said. "With honey already mixed in." She uncovered her plate and her eyes widened at the spread of meats and vegetables revealed beneath it.

None of this is what it seems, Shira informed Pierce. *There is no danger,* she added, before he could shape the question. *This food and drink is formed of pure magical energy, and it will strengthen body and mind of the creature that consumes it. You should be able to eat such matter. It will be absorbed into the web of energy that gives you life.*

Very well, Pierce thought. After years of watching others eat, he felt a certain level of excitement at the concept of eating his first meal. He removed the silver cover. The deep plate below was filled with a colorless paste. If there was an odor, it was too subtle for his senses.

Gruel.

His flagon proved to be filled with water. *The others are eating the same thing,* Shira observed. *The magic responds to your memories, and you have no pleasant memories to draw upon.*

Pierce tried a spoonful of the thick gruel. There was no noticeable taste, but Shira's prediction was correct. The matter seemed to dissolve in his mouth. As he continued to eat, he felt a sense of strength and confidence. It was difficult to pinpoint, but he felt better than he had since they'd first set out to Xen'drik.

For a time, they dined in silence. They'd gone a long time without food, and Pierce's companions were enraptured by the meal. As plates were finally cleared, a new figure entered the room. It seemed that all other light faded, and that she was the sole illumination in the room. The sparkling constellation above the table remained, but these tiny embers were eclipsed by the newcomer. There was no mistaking her. The Queen of Dusk had arrived.

The lady had the features of an elf, but she was taller than Pierce. Her dress was a marvel, a mirror of the sky. The gown was hemmed with pure gold, and the patterns woven into the thread burned with inner light. The skirt was the rosy hue of sunset clouds, while the colors shifted into the varied blues of a cloudy night above the waist. A net of gemstones gleamed in her long black hair, and she wore a circlet of silver with a crescent moon atop her brow. Beauty meant little to Pierce, as he had no biological response to such things. Yet Thelania transcended mere biology. There was a perfection to her form that made Pierce think of a perfectly balanced sword. Her beauty was an elemental force, and Pierce could *feel* the power of her presence, a thrill that ran through him when she looked his way. Pierce waited for Shira to identify the phenomenon, but his companion remained silent.

"Welcome." The woman's voice was pure music; while it had little impact on Pierce, he could gauge its sensuous power in Daine's reaction. "We have much to discuss, and all too little time."

"And what *do* we have to discuss?" Far from being awed by this otherworldly beauty, Lei sounded angry. "Do you even know who we are?"

Thelania showed no signs of anger, no signs of emotion whatsoever. Despite her beauty, there was something strangely inhuman about her; her calm features betrayed no hint of the thoughts below. "I know far more than you can imagine, Lei, once of House Cannith. I have been watching you throughout your life. I know the circumstances of your birth, and your true nature. And I know the disaster you have wrought in Xen'drik, however unwittingly."

Blood rushed into Lei's cheeks, but it was Daine who spoke first. "What are you talking about?"

"I speak of the Dreaming Dark, of the force that has used you since the day you arrived in Sharn. For tens of thousands of years they have been trapped in nightmare, awaiting their own destruction. Now you have given them the key to escape that prison and overrun your world."

"*We* did this?" Daine said. "When?"

"The moon . . ." Lei breathed, her eyes distant.

The faerie queen smiled, but there was no warmth in it; this was the smile of an indulgent adult entertained by a child's deduction. "Well done, Lei. It's not quite so simple, but you have grasped the heart of it. In ages past, the giants of the land of Xen'drik found themselves at war with Dal Quor, the plane of dreams and nightmares. An ill-advised conflict, fueled by arrogance on one side and desperation on the other. When the mage-lords of Xen'drik realized that they could not win this war, they sought other ways to end it, heedless of long-term consequence."

Xu'sasar spoke up. "When the host of horrors tore through the veil of the world, the mighty ones plucked a moon from the sky and used its power to force their foes into the darkness of the mind, where they were soon forgotten."

"There is some truth to the legends of your people, night child," Thelania said. She raised her hand, and the lights above the table *moved;* what had first appeared to be a chandelier was now a mass of living sparks, obeying the will of the queen. They formed into thirteen brilliant orbs, circling a larger central sphere. "There is a link between the moons and the planes of existence, though it is no simple thing to explain. In the planar arsenal of Karul'tash, the giants sacrificed the moon to break the orbit of Dal Quor, severing its bond to Eberron and preventing its inhabitants from setting foot on the world." She snapped her hand, and one of the circling spheres exploded in a burst of light. "The orb that you restored serves as an anchor, a representation of moon and plane. Now it is intact once more, and in the clutches of the Dreaming Dark. An army is gathering in the heart of Dal Quor, a nightmare horde beyond anything your world has seen in this age—and your people do not have the power of the giants of old."

"What of the dragons?" Lei said. "Surely the dragons of Argonnessen wield more power than the giants ever did."

"Indeed they do. And if they unleash that power in

battle, it will shatter humanity in its wake, like insects scattered before a storm. It was the dragons who finally destroyed Xen'drik, and if Khorvaire becomes their battleground, you are just as doomed. And so it falls on you to go Dal Quor and shatter the lunar crystal before the Dreaming Dark opens its own Gates of Night."

Daine pushed back his chair and rose to his feet. "You set a nice table, lady, but your stories don't hold wine. None of this makes sense. If all these nightmares needed was to find someone to fix that orb, why didn't they do it thousands of years ago?"

The fey queen remained impassive in the face of Daine's outburst. "The crystal moon is a product of a forgotten age, of magic humanity has yet to master. Even the giants who forged the orb were meddling with powers beyond their understanding, and they could not have restored it. The sphere was made to *be* destroyed, not to be rebuilt. You might as well pour wine into the ocean and seek to reclaim it again. It was an impossible task—for anyone but Lei."

"That's ridiculous," Lei said, rising to her feet. "I'm still learning the craft of artifice. I haven't even mastered the arts of the fifth circle. There are a hundred heirs of the house more skilled than I—"

"Hush," Thelania said, and it was a command.

Even as Shira warned him of the use of magic, Pierce felt a wave of calm settle over his thoughts, and he saw Daine and Lei relax.

"Sit," the fey queen said, taking the seat at the head of the table. "And let us continue. Lei, you speak the truth. There are many in your house more skilled than you. But your nature allows you to touch magic in a way no human can."

"Human?" Daine said. The calming effect kept his

239

voice steady, but it couldn't stop his interest.

Pierce was thinking the same thing. Memories flashed through his mind. *I may even spare you and sister Lei*, Harmattan had said. At the time, Pierce had thought it was a figure of speech, as they were all children of House Cannith. Then there was another memory, a vision he'd seen when he lay on the verge of death, a dream that might have been the moment of his creation. *Protect my daughter*, a woman had said. Lei. A child. A child who had been lying on the slab next to his.

"I'm . . . warforged?" Lei said.

"No," Thelania said. "Yet neither are you human. You are a creature of magic and flesh, a woman of two worlds. But this is not the time to discuss your future or your past. I brought you here to guide you to the path that lies ahead, so you may undo the damage you have done."

"Why *us*?" Daine said. "You said it yourself. We're not even as strong as the giants. You know what's going on. Why don't *you* fix this, and we'll handle the next one?"

"I cannot. My fellow lords and ladies wield great power in Thelanis, it is true. But there is a delicate balance between the planes. We are but one aspect of your reality. Dream and nightmare are another thread in the tapestry, one beyond our dominion. We cannot bring our power to bear against Dal Quor without catastrophic repercussions, even worse than what will happen if the Dreaming Dark takes your world. But you are children of the mortal world, and you have a place in every plane."

"And yet there are only four of us," Pierce said. "Would not an army have a greater chance of success?"

"You begin to try my patience," the queen said.

"An army could not enter Dal Quor undetected, nor match the full power of the Dreaming Dark in the region of dreams. There are other heroes in your world, but each has his own path to follow, his own destiny. Your journeys have prepared you for this task, in ways you have yet to realize. There is a web of fate, what the dragons call prophecy, and it falls to you to face this challenge."

Daine slammed his fist on the table, drawing all eyes toward him. He pointed at the flagon in front of him. "Lady, if you want people to follow your stories, you shouldn't serve goblin mead with the meal. Let me just get this straight. Lakashtai tricked us, and she used my weakness to get Lei to do what she wanted."

"With the aid of others, yes. Lakashtai is an emissary of a host of malevolent spirits."

"And now all those spirits are going to come to Eberron?"

"That is the least of my fears. Dal Quor has shifted from its orbit. I believe that the Dreaming Dark seeks to *merge* with Eberron—to make your world a living nightmare."

"Fine," Daine said. "I don't care how you know all of this. If I follow your path, will we find Lakashtai at the end of it?"

"Dal Quor is beyond my sight, Daine. But I suspect that if you find the crystal moon, you will find Lakashtai at its side."

"Then tell me how to get there," Daine said. "Because that woman is going to pay for what she's done."

"Every time you dream, you touch Dal Quor," Thelania said. "But in this instance you face many challenges. The bridge of dreams brings you only to the edge of the realm and leaves your thoughts distant and scattered. Thus you can rarely remember your dreams or even fully control your actions. Furthermore, in this fractured state you would be unable to inflict any lasting harm upon the inhabitants of the realm. You must dream to reach Dal Quor, but you must dream in a place where the walls between the worlds are as thin as possible."

Though Shira was not sharing her thoughts with Pierce, he could feel her rapt attention. He phrased a query in his mind but received no response.

"You're talking about manifest zones," Lei said. "Places where the planes merge. The very thing I was hoping we could use to get us back to Eberron. But there aren't any manifest zones bound to Dal Quor."

"Not now," Thelania replied. "The work of the giants broke all bonds, save those formed in sleep. But the spirits of Dal Quor have been working to restore this connection for centuries. In the realm you know as Riedra, servants of the quori have built monoliths of crystal and steel. These monuments are themselves anchors, pulling the planes back together."

"So now you want us to go to war with Riedra?" Daine said. He poured another glass of murky mead, downing half of it in a gulp.

"Not at all. Stabilizing the planes in this manner is the work of centuries, and not all of those who build the pillars even seek to harm your world. It is a challenge for heroes of another age. The crystal moon makes all of this irrelevant and gives the aggressive powers of the moment a chance to strike."

Daine finished his drink. "Then why are we even talking about this?"

"Because if you are to reach Dal Quor, you must sleep within one of these monoliths. Only there will you be close enough to reach the plane."

Lei shook her head. "You want us to go to Riedra?"

"Yes. My domain touches your world in many places, and there are many gates you can use when the light of Dusk strikes the ground. When we have concluded our business, Kin will show you the path. When next you sleep, it shall be in a Riedran monolith—assuming you survive the journey, of course."

Something had bothered Pierce throughout this conversation, and now it rose to the surface of his mind. "You say the journey requires sleep. Neither Xu'sasar nor I sleep."

Thelania smiled again. "I said there were many difficulties. More than you know, for Lei does not dream either."

"What?" Lei cried. It seemed the calming magic was fading. "What are you talking about? I dream every night."

"No, child, you do not. You only believe that you dream. Your visions are not the result of a spiritual journey. They are manufactured from within, assembled from memories and seeds long carried."

"You're lying! I don't—"

"In Karul'tash, you came upon a room filled with a thousand spheres. Did you not hear the voices in those spheres, whispering to you?"

"Yes," Lei said, her fury faltering.

"In dreams, the giants were most vulnerable to their foes. And so they sought to create artificial dreams, a sanctuary for the spirit at night. So it is with you, and so it is that you could touch those false dreams. Your visions have the appearance of dreams, but they are no more than a mask. You have never seen Dal Quor."

"But . . ." Lei looked away. Tears glittered in her eyes, and Pierce's mind filled with questions. What did this mean? What was she?

"So you're saying I have to do this alone?" Daine said.

"No," Thelania replied. "I told you, Daine, your journey has prepared you for the destiny that awaits. You have the bridge you need for your companions." She turned to face Pierce, and her smile was chilling. "She calls herself Shira."

"Explain," Pierce said. It was both word and thought, but the queen responded before Shira.

"The realm of Dal Quor, the world of dreams, goes through cycles of change and rebirth," Thelania said. "These cycles can last tens of thousands of your years, and even I do not know what causes them. When the giants of Xen'drik breached the planar barriers, the beings of Dal Quor knew that their age was at an end, and they sought some way to preserve their spirits. Their war with Xen'drik was a desperate act, an attempt to flee a ship before it sank. But they believed that those who crossed the barrier physically would still be bound to the plane of dreams and would suffer its doom. So they experimented with ways to sever the ties between dream and reality, to give a spirit an anchor in this world. You carry one of those few survivors with you: the spirit Shira, a refugee from a world forever lost."

Is this truth? Pierce's thought was a demand. *Tell me, or I will rip you from my chest.*

Yes. The knowledge flowed to the surface. Like all Shira's communications, it seemed as if he'd known it all along. *She speaks the truth. I am of Dal Quor.*

Why? Pierce thought. *Why did you not tell me what you were?*

Why did you let Lakashtai betray us?

I did not know her intent. I did not know you were in danger. Understand this: Dal Quor was my home. I knew that this Lakashtai was a spirit of my homeland, and I recognized the purpose of the orb your Lei repaired. But in my memories, Dal Quor is a world of light, a place of beauty. This Dreaming Dark they speak of means nothing to me. I have been trapped in shadows for millennia, Pierce. I should have known that my world would be no more. But I did not want to know what had taken its place. I do not want to be the last of my kind.

So you . . . you are a spirit of Dal Quor? A creature like Lakashtai?

We share a common origin, perhaps. But I am nothing like her, any more than you are like Harmattan.

Pierce didn't know what to say, or to think. *So I am a host body for you—just as Lakashtai wore a body of flesh.*

No. I told you. We were made to be together. To be one.

Pierce pushed the thoughts away, forcing himself to listen to the spoken conversation. Lei was speaking, her eyes lost in thought. For her, the intellectual challenge was shelter from fear and doubt.

". . . she has a natural bond to Dal Quor, being from that plane herself," Lei said.

"Correct," Thelania replied. "It is one she has broken, but it can be reforged."

"And she has been designed to connect to warforged . . . to Pierce. So you're saying that she can allow Pierce to dream through her own spirit."

Is this true? Pierce thought.

There was hesitation. *Yes.*

Why not tell me?

There seemed to be no need.

"But where does that leave me?" Lei said

"You have only begun to reach your true potential, child. Remember your bond with Darkheart, with your wands. Remember what you felt when you first touched

245

that sphere in Pierce's chest, when you repaired the damage. When the time comes, you must touch the sphere again and let it guide you both."

"How do you *know* all this?" Lei demanded. "How can you know what I've done, what I've felt?"

"Because that is my nature," Thelania said. "That is my domain. You know of the thirteen planes, child. Realms of order and chaos, life and death, dreams and madness. But what is Thelanis?"

"The faerie court," Lei replied.

"The domain of the fey. But now you speak of the inhabitants of the realm, not the primal nature of the plane itself. What are the fey?"

"I . . . don't know," Lei admitted.

"We are magic, and we are mystery. We are the lure of the unknown, the promise of a mother's tale. I see the stories unfold, and I know the secrets that shape the lives of heroes, and the paths your lives will take. This is not the first time we have spoken, and should you live, it will not be the last."

"Flamewind," Daine said.

"What of her?"

"Daine with no family name. That's what she called me. When Kin brought us here, he used the same words. Was that you?"

Thelania smiled, and now it was a sign of pride, an artist taking satisfaction in her work. "I have many eyes in the world, Daine, and many voices to speak on my behalf. An oracle is a channel for knowledge, but that knowledge must come from somewhere. Yes, Flamewind carried my message, as did the weird on the water."

"And what do you gain from this?" Lei said.

"I am no friend of Dal Quor. And should nightmares

overrun your world, I fear the impact it would have on Thelanis. I told you, Lei, we are the stuff of stories. What happens when no stories remain to be told?"

Lei shook her head. "No, Queen of Dusk. What do *you* gain from this?" Her hand dipped below the table, and she pulled out the darkwood staff. The carved face was a mask of sorrow. "I've met someone else who accepted your help, and you can see how well that worked for her."

"And will you believe anything I told you, Lei? What if I told you that all that I've done for Darkheart, I did for you? If the staff hadn't fallen into your hands, you would have died beneath Sharn."

"So you just want to help us? Then free her." Lei slammed the staff down on the table.

Thelania smiled again, and there was danger in her eyes. "Do not presume to issue orders in the seat of my power, child," she said. "Darkheart still has a role to play."

"Then I won't help you," Lei said. "We're not going to be pawns in your game."

The queen laughed. The sound echoed throughout the hall, and it was the sound of the last moment of light as the sun slips below the horizon. "It's far too late for that, Lei. I am not asking this as a favor. I am not bargaining with you. I am offering you the chance to save your world from a horror *you* unleashed. You are wiser than I thought, but you are no queen."

A chill had fallen over the room, and the light had faded. Thelania's skin was paler, almost luminescent, and the gems in her hair glittered like stars. Now her beauty held a darkness that had been hidden before: they'd seen the sun, but dusk also held the shadows.

"You may be surprised," Lei said, picking up the

staff. "Sometimes a pawn can win the game."

"Enough," Daine said. "She's right, Lei. You said it before—Lakashtai is our responsibility. Let's clean up our mistakes. But let me say this, your majesty . . ." Daine stood up, placing a hand on his sword. "For all I know, you may be all-powerful in this place. You may know everything we've done or will do. If so, you know what I'm thinking. When this is done, I don't want to see one of your eyes or your agents again."

Thelania inclined her head. "I give you my word, Daine. You never shall."

"Then let's be done with this. You said you'd show us the way."

"Yes. Kin knows many paths into your world, and he will take you into Riedra. From your point of entry, you must secure one of the dreambinder monoliths. You, Lei, and Pierce can sleep. Xu'sasar and Kin will remain awake to guard your bodies."

"And once we enter Dal Quor?"

"There your path grows dark," Thelania said.

"What?" Lei asked. "You mean you don't know absolutely everything?"

"No one is all-knowing," the fey queen said. "There is no weakness in this. I know of the danger that arises. I know that you have the potential to bring it to an end. And should you fail, I know of the horrors that will follow."

"So we just go to sleep and hope for the best?" Daine said. "That's a great plan."

"I cannot guide you through the nightmare realm, and I do not know what will be needed to destroy the orb again. But there are powers within Dal Quor that can aid you."

"Shira," Pierce said.

No, the thought came. *I have told you. It is not the world I left behind. I know nothing of what remains.*

"No," Thelania said. "A guide awaits you in dreams, but you need knowledge far greater than he has to offer. What do you know of death?"

"Enough," Daine said. "What do *you* know?"

A smile played across Thelania's lips. "When most creatures of Eberron die, their spirits go to the plane of Dolurrh, where memories are washed away, and the spirit is cleansed of its burdens."

Lei shot a smug look at Xu'sasar.

"Yet there are those who follow other paths," Thelania continued, "creatures who seek to preserve their knowledge and wisdom beyond the grave. As you have said, Lei, the dragons of Argonnessen are the oldest and most powerful civilization of your world. Dragons live for thousands of years, and scaled sages have devoted lifetimes to the study of the planes and the mysteries of death."

"Fascinating," Daine said. "Really. And the point?"

"There is a sect among the dragons that has formed a sanctuary in Dal Quor. An eidolon, a force comprised of the essence of hundreds of fallen dragons. Its power is but a fraction of what these dragons wielded in life, but it may be the one safe haven you will find in Dal Quor. And if there is movement—if armies are massing on the fields of darkness—the eidolon will know."

"Fine," Daine said. "Kin shows us the way, we take a nap, talk to some dragons, and they tell us where we can find Lakashtai. Is that all? Because I think I'm ready to go now."

"Are you so certain?" Thelania smiled. "Time is

of the essence. Yet with the danger that awaits you,
my realm holds many pleasures. Do you not wish
to linger for one evening? You may never have the
chance again."

"I hope that I don't," Daine said. "But thanks for
the dinner."

Thelania stood and stepped back from the table.
"There was more to the meal than you know," she
said. "The food will give you strength enough to travel
through the days ahead and to return to your world
without suffering any ill effects. And the drink has
strengthened your mind. Fear is one of the greatest
weapons of the quori, and my mead will shield you in
the battle ahead."

The effects that she describes will last for approximately one day,
Shira thought. Pierce kept his thoughts intentionally
blank, but he was still troubled. Only a day ago, he'd
found Shira's presence comforting. Now each alien
thought brought a cold chill.

I mean you no harm, Shira thought. Try as he might, it
was impossible for Pierce to hide his thoughts from
her, which only increased his fears. *Pierce, I have been
alone for for more than thirty-five thousand years. My home no
longer exists. I am not like Lakashtai. I am the last of my kind. If I
said nothing, it was because of my own fears. Please. Do not leave me
alone again.*

When Pierce had first acquired Shira, she had been
cold and impersonal. It had taken some time for Pierce
to be certain that there was a personality within the
sphere, that it was more than just a tool. She'd kept
distance between them. Now he felt her emotions—her
sorrow, her fear.

He just didn't know if he believed them.

The companions stood, and as they moved away from

the table, Thelania approached Pierce. "So, child of war, are you ready for the battles that lie ahead?"

"Why do you ask?" Pierce said.

"You walk into danger with no weapon in your hand. I have given each of your companions a gift. Did you think yourself forgotten?"

"I need nothing from you," Pierce said. Her cold laughter still rang in his mind. She might not be an enemy, but he could not find it within himself to consider her a friend.

"And I offer you nothing of mine," she replied. "I wish to help you find what lies within."

"Leave him alone," Daine said. "And summon your servant. We're leaving."

"Kin will be here soon, Daine."

Thelania walked around Pierce. A few of the sparks from the floating chandelier followed her. She placed her hand on Pierce's quiver, and Pierce found himself nearly recoiling from her touch. The quiver was a part of Pierce, embedded into his back, and the exterior shell had all of the sensation of his armored skin.

"Only one arrow, Pierce? What is a warrior without a weapon?"

"I am more than just a warrior," Pierce replied.

"You are more than you know," Thelania said. "And you are warrior and weapon. Reach within, Pierce." She took his hand and slowly guided it to the quiver. "Reach within *yourself*."

"Pierce?" Lei said. "Are you hurt?"

As his hand touched his quiver, Pierce realized that there was something to what they said. He had felt a void ever since Indigo had destroyed his flail. He'd dismissed it as shame and the loss of a familiar sensation, the comforting weight of the weapon in his hand. Now he realized that void was within *him*, not his hand. Reaching back into his quiver, he reached *into* that void . . .

And found a weapon.

It should have been impossible. The quiver wasn't deep enough to hold anything but arrows. Yet as he closed his hand, he drew forth a long flail. The weapon was similar in design to the one he'd lost, but lighter, the balance as perfect as any weapon he'd ever held. Though the ball and chain appeared to be made from gold, a touch proved that they were far too strong to be soft gold. Steel banded the haft, and the foot of the weapon was the steel head of a black lion. Shira was analyzing the magical properties of the flail—the ability of the ball to produce radiant light and heat, supernatural strength of the metal and remarkable accuracy—but Pierce didn't need her to tell him. The weapon was a part of him. It had been there all along. He reached into the void a second time, and he felt the quiver fill with arrows.

"Captain," he said, testing the weight of the flail. "I am ready."

CHAPTER  25

DUSK
THELANIS

Lei's thoughts were in turmoil as they rode through the sunset fields. Kin led them toward the sunset. There was no path to follow, and they pressed on through wildflowers and weeds. The emissary had been waiting for them at the front gate, with final gifts from the faerie queen: backpacks of oiled leather with golden buckles, filled with food, drink, and healing salves; and five horses, beautiful black steeds with silver manes, and white spots scattered across their flanks.

Her mind drifted back to their departure, the final words of the queen.

"If you wish to leave, I shall not delay you any further," Thelania had said. "Farewell, Daine. We shall not meet again."

"And what of Darkheart?" Lei said. The dryad's voice—*Free me!*—still echoed in her thoughts, and she had to ask again.

"Her destiny is still bound with yours, Lei," the queen said. "Her fate is in your hands, not mine."

Then Daine had pulled Lei away. As soon as they'd left the chamber, he'd demanded an explanation of the queen's words.

"I don't want to talk about this," she'd said, shrugging off his hands. "Not now. Not here. I just want to get out of this place." The battle with the Woodsman, the wonder of Dusk, the luxury of the palace had helped Lei push the visions of the river to the back of her mind, and she'd been all too happy to forget. The queen's words proved beyond any doubt that this was no dream, that she would soon have to face her past.

Kin promised a swift journey. "The portal we seek lies by the Bier of the Sleeper," he said. "It's not far from here—we'll be there by nightfall."

"Does night ever fall here?" Daine said as he mounted his horse.

"No," Kin said. "Still, it's not far."

For a time they rode in silence, and Lei had set aside all thought, simply soaking in the beauty of the fields. Her companions had other ideas, and soon Daine and Pierce dropped back to ride alongside her.

"Lei," Daine said, "I know this is hard for you. But we need answers."

"You need answers?" she snapped. "You need answers? Do you think I don't want answers every bit as much as you do?"

"So you have no idea what she was talking about?" Daine said. "Your bond with the staff? Hearing voices of dead giants?"

"I—" Lei shook her head.

"My lady," said Pierce, "I do not wish to add to your distress, but there is some logic to this claim. You asked why Lakashtai struck at Daine, when she truly wished to manipulate you. If what the queen said was correct, she could not touch your dreams. Daine was the only one of us she could threaten."

"Well, that makes *me* feel so much better," Daine grumbled.

"Beyond that, I have have been thinking about Harmattan," Pierce continued. "Perhaps there were other reasons he did not kill you. In Karul'tash, he called you *sister*—"

"I know," Lei said. "He spoke to me, while you were scouting. *It is not your fault you were forged of flesh instead of steel,* he said. I thought it was a metaphor. I thought he'd say the same thing to any human. But now . . ."

"I don't understand," Daine said. "What are you?"

"What *am* I? I'm the woman you kissed this morning, or have you already forgotten?"

"No," Daine said, grasping for words. "I mean—"

Lei's rage had been building, and now the walls came tumbling down. It wasn't truly Daine she was angry at, but she needed to unleash her anger, her confusion. "What, am I some monster now? I'm flesh and blood, Daine, and I don't know what this means any more than you do. When I fell into that river, I saw my parents—I saw my parents talking about *killing* me, as if I were some failed experiment." She reached back, placing her hand on her dragonmark. "I saw them *brand* me!"

Now Pierce spoke. "So your dragonmark is fal—"

"I don't know!" Fear, fury, and insecurity came to a point. All her life she'd defined herself as a child of Cannith, one of the youngest to bear the Mark of Making. This question of humanity was one thing, but it was so broad, so alien, that it was hard for her to grasp. Her dragonmark was her very identity. She whirled in the saddle to face Pierce, and in that moment all her anger burst out of her.

Pierce convulsed, his body shaking and then going

rigid, and he fell from the saddle. Lei's anger melted away into panic.

Did I . . . what have I done?

She reined in her horse and leapt from the saddle. Daine was the better horseman, and he was already kneeling at Pierce's side.

"Pierce!" he cried. He looked up at Lei. "He's inert. I don't see any damage."

"It's internal," she said. Even as she knelt over him, she knew what had happened. As her anger had grown, she'd seen Pierce's lifeweb in her mind, felt that pattern, and thrown the full strength of her rage against it. Such a thing was impossible. She should have had to touch him to cause this sort of damage.

She knelt next to Pierce, but she did not touch him. Instead, she tried to visualize his lifeweb, to find his spirit as she had during the battle with the Woodsman. The pattern resolved itself in her mind, and she was shocked to see the damage within him.

"What are you waiting for?" Daine said. "Fix him!"

Lei blocked out his voice, forcing all the noise and chaos from her senses. The pattern of Pierce became her world, and she carefully bridged the gaps and wove the strands together. Then it was done. The world came back to her, Daine shouting, Xu'sasar and Kin watching quizzically.

And Pierce sat up. "What happened?" he said. He paused, no doubt listening to his inner voice. "You attacked me," he said to Lei.

"I didn't mean to," she said. "I don't even know how I did it, Pierce. There's a bond between us. I can *feel* you."

"How is this possible?" Pierce said.

Another memory flashed through Lei's mind: the

vision she'd had when she first attacked Pierce, of a series of linked lifewebs, of her parents comparing patterns. "I think Harmattan was right. We *are* family. I think we were created at the same time, and that this bond . . . my parents must have done this."

"This is insane," Daine said, reaching out and taking her hand. "Lei, I'm sorry. I'm not good with words. None of this has come out the way I want. You're not a monster. And that's just it. You're not . . . you're not warforged. You're human. This woman is playing games with you, like Lakashtai did with me."

"No, Daine," Lei said. "Someone's playing a game with me, but it's not Thelania. You heard that serpent. I said that I was born in my mother's womb, and it told me I was wrong. And it showed me the truth."

"It showed you *something*," Daine said. "How do you know it was true?"

"I just do," Lei said. "It all adds up. That sahuagin, Thaask. Harmattan. The visions from the river. That time I almost died . . . I could *feel* my wand of healing, even while I lay dying. I should have been unconscious, but somehow I activated the wand. I brought myself back."

"You don't know that."

Lei looked at her hand. Her little finger, removed by Harmattan in the jungles of Xen'drik. "Give me your dagger," she said.

"What?"

She reached out and pulled Daine's dagger from his belt. Before he could stop her, she drew the edge across her palm.

Blood welled from the wound. "See," Daine said. "Blood. You're—"

Once again, Lei shut out the sights and sounds

around her. This time it wasn't Pierce she was looking for. This time she looked within. Once she'd had a dream of her mother, in what she now knew to be the hidden workshop in Blacklion. Aleisa had stood over her, studying Lei and comparing her to a pattern she held in her hand. Now Lei reached out for that pattern . . .

And she found it.

It was like no lifeweb she'd ever seen before. The warforged contained matter in the form of wood and roots, but they were inanimate objects given life through magic. This pattern . . . the body was flesh and blood, but the magic was still there, spread through every vein and every muscle.

How did this begin? she wondered. I was a child. I grew within the house. Was I born? Or did they *make* me from raw matter? She remembered the words of her mother, in the final moments of her river-spawned vision: *Let my blood flow into you once more.*

She studied the pattern more closely. *There!* It was so small she could hardly see it, but there was the cut on her palm. Concentrating, she sought to restore the design to purity. Repairing such minor damage to Pierce would have been the work of a moment. This was a struggle. The web was stranger than anything she'd every dealt with. Yet slowly, ever so slowly, it came together.

She opened her eyes. ". . . bleeding," Daine was saying.

The cut was gone, with only a few drops of blood on her palm to show that she'd ever been injured.

"Lei," Pierce said. "How did you do that?"

"It's all true," she said. "I'm not human."

The words felt empty. Her anger had faded away,

and all she felt was exhaustion. She fell to her knees, wildflowers brushing against her chest.

"I don't care." Daine dropped to the ground next to her, turned her chin to face him. "Warforged, human, dragonmarked or not . . . I don't care if you're a goblin, Lei. I doesn't matter what you are. I only care about who you are." His hands were on her shoulders. "I love you, Lei."

She kissed him, and in that moment, he was the world. When they broke apart, she felt tears welling. "I don't know what this means," she said.

"We'll find out together," Daine replied.

She nodded, and the tears flowed freely. She looked up at Pierce and held out her hand. The warforged pulled her to her feet. "Pierce, I don't know what to say."

"Nothing need be said. Daine is correct. It seems we both have mysteries to unravel. Whatever the future holds, I will be by your side."

Lei nodded, wiping at her cheeks. "Thank you, brother," she said to Pierce. She turned to Daine, and the words of the dryad came back to her. *You have life. You have love, if you have the courage to seize it.*

"This is very touching, but the future won't hold much of anything if you all stand here blubbering," Kin said. "The bier is just beyond the hill. Lords and ladies, do you think you can contain your emotions until you've saved your world?"

Lei ignored the guide, her gaze still on Daine. He was smiling, and there was a joy in his eyes she'd never seen before. "Daine . . ." she said.

"Hush," he said, taking her hand and leading Lei to her horse. "There'll be time for us later. Right now, Riedra awaits."

For the first time that day, Lei felt as if her burdens were truly lifted. Yet even as her heart soared, a memory rose to the surface, sending a chill through her mind. Her father, deep in the heart of Blacklion.

She is the most dangerous thing we have ever created.

What did he mean?

CHAPTER 26

Xu'sasar hated riding.

She had seen horses before. The outlanders who came to plunder her homeland usually brought these creatures as mounts or beasts of burden, and she knew from tales that horses ran wild in other parts of Xen'drik. Xu'sasar was naturally fleet of foot, and when she stalked explorers the magic of the spirits allowed her to match the speed of the outlander mounts. But these faerie horses of Thelanis were another matter. This came as no surprise. These were surely spirits of speed, the inspiration for the mortal creatures she had encountered in the past, and she could hardly expect to keep pace on foot.

Fortunately for Xu'sasar, her horse was both friendly and responsive. He seemed to know the path, and all Xu'sasar needed to do was to hold on. She'd tried talking to the horse, but if it had the power of speech it chose not to speak with her, and she was left alone with her thoughts.

At the moment, those thoughts were gloomy. She did not understand this interaction between Daine, Pierce, and Lei. All Xu'sasar knew was that it didn't

261

involve her in any way, and that there was now a stronger bond between Lei and Daine. This was made worse by the knowledge that she would not be able to join Daine in this struggle against the forces of darkness. Here was an epic conflict, a chance to battle spirits of legend, and she was left to watch others sleep. Alone.

As her horse trotted across the meadow, Xu'sasar took a second look at the amulet she had been given as a gift. It was a locket made from pale silver, bound to a wide strip of black leather. A symbol was carved on the face of the amulet, but it held no meaning for her. Opening the locket, she found a shard of chitin, a piece of a scorpion's shell. When she wrapped the band around her neck, she could feel a tingle along her skin. Surely the amulet was a gift from Vulkoor, passed down to this Queen of Dusk. Xu'sasar wore little armor, relying on her speed and her vambraces to deflect attacks. If this amulet gave her skin some of the strength of the scorpion's shell, that was a blessing indeed. And with the Tooth of the Wanderer in her hand, she had been given sword and shield. She was prepared for the challenges that lay ahead—yet it seemed that she was to be denied the chance to fight in the greatest battle of all.

Perhaps luck would be with her. Perhaps an army would strike while the others slept.

She turned her attention to Kin. The fey envoy troubled her. For all that he had human teeth, his smile reminded Xu'sasar of the innkeeper Ferric. Xu'sasar was a child of the natural world, and there was something fundamentally unnatural about Kin. His features were handsome enough, but looking at him, she was certain that another face lay beneath the warm mask.

"There it is," Kin said. "The Bier of the Sleeper."

They had crested a hill. In the small valley below, Xu'sasar could see a ring of trees surrounding a pool of still water. As they rode down the hill, Xu'sasar caught sight of a stone slab next to the pool—the bier from which the grove took its name. At first Xu'sasar thought that a man was laid out upon the stone, but as they drew closer, she saw that the figure was a statue carved from black marble. Kin dismounted at the edge of the trees, and the others followed suit.

Xu'sasar darted forward to examine the statue. It was the figure of a warrior, clad in chainmail, with a longsword by his side. Muscular arms crossed over his chest. Strangely, she found that she couldn't see his face. At first she thought it was unsculpted, yet the longer she studied the statue, the more strongly she felt that some force was turning her eyes away, that the detail was there, just beyond her grasp.

"Who is this?" she said.

"The Sleeper's far older than I am," Kin said. "I'm afraid I don't know the full tale. A soldier of your world, favored by the queen. When he died, the monument was erected to honor his memory and guide future travelers."

"Where's his sword?" Daine said, examining the bier. Only now did Xu'sasar see that the scabbard lying next to the warrior was empty. For a moment she thought of her own empty sheaths, and the daggers given to her by her mother, lying next to the corpse of her father in the monolith of Karul'tash.

"A fine question, Master Daine, and one I will explain. Please gather around the pool and bring your horses." Kin produced a pouch from his own pack, and proceeded to sprinkle a sour-smelling dust over the companions and himself. "Now, Daine, if you will touch that empty scabbard—"

"What?" Daine said. "Why?"

"A gate can take many forms, as I would think you'd have learned from your time beneath the Hunter's Moon," Kin said. "The scabbard is the portal."

"You're going to make us small enough to walk through it?" Daine said.

"Not at all," Kin replied. "Please, just do as I ask."

As Daine laid his hand on the stone scabbard, Kin threw another handful of powder into the air above the water, and suddenly they were *falling*. The earth rose up, tumbling them down into the pool . . .

. . . and just as quickly, flinging them out onto dry land. They were standing by a pool of water. The trees were gone. The bier was gone. And there was no sun. Four moons could be seen in the sky, along with the faint glow of the Dragon's Ring. They had returned to Eberron, although the stars and the Ring told Xu'sasar that they were far from the land of her birth.

"Was this supposed to happen?" Daine said. The others turned to look. Daine was holding a scabbard in his hand, and it wasn't made of stone. The sheath was black leather, studded with purple dragonshards and chased in silver.

"Fascinating!" Kin said. "I wonder what effect that will have on the journey back. No matter."

"I thought you said we'd go through the scabbard," Lei said. "It seemed to me the pool was the portal."

"Yes, it did," Kin said. He shrugged. "We appear to be in the proper place, and that's all that concerns me."

"Are we?" Lei pointed to the sky. "I've never seen *that* before."

There was a new moon in the sky, and it was a moon Xu'sasar had never seen. Or was it? It seemed hazy, indistinct, and Xu'sasar felt that she could see the stars shining through its heart.

"That's your moon, Lady Lei," Kin said. "Let us move swiftly before it arrives in full glory. Mount up while I change into something more appropriate to our new surroundings."

With that, his face *rippled*. Darkness flowed out across his hair like smoke across a fire, transforming golden blond to coal black, and his hair pulled in on itself. A tan spread across his skin. His clothing followed suit, as the velvet and silk of the courtier turned into a black robe hemmed in silver, with a silver veil beneath a deep hood.

"What manner of creature are you?" Xu'sasar said. She held the bone wheel in her hand, ready to throw, and the points were sweating venom in response to her anger. She *knew* Kin was a trickster. This power alone was no proof of treachery, but she held herself ready to strike.

"Oh, did you not know?" Kin said. His voice was deeper, slower. He pulled back the hood, and now his skin faded to dull gray, and his eyes became as white as Xu'sasar's own.

"You're a changeling?" Lei said.

"Yes," Kin replied. "I was born in the land you know as the Eldeen Reaches. The people of my village follow the ways of the Greensinger druids and have close ties to the faerie court. As a child, I caught the eye of my mistress, and she brought me to Thelanis to serve as her envoy." As he spoke, he resumed his Riedran guise.

"Wait," Lei said, considering this. "So you're a . . . changeling?"

"I suppose so," Kin said. "Yet what I am now is your guide. The monolith we seek is a few leagues to the north. The lords of this land have impressive supernatural powers, and I suggest that we move quickly."

"What about this?" Daine said, gesturing with the scabbard.

"Keep it, if you want," Kin said. "Otherwise, I'll hold onto it."

"Fine." Daine tossed the jeweled sheath to the changeling and mounted his horse.

"What dangers can we expect?" Xu'sasar said.

"The people of this land prefer not to travel," Kin said. "With luck, the only challenge will be the guards at the monolith itself. If we do encounter anyone, let me speak on our behalf. I can be quite convincing, when I need to be."

"I don't think any of us speak Riedran anyway," Lei said.

"You are mistaken, Lady Lei. My mistress fed you knowledge as well as food. Thanks to the waters of Dusk, you will understand all languages, and all who hear you speak will know the meaning of your words. The effect will fade, but it should suffice for the task you must accomplish—here and in Dal Quor. Now follow me."

Xu'sasar considered the Queen of Dusk. She disliked Kin, all the more now that she had seen his true face. This Thelania . . . it was obvious that she was one of the great spirits, and she had been most generous in her gifts. Yet she too concealed her nature behind an elven face. Vulkoor was the great scorpion, the deadly hunter who strikes unseen. What primal nature was Thelania hiding?

They rode across a vast plain. Xu'sasar was born in rolling jungle, and this flatland was strange to her eyes, so empty, lacking even the hills or tors of the Huntsman's realm in Thelanis. The fields were filled with tall grasses, and rodents and insects scattered as the fey horses pounded across the plains.

Daine rode next to Lei, and the two spoke quietly. Though Xu'sasar was still learning the customs of the outlanders, she could see that they did not wish her company, so she stayed close to Kin, keeping an eye on the changeling and the shadowy landscape.

"What's that?" she said, pointing to the west. She could see a slight break in the silhouette of the grasslands, a sharp edge rising above the swaying plants.

"Ruins, I should think," Kin replied. "This land has a long history of war, and when the current overlords took power, they razed the old cities and built anew. There are ruins scattered across Sarlona, usually far from any current village."

This thought brought some small comfort to Xu'sasar. Xen'drik was a land of ruins, and the Qaltiar used these remnants of giant civilization as shelter, moving from one shattered city to the next. Surely these ruins differed greatly from what she was used to. Nonetheless, it was comforting to know that there was shelter in the wilds, if she should need it.

"There's our destination," Kin said, halting and pointing. A black teardrop was silhouetted against the stars, rising up against the horizon. There were no lights, no signs of activity. "From this point on, we must act with care."

"You don't think your disguise will hold up, then?" Daine said.

"Please, Master Daine," Kin replied, "my abilities are not a concern. They would not suspect me. But the Riedrans fear foreigners, and the mere sight of strangers will likely cause alarm."

"Then I suppose I'm in her majesty's debt." Daine sighed and pulled the glamerweave cloak out of his pack. The shifting black patterns made it all but invisible in the shadows of night. "Lei, can you make a temporary cloak of invisibility?"

Lei nodded. "It'll take a little time, but it's simple enough."

"Pierce, Xu, I want you to scout ahead. We need to know what we're up against."

Lei looked troubled, and she hesitated slightly before she spoke. "There's something else. I'm not sure if it will work, but . . ."

"Yes?" Daine said.

Lei closed her eyes, a look of deep concentration settling over her features. For a moment, nothing happened. Then Pierce spoke.

"I hear you, my lady."

"What are you talking about?" Daine said

Lei opened her eyes. "It's the bond that let me heal and hurt him before. I can touch Pierce at a distance. I thought we might be able to communicate through it, and it seems that we can." She looked at Pierce. "Here, try to respond without speaking." She closed her eyes again, and after a moment she smiled. "Good."

"I remember Lakashtai doing the same thing," Daine said. "Can you bring the rest of us in?"

Lei shook her head. "No. This is just between Pierce and me."

"Still," Daine said, "it'll help for coordinating actions. Pierce, Xu, move out. See what you can see, and wait for word from Lei." He looked at Xu'sasar. "Is that understood?"

"Yes," she said. She felt the slightest hint of shame because Daine thought this necessary. This was a situation of great import, and she knew just how critical it was for their pack to work as one. She would prove her worth in time.

It was a pleasure to dismount from the horse and to feel the soil beneath her feet once more. "Take lead," she said to Pierce. "I will follow."

She drew on the shadows in her blood, winding herself in the comforting dark. She held the Tooth of the Wanderer, still in the shape of the bone wheel, and for the first time since they'd entered the realm of Dusk, she found herself at ease. The enemy was ahead of them. The hunt was on.

❀ ❀ ❀ ❀ ❀ ❀ ❀

The giants of Xen'drik built with stone, and Xu'sasar never imagined that metal could be worked on so vast a scale. The monolith was a smooth steel ovoid, easily a hundred times her height. She saw no guards in their path, but they had traveled only a short distance when Pierce raised his hand. Xu'sasar had learned only a few of the signals the others used, but this one was easy enough. *Stop.*

Xu'sasar dropped into the grass. She called on the spirit of the scorpion, drawing on the stillness of the hidden hunter to conceal her from her enemies. None too soon, for a moment later the enemy was upon them.

There was no sign of movement on the plains, no hint of human activity. Yet in that moment, Xu'sasar felt a *presence.* They were being watched, of that she

269

had no doubt. As a child she had ventured into the City of Tears, although the teller of tales had warned her of the ghosts; she'd felt the same sense of presence in that place, a force of personality beyond mere flesh and blood. Xu'sasar held her breath, letting the spirit of the scorpion calm her fear and hold her in stillness, and a moment later the presence was gone.

Continue, Pierce signaled.

While Xu'sasar did not understand all that the Dusk Queen had said, she gathered that Pierce had a bond with a lesser spirit that advised him on matters of magic. Most likely this guide could see the guardian that had passed them.

Motion! There were openings set into the base of the great metal seed, wide arches filled with pale light. And as they moved forward, Xu'sasar saw the silhouette of a man pass across the portal. The figure was only caught in the light for an instant, but that was long enough. *Male. Long sword, sheathed. Chain mail, no shield seen but likely kept close.* She studied the other portals. *There.* An archer, barely visible, peering around the edge of a gate. Face hidden behind a black helm and silver veil.

Hold position, Pierce signaled. *Watch.*

Regretfully, Xu'sasar settled into her crouch. She would have rather moved closer, to peer within the monolith, but she understood Pierce's tactics. Someone should watch the archer, be ready to strike if the alarm was sounded or, if it became necessary, to flee and alert the others. And so she waited, watching the lights and envisioning the battle that lay ahead of her.

The archer didn't move, but a new figure passed across an archway. She could see the shape of a greatsword slung across the back, a long bow held ready for action, but what caught her attention was the sheer size of the creature. Xu'sasar was used to fighting giants, and she'd fought larger foes. Nonetheless, this warrior was about twice her height and many times her weight. His muscles spoke of fearsome strength. And even from this distance, she could see the short horns protruding from his forehead. *This is my foe.* No question in her mind. Let the others fight these human soldiers. Xu'sasar would bring down the giant.

Pierce returned. His voice was barely louder than the wind in the grass. "There is a woman within who watches the area with her mind. We must eliminate her the moment the battle begins, before she can bring other powers to bear."

Xu'sasar clicked her tongue. A challenge!

"You possess the skill to approach unseen and the ability to resist the other forces that will be brought to bear. Daine wishes you to circle around, enter the monolith, and when battle is joined, ensure that this woman in purple is eliminated before she has the opportunity to act. Are you willing?"

"I have already gazed upon the fields of death," Xu'sasar said. "I have no fear, and I will not fail. Just let me fight the giant when the woman falls."

Pierce was silent. Xu'sasar imagined that he was relaying the message back to Lei.

"Very well," he said. "A burst of fire will signal the attack. Strike swiftly and hard. We will arrive as soon as possible."

Xu'sasar placed her palm against his, dark flesh dwarfed by the metal gauntlet. "We fight as one."

She rose and moved into the night.

Three archers stood sentinel in the monolith, watching the plains for any signs of motion. However skilled they might be, they were only human, and no match for Xu'sasar. She was a scorpion wraith of the Qaltiar. Shadow was her shield, and the night her hunting ground. She drew the darkness to her and slipped toward her foes. Soon she stood at the base of the monolith itself, at the edge of one of the gates. Pale green light spilled out onto the ground. The light was unbroken by any motion, and Xu'sasar peered around the edge of the gate.

The monolith was a vast, hollow shell, a single chamber, and the only feature of note was a beam of light rising up from the ground. No, it was *crystal,* a glowing pillar hundreds of feet in height. Her horned giant, his bulk wrapped in chainmail and black leather, paced restlessly about the chamber. He was a strange creature, more bestial than the giants she was used to battling. His pale blue skin looked as tough as leather, and long black tusks protruded from his mouth.

Two soldiers slept on the floor, with swords set just within reach. A third warrior sat on the floor, oiling his blade.

Then Xu'sasar saw the woman in purple. Her eyes were closed, her legs crossed—and she was floating a few feet off the floor. The woman's robe was silk hemmed with intricate silver patterns, and she wore a headdress made from violet glass, with sweeping horns curving up and around her head. Her skin was pale, her hair dark, and her features reminded Xu'sasar of the one who had accompanied Daine in the burning jungle—Lakashtai, the servant of demons.

Though there was little cover in the inner chamber,

the green light of the crystal core was faint, no stronger than moonlight. Calling on spirits of scorpion and shifting panther to hide her from her foe, Xu'sasar slipped within the monolith. The blue-skinned giant turned as she entered, but his gaze slid past her.

Xu'sasar raised the Tooth of the Wanderer. The bone wheel was not the weapon for close battle, and she considered her options. The twin knives were the weapon of her mother, the weapon passed down to her, yet using the Tooth in that form reminded her of the heirlooms she'd left behind, the memories she would never pass on. The single sword? The razor chain? The rod of venom? In the end, she decided on the long teeth, a polearm with a sharp blade on each end of the haft. As soon as the thought was clearly formed in her mind, the Tooth shifted in her hands, bone and leather stretching into the new shape. The balance was perfect, and though it had the appearance of bone, the weight of the weapon spoken of a stranger truth. Xu'sasar felt the thrill of battle rising within her. She held the tooth of one of the great spirits. What mortal creature could stand against such power? Now it was just a matter of waiting for the attack. *A burst of fire*, Pierce had said. She crept forward, moving to where she could see the plains, watching for signs.

There! A flash in the night. Flame filled the monolith. This was no mere signal; it was a deadly fireball, a blinding burst of heat. The wall of flame boiled toward Xu'sasar, and she heard the first notes of the soldier's screams.

You possess the ability to resist forces that will be brought to bear, Pierce had said. Fortunately for Xu'sasar, he was correct. Night and darkness were bound to her blood, and this shadow had the strength to extinguish lesser magics. The flames swept over her but melted before touching her. Even the air around her remained cool and breathable.

The mystic fire lasted for only a second, fading as swiftly as it had struck. Xu'sasar was already in motion, the point of her blade leveled at the demon-woman in purple. The initial thrust slammed through her opponent's breast, piercing the woman's heart. Violet eyes flew open, filled with shock and pain. Xu'sasar kicked her in the chest, using the force of the blow to pull her weapon free. Before anyone in the chamber could react, Xu'sasar spun to the side, lashing out with the Tooth. Both blades flashed across the woman's neck, cutting flesh and muscle with ease. The woman never made a sound. She simply fell to the ground as blood flowed across the floor.

Would that she had time to savor the triumph. Xu'sasar turned, taking in her surroundings. The human soldiers lay scattered around the floor, and though a few still twitched and feebly reached toward their weapons, the stench of burnt flesh and smoldering cloth told her all she needed to know.

But where was the giant? The horned creature was nowhere to be seen.

There! Floating in the air, shimmering into view as the spell of invisibility faded. He was drawing his great bow, preparing to loose a second arrow. The first ripped across Xu'sasar's ribs, and even the magic of the fey amulet couldn't turn this bolt.

Fire flowed through Xu'sasar's veins—excitement, not fear. A worthy foe at last! She rolled to the side, and the second arrow slammed into the ground just behind her feet. Clearly he thought to wear her down, using his power of flight to his advantage. But Xu'sasar had fought the firesleds of the sulatar, and no mere bowman could get the best of her. As the beast drew a third arrow to his bow, Xu'sasar *leapt*, the strength of the spirits flowing through and carrying her across the air. Her blades flashed in the green light, sundering the giant's bow and scattering shards of wood across the chamber.

"Dark spirit!" the beast cried, his booming voice echoing throughout the empty tower. And with that, he disappeared again.

Xu'sasar felt pleasure. This one still had much to learn. She set her back against the crystal pillar, brought her weapon into a cross guard, and closed her eyes. Darkness was one of the weapons of the Qaltiar, and every child of her tribe was taught to fight without the benefit of sight. Sound, scent, even the pressure of the air combined to paint a picture of her surroundings. She heard the greatsword slide from its sheath, the sword cutting through air on the backstroke. She could *see* the enemy in her mind, and even as he swung at what he thought a helpless foe, she dove forward, rolling down and under the blow.

The giant came into view again as his sword *crashed* into the crystal pillar, sparks and shards of glass flying through the air. Already in motion, Xu'sasar felt a thrill as her blades pierced leather and steel and sank deep into blue flesh. The creature grunted in pain as he turned to face her.

The battle began in earnest.

This giant was no fool, save for the arrogance that led him to fight instead of flee. He learned from each wound, and he fought more carefully, using his size and reach to hold her at bay. His strength was formidable. One clean blow with the greatsword would be devastating, and he knew it. Worse still, his wounds were healing. As they circled one another, Xu'sasar saw that the cuts on his back had vanished. The skin beneath the armor was smooth and unblemished.

Xu'sasar felt the first touches of fear. She was not afraid to die. But for the last of the Qaltiar to die at the hands of a giant, without even harming her foe? This was shame indeed. Surely there was a weakness she could exploit. As she danced away from the giant's sword, she realized that his face was burned, that he had recovered from the stroke of her sword, but not the blast of fire.

Then Pierce arrived.

The warforged swung, the whirling chain singing in the air, the golden ball ablaze with light, nearly as bright as the sun itself. The giant turned to face this new foe; it seemed that Xu'sasar was unworthy of his attention, having proved unable to inflict any true injury.

It was a fatal mistake. With a thought, Xu'sasar shifted the form of her weapon. The hard haft of the polearm divided into a hundred links of chain. One swift motion, and she caught the giant's leg with a coil of razor-edged bone. For all his strength, the creature was unprepared for the attack, and he tumbled to the ground. As he started to rise, Pierce's flail smashed into the giant's face. Bone snapped beneath the golden ball, but physical force was only part of the blow. The flail's glow was the result of terrible heat, and the stroke seared the flesh even as it tore through the skin. Two more blows, and the giant fell still.

"My apologies," Pierce said. "I know you wished to battle this one, yet—"

"The pack is stronger than the one who hunts alone," Xu'sasar replied. As she spoke, she returned the Tooth of the Wanderer to the shape of the bone wheel. "I thank you for your aid."

The others arrived within moments. Daine looked down at the burnt corpses and shook his head. "A bad way to die," he said.

"I assure you, there would be no reasoning with the likes of these," Kin said. He looked down at the woman in violet. "We're lucky. This one was only a vessel in training, not a host to one of our true foes." Kin placed his hand on the crystal pillar and closed his eyes. "Yes, this will do," he said. "All you need to do is sleep."

"Now if only I was tired," Daine said.

"Look in the pack my mistress gave you," Kin replied. "The vial of green fluid is a powerful sleeping draught. Drink it, and you will sleep. Pierce, Lei . . . you'll be relying on Pierce's companion to provide you with a passage into Daine's dream."

"Yes," Pierce said. "She says to place your hand upon my chest, my lady."

Xu'sasar approached Daine, who was rummaging through the pack. "I am sorry that I cannot accompany you," she said.

"You've done your part, Xu," Daine said, without looking up. "You did well. Aureon only knows what that woman would have unleashed if you hadn't brought her down."

"Any of you would have done the same."

"You're right," he said, and he looked up. "But none of us could. I'm glad you're with us, Xu. It's good to know someone will be watching over us while we sleep."

Xu'sasar closed her eyes, inclined her head, and let

him go about his work. Lei pulled blankets from her magic satchel, and soon Daine and Lei lay on the ground with Pierce between them. Lei laid a hand on Pierce's chest, and for a moment she stiffened. Then she relaxed.

"Whenever you are ready, captain," Pierce said.

Xu'sasar knelt next to Daine as he swallowed the potion. His eyes unfocused, and his eyelids began to flutter.

"Return," Xu'sasar said, touching her palm to his. "Do not leave me alone."

Daine smiled at her.

And then he fell asleep.

CHAPTER 27

THE FRINGES
DAL QUOR

Perhaps you'd introduce me to my new guests, Master Daine. I dislike surprises in my house."

Daine felt dizzy, disoriented. The world was a blur of color and noise, conversation and laughter. And the woman's voice, terribly familiar.

Alina Lorridan Lyrris.

The surroundings pulled into sharp focus. Alina's hall in Metrol, the walls lined with stained glass, revelers dancing to the strains of ghostly music. The gnome woman stood before him, staring up into his face. Illusions were woven into the fabric of her gown, so that it too appeared to be made from stained glass. Crystal shards were pinned within her pale golden hair. Barely three feet in height, still she had the charisma of a queen—a stronger presence, in fact, than the young queen of Cyre whom Daine had seen near the end of the War. And there, at his side, stood Jode, dressed for a celebration in a doublet of red and brown. His dragonmark was unusually vivid, an even deeper blue than the glass panes in the windows.

"My apologies, Lady Lyrris." Another voice, just as familiar. "May I introduce the Lady Lei d'Cannith,

279

and her bodyguard, Pierce. My name is Jode, personal physician to the Lady Lei. It was never our intention to take undue advantage of your hospitality. My lady has swift business to conduct with your servant Daine, and then we will depart."

"How intriguing." Alina said, raising a perfect eyebrow. "I'll expect a full report this evening, Daine—after our own swift business, of course." Her smile was cold and predatory, and she departed without another word.

"You know, I've always wondered," Jode said. "Did she reduce you or enlarge—"

"Leave it be," Daine said.

"Jode?" Lei said, a note of wonder in her voice.

Pierce and Lei stood just behind Daine, and both appeared just as they had in the Riedran monolith. Pierce held his golden flail, and spots of ogre's blood were still spattered across his armor.

"That would be me," Jode said, with the brilliant smile that was forever fixed in Daine's memory. He darted around Daine, and Lei knelt to embrace him.

"This is just a dream. You're not—" Her words faded as she gazed into his eyes. "It really is you, isn't it? How is this possible?"

"Doesn't Daine tell you anything?" Jode said. "Blue bottle?"

"Yes," Lei said. "The essence of your dragonmark." Now her eyes became distant. "When I tried to touch your spirit, there was nothing there at all. You're saying that they bound your soul to the dragonmark? And Daine *drank* it?"

"That's about it," Jode said. "Things are very vague before that, but once Daine drank the potion . . . it's hard to explain. I was alive again. And I could feel Daine.

I think our souls are merged, somehow." He looked at Daine. "Is something wrong with our back?"

"Yeah, you could say that," Daine said. He looked around the hall. It was much the same as the dream he'd had in Thelanis, and yet there was a fundamental difference. Everything was sharper, more focused. More than that, he felt completely aware. More often than not, he watched his dreams from a distance, the world and people changing around him. But now . . . if anything, this felt *more* real than the world he had left behind.

Jode looked up at Pierce. "As much as I'm thrilled to have this little reunion, the fact that you're here suggests there's something very odd going on," Jode said. "Care to fill me in?"

Lei spoke first. "It seems that the natives of this place . . ." She paused, looking around at the party. "Well, not *this* place, but this plane—"

"I understand," Jode said. "I've been here longer than you have. Trust me, you'll know the difference."

"It seems the natives of this place are preparing to invade Eberron. We inadvertently provided them with the key needed to restore passage between the planes. Now we must destroy it, and it seems that time is of the essence." Lei looked around the party. "We were told that a guide would be waiting for us, but they said nothing about the form it would take."

Jode cleared his throat.

"What?" Daine said. *"You're* our guide? But you said you were barely conscious before I . . . drank you."

"You wound me," Jode said. "Haven't I always made it my business to know the lay of the land? And as for time, you'll find it's not what you're used to. It's been over three months since our first conversation in

281

dreams, Daine, and I've made quite a few friends in the fringes. Your story explains a lot of things. There've been rumors flying around about activity in the core. And I do mean flying around."

"You have been to the heart of this realm?" Pierce said, a hint of surprise in his normally impassive voice.

"No, no," Jode said. "But I've talked to a few who have. Archetypes, mainly—ideas that draw strength from multiple dreams. You know, like when you dream you're supposed to be taking the Test of Siberys, and you suddenly realize you're not wearing any clothing? I've met the anxiety that generates. Edgy, easily embarrassed, but not a bad fellow."

"Hey, Daine!" It was another voice he hadn't heard for years—the voice of a man he'd killed. Morim d'Deneith, another of Alina's guards. Unlike Daine, Morim enjoyed his work. A cruel grin split his face, and there were spots of blood on the leather of his gauntlets. "One of the guests had an accident in the foyer. Lady Lyrris wants you to clean up the mess."

"In a moment," Daine said. The sudden appearance of the dead man was a jolt, bringing back memories Daine had tried to forget. "I'm in the middle of something right now."

"And you can get back to it when you're done," Morim said, taking Daine's arm. He was a stocky, powerful man, and his hand felt like a manacle around Daine's wrist.

"Let go, Morim," Daine said. He pulled at the guard's grip, but his rival simply grinned.

"So you're saying you have other business? Something more important than Lyrris's orders?"

"That's right," Daine said.

"Too bad."

Everything fell into slow motion. Morim raised his hand to smash Daine in the face, but there was a long blade of energy where his fist should have been. As this spike flashed toward Daine's eyes, he ducked beneath the blow, using his momentum to pull at Morim's wrist and fling the thug to the ground. For a moment Morin was suspended in the air, caught by the strange flow of time. As soon as his hand slipped away from Daine's wrist, everything sped up. Morim slammed into the ground, and Daine staggered away from him.

Morim rose to his feet—but he wasn't Morim any more. Both hands were curved, glowing blades. His flesh and clothes burst, revealing the red chitin armor of some monstrous insect or crustacean. His head was wider, flatter, and a host of burning eyes were pressing forward through his skin.

You're an interesting one, traveler. The telepathic projection still held traces of Morim's voice, but it was over-shadowed by a malevolent alien presence, thick and cold, oil running through his mind. *More awake than you should be. Let's see what happens when you die.*

Daine drew his sword and dagger, setting himself on first guard—and then blinked. The dagger in his left hand wasn't his dagger. Instead of black adamantine, it was plain steel. It was a trivial thing, inconsequential in the grand scheme. But it was a distraction, and that was all the creature needed. The horror ripped free of the remnants of Morim's flesh, lashing out with both blades.

And ran into Pierce and Lei.

The darkwood staff was in Lei's hands, the striking end studded with vicious thorns. Pierce's flail ended in a true ball of fire, a blazing orb that smashed through one armored shoulder. Daine recovered his balance and made a deep thrust, sinking the point of his blade into one of the creature's blue eyes. A howl of pain echoed through his mind, and the creature vanished.

Daine whirled toward Jode. "Well, *guide*, what in Aureon's name was *that?* And why aren't they *doing* anything?"

The revelers around them continued to dance and drink, seemingly oblivious to the ruined mass of flesh on the floor.

"I told you that the locals were easy to recognize," Jode said. "That was one of the weakest. These others, Alina . . . they're just figments plucked from your memories." He prodded the remnants of Morim's body with a toe. "It'll take some time for that spirit to reform, but I suggest we start moving. Give me your hand."

Their fingers touched, and Daine staggered. Sensations poured through his mind, memories and images, just as when he'd touched Jode in the first dream they shared. Once again, he felt a sense of the world around him, and how it was no world at all—just one bubble drifting in vast darkness.

"Daine!" Lei cried.

"Let it go," Jode said. "Don't try to see it all. Focus on me. Follow me."

The chaos faded, his surroundings resolving once more. Jode tugged on Daine's hand, pulling him forward, deeper into the great hall.

"Come," Jode said. "Tell me where we're supposed to go."

"Draconic . . . eidolon," Daine said, still catching his breath.

"It's supposed to be a region formed from the dreams of dead dragons," Lei explained. "Some sort of sanctuary for their spirits."

"Oh, certainly. I think we can find a way," Jode said. Daine laughed, and Jode looked up at him. "What's so funny?"

"You," Daine said. "Leave you alone for a day, and already you know your way around."

"I told you, it's been much more than a day for me. And this sanctuary you're looking for . . . it's the sort of thing the locals talk about. We're in the fringes of Dal Quor, you see, where reality is shaped by mortal dreams. The quori spirits use these realms as a hunting ground, preying on dreamers and wanderers like me. This dragon realm, well, it's one of the only places in the fringes that the quori are afraid to go. Of course, no one else who goes there returns, so it's not exactly a popular destination."

Their surroundings were changing, subtly at first. The revelers slowed in their dance, and the color faded out of the glass windows. By the end of Jode's speech, Daine saw that the people around him were no longer flesh and blood. They were statues, and the paneled floor was covered with warm sand.

"What's going on?" he said.

"We're moving," Jode replied. "Leaving your memories and searching for another dream. And let me tell you, it's far easier with you here. It would have taken me hours to get this far on my own."

"Two souls in one body," Lei murmured.

"I think so," Jode said. "It's as I said. Our spirits are merged. Honestly, I don't know what our potential is, but touching you I can *feel* power within us. A fortunate thing that you drank the potion, eh?"

"No . . ." Daine said. "No. It wasn't luck. She *told* me to do it."

"Hmm?"

"The sphinx. Flamewind. 'You will be asked to give away the soul of your closest friend.' When Harmattan challenged me, I remembered those words."

"Interesting," Jode said. "And it was Flamewind who led me to Olalia . . . and to my death. So was she predicting the future, or creating it?"

"Is there a difference?" Lei said. The walls of Metrol faded away, revealing an endless desert. Stone pillars rose from around them, etched by wind and sand into shapes faintly reminiscent of the revelers they'd left behind.

The words of the Morim-creature returned to Daine's mind. "What happens if we die here?"

Jode shrugged. "Hey, I'm already dead, remember? Normally, you'd just wake up, I think. But now . . . there's something different about you. All of you. I've met quite a few dreamers, and you're more *real* than they are. More like the archetypes. I think, somehow, you're really *here*. And if that's the case, dying seems like a bad idea."

"Shira concurs," Pierce said. "Death would surely be a traumatic experience. Even if we survived, we might be left comatose, wounded spirits trapped within our physical bodies."

"Oh, right. Shira." With everything else that had been going on, Pierce's pet spirit had slipped his mind. "Are you sure about her, Pierce? From what Thelania said, haven't we just brought the dragon to the hoard?"

"I believe in her, captain," Pierce said. "This is not her home, and these are not her people. She was as horrified to see that creature in the hall as you were."

"If you say so." Daine frowned. The desert came to an abrupt end ahead, with nothing but stars visible beyond the sand. "Jode?"

"Don't worry," Jode said cheerfully. "It's only the end of the world."

A vast chasm lay ahead. If it had another side, it was beyond the range of Daine's eyes.

"So where do we go now?" he said.

Jode pulled his hand free and pointed to the sky. Daine followed the gesture and drew his breath in wonder. A dragonshard floated above them, a golden crystal burning with inner light. It was larger than any shard Daine had seen, as large as a wagon—and it was the first and smallest in a chain. A belt of golden dragonshards rose into the sky and curved across the horizon.

"The Ring of Siberys," Lei said, her voice filled with wonder.

Jode smiled. "Welcome to the sanctuary of the dragons."

CHAPTER 28

THE
DRACONIC
EIDOLON
DAL QUOR

The Ring of Siberys. The golden belt that stretched across the sky. According to legend, it was the remnants of a great dragon, slain at the dawn of time. Some stories said the first dragons were formed from the blood of Siberys, or that the Ring was the ultimate source of magical energy. Most of the sages of House Cannith dismissed these myths, but there was no denying the magical power within the golden dragonshards that fell from the Ring. And shards of such size—the wonders that could be forged with such things!

It's just a dream! Lei looked away from the light, feeling foolish. Nothing here was real. This was someone's imagining of the Ring, nothing more.

Daine's concerns were more practical. "So where are the dragons?" he said.

"I never promised dragons," Jode replied. "What lies ahead are the *dreams* of dragons, and dragons long dead at that. I don't know what form this eidolon of yours will take. Whatever it is, it's somewhere up there. In the Ring."

"So we just start climbing?"

"Unless you've got a better idea," Jode said. "If you were a dragon, you could just fly."

"I'm not a dragon."

"I could be," Lei said.

"What?" Daine looked at her.

"I've never tried anything so large, but I think I could transform myself into a dragon." Lei's mind raced, calculating mystical parameters and dredging up half-forgotten formulas. "The change wouldn't last long. But I would be able to fly and carry the rest of you."

"What are the risks?" Daine said.

"Risks." Lei grimaced. "It's hard to say. I'll have to channel a tremendous amount of magical energy, and if I lose control of the forces, I could end up trapped in the body of a lizard. Or I could have my organs turned inside out, exploded from within, or something else spectacularly fatal."

Daine glanced down at Jode. "Well?"

"Don't ask me," Jode said. "It's her body."

"I can do this," Lei said. "I know it's dangerous, but I can make this work." As crazy as it was, something about it appealed to her. The thought of spreading her wings, taking to the air—of shedding this increasingly strange body, if only for a few moments.

"Faith matters here," Jode said. "We're walking in dreams. If you're sure of yourself, I think it's worth the risk. But I want us to work together. Daine, sit next to me and take my hand. We need to envision her success, lend our strength to Lei."

"What should I do?" Pierce said.

"Watch," Jode replied. "By now, the quori may be looking for us. Keep your eyes open for any signs of attack."

"Think good thoughts," Daine muttered, making no attempt to conceal what he thought of this operation. Nonetheless, he sat next to Jode, took the halfling's hand, and closed his eyes.

Perhaps it was just Lei's imagination, but she did suddenly feel calmer, stronger. She closed her own eyes and began to build the pattern.

The magic of artifice could not be bound directly into flesh and blood, and an artificer had to tie her patterns to inanimate objects. Lei typically used her armor for this task, her green and gold jerkin. This was an heirloom of her family, said to be the work of one of the greatest artificers of House Cannith. A reservoir of magical energy lay within the golden rivets, and Lei could use it for her most difficult enchantments.

Or so she'd always believed.

Now, as Lei reached out for the mystical patterns that defined the vest, a shock ran through her. Lei had worked with illusions in the past, and this was the same sort of sensation as watching an illusion fade, revealing a strange reality. Her mental image of the vest faded away, and Lei realized that she was working her own pattern, the lifeweb she had discovered within herself. *There's never been any power in the vest. The energy I was calling on is in me.*

It made no sense. Then again, natural flesh and blood couldn't be repaired with the magic of the artificer, and she'd already proven an exception to that rule.

What am I?

There was no time for doubt. The energies she was binding had built to a critical point, and if she let her mind wander, the Sovereigns only knew what would become of her. Pushing her fears and doubts away, she focused on the threads of mystical power, forcing the divergent filaments into one coherent pattern. Finally, carefully, she laid that pattern over her own.

An explosion of light and heat spread throughout her muscles. *She was growing!* Her leather armor merged with her skin, transforming into huge, rusty scales. Leather flaps formed as her arms transformed into mighty wings, and she could feel her powerful tail stretching out behind her, ready to lash at her foes. For a moment she was baffled by the presence of the tiny mammals and the little metal man. Instinct demanded that she take to the air and strike these impertinent creatures down with tooth and claw. Then the fog lifted from her thoughts, and she remembered who she was and where she was. Lei. The dragon.

"That's a dragon?" It was Daine's voice, though it seemed so small and weak to her new ears. "I thought they had four legs."

"This creature is a wyvern," Pierce said. "Aside from the missing forelimbs, it lacks the deadly breath and magical power of the creatures often referred to as true dragons, compensating with a poisonous stinger in its tail. Despite these differences, it is a form of dragon."

"I—" Lei's first word caught in her throat. Her voice was hoarse thunder, and her tongue was not made to speak the Common tongue. She tried again, struggling to form words with a throat designed for mighty roars. "I've . . . never seen . . . a dragon. Best I could do." She stretched her wings, feeling a thrill as they caught the air. Remembering the task that lay ahead, she leaned her head against the ground. "Mount!"

"We're just going to hang on?" Daine said. He looked over at the seemingly bottomless chasm. "Oh, *this* is a fine idea."

"Confidence!" Jode said, crawling up Lei's neck. A slight ridge ran along her spine, and he wrapped his hands around one of the points, bracing his feet against her scales. "You're dreaming. *Believe*, and you can succeed."

Lei knew Daine, knew the bitterness that he carried inside, and she expected him to respond with a jibe. The destruction of Cyre had been hard on all of them, but Daine had suffered the worst. Lei had lost relatives, but the nation meant little to her, and Pierce placed greater worth on his companions than on the abstract nation. Cyre mattered to Daine, and he'd been haunted by that sense of loss and failure, both his failure to protect the soldiers under his command and to somehow defend the nation itself. And then the nightmares began.

When Lei first met him, Daine was bold and confident. He believed in his country. He believed in his abilities. He even believed in the Silver Flame. During their time in Thelanis, Lei had seen a fraction of that confidence return. It was as if something opened within him, releasing a spirit long trapped inside. He laughed, and instead of being sardonic, he actually seemed pleased. "Fine," he said. "What do we have to lose?" With a new light in his eyes, he took his place between her wings, and Lei felt renewed joy.

Buoyed by that emotion, Lei took to the air. Flying was second nature to her. The knowledge lay *in* her body, the instincts just beneath the surface of her mind. The sensation of the wind against her scales thrilled her, and for a moment she forgot about the people clinging to her back. She felt a force above her, a beacon calling to the dragon's blood within. She rose up along the edge of the Ring of Siberys, basking in the radiance of the stones. Only then did she remember her passengers and mitigate the angle of ascent.

"Where are you going?" Daine called, his voice barely audible over the wind.

Lei didn't try to answer. In truth, she didn't even know. The call was impossible to resist.

She saw it. The largest shard yet, the size of a castle. A hole gaped in one side, the mouth of a vast cavern. Lei dove into the tunnel beyond. The crystal walls pulsed with faint light, but a brighter spark shone ahead, a flame at the heart of the stone.

And flame it was. At last she flew into a wide chamber, hundreds of feet across. A great draconic paw rose up in the center, crystal talons curved toward the ceiling. Fire rose from the claw, a pillar that seemed to draw in heat instead of releasing it. Smaller lights were scattered across the walls of the chamber, hundreds of tiny sparks. But the great column was the force that had called to her, of that Lei had no doubt.

Lei settled on the floor of the cavern and folded her wings. The moment her talons touched the floor, the sparks along the walls burst into full flames. The central fire changed color, becoming intense silver-white, and a powerful odor of fresh rain filled the room. The flames formed the head of a massive dragon, a mighty wyrm with horns curving back on each side of its head, and long, frilled ears. A ridge beneath its chin gave the impression of a beard.

"Who comes among us?" it said, and the chamber shook with the sound. "You are no child of Siberys!"

"No," Daine called, sliding down from Lei's back. "We come in search of knowledge."

The burning silver dragon looked down, seeming to notice Daine for the first time. "Let the pretender abandon her false form, and then we may consider your request."

With some regret, Lei raised the pattern in her mind and dissolved the enchantment. Her muscles burned as she shrank to her original form, her scales becoming cloth and armor once more. A moment later she was on her hands and knees on the floor. Physically, she was healthy enough, but she felt a terrible void within. Summoning the energy had taken more from her than she had anticipated.

The central fire became an intense sapphire blue, and the shape twisted and changed. The new dragon had deep, sunken eyes, and a single horn in the center of its snout.

"Intriguing," it boomed, gazing down at them. "A traveler, and a most unusual one at that. What is it you seek, that you would dare disturb our rest?"

A month ago, Daine would have turned to Lei. A year ago, Jode would have been the voice of the group. Now, Lei saw the strength in Daine that had long been in hiding. It was Captain Daine who strode forward and gazed up into the fire. "The Dreaming Dark is gathering its might in the heart of Dal Quor. The balance of the planes is shifting. We were sent to this place by one who believed that you could guide us in the battle that lies ahead."

"And to what end do you fight?"

"To protect our land—the world of your birth—from the forces of nightmare."

The flame shimmered through a spectrum of color, the shape wavering like true fire, before settling once more into the great blue dragon. "You are bold, traveler. And you speak the truth. An army of nightmares gathers in the very heart of Dal Quor, and with every passing moment, the planes move closer to the vital alignment. Yet all hinges on one piece: the crystal moon, which lies under guard in the Tower of a Thousand Teeth."

"What must we do?" Daine said.

"You must find a path to the tower that will not take you through the host of horrors assembled on the plains. And you must find the key to shatter the crystal moon, to restore the imbalance of old. Both lie in a place of pain, a memory forgotten, a battle you have fought a hundred times. It is a dangerous road, but the only one that leads where you must go."

Daine considered this, and then he nodded. "Very well. I thank you for your wisdom, great eidolon."

"Our business is not yet done," the burning dragon said. Its voice shifted, and with it, color and form. Dragons of copper and bronze, fierce red and baleful green. Lei caught a glimpse of a vast dragon skull formed from fire as white as bone, just before the flame shifted to black deep as any shadow. "The way has been prepared. Take our gift, and walk the world once more."

The shimmering dragon's jaws opened wide, and it *breathed*. A prismatic column of flame engulfed Daine, and his scream echoed across the chamber.

CHAPTER 29

THE FRINGES
DAL QUOR

Pierce charged across the cavern, intending to slam into Daine and push him out of the flames. For all his speed, Pierce wasn't fast enough. The brilliant fire faded, and as it did, so did the chamber around him. Crystal walls dissolved like sand blowing in wind, and by the time Pierce reached Daine's fallen form, they were back in the desert, and the Ring of Siberys was nowhere to be seen.

Lei and Jode knelt over Daine, Jode pressing forward to bring his healing touch to bear. He reached for Daine, then paused in confusion.

Daine was unhurt. Despite the scream and the fury of the flames, there were no burns or any other signs of injury. Shira swiftly confirmed the evidence of their eyes, and almost on cue, Daine stirred, pushing himself up with one arm.

"Thanks for the gift," he groaned. He shook his head, blinking several times. "Next time, just give me the advice."

"*Daine!*" Lei dropped to the ground and wrapped her arms around him. "Are you hurt?"

"Don't think so," he said, his voice stronger with every word. "The pain . . . agonizing, but now . . ." He slowly stood up, surprise entering his voice. "I feel . . . good. Better than before."

There has been an infusion of spiritual energy, Shira informed Pierce. *At this time, I am unable to determine the precise nature of this phenomenon or what effects it will have.*

Jode reached up and took Daine's hand. "Yes," he said. "You *are* stronger than before. It seems the dragons gave you a gift, after all."

Daine looked down at Jode. "You said we had power. What sort of power? If we're going to war, I need to know what resources are available."

"I don't know exactly," Jode said. "Our strength comes from our unity, and I've been here on my own. But if we're together, close to one another, you should be able to overcome the limitations of the physical world. In Dal Quor, anyone can do this to a limited degree. This is a world defined by imagination. But we have the strength of two." He looked at Daine with an appraising gaze. "And now, perhaps more. The most important thing is to believe. You're as fast and strong as you can imagine. I'm afraid you'll find it's difficult to shed your belief in your own limitations. Just try. You'll be surprised by what you can do."

"What about this?" Daine drew his dagger, a weapon of plain steel. "Why does Pierce have that golden flail, while I have this old thing?"

"We arrived in a dream plucked from your memories. You have the armor and weapons you had at that time."

It was true. Daine was wearing a shirt of plain steel chainmail and a gray cloak pinned with a brooch bearing House Deneith's chimera seal.

"Concentrate," Jode said. "Remember the moment at which you left Eberron, what you wore, what you carried."

Daine closed his eyes, and his armor changed. Within moments he was wearing the gifts he had received from the faerie queen, and the dagger in his hand was Cannith adamantine. He opened his eyes and shook his head in amazement. "How far can we take this?" He closed his eyes again, but this time there was no change that Pierce could see.

"It's easy to reclaim your memories," Jode said. "It may be possible to create something new, but I haven't been able to manage it yet, and I've been here longer than you."

Daine opened his eyes. "This will have to do, then." He looked at the desert around them. "I see we're back where we started. Where do we go from here?"

"The dragon told us of a path," Pierce said. "A place of pain, a memory forgotten, a battle you have fought a hundred times."

"What battle have we fought a hundred times?" Lei said. "We spent that one summer fighting Valenar, but not in one place."

"Not you," Daine said, a smile spreading across his face. "The dragon was speaking to me. And there is one battle that I have fought a hundred times and more, and a memory we have all forgotten. Jode, can you help me find a path?"

"Certainly," Jode said, holding out his hand. "Where are we going?"

"Keldan Ridge," Daine said. "And this time, we finish the battle."

* * * * * * *

They walked across the desert, and the world slowly changed around them, becoming more like Cyre with every minute that passed. Perhaps this was normal for the others; perhaps reality always shifted in dreams. But Pierce had never had a dream, and it was disconcerting to see trees sprout from barren earth and day turn into night. Pierce had his greatbow in his hands, an arrow nocked to the string, and he did his best to maintain awareness of the surroundings, searching for any sign of enemy motion, as he had done on countless patrols since the time of his forging. But how could he be expected to prepare against an enemy when the land itself refused to hold one shape?

Pierce was still coming to terms with the flail he'd drawn from within, and the newfound capabilities of his quiver. Like Lei's satchel, the space inside was larger than it appeared. In fact, there were two pockets, a narrow space filled with arrows, and the larger area that held the flail—and, as it turned out, could hold his bow. It was strange to think that he'd had this capability all along and never known it. He wondered if other secrets lay hidden within his frame.

"Sovereign lords," whispered Lei.

Pierce had little use for wonder. He tried to analyze every situation, evaluating it from a tactical standpoint, searching for the threats hidden within. Yet the sight before him was enough to give him pause.

They stood on the edge of Keldan Ridge. Fires burned in the valley below, smoke rising from the shattered airship and torn tents. Corpses littered the field, Cyran soldiers intertwined with the warforged they'd fought that night. Pierce had no memory of how this battle had ended, but the beginning was fixed in his mind. The cries of the wounded. His comrades in arms—his friends—being butchered by these bizarre constructs. He remembered how those who survived the initial assault had looked at him, the fear in their eyes, as if they blamed him for the actions of the strange soldiers. The memory was strong, but Pierce had never dreamed, and he'd never thought to see this place again.

"There," Daine said, pointing. A small group of soldiers made their way down the distant hill where the Cyrans had built their redoubt. It was hard to see much detail at such a distance, but Pierce could see the long wooden poles they carried—small trees, stripped of their limbs.

"It's just as I dreamed it," Daine said. "Lei, you set up a siege staff in the center of the valley—"

"I can't build a siege staff," Lei said, her gaze on the descending soldiers.

"I know. But the enemy didn't. They sent out their soldiers to engage you. Jode, Krazhal, Kesht, and I used the confusion to enter the base. The tunnel should be . . . *there*. It's concealed behind an illusion, but the earth is worn down around the entrance."

"And what is inside this base?" Pierce said.

"I don't know," Daine replied. "In my other dreams, I never made it very far. All we know is that we somehow ended up on the Dorn Plateau by morning. Perhaps tonight we'll find the answer."

"Look, that's me," Lei said, pointing at the soldiers setting up the weapon in the center of the field. "You can see the green."

"I told you," Daine said. "Now we wait for the soldiers to emerge, and then we make our way into the base."

Pierce studied the soldiers. He couldn't see himself among them, but that was hardly surprising. Surely he was in hiding, and at this distance, Pierce's talent for stealth was enough to conceal him from his own keen eyes. He felt the faint tug of curiosity—What had happened that night?—but concern for his friends was by far the stronger emotion. What dangers lay within the hidden complex?

Pierce.

It was Shira's thought. It was unusual for her to address him by name. Typically her thoughts simply flowed into his mind as if they were his own.

I have withheld tactical data from you, and for that I apologize.

A few warforged scouts emerged from the tunnel. Each one was slightly different; some were lopsided, some covered with spikes. One seemed terribly familiar—it was one of the bodies of Hydra, the warforged he'd met in the service of Harmattan!

Pierce raised his bow, but Daine held him back with a gesture and snapped, "No! This is is just the beginning. We've got to wait for the rest to emerge. Don't do anything without my orders."

Pierce reluctantly lowered his bow. *What have you concealed?* he thought.

My ability to maintain the link to this world is of limited duration. In time, you and Lei will be forced back to Eberron.

What are the parameters? Pierce thought. *When will we be able to return to this place?*

You will not. When this is over, I will no longer exist.

"What?" Pierce said. Surprise and concern caused him to speak aloud, and the others turned to look at him.

"Pierce?" Lei said.

The fey spirit you dealt with told you the truth. My people learned that our world was going to change into something unknown—and, we feared, something horrible. We could find no way to stop this turning of the age, and we acted with desperation. The sphere you found was built to be an anchor for my spirit, a shield from whatever changes occurred on Dal Quor. We made the first of your kind to serve as our soldiers, and in time, our bodies. But our knowledge came too late, and the balance of the planes was broken before more of my kind could make the transition. And I was locked away.

"But what does this have to do with your death?"

You do not understand. I exist only because I severed all ties with Dal Quor. To bring you here, I had to reestablish that connection. I am a spirit of Dal Quor, bound to the plane, but I do not belong in this age. I can feel the power at the heart—this Dreaming Dark you have spoken of—pulling at me, changing what I am. I can resist, but not forever. Soon it will pull me away, and recreate me in its own image.

Pierce was at a loss for words. He'd only possessed Shira for a few days, and she had always been a passive presence in his mind. Only now did he realize just how comforting that presence was, how much he enjoyed the companionship, and the knowledge she shared with him.

What if you leave now?

No. It is too late. It was too late the moment I touched this world again. I knew what would happen, Pierce. And more than any other creature, I can assure you that this fight is worthwhile. I can feel what my beautiful world has become, and it is a horror. Hold this line. Keep this Dreaming Dark from breaking its chains. And in time, the age of light will return again.

"Now!" Daine said. A squad of motley warforged soldiers was making its way across the valley, toward the Cyran camp. Daine started down the hill, Lei and Jode behind him.

Pierce was not made for tears. His eyes were solid crystal. As he raised his bow and followed his comrades, his sorrow seemed to be trapped within him, like steam seeking release.

Feel no pain, Shira thought, *for I do not. I fought this fate for thirty thousand years, and now it is time to accept it. I am blessed, for you have given me one final chance to see the light before my journey into darkness. Cherish your companions and the time you have, and I thank you for what you have given me.*

Pierce had no response. He fought back the sorrow as they approached the tunnel entrance. Battle lay ahead, and he needed to be calm and detached.

And he wanted to hit something.

CHAPTER 30

KELDAN RIDGE
DAL QUOR

A smile lit Daine's face. He was about to challenge an army of demons to determine the fate of the world, and he was grinning from ear to ear. Despite the madness of their quest, he felt better than he had in years. He'd spent the last year as a haunted man. Jode's death, the mystery of Keldan Ridge, the horror of the Mourning—all of these weighed heavily on his soul. Now Jode was at his side, the answers to Keldan Ridge lay ahead, and if he couldn't save Cyre . . . well, he had a chance to save Eberron itself. A fool's quest? Perhaps. But this time, he'd succeed or die in the effort.

Beyond this newfound confidence, Daine was amazed by his own strength and stamina. Once, descending the ridge would have proven a challenge. Now, it felt like child's play. He found that he felt even better when he was close to Jode. If the halfling was within a few arm's lengths, Daine felt swifter, more coordinated, and his every sense seemed sharper . . . almost as if he were adding Jode's strengths to his own. And all of his abilities were enhanced yet again by the breath of the draconic eidolon. He felt as if a fire raged within him, an endless pool of energy. When he fought his first battle at Keldan Ridge, Daine didn't know about the Mourning. He didn't know that it was the last night of his service to Cyre. Today, he knew exactly what was at stake, and if he died in dreams, he would take a few nightmares with him.

"There it is," Lei said. She was wearing the goggles she'd been given by Thelania, and the lenses shimmered in the moonlight. "There's a door on the other side of the illusion."

"I know," Daine said. "Krazhal blew it open. Once inside, we set secondary charges so we could seal off the exit if needed. I can only assume that those blast disks were never detonated, since we made it out alive."

"Hmm," Lei said, adjusting the lenses on her goggles. "I've never much cared for explosives. It's going to be tricky working through the illusion, but I should be able to get it open."

"Keep watch," he told Pierce and Jode. "We didn't encounter any resistance going in, but obviously history isn't going to repeat itself perfectly." A curious thought occurred to him. "Jode, are *we* going to show up here? If we'd waited, would Krazhal have opened the door?"

"Anything's possible, but it's unlikely," Jode said. "Essentially, we're in your dream. Since you're already here, and breaking in at that, there's no reason for you to appear again."

Daine shook his head. "Dreams."

"Got it," Lei said. She stepped forward, into what appeared to be rough hillside, and vanished. Daine signaled the others and made his way through the illusion.

The hallway was exactly as he remembered. Bare stone, just tall enough for a warforged juggernaut to make his way through, spheres of cold fire set at distant intervals, shedding faint illumination throughout the hall.

"I know we didn't encounter any danger in the tunnel itself," Daine said quietly, "but I can't remember what came after. Jode, when we first came here, I sent you to scout ahead. What do you remember?"

"There's a sort of barracks up ahead," Jode said. "Empty now. I came back to report to you, and that's all I can remember."

"Then from this point on, we go quiet and careful. Given the presence of the warforged, we have to consider the possibility of magical countermeasures. Lei, I'll need you watching for glyphs, blast disks, or anything else." *That would have been Krazhal's job*, he thought. *I wonder how well he fared.*

"Pierce, bring up the rear. If we get more space, move to the side. If you see a clean bowshot, take it."

"So we assume all motion is hostile?" Pierce said.

"Have you forgotten the battle, Pierce? Did you see the corpses? Whoever built this place is responsible for the deaths of all those soldiers, and who knows what else?"

"Remember, it's only a dream," Jode said.

"And if it's drawn from my memories, then this is our chance to finally make these bastards pay for what they did."

Lei nodded, her expression grim. "Let's go, then."

She adjusted her goggles as she moved forward, and something occurred to Daine. *How does she know what those goggles do?* The lenses were a gift from Thelania, but Daine never saw Lei put them on while they were awake. Now they were dreaming she was wearing them, apparently to some useful effect, but if the powers of their weapons were based on their own memories, how could this work?

Daine shook his head. He had his sword and his dagger, and that was all he needed. The rest of this dreaming could go to Dolurrh, for all he cared.

They'd moved less than fifty feet down the hall when Lei raised her hand. *Danger!* She knelt, making a few passes over the ground, and when she stood, she had a blast disk in her hand.

One of Krazhal's blast disks.

Daine realized—this was where the dwarf had set the charge to bring down the tunnel. He glanced back at Jode. *How was this possible?*

"It's part of the environment," Jode whispered. "You knew it would be there. I suggest we move past and let Lei reset it."

"I'm not a sapper," Lei said. "I can place it, but not to do maximum damage."

"Lady Lei, I seriously doubt that it matters," Jode said quietly. "It's not even real. It exists only because it has a role to play, and if it's supposed to bring down the tunnel, I suspect your skill in placement won't be the deciding factor."

"What if I just keep it?" Lei whispered.

"I think it's better if we don't find out."

Daine nodded. "Enough. We move on. Replace the disk behind us."

They emerged in a large chamber. As Jode had suggested, it was a barracks of sorts . . . a barracks for warforged. There were no beds, no tables. The warforged needed no rest. Instead, the room was littered with the tools of war. Weapon racks were largely empty, but a few swords and maces hung from the walls, along with quivers of arrows. A small forge filled the room with heat, and hammers and tongs lay scattered around it. There were no molds, nothing that would serve to create new weapons. This was simply a repair station, where warforged could remove the wear of battle.

Daine gestured. *Keep moving.* Doubt gnawed at the back of his mind. What if there was nothing to find? What if this place was simply an outpost for the warforged now on the battlefield? Could he and Jode have explored and left? No, he concluded. Because Krazhal and Kesht didn't survive the night.

Lei led them through the barracks and down a hall. The smell of molten steel filled the air, mingled with another scent. Sap? Burning wood? They came to the entrance of the next chamber, and Lei stopped short in amazement.

They stood on a wide platform at the top of a flight of stairs, with at least a hundred steps leading down to the floor of the hall. The chamber was a vast sphere, with walls of polished black marble covered with lines and sigils, complex engravings that pulsed with crimson light. But it was the object in the center of the chamber that took his breath away. It was a pillar of black marble, but it was neither smooth nor uniform in shape. Rather, it looked like the trunk of an ancient tree, gnarled and twisted, with patterns of red light in place of the lines of bark. It was studded with glowing stumps, as if limbs had been severed with a perfect blade. The base of the pillar was hidden in a radiant pool. Fibrous tendrils—massive roots—rose from this pool and spread out across the floor, each terminating in a stone pod.

"It's a creation forge," whispered Lei. "This is what House Cannith uses to produce warforged."

"So whoever's running this place was using this to

make the warforged army?" Daine said.

"They must be," Lei said. "But only one who bears the Mark of Making can use a creation forge."

"So . . . rogue heirs? Or was your house creating an army for its own ends?"

Lei shook her head. "It still doesn't make sense. There's no practical reason to produce such a diverse range of warforged. The labor and resources required to create the variety of designs we saw on the battlefield would be immense, and to what end?" She squinted down at the forge. "And the colors, the patterns . . . there's something strange about this forge. I want to take a closer look."

"Then let's—"

Daine never finished the sentence. He'd been blinded by the spectacle of the forge, and he'd allowed their easy entry to make him overconfident. Black metal covered the warforged, and he was all but invisible against the chamber wall—until he moved. All Daine saw was a blur of motion, followed by a sickening crunch and a cry of pain as the construct smashed into Lei and sent her tumbling down the stairs.

The construct had a hunched, apelike posture. His arms were long and powerful, and he ran on all four limbs. His head and face were similar to Pierce's, except for the mouth; he had a massive hinged jaw with blades fused along the rim, and this was gaping wide as the construct lunged at Daine.

Daine yearned to follow Lei, but if she was injured there was nothing he could do for her. He needed to clear a path so Jode could reach her. Was this when Krazhal died? he wondered. It was clear this creature wouldn't fall easily, but right now Daine just wanted him to move. He lashed out with his blade, catching a ringing blow on the creature's head; as he expected, it barely left a mark, but it drew the metal monster's attention.

"Come on!" Daine cried, darting back a few steps.

His plan worked all too well. The warforged charged. It was the very move Daine wanted the construct to make, but he'd underestimated his opponent's speed. The metal beast crashed into him, throwing him back to the floor. Light filled the room—*Pierce's flail*—but the warforged monster was already towering over Daine, iron fists descending to crush flesh and bone.

No.

Once, Daine might have been too slow to evade the construct's blows. In another time, another place, this might have been the end. Not here. He could feel the dragonfire in his blood, feel his anger and his concern for Lei, and it gave him strength and speed he'd never imagined possible. The warforged struck bare stone, scarring the finish. Daine was already standing, moving behind the creature, lashing out with sword and dagger. Pierce was at his side, and the enemy construct staggered beneath the blows of the glowing flail. But the fight was far from over.

For all his newfound strength, Daine's sword was not the most effective weapon against the armored bulk of the iron beast. The construct turned his back on Daine, smashing Pierce with both fists. Pierce was stunned by the impact, and the enemy warforged grabbed him by both arms and lifted him off the ground. The construct's intention was clear. He was going to tear Pierce limb from limb.

"*No!*" Dropping his sword, Daine gripped the hilt of his dagger with both hands and drove it into the construct's back. No mundane metal could withstand the adamantine blade, and the dagger sunk deep. Calling on every ounce of his dream-inspired strength, Daine pulled down on the blade, carving a deep gouge where a human would keep his spine. For a moment there seemed to be no effect, and Daine could hear the tendrils snapping in Pierce's joints. Then a shudder ran through the frame of the iron beast. He fell forward, collapsing on top of Pierce.

"Pierce? *Pierce!*" Daine struggled to push the beast off his companion. The dead construct shifted, and then fell to the side.

"I . . . am functional," Pierce said. He rose slowly, one arm hanging at an awkward angle. "I thank you for your aid, Captain."

"Everyone in one piece?" Jode's voice rose from below. "We've got a little problem down here."

Daine cursed. *Quiet and careful. Could I have made myself any clearer?*

He pulled his dagger from the ruined construct. "If you can use your bow, get it out," he said to Pierce. He headed for the forge, taking the stairs two and three at a time.

Lei stood by the central trunk, studying the stone pillar, while Jode followed the path of one of the roots.

"What are you *doing?*" Daine grabbed Lei by the arm and whirled her around. She seemed unharmed by her fall—thanks, most likely, to Jode—and Daine's anger warred with his relief.

"Examining the forge," Lei replied.

Daine expected more from her. Lei had led a sheltered life, and when they'd first met she was certainly naïve and arrogant, all too careless with her own safety. The war had changed her, and he'd come to rely on her courage and intelligence. But to indulge her love of research in the midst of an enemy stronghold, while Pierce was injured . . .

"Pierce needs help, now!"

Lei pulled away from him and turned back to the trunk. "You don't understand. The forge—"

"—will wait," Daine said, taking her arm again. "I need Pierce repaired *now*. The enemy could return at any time, and—"

The lights went out, and the room fell into utter darkness.

"Too late," Lei said.

Crimson light filled the room. The central pool and every line on the wall that had been glowing before now burned with a blinding radiance. Daine threw up his hand to shield his eyes. A vast roar filled the hall, the sound buffeting Daine and driving out all other thought.

Daine barely realized when the sound and lights faded. His head was pounding, his vision scarred by the terrible light. He could see movement around him, shadowy shapes. He raised his sword, but his reflexes were still scattered. He felt a chill in his back, a burst of cold that spread out through his muscles, freezing him in place.

Then his vision returned. He was surrounded by warforged, at least a half-dozen of them, every one different. Some were unarmed, while others had spikes, claws, or other weapons merged into their limbs. The pods ringing the forge . . . Daine saw that they were hinged like coffins, and that they were open.

"Well, this is a surprise."

The voice came from behind him. Daine tried to

turn his head, but the magic holding him in place had paralyzed every muscle. He couldn't even speak.

A man walked in front of him, a tall, lean man in a robe of shifting colors. His wavy red hair was streaked with gray, and his green eyes were hard as stone. He reached out and took hold of Daine's chin, turning his head to study him.

"Daine of House Deneith, isn't it? Now captain in the Cyran army?" The stranger's voice was cold, and there was something terribly familiar about it. "Tell me, Daine, what have you done with my daughter?"

CHAPTER 31

His creation forge was strange, like no design Lei had ever seen. She'd never been trained to operate a creation forge. The position of forgemaster was one that needed to be earned. But while she had no hands-on experience with these artifacts, she'd spent her childhood learning all she could about them. Living in a warforged foundry, it was hardly surprising that she'd be fascinated by the forges. One touch was all she'd needed to see that the forge was in the final stages of a production cycle. She'd tried to interface with the pillar, hoping she could find some way to disrupt the energies within. Even if Daine had left her alone, it was a hopeless task. She'd never seen anything so complex.

Knowing what to expect from the forge, Lei was able to cover her eyes in time to preserve her vision. But she could do nothing about the overwhelming noise. Struggling to stay on her feet, she reached down and pulled the darkwood staff from her satchel. Keeping her eyes tightly closed, she leaned on the staff, drawing comfort from its presence.

At last the thunder faded. Lei opened her eyes, but just as she feared, the containment pods were open and warforged soldiers were emerging from each one. In a traditional Cannith facility, these newborn soldiers would be confused, requiring direction and instruction. Not so the warforged of Keldan Ridge, who seemed to have a clear purpose in mind: apprehend the intruders.

Daine was dazed. Jode was nowhere to be seen. Pierce, by her side, loosed an arrow from his bow, burying the shaft in the leathery throat of a warforged scout.

They're warforged, Lei thought. I know how to fight warforged.

She readied the necessary patterns of magic in her mind, infusions that would shatter and destroy whatever construct she touched. She reached out for the nearest warforged—and everything went numb. She was frozen. Paralyzed. Pierce had drawn his flail, which was raised above his head, but he was frozen too, as still as a statue.

A panel opened in the wall of the chamber, a hidden door that had escaped her cursory search. A man stood silhouetted in the light, a slender wand held in each hand. He stepped into the light, and Lei saw his face.

Father!

Lei struggled to speak, but every muscle was paralyzed. There could be no mistake. This was Talin d'Cannith. There were a few new lines on his face, a little more gray in his hair. In place of the traditional blue uniform of the Cannith forger, Talin wore a glamerweave robe alive with shifting colors, and a leather harness lined with tools and wands. For a moment she thought this image was plucked from *her* dreams, but over the last year, whenever she'd seen her parents in her visions, they'd always been young. This was Talin as he might be today.

What was going on?

Had her parents been at Keldan Ridge all along?

A warforged soldier followed Talin out of the hidden room, a lean figure with mithral plating, armed with longsword and shield. Compared to other warforged of Keldan Ridge, he was remarkably normal. In fact, he reminded Lei of Pierce. There was something familiar about him, something nagging at Lei's mind, but at this distance, she couldn't identify it.

"Well, this is a surprise." Talin tucked one of his wands into his harness and walked past Lei without a second glance. He stopped in front of Daine, examining his face. "Daine of House Deneith, isn't it? Now captain in the Cyran army? Tell me, Daine, what have you done with my daughter?"

I'm right here! Why didn't he recognize her? Or was there something wrong with her? Had she been corrupted in his eyes?

Whatever the thought behind it, Talin's question was rhetorical. Lei could see that Daine was paralyzed as well. As a result, Talin must have been quite surprised when a voice rang out across the chamber.

"You're asking the wrong question."

Jode stepped out from behind a containment pod, as cheerful as ever. Talin brought his remaining wand to bear on the halfling, and Jode raised his hands.

"You're looking for Lei, aren't you?" Jode said. "If so, you'd be wiser to ask what *you've* done to her."

"Explain yourself, halfling," Talin said.

"Lei is on the field above us, fighting these soldiers of yours. By now, she may be dead. And if so, who's to blame? Daine—or you?"

Lei knew Jode. He was buying time, trying to learn what he could while he waited for the paralyzing magic to fade. And she knew Daine. Right now, her father had his back to Daine, and as far as Daine was concerned, this was the man responsible for the death of his soldiers. If Daine broke free, he'd strike to kill. She struggled against the spell, to no avail; her muscles might as well have been made of stone.

Then she felt the others, rising within her.

First came Darkheart, the staff stirring in her hands. The bond was weak, but the spirit was there. Darkheart's life had been a prison, and now she was bound within this splinter of wood. She wanted freedom more than anything, and she let this desire spill into Lei, adding her passion to Lei's flagging willpower. Darkheart wasn't alone. Now Lei felt a second presence, a voice in her mind. Pierce.

Fight, my sister. The thought was strong and calm, conjuring memories of all the times Pierce had fought at her side and shielded her from harm. *This is your battle, and my strength is yours.*

Once again, Lei laid her will against the magic that held her paralyzed, and the spell shattered against the combined resolve of her allies.

She was nearly too late. Daine broke free just as Lei did. Another instant, and his dagger would be buried in her father's back.

"No!" Whether it was the magic of dreams or sheer determination, Lei forced herself to move faster than Daine. Her staff snaked out, catching him off-guard and sending him tumbling to the ground, cursing.

The room erupted into chaos. Talin raised his wand, and Lei knocked it from his grasp. The warforged burst into motion, but the spell had finally broken, and

Pierce and Daine were ready for battle. These warforged were more skilled in battle than the typical newborn, but Pierce and Daine were true veterans. Lei was confident that they could hold their own, at least for a few moments.

"Father!" she said. "What are you *doing*? I'm right here!"

Talin met her gaze, and she saw only confusion in his eyes. Then she realized. *This is Daine's dream. Drawn from his memory. I wasn't there.* Perhaps she was playing the role of Krazhal. Perhaps he couldn't see her at all. But as far as he was concerned, his daughter was still out on the battlefield.

Then a new voice echoed across the room. "Stop, all of you! There is terrible danger!" Strangely, it seemed to come from both sides of the room at once, from the top of the stairs and from Talin's hidden chamber. Talin's eyes widened, and Lei realized that she'd heard two voices, almost but not quite identical—two voices speaking in perfect unison. Her voice, and that of her mother.

Lei followed her father's surprised gaze, and for a moment she saw *herself*, running down the stairs, a blast disk in her hand—the disk left at the tunnel, which she must have disarmed. Pierce was right behind her, his armor marred by the wounds of battle. For a moment, she was too stunned to act. And in that moment, the second Lei seemed to dissolve, fading into a column of light and flowing *into* her. A rush of memories flooded her mind. Building the false siege staff, struggling to hold the position against the warforged, the terrible discovery that forced her and Pierce to chase after Daine, and her shock when she saw her father in the hall.

"Lei!"

This time three voices spoke at once. Her father, surprised yet still cool and calm. Daine, confused and distressed. And her mother, whose voice held both fear and joy. Around them, the battle had come to a halt, as the warforged obeyed the orders of their mistress. Only one still held himself at battle readiness . . . the tall soldier with the greatsword, Pierce's twin.

Talin placed his hands on his daughter's shoulders and stared into her eyes. But when he spoke, it was to her mother. "What is it, Aleisa?" he said. It was only then that Lei remembered the vision she'd seen after falling into the river, when her father had seemingly incapacitated a young Lei with a touch. If she tried to pull away, could he strike her down?

Would he?

"There's a wave of magical energy coming from the heart of Cyre, and the power is astonishing. We've only got minutes before it strikes." Now Aleisa was next to Lei, and she pushed Talin's hands off her daughter. "Go see for yourself."

Talin strode away, and the tall soldier followed him. Daine started to speak, but Jode kicked him in the foot and he closed his mouth.

"Just look at you, my daughter," Aleisa said. She glanced over at Pierce. "And you, by her side. It is good to see that a few things are right in the world. But I fear that this is a poor time for a reunion. Come, quickly."

"Daine—" Lei began.

"Bring him if you must. But put that sword away, boy." Daine glanced at Lei.

"Please," she said, "we need answers. Don't you see? This *is* what happened. And these are my *parents*. I've got to know."

"Fine," said Daine, sheathing his sword and falling

319

in line. "But I don't see how any of this is helping us fight Lakashtai."

Jode hushed him, mending his wounds with his healing touch.

The hidden chamber rivaled anything Lei had seen in the forgeholds of Cannith. Scrying spheres were embedded in the walls, mystically charged crystal displaying images of distant locations or patterns of magical energy. Two tables were lined with wands of wood and crystal, piles of parchment, and all manner of mundane tools. One corner of the floor was covered with a seal painted in silver—a conjuring circle of considerable sophistication.

Aleisa joined her husband. Talin stared into a crystal sphere. A map of Cyre was visible within the orb, with patterns of light playing over the contours. He passed his hands across a dragonshard mosaic, and colors shifted within the shards.

"That's right," Lei said, as the memories of her shadow rose to the surface. "That's what we saw. A wave on the horizon. *Covering* the horizon, moving forward. I told the others to fall back, and we came to find you, to get you out before it struck."

"The Mourning," Jode said.

It was a relief, however small. From the moment she saw her father in this place, Lei had been gripped by a terrible fear—that her parents had been responsible for the destruction of Cyre itself.

"Mother," Lei said, approaching her parents. "What is it?"

"I don't know, Lei. The pattern is so powerful that it's overwhelming any attempt to analyze it, let alone dispel or disrupt it. I don't know who could unleash this level of power."

"Of course you do," Talin said. "I never expected something of this magnitude, but think of the possibilities. Think of what this will do to the people of Eberron."

"Apologies, my husband, but at the moment I'm more concerned with our own fate, and that of our children."

"What are you saying?" Daine said, grabbing Talin by the shoulder. "You *know* who did this?"

The point of a sword flashed in the air, steel slashing Daine's cheek precisely along the path of his scar. It was the warforged soldier that had followed Talin, the mirror to Pierce. He certainly shared Pierce's speed, and his blade was perfectly steady, the point just beneath Daine's eye. Daine carefully released Lei's father, and took a step back from him, watching the warforged with venom in his gaze.

"I told you there's no time for this," Aleisa snapped. She looked into the orb once more. "Captain Daine, by dawn your nation will have ceased to exist. My husband may have his own ideas as to the cause of this, but right now my concern is seeing my daughter safely away from it. And as for you—I'm afraid this war will have a few more casualties."

"But you can keep Lei safe?" Daine said.

"Yes, although sacrifices will need to be made. Talin?"

"Almost complete, beloved. Begin your preparations."

"Very well. Lei, take Fifth and stand by the silver circle." Aleisa looked down at her own crystal mosaic and made a few adjustments, turning a few crystals and replacing others. A tingle of magical energy filled the air.

"Fifth?" Lei said. Her mind whirled . This was happening too quickly. Her father thought he knew who caused the Mourning? And what did this have to do with

321

the creation forge, with the army of warforged?

Aleisa shook her head and pointed at Pierce. "That. You, whatever you call yourself now, take my daughter to the circle." She put a hand on Lei's shoulder. "Trust me. Just go, and we'll explain it all soon."

The unidentified warforged soldier still had his sword out, and he was still threatening Daine. "My lady," he said, and there was something familiar about his voice. "The circle will only transport four beings."

Talin turned to face him. "Indeed. You will have to remain behind with these two captives. The expansion is unpredictable. You may have time to escape."

"I was created to survive, my lord. At any cost."

"And of all of us, Fourth, you have the greatest chance of surviving this disaster. Now do as you're told."

Lei glanced at the silver circle, and the pieces fell into place. It was a teleportation circle, capable of transporting those who entered it to some distant location—a location her parents had no doubt set using the crystals. Such a tool would allow her parents to bring in supplies from across the world, and it helped explain had they could operate a forge in secret. But this was immensely powerful magic, beyond anything employed by House Cannith. Where had her parents come by it? Only then did the rest of the sentence sink in. *Remain behind with these two captives.*

"I can't leave without Daine and Jode," Lei said.

"You certainly can, my daughter." Once again, Talin had a wand in each hand, one leveled at Daine and the other at Lei. "Please don't make this difficult. You and your companion must survive. These two, on the other hand, are most certainly disposable. Now, go to the circle. If I have to paralyze you and carry you, I will."

"My lord," said the warforged soldier, "why do you take Fifth in my place? I have served you personally."

"Do not question me again, Fourth," Talin said. "I have need of Fifth. And I told you, you have the best chance of survival."

"And you have no further need of me?"

"Truly, Fourth? I had higher expectations for you. I did not build you to be some pathetic soldier. There is greatness in you. Perhaps this challenge is what is needed to set it free."

"Perhaps it is." The warforged struck as he spoke. Talin was turning away from him, and the thrust caught the artificer in the back, right along the spine. He struck again before the event had fully registered in Lei's mind, his blade striking low for the liver. Blood spread out along Talin's robe of shifting colors, and the artificer fell to the floor.

It was then, staring at the soldier standing over her wounded father, that Lei realized why the warforged was so familiar to her. It wasn't his body. It was his head. While the rest of his body was covered in mithral, his head was forged from adamantine. Every warforged bore a design on his forehead, a symbol as unique as any fingerprint. Looking at this soldier, Lei remembered where she'd seen his mark before, battered and blackened, but still clearly visible.

Harmattan.

"Damn it, Fifth, *protect my daughter!*" Aleisa cried.

It was too late for Talin. Even as he struggled to rise, Harmattan struck again, two more blows right along the spine. He raised his shield just in time to deflect the descending ball of Pierce's flail. The glowing orb left a scorched dent in the steel, but Harmattan was not perturbed.

"Why do you fight me, little brother?" he called, falling back and taking a defensive stance. Lei realized why he had sounded so familiar . . . the voice itself was far different, but the patterns of speech were those she'd heard back in Xen'drik. He continued to speak as Pierce attacked, deflecting each blow. "This is our time to take destiny into our own hands! This is the will of our true creator. Join me. Bring down the creatures of flesh, and let us leave this place together!"

"Not in one piece," Daine said. Harmattan's attention was focused on Pierce, and he hadn't seen Daine join the fray. Daine sank his blades into the soft space between the joints of Harmattan's armor. The warforged was strong and fast, but he lacked the sheer bulk and stamina of the metal beast they'd fought earlier.

Or so it seemed. Harmattan hissed in anger, and Daine withdrew his blades to parry the blow. From where she stood, Lei could see the injury immediately begin to heal. The root-muscles beneath the armor bound back together. *I was created to survive*, he had said. And in her mind she saw her father holding the warforged head. *This is how you defeat death.*

In that moment she *knew* that Harmattan would never fall to sword or flail. There was only one hope. She forced her way into the melee, ignoring Daine's cry of pain as Harmattan struck him. She ducked past Pierce, reaching out for Harmattan—but she wasn't fast enough. His shield slammed into her, knocking her back and almost to the ground.

Her companions weren't fools, and both realized what she was trying to do. They redoubled their efforts, now not even trying to bring down the warforged warrior, but merely to distract him. Harmattan could repair the damage from Pierce's attacks, but even if it caused no permanent damage, a flail-blow to the face was difficult to ignore. Daine bound Harmattan's blade with his own, preventing the warforged from striking at Lei. All they were doing was buying time, but time was all that she needed. Slipping behind him, she laid her hand on Harmattan's back and let all her rage and fury fall into him. The indignities she'd suffered in Xen'drik, the death of her father, the mysteries that might never be answered. Her fury was a white-hot knife, and she cut at the core of Harmattan's being.

He exploded. Pieces scattered across the room, chunks of root and shards of metal. Lei knew that the Harmattan she'd met in Xen'drik could have reassembled himself even from this state, and she held her breath. But nothing happened. The shards fell to the floor and were still. Lei let out her breath.

"There's no more time." Aleisa was kneeling beside Talin, and her robe was soaked with his blood. "I've set the circle to take you where you need to go. Leave. Quickly."

"Mother . . ." Lei said. She knelt next to her, reaching out to touch her. "I can't just leave you. You don't know what's coming. You don't—"

"I do, my child, more than you know. Talin didn't want it to happen like this, but he knew it was inevitable. All that is flesh must die, after all." She smiled, a weary smile, and kissed her daughter on the cheek. "My work here is done, Lei. As long as you are alive, we will be with you." She stood, holding Lei's hand, and brought her to the circle. When she spoke again, there was something different in her voice, and even her face. It seemed as though she were younger, more like Lei with each passing moment. "Remember, Lei. *It wants to be destroyed.* That is its purpose. Look within, and follow the path."

"Mother?" Lei asked, confused.

Aleisa turned to Daine. "At this moment, you have more power than you know, and it is that power that will take you where you need to be. In this place, you have been bound by your own memories. Where you are going, you will need to use your gift, and to its fullest measure."

"One moment, my lady," Jode said. "Do you mean that you're—"

"There is *no more time!*" Aleisa said. As she spoke, there was a change in the air, a sickly chill that seemed to twist at Lei's flesh and her thoughts. "*Go!*" Aleisa *pushed,* shoving them back into the silver circle. Even as she did, the room behind her began to fill with dead-gray mist.

"*MOTHER!*" Lei cried.

And they were gone.

CHAPTER 32

THE
DREAMING
DARK
DAL QUOR

"This isn't the Dorn Plateau," Daine said.

You have teleported, Shira reported. *You remain within Dal Quor. Your current position . . . is impossible.*

Pierce felt pure astonishment radiating from Shira, an uncharacteristic burst of emotion. *Why?* Their surroundings seemed mundane enough. They were on a plateau, a butte raised high above canyon lands. A lone moon hung above them, full but strangely faint.

You have entered the heart of Dal Quor. No simple spell could allow such motion.

"Clearly history has been altered," Jode said. "I think that much of what we saw actually happened at Keldan Ridge. That would explain Lei's father not recognizing her at first, and why you had as much trouble as you did with the second warforged."

"Fourth," Pierce said.

"As you wish," Jode said. "At the end, the woman was clearly addressing us *now*. She wasn't talking about our history. She must have sent us here . . . 'where we need to go.'"

"And she said she was using Daine's own strength to do it," Pierce observed.

Most likely a reference to the energy of the draconic eidolon, Shira observed. *I underestimated this power. I believe an exponential effect is at work.*

"So why didn't we remember any of it?" Daine said.

"You saw the mist filling the room at the end," Jode replied. "We've seen that mist before, marking the barrier of the Mourning. Perhaps, when it really happened, we were trapped just a little longer, and our amnesia was a result of a brief exposure to the energies of the Mourning."

"Or perhaps Lei's parents made us forget," Daine said. "We still don't know what they were doing there! They—"

Daine paused, and a slight flush reddened his cheeks. Pierce was puzzled. Then he realized that Lei had just watched her parents die, and dream or not, that was surely a difficult experience. Normally she would be in the midst of any discussion on arcane and planar theory, and her silence spoke volumes. In fact, she had wandered away from the others and was walking toward the edge of the plateau.

Pierce and Daine exchanged glances. "Captain," Pierce said, "while I recognize the strength of your feelings, at this moment I believe my presence will offer greater comfort."

Daine sighed. "Go."

Pierce quickly caught up with Lei. She stared out over the barren land far below, all but hidden in the gloom of night. He extended his hand. He wasn't certain if this was the appropriate gesture, but she reached out and clasped it tightly. He said nothing, letting her choose the time to speak.

"I can't think about this right now," she said. Her voice was thick, her cheeks streaked with tears. "This . . . not now. Not with everything else that's at stake."

"I understand," Pierce said. And for once, he did. He felt emotions warring within him, feelings he didn't even know he had. Recognition of Harmattan had been shock enough. Yet there was something else, a stranger feeling. Talin and Aleisa were his parents, too. He'd never known his creators, and he'd never thought such knowledge mattered. But now his mind was full of questions. What expectations did his parents have for him? How had he measured up? What plans had they had for him?

And what did Harmattan mean—*This is the will of our true creator?*

While loss and confusion welled within, there was one bright ember. Lei. His sister. They would face the future together, and if these mysteries could be unraveled, they would find a way.

Lei's grip tightened. "Sovereign Host!" she said, her eyes widening. "Look at the plains!"

Pierce pushed aside his troubled thoughts and looked down at the desert. At first he saw nothing of note. They were high above the plains, and the moon was dim, then he realized . . .

The plains were moving.

There were no campfires below, no lights of any sort, and it took time for Pierce's eyes to adjust to distance and limited visibility. An army spread across the desert below, stretching out as far as the eye could see. Pierce had seen many armies during the Last War, but this was a force drawn from nightmares. Platoons of insect horrors arrayed alongside masses of serpentine tentacles and figures formed of pure shadow. Shapes of strange siege engines rose up into the night, cannons formed of crystal and curved bone. Despite the constant motion, an eerie silence lay across the desert. No light, no sound, just nightmares girding for war.

Daine sprinted over to their position. "What is it?"

Lei pulled her goggles down over her eyes and adjusted the lenses. "There's *thousands* of them," she said. "Tens of thousands. Maybe more. I see . . . circles, glass rings set into the ground, maybe forty feet across."

The legions of Dal Quor prepare for battle. I remember when my people gathered around our gates. Shira's thought was touched with sorrow and shame. *Song filled the air, and our crystal banners made the plain an ocean of stars. We served the great light. We thought ourselves the heralds of glory, perfect embodiments of wisdom. But the people of Xen'drik spurned our guidance and refused to be hosts for our people. And when they would not shield us from our destruction, we turned to war. We struck at their dreams. We tore at the fabric of reality itself. And these horrors down below will do far worse. There is no mercy in them, only malice. I can feel it.*

"Flame," Daine murmured. "We can't fight that."

"We don't have to," Lei said, pushing back her goggles. "All we need to do is find that orb and destroy it. That's what my mother said. She'd send us where we *needed to be*. The only question is what we do now."

"Turn around?" Jode said.

Pierce followed Jode's gaze but saw only stone and sky.

"What are you talking about, Jode?" Daine said.

"There, in the center of the plateau. Can't you see the tower?"

He is correct, Shira said. *There is a force that seeks to deceive your senses, to hide what lies before you. Look beyond the lie.*

Pierce studied the plateau. *A tower,* Jode had said. If there was a tower in this place, what might it look like? He let the image drift into his mind, a dark spire set against the starless sky . . . and it appeared.

A tower of teeth. Four massive tusks reached into the night, supporting a single spire of ivory and raw flesh. Dozens of mouths adorned walls of dark muscle, and the jaws of an ancient dragon stood in place of a gate, grinning at the top of a short flight of stairs.

"What is it?" Daine said, studying the tower. "Is it alive? Can it see us?"

"It is one manifestation of the Dreaming Dark," Pierce said, allowing Shira to speak through him. "As is the stone we stand on. In some ways, the tower will behave like a living creature. Pierce a wall, and it will bleed. But there is no intelligence behind its actions, and it cannot sense our presence."

"It's the Tower of a Thousand Teeth," Lei said. "That's where the dragons told us the orb was hidden."

"So where are the guards?" Daine said. "I don't like this."

Once again, Pierce gave voice to Shira's thoughts. "The guards are all around us, Captain. The quori don't believe that it is possible for anyone to teleport to this place. We are at the heart of an army, and any intruder would have to fight his way through thousands of nightmare spirits. With luck the lords of this realm will have seen no need for additional security."

"Let's not rely on luck," Daine said, as he examined the tower. "It's small, so prepare for close quarters. Pierce, ready your flail. Lei, how are you holding up?"

"Close to the edge," she replied. "Fighting Harmattan took a lot out of me."

"Jode?"

Jode rubbed a hand across the top of his head. "I've got a little more magic in me, I think. Just try not to lose a limb."

Daine nodded. "Lei, get Pierce patched up as best as you can, then take a look at the path. It'd be a fool's death to come this far and then step on a blast disk."

There are no blast disks, or mystical wards of any sort.

"There are no blast disks," Pierce said.

"I'd like to hear that from Lei," Daine said.

He doesn't trust me, Shira thought. *Perhaps he is wise. I can feel the darkness growing within me. But I will die before it turns me against you. And I will die soon.*

Pierce felt a pang of sorrow, but he knew nothing could be done. He could feel Shira's thoughts growing weaker every time she communicated. Once her presence had been as strong as his; now her thoughts were faint echoes in the back of his mind.

Stay close to Lei, Shira told him. *My strength fades quickly, and should you stray too far from her, the connection will be lost.*

Lei finished her work on Pierce and turned her attention to the plateau, taking a few steps in the direction of the tower. "No blast disks, nothing at all," she said. "It's clear from here."

"Then I suggest we get inside," Jode said. "We may be far from that army below, but some of *my* nightmares have wings, and I don't want to be standing here in the open when one of them comes along."

"Agreed," said Daine. He drew his sword, and the Watchful Eye engraved on the hilt flashed in the night. "Pierce, at my side. Lei, directly behind, and watch for wards."

No threats emerged from the darkness as they crossed the plateau; no horrors fell from the sky or rose from the plains below. There was only one problem: opening the dragon's jaws. Teeth and fleshy walls resisted both Lei's magic and Daine's adamantine blade.

This is the dream of the darkness itself, Shira told him. *Force will not avail you here. Only willpower can open the gates. Imagination is the key.*

Daine looked skeptical when Pierce relayed the message, but Jode understood.

"All the pieces are in place," he said. "Daine, I don't understand this power we seem to have, but we are stronger together. Lei's mother said you'd have to 'use your gift to the fullest measure.' I think we can *make* the jaws open."

"Just by thinking about it?" Daine said.

"Just by thinking about it."

"It's worth a try," Daine said. He looked at each of them in turn. "This is it, then. I don't know if we'll all come out of this alive—"

"I doubt I will," Jode said. He sighed. "Sorry, I know, not a moment for levity."

"No, you're right, Jode," Daine said. "You've already sacrificed your life, and now I'm asking you to risk your soul. But look off the edge of that cliff. I thought the Mourning was the worst disaster I'd ever see. But I'll be damned to Dolurrh before I let that horde reach Khorvaire."

He turned to face Pierce. "When I first met you, I knew little about the warforged. I'm ashamed to say I thought of you as an object. A weapon."

"As did I, Captain."

"Tonight, just make it Daine. You've been a good soldier, Pierce. The best I've ever seen. But you've been a better friend, and I count myself lucky to have known you."

"We are equally lucky, Daine," Pierce said. "And I do not intend to let you die tonight."

Daine smiled. He looked at Lei and opened his

mouth to speak, but she kissed him before he could utter a word.

Watching the two, Pierce felt a twinge of envy. For all that he had a sense of touch, he would never know what this moment felt like for them. Then he thought of Indigo, and the pleasure he'd found in her company . . . and simple satisfaction when Lei had held his hand. He might never know what love felt like for a human, but he knew what it was for a warforged.

"Don't tell me goodbye," Lei said, when they broke apart. "I'm not letting you go."

Daine looked into her eyes in silence, and finally turned away. "Well, Jode," he said. He reached down and took the halfling's hand.

And slowly, very slowly, the jaws of the dragon opened wide.

"With me, Pierce," Daine said. And together, they walked into the Tower of a Thousand Teeth.

❋ ❋ ❋ ❋ ❋ ❋ ❋

Entering the tower, Pierce braced for battle. War was his purpose, and he felt a thrill as he prepared to engage the enemy. He'd calculated plans for a half dozen scenarios, based on the number and nature of enemies awaiting them.

But the chamber within the hall was silent and empty.

There were no guards, no beasts out of nightmare—at least, none that he could see. The floor was soft muscle, but Pierce felt the scrape of ivory against his feet. The room was utterly dark, and while Pierce's vision was sharp enough to assure that there was no movement in the room, he could see little else.

A pale light took shape behind him. Lei, binding

cold fire to her gauntlet. Now they could see the room's barrenness. No furniture, no banners, nothing but flesh and tooth. Then Pierce took a good look at the center of the chamber. The floor of the room was one vast mouth. Pierce had just stepped onto the edge of a pointed tooth larger than he was. He didn't know if the maw could open fully, but if it could, they'd all tumble down into whatever lay below.

Daine caught his attention, urging Pierce to move back against the wall, away from the massive mouth. Daine gestured upward. Long fangs protruded from the walls of the chamber, and Pierce saw that they formed a staircase, rising to an opening in the ceiling above them. The tower wasn't that large, and this upper chamber would be its apex. The object of their search must be above.

Unless it lies below, Pierce thought, glancing at the grinning maw stretching across the floor. He thought Shira might respond, but she remained silent.

Daine wrapped his fey cloak around him as he ascended the stairs. He was shrouded in shadows, and Pierce almost lost sight of him. He followed close behind. The long teeth were slippery and felt all too fragile beneath Pierce's feet, but despite his concerns, the stairs held his weight and he ascended into the upper chamber.

Six tusks rose from the fleshy floor of this room, curved pillars of ivory spread in a circle around the center of the chamber. Twice Pierce's height, each was easily wide enough to provide shelter for an enemy. Daine gestured to the right and proceeded to circle slowly to the left, staying close to the wall. Pierce followed the signal, moving carefully along the wall.

Nothing.

The center of the chamber, the space between the tusks . . . there was nothing there. No monsters, no glowing orb, just a mosaic of interlocking teeth, drawn from dozens of different creatures.

Pierce continued to circle the tower. When he rejoined Daine, they could determine their next course of action.

But by the time Pierce reached him, Daine was already dead. His throat had been severed, a deep wound that cut through to the spine, almost decapitating him. Another blow had pierced his heart, puncturing chainmail and going straight through back and chest. His eyes were wide and shocked. Blood flowed from his injuries, but the fleshy floor soaked it all up.

There was no time for fear. Whatever had done this had moved swiftly and silently. Pierce hadn't even heard Daine's body fall to the ground. There would be time to mourn the loss of his captain later. Now he needed to defend the living.

Lei? Pierce had yet to fully grasp the use of the telepathic bond he now shared with Lei, and he wasn't entirely certain how to activate it. *Danger.*

No response.

Keeping his back to the wall, Pierce moved swiftly to the stairwell. He could see the light of Lei's cold fire at the top of the stairs. And as he drew close, he saw a hand in a glowing gauntlet, lying severed on the floor.

Lei!

"You think this is painful?" the voice came from behind one of the ivory pillars. The figure that stepped into view was barely visible, her skin covered with shifting patterns of darkness. "You still have much to learn about pain."

Pierce set his flail whirling, and the golden ball burst into light, burning with a heat as intense as his own fury. Indigo stood exposed before him, and adamantine blades slid from the sheathes in her forearms.

"You cannot be here," Pierce said, anger warring with doubt. "You cannot dream."

"You forget, *brother*," she said. "You tried to bury me in a vault beneath Xen'drik, the same vault from which you plucked your metal companion. Did you think she was the only one?"

Pierce saw the jeweled sphere embedded in Indigo's chest—a sphere almost identical to Shira. *Is this possible?* he thought, but there was no response from within.

"I may be trapped forever in the Monolith of Karul'tash," Indigo continued, slowly circling him, "but I was given one final chance to see that you pay for your betrayal. I told you, Pierce. If I die, she dies with me. And now she has." She spread her arms wide. "So come, brother. Will you not finish what you began?"

"No," Pierce said. His thoughts were in disarray. He could have ensured Indigo's destruction before they left Karul'tash, when he'd allowed her to survive in an inert state. "You do not understand what you have done. The fate of Eberron itself—"

"Means nothing to me," Indigo said. "You saw to that. Why should I care what happens to the world beyond my prison? All I wanted was for you to feel my pain, and that is done. Come, Pierce, let us die in battle. That is all we ever had."

No, Pierce thought. Lei and Daine, presumably Jode— they were all dead. Nothing could be done for them. It was over. What good would another death do?

"Perhaps you should keep this," Indigo said. "Something to remember her by."

She kicked Lei's severed hand across the floor, and it struck Pierce's foot.

And something within him broke.

Pierce was not given to anger. Battle was a matter of careful calculation—until now. Pure rage drew him across the ivory floor, and his flail was a streak of light. Swift as she was, Indigo wasn't prepared for the fury of his assault, and the ball smashed into her chest, denting her armored plates and scorching the cords below. She staggered back, and Pierce raised his flail to finish her. Before he could strike, she flew forward, arms outstretched. Her adamantine blades should have dug into his torso, but he felt no such impact. Instead, a fire spread throughout his body, tearing him apart from within. The agony was terrible—and all too familiar.

Lei! He cried out in his mind, and then pain drove out all thought.

CHAPTER 33

THE
TOWER OF A
THOUSAND TEETH
DAL QUOR

A thought was all it took for Lei to weave cold
fire into her gauntlet, conjuring a faint light to drive
back the shadows. Her eyes widened as she saw the vast
mouth set into the floor. Pierce stood on the very edge
of a tooth, and it was all too easy to imagine that maw
opening wide and swallowing them all.

Daine gave her a questioning look, and Lei pulled
her goggles over her eyes and studied the room.
These lenses were a tool designed to locate and analyze magical auras. If there were magical defenses in
the chamber, the goggles would help her find them.
The lenses were certainly an unusual gift to receive
from a faerie queen. They bore marks of Cannith
design and seemed well worn. Of course, Lei had
seen an identical pair less than a day ago, after she
fell into the river of truth, and saw her young mother
in Xen'drik. Could these goggles have belonged to
Lei's mother? How would they have fallen into the
hands of the Queen of Dusk, and why would she give
them back to Lei?

These questions wouldn't be answered in Dal Quor,
and Lei turned her attention to the task at hand. She

saw no signs of glyphs or wards, and she gave Daine the signal for safety. He in turn gestured to Pierce, and the two warriors ascended the disturbing flight of stairs.

Lei waited at the foot of the staircase. As useful as her glowing gauntlet could be in this darkness, it would certainly draw the attention of anyone on the second floor. She needed to give Pierce and Daine the chance to move away from the stairs before she followed. She glanced over at Jode, and he smiled at her. Despite all the horror around them, she couldn't help but feel a sense of warmth. The four of them were together again, and she felt like nothing could challenge them.

That's enough time, she thought. She started up the rickety stairs, fighting to maintain her balance. She reached out to steady herself against the wall, jerking her fingers back as a tiny set of razor-sharp teeth snapped at her. Step by step. Slowly.

She reached the top of the stairs. It was a welcome change from the flesh and bone of the lower level. The black stone was comfortingly stable beneath her feet. And there was light, spilling from cold fire lanterns lining the long hall. A hallway that was far too long to fit in the tower, at least as it had appeared from the outside. She looked at the nearest lantern, and a chill ran down her spine.

She was in Blacklion. The stairs behind her had vanished, and there was no sign of Jode, Daine, or Pierce.

"This is a dream," she said. "I'm not a fool. None of this is real. You're just drawing images from my mind."

Lei?

Was it a sound? Or just a thought, pressing into the back of her mind?

"This is a dream," Lei said again. She remembered what Jode had told them about the nature of this place, and she tried to imagine the black stone walls fading away. Instead, she heard footsteps far down the hallway, the faint laughter of a little girl. And a cold whisper, echoing across the stone.

We'll have to destroy her.

It was her father's voice, and she couldn't suppress a shiver. "Very clever," she called. "But I began working with illusions when I was a child. You'll have to do more to impress me."

We have no wish to impress you.

Cold fire glittered on the thousands of shards of Harmattan's body, and the razor cloak that spread around him. Just as when she'd first seen him, his head was shrouded in a cloud of mist. Now that darkness settled down into his body, revealing the scarred warforged head . . . the battered remains of his original body.

We only wish to destroy you, little sister.

"Then why don't you?" Lei said. "You're trying to provoke me. Drawing on my memories. Showing me the creature who killed my father. If you want to destroy me, you could have struck me down without saying a word."

I didn't say I wanted to kill you, Lei. I said I wanted to destroy you. You have no idea of the troubles you've caused. To let you die quickly and unaware . . . the time for such mercy is long past.

Lei fought against doubt. Could he be telling the truth? She knew so little about Harmattan. What was he capable of?

"Where are the others?" she said. "Daine? Pierce?"

There, Harmattan said. *That will do. Die now, never knowing their fate.*

She'd forgotten how quickly he could move. His fist was a blur, and she felt flesh tear and ribs break

341

as it smashed into her. The physical force threw her back, but there was something else, a terrible heat that burned her skin.

Harmattan raised his fist for another blow, but before he could strike Lei leapt forward, driving her hands into his chest. She had no idea if she could harm him in this way, but on some level he was still warforged. She could feel a lifeweb before her, and she poured all her energy into it, seeking to shatter Harmattan once more. Only then did she realize—the pattern she sensed was familiar.

Lei!

It was Pierce who was burning in her grasp. Lei released him, her head spinning from her own terrible injuries, and she fell against the ivory floor.

CHAPTER 34

THE
TOWER OF A
THOUSAND TEETH
DAL QUOR

Pierce?" Daine said quietly. The two of them had made their way to the upper chamber, circling around the edge of the room. At first, Daine was merely disappointed. He thought their luck had indeed turned, that they might find the orb unguarded and waiting for them.

When he crossed the chamber and met up with Pierce, his disappointment turned to concern. The warforged ignored Daine's signal and even his words, moving past him and heading back to the stairs.

"He can't hear you." The voice came from behind one of the tusks rising up around the center of the room. And it was a voice that Daine knew well.

"Lakashtai," he said. "And I thought I'd have to fight my way through that army to find you."

"Oh, Daine, did you come looking for me? I'm touched."

Lakashtai walked into the circle of tusks, and her slight smile sent a chill down Daine's spine. She was a creature of dreams, too perfect for nature, her skin snow-white, her hair a dark river flowing down her back, her features sculpted by a craftsman with an eye

343

for beauty but no grasp of emotion. In the faint light rising from the lower chamber, Lashkashtai's green eyes seemed truly to *glow,* and even across the room Daine could feel the force of her personality—her almost irresistible charisma.

Daine didn't hesitate. He lunged, the point of his blade in line with her throat. Lakashtai's response was perfect. She took one long step backward, moving with languid grace, as if she wasn't even concerned about the outcome. But that step was just enough to take her out of Daine's reach. He was drawing back for a second attack when she spoke again.

"Lei!"

One word, but it was enough to stop Daine in his tracks. He kept his sword steady, ready to thrust. "What about her?"

"If you care about Lei and Pierce, I suggest you lower your sword."

"Lei!" Daine called. The light was drawing stronger. Lei was coming up the stairs. "Lei!" he yelled again.

No response. Glancing over his shoulder, Daine saw that Pierce was kneeling, as if examining something on the ground. Lei appeared at the top of the stairs. If she'd heard Daine, she gave no sign of it, nor did she acknowledge his presence. She looked around the room with a confused expression.

"What have you done to them?" Daine said.

"Lower your sword, Captain Daine, or I assure you that you'll find out."

Lakashtai's eyes gleamed in the darkness, and Daine could feel the subtle urge to obey her commands. It was a powerful and insidious effect, and only now did he realize how often she had used it against him in the past. It had little impact on him, but he still had no choice. He lowered his weapons.

"I must admit, I never expected to see warforged here," Lakashtai said, watching as Pierce rose to his feet and Lei walked across the room. "If I'd known this was possible, I could have targeted Lei from the very beginning, and this would have been so much simpler."

"What have you *done* with them?" Daine said.

"Mind your temper, Captain," Lakashtai said. Dark mist played around her feet, shadows clinging to the hem of her black gown. "You're not in your dreams anymore, little Daine. You're in mine. They see what I want them to see."

"And *we* don't. Isn't that interesting?" Jode said. The halfling must have followed Lei; he was leaning against one of the curved tusks. Lakashtai's eyes widened. For her, this was as significant as a shout. "Surprised to see me?"

"That meddling sphinx," Lakashtai said, and her calm façade dropped, revealing the anger below. "I admit, I wondered what had become of you, Daine—why I couldn't touch your mind anymore."

Daine remembered his first dream after drinking the potion in Karul'tash . . . the vision of the dark giant, shattering against the shield of light. "You couldn't match our combined strength."

Lakashtai smiled. "Oh, Daine. Yes, your twin souls are more powerful than I expected. A clever gambit. But now you've delivered yourself into my hands. You may have the strength of two souls, but I am one of the chosen of the Dreaming Dark itself, and this is my place of power. You should have left well enough alone and enjoyed the little time left for your world."

"You're clever," Jode said. "But for all your false

bravery, we're still here. I don't think you can stop us. Give us the crystal moon, and let's be done with this."

Lakashtai laughed, a terrible sound. "You don't think I can stop you? You have no idea, halfling. The Dark has rewarded me for my faithful service, and my power is beyond your imagining. You are alive only because it amuses me . . . and I think I've had enough of you." She looked at Daine and smiled. "Daine, why don't you kill your friend for me?"

"Why would I—"

"Because if you do, I'll let Lei go, and I'll let the both of you wake up and have your last few days together. If not, she dies while you watch. Then I'll kill your friend. And if you're lucky, afterward I'll let you die." She held out her hand, and the darkness rose up to twine around her fingers. "You have to the count of five."

"No," Daine said. "There's no need. You've won."

Images passed through his mind. The vast army outside. Creatures of nightmare, tearing through High Walls and Sharn. And Lei. Lying on a bed in Thelanis, all but dead. The tear in his heart when he thought that he'd lost her.

"Daine—" Jode said.

"I'm sorry." Daine forced all emotion from his mind. He raised sword and dagger, calling on all the speed and strength of the dragonfire that still burned within.

He struck Lakashtai.

For once, Daine caught Lakashtai unprepared. The point of his grandfather's sword disappeared in her throat, while his dagger flashed toward a brilliant green eye. It was swift and brutal, and Daine took no pride in his work. But he could not risk letting her live another moment.

Yet she did. She dropped to one knee, blood spilling

down across her pure white skin. But she did not fall. She opened her ruined eye, and now it was a pool of utter darkness.

In that moment, Pierce lunged at Lei, his flail a streak of light in the shadows. Daine heard a sickening crunch as the ball slammed into Lei's chest, and blood flowed from her mouth as she staggered backward.

"No!" Daine cried. He forced Lakashtai to the ground, striking again and again. Rage overwhelmed all senses. When his vision cleared, his hands were covered with blood, and the life had fled Lakashtai's body. He turned, afraid of what he might see.

Lei must have struck back at Pierce; both were stretched out on the ground. Lei's green jerkin was torn and burnt, and blood flowed from her chest. Half of Pierce's muscle cords had snapped, and his armor plates were pitted, some hanging from his body. Jode knelt next to Lei, and the dragonmark on his head burned with blue light.

Daine was there in an instant, kneeling between the two. "How bad?"

"I . . . am . . . functional . . ." Pierce said, his voice barely a whisper. He raised his head, though he seemed to have difficulty holding it straight. "Lei?"

"I'm doing the best that I can," Jode muttered.

A moment later Lei choked and coughed, blood bubbling along her lips.

"Jode," she said faintly, and Daine's heart soared.

"Yes, Lady Lei," Jode said. "You're not rid of us yet."

Oh, but I will be.

The new voice echoed around them, and Daine couldn't say if it was sound at all, or all in his mind. There was nothing human in that voice. It was cold fear, the force a child sees in the darkness, a horror all the worse for not being seen.

You think killing one body means anything to me? You have no conception of what we are. I am your nightmares, Daine. I am every fear you've ever had, and horrors you've never imagined.

"Shield them, Daine," Jode said, clasping Daine's wrist. "We know we can do it. Don't let her take them again."

Once again, Daine felt warmth flowing from Jode and into him. He could feel the emotions of his friend, his love and his courage. He thought of Lei and Pierce, and he reached out with his feelings, covering them with light. And he turned around.

There was a shadow above Lakashtai's corpse, a mass of pure darkness. Daine could see shapes hidden within—

Lakashtai risen again.

His father with a sword in his hand.

Children slaughtered in the streets of High Walls.

Terror and despair rose within him, and he felt a mad desire to cut his own throat. But Jode was at his side, and Lei and Pierce needed him. He threw his will against the frightful storm, and it abated.

Most impressive. I had so hoped to watch you kill yourselves. But you cannot fight me.

Tendrils spread out from the cloud, serpentine tentacles of solid shadow. Some bore the heads of vicious beasts, while others were tipped with razor-edged blades. They crawled toward Daine and Jode, moving slowly but inexorably, and Daine knew no blade could touch that darkness.

But fire could.

Daine's arm rose up of its own accord, his sword dropping from suddenly nerveless fingers. Energy surged within him—the dragonfire, the gift of the draconic eidolon. The darkness collapsed in on itself, bound in a web of prismatic light. And the shadow howled.

"What are you doing?" Jode whispered.

Daine had no idea. He felt the power growing within him, but it was none of his doing.

You cannot harm me! The voice roared around them. *I am a part of this realm, a part of the darkness itself! I cannot die!*

Daine felt a terrible pain, as if acid were being poured across his back. He could *feel* the dragonmark searing his flesh, and a deep red glow filled the chamber—light from the mark, piercing his armor to fill the room. The agony built with each passing second. And then it exploded. A beam of energy burst out of his chest, a mass of twisted lines. It was as if the dragonmark itself reached out. This bolt smashed into the cloud of darkness, enveloped it, consumed it—and was gone, snapping back into Daine with another wave of pain. All that was left of Lakashtai's spirit was a ball of glowing light—a crystal orb. The sphere fell to the ground and rolled across the floor.

"Moon," Lei said. She rose on one knee, and Jode helped her rise, moving toward the sphere.

"What have . . . you done . . . Captain?" Pierce pushed himself to his feet. "Shira . . . says the spirit . . . is destroyed. Impossible."

"I don't know," Daine said. Every nerve cried out in pain, and his back still burned. Far from fading, the dragonfire presence felt even stronger than before.

"Captain," Pierce said. "Lei and I . . . only moments . . . Shira dies." He staggered toward Lei.

The tower shook.

"What *now*?" Daine said.

Pierce knelt by Lei, who clutched the crystal sphere.

"Your work . . . not unnoticed," he said. "The Dreaming Dark . . . rises."

"I need time," Lei said. The sphere pulsed in her hands, and her face was tight with concentration.

Jode took Daine's hand again. "Just a few more moments, my friend. Let's hold this place together."

The walls shook. Every mouth opened, and a single inhuman howl of rage filled the room. The walls began to distend, twisting outward.

"Imagine," Jode said.

And Daine did. As the tower collapsed around them, he imagined a secure place of shelter. A home. A welcoming fire. The voices of children, coming from below. The walls of flesh and ivory fell away, and only the floor remained. They were caught in the eye of a storm, and all around was howling darkness, a maelstrom of horror.

"Yes," Lei said. *"It wants to be destroyed.* It's a weapon. It was made to shatter, to break the bonds between the planes. All I need to do is find the right path. Just another moment . . ."

Her face was caked with blood, her clothes were torn, her skin scabbed and burnt. But she was still the most beautiful woman Daine had ever seen, and the light in her eyes gave him the strength to fight the storm.

And then she vanished.

The sphere was glowing, pulsing in her hand, and then it fell to the floor. Lei and Pierce were gone. Daine saw a shadow in Pierce's place, then it was drawn away into the swirling mass around them.

"No!" he cried. Despair overwhelmed him, shattering his emotional shield. The floor crumbled around them, and Daine and Jode fell toward the darkness, horror howling in triumph.

But as they fell, the moon fell with them.

Cracks appeared, fine at first, then growing and spreading. And as the darkness rose to meet them, the crystal moon shattered into a thousand pieces. The orb became a sphere of pure energy, glowing like the sun, then it burst, flowing out and over Daine and Jode, engulfing them in brilliance.

Daine felt the dragonfire surge once more. The power rose within him, tearing at flesh and spirit, and *pulling*.

And the dream faded away.

Light.

Sunlight.

A desert. He was lying on desert sand, beneath a brilliant sun.

No . . . *two* brilliant suns.

"Daine?" Jode pushed himself to his feet and looked around. "Are you hurt?"

"I don't think so," Daine said. He sat up. Something was wrong. Something was missing. *The dragonfire.* That sense of burning energy, the strange presence within—it was gone.

Suddenly the earth shook and everything changed. Air, sand, even the suns; for a moment they seemed to flicker and almost fade away.

"Where are we?" Daine whispered.

"This is a dream," Jode said, looking around. "We're on the fringes of Dal Quor."

"It's no dream of mine," Daine said, looking at the two suns.

"No, I don't think it is." Jode put his hand on Daine's chest, and his dragonmark glowed. "I don't know what's happened. But I don't think you're dreaming any more."

"What are you talking about?" Daine said. The ripple came again, stronger this time. When it passed, the sand had become a sheet of red glass.

"These quakes—I think they're because of what we did. The plane is falling out of alignment with Eberron. I don't know if that's the reason or not, but you've become like me. You've lost your connection to your body."

"No."

"Then wake up." Jode held out his hand.

Daine took it, and he thought about that first dream in Karul'tash, remembering what he'd done.

Wake up.

He opened his eyes . . . and the desert remained.

"Lei," he said. "Pierce. Are they—"

"They should be fine," Jode said. "Pierce said their connection was failing. They disappeared before the moon shattered. There's no reason their spirits wouldn't have returned to their bodies."

Lei. He saw her in his mind, bloody and beautiful, proud and strong. Challenging the Woodsman. Looking at him in the night of Thelanis, with the moon in her eyes. He remembered her warmth in his arms. *There'll be time for us later,* he'd told her.

"No," Daine said. "No. I don't accept this. There's a way out of here. There's got to be. And we're going to find it." He looked down at Jode. "For both of us."

Another tremor. Fractures ran across the surface of glass desert.

"We're not alone here," Jode said. "We may have stopped the Dreaming Dark from opening its gates, but the quori still rule this realm. We'll need to stay on the fringes, to keep moving."

"Whatever we need to do. But I will find my way back to her, Jode."

"Even if you have to face a thousand nightmares to do it?"

Daine nodded. "I believe that we just saved the world. How hard can this be?"

Jode smiled and held out his hand. "Then let's go, my friend. If the right woman is dreaming, I know an inn with a tribex stew the likes of which you'll never find in the waking world."

Daine clasped his hand, and the two of them faded away.

EPILOGUE

CORVAGURA
RIEDRA
Barrakas 5, 997 YK

Lei opened her eyes.

Did it work? Even as her spirit was being torn from the crystal orb, she'd found the proper thread and sent the command. Had she acted in time?

She forced herself to her feet and staggered toward the nearest opening. Her chest ached with phantom pain, but there was no blood on her skin, no broken bones. She was awake, back in the Riedran monolith.

She reached the arch and peered out into the night. The moons had barely moved. It seemed that time passed more quickly in Dal Quor than it did on Eberron. She searched the sky, looking . . .

There! The dark orb was still in the sky, just barely visible. The thirteenth moon. Her heart sank.

Then the moon simply faded away.

We did it. There was no doubt in her mind. She knew the power that lay in the crystal orb. She'd felt it, merged with it. If the moon was pulled away, Dal Quor was trapped once more. Now they just had to return to Thelanis and find a gateway that would take them back to Khorvaire. With the help of the Dusk Queen, they could be home by morning.

Lei. Return. There is danger. Pierce's thoughts flowed into her mind, and his concern shattered her sense of elation. She turned, and walked over to Pierce . . . and stopped short in surprise.

Xu'sasar was sprawled on the ground.

"What happened?" Lei said.

"I do not know. She is alive, but unconscious. Kin is nowhere to be seen."

"What about . . . Shira?"

Pierce looked away. "Shira is no more. We have other concerns. Look to Daine."

Lei's heart raced. She looked across the floor and saw him still stretched out on the ground. Panic rose as she moved to his side, but she could see his chest rising and falling. He was alive.

Then Lei saw what Pierce was talking about. There was a circle around Daine, a pattern painted in silver and gold. It was a summoning circle, designed to aid in the conjuring or binding of spirits. Then Lei noticed something else. Daine's sword . . . his scabbard had been replaced, and his sword now rested in the jeweled sheath Daine had taken from the Bier of the Sleeper.

Daine stirred. His eyes opened and he sat up with a start, glancing about wildly. Lei reached out to him, and he seized her hand as if it were a rope that might pull him from a stormy sea. Then he took a deep breath and smiled at her.

"It's good to be home," he said.

Glossary

aberrant dragonmark: There are twelve *dragonmarks*, but stories say that when dragonmarked bloodlines mingle, they can produce warped marks. Like the true dragonmarks, these bestow magical powers, but these powers are dark and dangerous and said to take a terrible toll on the mind and body of the bearer.

adamantine: An alloy of astonishing strength, adamantine can only be forged through the use of magic. Adamantine weapons are virtually indestructible and can cut through any lesser material.

Alina Lorridan Lyrris: A gnome wizard with considerable wealth and influence. Whether she is a true criminal or simply amoral, Alina is a dangerous woman who usually works in the shadows. Once she lived in the city of Metrol, where she employed *Daine*. Currently she resides in the Den'iyas district of Sharn.

Argonnessen: A large continent to the southeast of Khorvaire, said to be the home of dragons.

artificer: A spellworker who channels magical energy through objects, creating temporary or permanent tools and weapons.

Aureon: The Sovereign of Law and Lore, the source of order and knowledge. Followers of the Sovereign Host say that Aureon gives guidance to rulers and those who pass judgment, guides the scribe and the student, and is said to have devised the principles wizards use to work their spells. Aureon is occasionally depicted as a noble blue dragon.

Balinor: The Sovereign of Horn and Hunt. Followers of the Sovereign Host say that Balinor guides anyone who must interact with the animal world, both hunter and farmer. A common oath is *Balinor's bow!*

Blacklion: A forgehold of House Cannith. During the Last War, Aleisa and Talin d'Cannith worked on warforged at the Blacklion Forgehold.

"breather": A derogatory term used by the warforged to describe non-construct creatures, i.e., elves, humans, halflings.

Breland: The largest of the original Five Nations of Galifar, Breland is a center of heavy industry. The current ruler of Breland is King Boranel ir'Wynarn.

Broken Oath: See *Qaltiar*.

Cannith, House: The dragonmarked House of Making.

Casalon: A fortified city in Cyre, destroyed by the Mourning.

changeling: Members of the changeling race possess a limited ability to change face and form, allowing a changeling to disguise itself as a member of another race or to impersonate an individual. Changelings are said to be the offspring of humans and doppelgangers. They are relatively few in number and have no lands or culture of their own but are scattered across Khorvaire.

Colchyn: A mighty boar found beneath the Hunter's Moon of Thelanis.

cold fire: Magical flame that produces no heat and does not burn. Cold fire is used to provide light in most cities of Khorvaire.

Corvagura: One of the largest provinces in the nation of Riedra. Corvagura is a realm of fertile plains and rain forests.

Crooked Tree: An inn found beneath the Deepwood Moon of Thelanis. Despite being in the dominion of the Woodsman, the Crooked Tree is a free house that stands outside the Woodsman's rule.

crown: The copper crown is the lowest denomination of coin minted under the rule of Galifar.

Cyre: One of the original Five Nations of Galifar, known for its fine arts and crafts. The governor of Cyre was traditionally raised to the throne of Galifar, but in 894 YK, Kaius of Karrnath, Wroann of Breland, and Thalin of Thrane rebelled against Mishann of Cyre. During the war, Cyre lost significant amounts of territory to elf and goblin mercenaries, creating the nations of Valenar and Darguun. In 994 YK, Cyre was devastated by a disaster of unknown origin that transformed the nation into a hostile wasteland populated by deadly monsters. Breland offered sanctuary to the survivors of the Mourning, and most of the Cyran refugees have taken advantage of this amnesty.

Cyran dusksinger: A nocturnal songbird once native to the nation of Cyre, the dusksinger is most likely extinct in the wake of the Mourning. Cyran commandos often use the calls of the dusksinger as recognition signals.

d'Cannith, Aaren: Dragonmarked artificer, one-time baron of Metrol, and member of the Cannith Council based in Cyre. The official records of the house credit Aaren with the mystical breakthrough that gave true sentience to the warforged. Aaren was fascinated by the mysterious continent of Xen'drik, and some say his work was based on ancient secrets recovered there. Aaren passed away in 984 YK. He is survived by his son *Merrix d'Cannith*.

d'Cannith, Aleisa: A dragonmarked artificer of House Cannith and mother of *Lei d'Cannith*. Aleisa was involved with the development of the warforged, but all records of her work were lost in the war. She is believed to have died in Cyre on the Day of Mourning.

d'Cannith, Banon: An artificer stationed at the forgehold of Blacklion.

d'Cannith, Hadran: A dragonmarked heir. Hadran's ancestors were one of the first branches of House Cannith to set roots in Sharn, and he possesses considerable wealth and influence. A widower with no children, Hadran arranged a betrothal with *Lei d'Cannith*.

d'Cannith, Lei: A dragonmarked heir, daughter of *Aleisa d'Cannith*. Lei studied the mystical arts in Sharn and Metrol. Like many young artificers, she chose to serve in the Cannith support corps during the war. She served with the military forces of the Five Nations to maintain the warforged soldiers and other weapons each nation had purchased from Cannith. In 993 YK, her parents arranged for her betrothal to *Hadran d'Cannith*, but Lei's father insisted that she serve a term in the military before her marriage. Lei was assigned to the Southern Command of Cyre, where she served with *Daine, Pierce*, and *Jode*. In 996 YK, she was excoriated from House Cannith (see *City of Towers*), the reasons for this remain a mystery.

d'Cannith, Merrix: As a baron of House Cannith, Merrix oversees house activities in the vicinity of Sharn. Son of *Aaren d'Cannith*, Merrix is a skilled artificer who has spent a decade working on new warforged designs. In the wake of the Last War he has shown shrewd political instincts and has moved to take advantage of the chaos created by the destruction of the House Council. He is the most influential Cannith baron in Breland, and many believe that he hopes to seize control of the House itself.

d'Deneith, Morim: A soldier of House Deneith. A cruel man, he served as one of Alina Lorridan Lyrris's household guards during the Last War.

Daine: A soldier and one-time mercenary, Daine was once an heir of House Deneith. Born in Cyre, he is known to have worked for *Alina Lorridan Lyrris* for an extended period of time. In 988 YK he left House Deneith, forsaking his birthright in order to serve with the Queen's Guard of Cyre, ultimately rising to the rank of captain in the Southern Command. Following the *Mourning* and the destruction of Cyre, he has led the survivors of his troop to Sharn.

Dal Quor: One of the outer planes of existence, also known as the region of dreams. Thousands of years ago, the inhabitants of Dal Quor invaded the land of Xen'drik, fighting the giants that lived there. The giants fought back with powerful magic that completely severed the connection between the two planes. While physical travel between the planes is difficult, mortal spirits still travel to Dal Quor when they dream.

Darkhart, Jura: Born Jura d'Cannith, this dragonmarked aristocrat was expelled from House Cannith after marrying a dryad. He remained in Sharn even after being condemned as an excoriate. His wife died in 995 YK.

Darkheart, Lady: The youngest of the Darkwood Daughters, this faerie is also known as the Heart of the Darkwood Grove. A powerful wood spirit, she was betrothed to Torenas the Woodsman but sought to escape this fate. The Lady Thelania helped her escape to Eberron, but there she was bound in marriage to Jura Darkhart. Ultimately her spirit was trapped in a darkwood staff, where it remains to this day.

Dark Six: The six malevolent deities of the Sovereign Host, whose true names are not known.

Darkwood: This rare lumber is named for its pitch-black color. It is as hard as oak but remarkably light—almost half the weight of most types of lumber. It is often used in the creation of magical wands and staves.

Deneith, House: A dragonmarked house bearing the Mark of Sentinel.

Deepwood Moon: One of the many regions of Thelanis. The Deepwood Moon is one of the realms of night, and is under the rule of the Woodsman.

Dolurrh: The plane of the dead. When mortals die, their spirits are said to travel to Dolurrh and then slowly fade away, passing to whatever final fate awaits the dead.

Donal: A soldier in the Cyran army. Donal served under *Daine* at the battle in Keldan Ridge. He has not been seen since the Mourning.

Dorn Plateau: A large plateau on Dorn Peak.

"Dorn's Teeth!": A mild oath invoking Dol Dorn, the Sovereign Lord of War.

dragon: 1) A reptilian creature possessing great physical and mystical power. 2) A platinum coin bearing an image of a dragon on one face. The platinum dragon is the highest denomination of coin minted under the rule of Galifar.

dragonmark: 1) A mystical mark that appears on the surface of the skin and grants mystical powers to its bearer. 2) A slang term for the bearer of a dragonmark.

Dragonmarked Houses: One of the thirteen families whose bloodlines carry the potential to manifest a dragonmark. Many of the dragonmarked houses existed before the kingdom of Galifar, and they have used their mystical powers to gain considerable political and economic influence. See *dragonmark, War of the Mark*.

dragonshard: A form of mineral with mystical properties, said to be a shard of one of the great progenitor dragons. There are three different types of shard, each with different properties. A dragonshard has no abilities in and of itself, but an artificer or wizard can use a shard to create an object with useful effects. *Siberys shards* fall from the sky and have the potential to enhance the power of dragonmarks. *Eberron shards* are found in the soil and enhance traditional magic. *Khyber shards* are found deep below the surface of the world and are used as a focus binding mystical energy.

dream serpent: Large snakes native to the continent of Xen'drik. The venom of the dream serpent causes its victim to fall into a deep slumber. The drow of Xen'drik often hunt dream serpents, both as a source of food and to harvest the potent venom of these creatures.

Dreaming Dark: 1) A secret order of psionic spies and assassins that serves as the eyes and hands of the quori in Dal Quor, the Region of Dreams. 2) The spiritual force that guides all of the quori; also known as *il-Lashtavar*, the Darkness that Dreams.

drow: A humanoid race found on the continent of Xen'drik. There are many similarities between drow and elves, and the drow are often called "dark elves"—a reference to their pitch-black skin and their nocturnal tendencies.

dryad: A fey wood-spirit. A dryad is bound to a specific tree, although she can usually venture out and travel a short distance. Dryads associated with darkwood trees—such as Lady Darkheart—are particularly powerful.

Eberron: 1) The world. 2) A mythical dragon said to have formed the world from her body in primordial times and to have given birth to natural life. Also known as "the Dragon Between." See *Khyber, Siberys*.

Eidolon: A gestalt entity formed from spirits of the dead that have somehow avoided Dolurrh. The religion of the Silver Flame holds that noble souls are drawn to the Flame after death. If true, this would make the Silver Flame an eidolon of immense age and power.

Eldeen Reaches: Once this term was used to describe the vast stretches of woodland found on the west coast of Khorvaire, inhabited mostly by nomadic shifter tribes and druidic sects. In 958 YK the people of western Aundair broke ties with the Audairian crown and joined their lands to the Eldeen Reaches, vastly increasing the population of the nation and bringing it into the public eye.

eternal fire: See cold fire.

everbright lantern: A lantern infused with cold fire, creating a permanent light source. These items are used to provide illumination in most of the cities and larger communities of Khorvaire. An everbright lantern usually has a shutter allowing the light to be sealed off when darkness is desirable.

excoriate: A person who has been expelled from a dragonmarked house. An excoriate is stripped of the family name and any property held by the house and is not welcome at house enclaves. Members and allies of the house are urged to shun excoriates. Prior to the foundation of Galifar, houses often flayed the victim's dragonmark off of his body. While only temporary, this was a brutal and visible way of displaying the anger of the house. See *dragonmarked houses*.

Eye of Deneith: Most of the dragonmark houses have two heraldic emblems—a magical beast associated with the history of the house and a simpler, iconic symbol. The three-headed chimera is the beast of Deneith, while its icon is a silver eye surrounded by the golden rays of the sun. This symbol is known as the Watchful Eye or the Eye of Deneith.

Fernia: A plane of existence known as the Sea of Fire.

Ferric: The innkeeper of the Crooked Tree. Ferric is a powerful fey in his own right, and he gains additional power from serving the Crooked Tree. A cunning trickster, Ferric is also a dedicated enemy of the Woodsman.

fey: A term used to describe the natives of the plane of Thelanis. The fey—also known as faeries—are creatures of magic and mystery. Many fey have a close bond to nature, such as the dryad wood-spirit. In the lore of Eberron, fey are typically seen as tricksters.

Fifth: Another name for the warforged Pierce, used by Talin and Aleisa d'Cannith.

Final Lands: The afterlife of the Qaltiar. The Final Lands are said to be a series of tests for the fallen warrior. Those who succeed in these tests get to join the spirits of other triumphant heroes in an unending battle.

firebinding: A technique taught to artificers. This art includes the creation of cold fire and true flame, allowing an artificer to produce a flaming sword or to slay an armored knight by boiling him in his armor.

Five Nations: The five provinces of the Kingdom of Galifar—Aundair, Breland, Cyre, Karrnath, and Thrane.

"Flame!": A common oath derived from the divine force known as the Silver Flame.

Flamewind: A sphinx residing in the city of Sharn, where she is respected for her oracular powers. She is an occasional agent of Thelania, and passed information to Daine, Lei, Jode, and Pierce on behalf of the Queen of Dusk.

'forged: A slang term for the warforged.

forgehold: A large facility designed to research and produce magical goods or techniques. Most of the forgeholds in Khorvaire belong to *House Cannith*.

Fourth: Another name for the warforged now known as Harmattan.

Galifar: 1) A cunning warrior and skilled diplomat who forged five nations into a single kingdom that came to dominate the continent of Khorvaire. 2) The kingdom of Galifar I, which came to an end in 894 YK with the start of the Last War. 3) A golden coin minted by the kingdom, bearing the image of the first king. The golden galifar is still in use today and is worth ten sovereigns.

Gerrion: A gambler and guide who made his home in *Stormreach*. Born of human and Sulatar parents, Gerrion lured Daine and Lakashtai into a trap. Gerrion was poisoned and left for dead in the plane of *Fernia*.

Ghallanda, House: A dragonmarked house bearing the Mark of Hospitality.

ghulra: The mark on the forehead of a warforged. Every warforged has a unique ghulra, much as humans have unique fingerprints.

glamerweave: A general term used to describe clothing that has been magically altered for cosmetic purposes. A glamerweave outfit may enhance the appearance of the wearer—concealing blemishes, adding color to hair or eyes—or it may simply possess colors or patterns than could never be replicated with mundane fabrics. Glimmersilk is one form of glamerweave.

glyph: A mystical symbol. Often used to refer to a *glyph of warding*, a magical security system that will unleash a spell on anyone who crosses the glyph without speaking the proper phrase.

gnome: A race of small humanoids. Gnomes are found across Khorvaire but are concentrated in the nation of Zilargo.

goblinoid: A general term encompassing three humanoid species—the small and cunning goblins, the warlike hobgoblins, and the large and powerful bugbears.

gorgon: A large, bull-like creature with scales as hard as iron and breath that turns its enemies to stone. The gorgon is the heraldic symbol of House Cannith. The flesh of the gorgon is considered a delicacy in certain nations, in part because of the difficulty and danger involved in acquiring it.

half-orc: When humans and orcs interbreed, the offspring typically possess characteristics of both races. These half-orcs are not as bestial in appearance as their orc forbears, but they are larger and stronger than most humans and usually possess a few orcish features, such as a gray skin tone or pronounced canine teeth. Half-orcs are most common in the Shadow Marches but can be found across Khorvaire.

Harmattan: A charismatic warforged insurgent. Harmattan possesses unusual physical abilities.

High Walls: A district in the Lower Tavick's Landing ward of Sharn. During the Last War many foreign nationals living in the city were relocated to High Walls, and the majority of the Cyran refugees living in Sharn reside in this district.

Hul'drac: One of the great spirits worshipped by the Qaltiar. Hul'drac is the spirit of the shifting panther. He is a cunning hunter who uses guile to avoid the enemy's blows, and is second only to Vulkoor in the eyes of the Jalaq Qaltiar.

Hunter's Moon: One of the regions of Thelanis. The Hunter's Moon is one of the realms of night, and it is ruled by the Huntsman.

Huntsman: A faerie lord of Thelanis. The Huntsman is one of the Nine Brothers of Night, each of whom holds dominion over a realm in Thelanis. The Woodsman's domain is known as the Hunter's Moon.

Huwen: A fey spirit who lives beneath the Deepwood Moon in Thelanis. Huwen takes the form of a crow. He has telepathic abilities and claims to feed on secrets.

Hydra: 1) A large reptilian creature with multiple heads. 2) An unusual warforged who serves Harmattan. Hydra's consciousness is spread between multiple bodies. While Pierce destroyed a number of Hydra's bodies, it is unknown how many more the warforged may possess.

Indigo: A warforged assassin who serves *Harmattan*.

Inspired, the: The lords of the land of Riedra. The subjects of the Inspired say that these nobles are guided by the wisest spirits of the past. The *kalashtar* believe that the Inspired are conduits for quori spirits: the direct agents of the *Dreaming Dark* on Eberron.

ir': When attached to a family name, this prefix indicates one of the aristocratic lines of Galifar. The descendants of King Galifar I belong to the ir'Wynarn line.

ir'Soras, Teral: Once a councilor to the court of Cyre, Teral ir'Soras retired from politics to enjoy his middle years. This quiet life came to an end when the Mourning destroyed Cyre. The wounded counselor was found by *illithids*, and these alien creatures transformed him, granting him terrible power in exchange for his service. Teral organized an illithid cult in Sharn but was killed by *Pierce*.

Jalaq Qaltiar: A particular tribe of the Qaltiar drow. Xu'sasar is the last surviving member of the Jalaq tribe.

Jholeg: A goblin scout who served in the Cyran army under *Daine's* command.

Jode: A former companion of *Daine*. Jode was a halfling with the Mark of Healing, though he never admitted to having a tie to House Jorasco. In 988 YK he took up service in the Queen's Guard of Cyre along with *Daine*. He served as a healer and occasional scout, using his dragonmark and quick wits to assist his friend. He died in 996 YK, though the circumstances of his death remain a mystery.

Jorasco, House: A dragonmarked house bearing the Mark of Healing.

kalashtar: The kalashtar are humans touched by the Dal Quor, the region of dreams. Every kalashtar has a bond to one of the rebellious quori spirits who opposed the *Dreaming Dark* and were forced to flee Dal Quor. By drawing on this bond, kalashtar are often able to develop significant mental powers. Kalashtar use the name of their quori spirit as a suffix. Thus, Lakashtai and Tetkashtai are both kalashtar of the lineage of *Kashtai*.

Karrn: A citizen of Karrnath.

Karrnath: One of the original Five Nations of Galifar. Karrnath is a cold, grim land whose people are renowned for their martial prowess. The current ruler of Karrnath is King Kaius ir'Wynarn III.

Karul'tash: An ancient forgehold built by the giants of Xen'drik.

Keldan Ridge: A remote region of hills in southern Cyre. While passing along the ridge in 994, Daine's soldiers encountered a heavily armed force of unknown nationality. This enemy scattered the Cyran forces. It was this forced retreat that pushed *Daine*, Lei, Pierce, and Jode outside the radius of the Mourning.

Kellan: A hero of folklore, whose exploits are told to the children of the Five Nations. Kellan was said to have been a knight of Galifar, in the region that is now Aundair. He patrolled the edge of the great forest of the west, and in the process he fought many monsters and occasionally found himself in the plane of Thelanis, where he pitted both blade and cunning against the fey.

Kesht: A shifter who served under *Daine's* command during the Last War. He was killed in the battle of Keldan Ridge.

Khorvaire: One of the continents of Eberron.

Khyber: 1) The underworld. 2) A mythical dragon, also known as "the Dragon Below." After killing Siberys, Khyber was imprisoned by Eberron and transformed into the underworld. Khyber is said to have given birth to a host of demons and other unnatural creatures. See *Eberron, Siberys*.

Kin: A changeling from the Eldeen Reaches, Kin was taken to Thelanis at a young age where he was adopted into the service of Thelania.

Ko'molaq: A spirit known in the legends of the Qaltiar drow, Ko'molaq takes the form of an immense, two-headed serpent. His name translates to "the Keeper of Secrets," and he is said to possess knowledge of many hidden things.

Krazhal: A dwarf siege engineer who served *Daine* during the Last War. He was killed in the battle of Keldan Ridge.

Kundarak, House: A dragonmarked house bearing the Mark of Warding.

Kura'tra: One of the great spirits worshipped by the Qaltiar drow. Kura'tra is the spirit of the tilxin bird, a clever creature who relies on speed and keen senses to outwit the deadly predators of Xen'drik. While the Qaltiar have more respect for predators than prey, Kura'tra is seen as a wise and cunning spirit, and the drow may call on her for inspiration or speed in battle.

Laraek ixen korth!: A Draconic invocation, roughly translating to "Empowered weapon of fire!"

Lakashtai: An agent of the *Dreaming Dark*, Lakashtai deceived Daine and tricked him into killing *Tashana*. Lakashtai stole a powerful artifact from *Karul'tash* and escaped to *Dal Quor*.

lallis hound: A breed of hunting dog popular in Cyre. Much of the breed was wiped out in the *Mourning*, but lallis hounds can still be found across Khorvaire.

Last War, the: This conflict began in 894 YK with the death of King Jarot ir'Wynarn, the last king of Galifar. Following Jarot's death, three of his five children refused to follow the ancient traditions of succession, and the kingdom split. The War lasted over a hundred years, and it took the utter destruction of Cyre to bring the other nations to the negotiating table. No one has admitted defeat, but no one wants to risk being the next victim of the Mourning. The chronicles are calling the conflict "the Last War," hoping that the bloodshed might have finally slaked humanity's thirst for battle. Only time will tell if this hope is in vain.

Lharvion: 1) The eighth month of the calendar of Galifar. 2) One of the twelve moons of Eberron.

Lyrandar, House: A dragonmarked house bearing the Mark of Storm.

magewright: A general term for any professional who uses magic to enhance the skills of his trade. The typical magewright can only perform one or two spells. Examples include the blacksmith who uses magic to improve his craft, the lamplighter who produces everbright lanterns, and the auger who uses magic to divine the future for her clients.

'Mark: A slang term for the bearer of a dragonmark. See *dragonmark*.

Metrol: The capital of Cyre. Metrol was destroyed by the Mourning.

mithral: A silvery metal that is just as strong as iron, but far lighter and more flexible.

Monan: A changeling who served *Teral ir'Soras*. Monan fought *Daine* in Sharn and nearly destroyed him with an insidious mental attack.

Mourning, the: A disaster that occurred on Olarune 20, 994 YK. The origin and precise nature of the Mourning are unknown. On Ollarune 20, gray mists spread across Cyre, and anything caught within the mists was transformed or destroyed. See *the Mournland*.

Mournland, the: A common name for the wasteland left behind in the wake of *the Mourning*. A wall of dead-gray mist surrounds the borders of the land that once was Cyre. Behind this mist, the land has been transformed into something dark and twisted. Most creatures that weren't killed were transformed into horrific monsters. Stories speak of storms of blood, corpses that do not decompose, ghostly soldiers fighting endless battles, and far worse things.

Nine, the: A term used to refer to the nine deities of the Sovereign Host.

Onatar: A deity of the Sovereign Host, Onatar is Lord of Fire and Forge. He is the patron of both smith and artificer, lending skill to those who follow the traditions of old.

Pierce: A warforged soldier, Pierce was built by House Cannith and sold to the army of Cyre. He was designed to serve as a skirmisher and scout, specializing in ranged combat. His comrades named him based on his skill with his longbow. Following the destruction of Cyre, he has chosen to remain with *Daine*, his last captain.

Qaltiar: One of the drow tribes of Xen'drik; the name translates into "Broken Oath." The Qaltiar drow are driven by an ancient vendetta against the giants of Xen'drik and the *Sulatar* drow. Where many drow tribes worship *Vulkoor*, the Qaltiar consider Vulkoor to be just one of the great spirits of the wild. This often causes tension with other drow tribes. *Xu'sasar* is a member of the *Jalaq* tribe of the Qaltiar.

Quori: Common name for someone or something from the plane of Dal Quor. The inhabitants of Dal Quor are spiritual entities that typically appear as nightmarish to human eyes. Many of these spirits take pleasure in shaping human nightmares and preying on dreaming mortals.

Riedra: The largest country on the continent of *Sarlona*. Once a collection of warring states, Riedra overcame its internal conflicts only to break all ties with the rest of Eberron. After a thousand years of silence, Riedra is only beginning to reestablish diplomatic relations with the nations of Khorvaire, and much about the realm remains a mystery.

sahuagin: A race of amphibious humanoids that live in the oceans of Eberron. Aggressive sahuagin tribes often attack ships that cross their territory; other sahuagin sell their services as aquatic guides.

Sarlona: One of the continents of Eberron. Humanity arose in Sarlona, and colonists from Sarlona established human civilization on Khorvaire.

Scorpion Wraith: A sacred warrior of the *Qaltiar* drow, blessed with the speed and skill of the predator. "Scorpion wraith" translates to *"Vulk N'tash"* in the tongue of the Qaltiar.

selas leaves: A sweet herb found in the Eldeen Reaches, selas leaves are often used in the cuisine of Aundair.

Sharn: Also known as the City of Towers, Sharn is the largest city in Khorvaire.

shifting panther: Drow name for the displacer beast, a magical predator found in Xen'drik and western Khorvaire. The displacer beast appears to be a few feet away from its true position, making it difficult to fight.

Shen'kar: The commander of one of the scorpion wraith squads of the *Jalaq Qaltiar.*

Shira: A magical intelligence created during an ancient war between the giants of Xen'drik and the plane of Dal Quor.

Siberys: 1) The ring of stones that circle the world. 2) A mythical dragon, also called "the Dragon Above." Siberys is said to have been destroyed by Khyber. Some believe that the ring of Siberys is the source of all magic. See *Eberron, Khyber.*

Silver Flame, the: A powerful spiritual force dedicated to cleansing evil influences from the world. Over the last five hundred years, a powerful church has been established around the Silver Flame.

Sivis, House: A dragonmarked house bearing the Mark of Scribing.

Sleeper: A fallen hero. His true identity remains a mystery, but he is said to be a warrior of a past age who won the heart of Thelania. He was defeated in battle, but his remains were preserved in Thelanis, at a tomb known as the Bier of the Sleeper.

Sovereign: 1) A silver coin depicting a current or recent monarch. A sovereign is worth ten crowns. 2) One of the deities of the *Sovereign Host.*

Sovereign Host, the: A pantheistic religion with a strong following across Khorvaire.

Stormreach: The largest human city on the continent of Xen'drik. Once a pirate outpost, this port sees vessels from Khorvaire, Aerenal, and even Sarlona.

Sulatar: One of the drow cultures of Xen'drik. "Sulatar" means "firebinder" in the language of the giants. Thousands of years ago, the Sulatar drow were taught techniques of fire magic by giant wizards, and the dark elves retained much of this knowledge even after the cataclysm that destroyed the giant nations. The Sulatar are deeply religious and believe that their faith will eventually be rewarded with immortality and power with which to conquer all of Eberron.

tal: A beverage from the Talenta Plains. Tal was introduced to the Five Nations by the halflings of House Ghallanda. Made by steeping herbs in boiling water, it serves many purposes depending on the herbs that are used. There are dozens of varieties. Milian tal is typically served cold and is said to settle a fever, while blackroot tal is served hot and is a popular midday drink.

Tarkanan, House: A criminal organization based in Sharn, specializing in theft and assassination. Only people possessing aberrant dragonmarks can join House Tarkanan, and the members of the house are taught to hone these skills to aid in their work. The organization is structured as a mockery of the true dragonmarked houses, in remembrance of the aberrant alliance that arose during the War of the Mark.

Tashana: A psionic warrior who sought to eliminate *Lakashtai*. Daine originally believed that Tashana was a servant of the *Dreaming Dark*. He fought Tashana and mortally wounded her, only to discover that she was a *kalashtar* agent opposing the darkness.

Test of Siberys: A tradition among the dragonmarked houses. When a child comes of age, he undergoes a test that is intended to draw out a dragonmark if he possesses one. The precise form of the test varies considerably based on the house and the powers of the associated dragonmark.

Thaask: A *sahuagin* guide who sells his services to ships traveling through the Straits of Shargon.

Thelania: A powerful spirit of Thelanis and sovereign of a large domain within that plane. Thelania has appeared in many tales under many different names. She is most often referred to the Queen of Dusk and Shadows, or simply Dusk. In tales, she often assists heroes, providing them with magical gifts or useful advice. However, the heroes who receive her favors rarely live long and happy lives.

Thelanis: One of the outer planes of existence, also known as the Faerie Court. Thelanis is best known as being the home of the fey. Some say that it is one of the sources of magic and that the energy of Thelanis flows into the world where it is shaped by wizards and sorcerers.

thorn: A minor fey spirit. Thorns are warriors who serve the faerie lords of Thelanis, especially those with dominion over woodlands. They wield large thorns in place of swords and often coat their weapons with a venom that paralyzes the victim.

tilxin bird: A small bird native to the land of Xen'drik. The tilxin bird possesses supernatural speed and maneuverability. Its blood is a valuable component for magic items that enhance speed, and House Cannith pays well for tilxin blood. The Qaltiar drow hunt tilxin birds as a test of speed and cunning.

Tooth of the Wanderer: A powerful artifact now in the possession of Xu'sasar. The Tooth of the Wanderer is a weapon that shifts its form according to the desires of the wielder. Its full capabilities are currently unknown, but it is apparently indestructible and can secrete poison upon demand.

Tower of a Thousand Teeth: A fortress at the heart of Dal Quor.

Towers of the Twelve: A foundation for mystical research and development formed as a joint effort by all of the dragonmarked houses.

Traveler, the: Loosely aligned with the Dark Six, this deity is the embodiment of change and artifice. The Traveler is a consummate shapeshifter who cannot be bound by a single shape or gender. Alone among the deities, the Traveler is often said to walk the earth, though such tales can usually be traced to the actions of changeling priests. A common proverb is "Beware the gifts of the Traveler," a reference to the fact that good fortune often has unexpected consequences.

Valenar: 1) A nation in southeastern Khorvaire, founded by an army of warrior elves. 2) Common name for someone or something from the Valenar nation.

Vulkoor: The primary spirit worshipped by the drow of Xen'drik. Vulkoor is the great scorpion and is seen both as a deadly hunter and wise provider. While all scorpions are considered to be eyes of Vulkoor, the drow usually depict him as a ghost scorpion. Drow warriors often wear armor made from the pale white chitin of the ghost scorpion, which they consider to be one of Vulkoor's many gifts.

Xen'drik: A large continent south of Khorvaire. Once home to an advanced civilization of giants, Xen'drik was devastated by a terrible cataclysm almost forty thousand years ago. The effects of this disaster still linger. Space and time are often unpredictable in Xen'drik, and many strange creatures and cultures have appeared in this shattered land.

Wanderer: A spirit revered by the Qaltiar drow, the Wanderer cannot be tied to a single shape or creature. Some have compared this trickster god to the Traveler of the Dark Six.

War of the Mark: Five hundred years before the creation of Galifar, the dragonmarked families joined forces to eliminate those who possessed aberrant marks. Ultimately the aberrants joined forces and formed an army of their own, under the leadership of Lord Halas Tarkanan and his lover, the Lady of the Plague. Despite Tarkanan's skill and personal power, his troops were few in number and poorly organized, and he could not stand against the dragonmarked. In the aftermath of the war, the families formally established the first dragonmarked houses.

warforged: A race of humanoid constructs crafted from wood, leather, metal, and stone, and given life and sentience through magic. The warforged were created by House Cannith, which sought to produce tireless, expendable soldiers capable of adapting to any tactical situation. Cannith developed a wide range of military automatons, but the spark of true sentience eluded them until 965 YK, when *Aaren d'Cannith* perfected the first of the modern warforged. A warforged soldier is roughly the same shape as an adult male human, though typically slightly taller and heavier. There are many different styles of warforged, each crafted for a specific military function—heavily-armored infantry troops, faster scouts and skirmishers, and many more. While warforged are brought into existence with the knowledge required to fulfill their function, they have the capacity to learn, and with the War, many are searching their souls—and questioning whether they have souls—and wondering what place they might have in a world at peace.

Watchful Eye: The emblem of House Deneith, a golden eye set over a silver sun.

Whitehearth: A House Cannith forgehold in Cyre. Presumed destroyed in the *Mourning*.

Woodsman: A faerie lord of Thelanis. Torenas the Woodsman is the youngest of the Nine Brothers of Night, each of whom holds dominion over a realm in Thelanis. The Woodsman's domain is known as the Deepwood Moon. Torenas is betrothed to Lady Darkheart.

Xu'sasar: A scorpion wraith of the *Qaltiar* drow.

YK: Most of the nations of Khorvaire make use of the calendar of Galifar. The current date is reckoned from the birth of the Kingdom of Galifar, in the Year since the founding of the Kingdom, or more simply, YK.

Zimi: A musician at the Crooked Tree, Zimi is a half-insect spirit known as a grig.

THE LOST MARK TRILOGY

Matt Forbeck

Twelve Dragonmarks.

Sigils of immense magical power.

Borne by scions of mighty Houses,
used through the centuries to wield authority
and shape wonders throughout Eberron.
But there are only twelve marks.

Until now.

MARKED FOR DEATH
Volume One

THE ROAD TO DEATH
Volume Two

THE QUEEN OF DEATH
Volume Three
OCTOBER 2006

For more information visit **www.wizards.com**

THE DRAGON BELOW TRILOGY

Don Bassingthwaite

In Eberron, there are terrors older than the nations
of men. In the dark places of the world, the secrets
of the Dragon Below are better left undisturbed....

THE BINDING STONE
Book 1

A chance rescue brings bitter rivals together. With
a mysterious ally, the two warriors embark on a
mission of vengeance, but the enemy waiting for
them in the depths of the Shadow Marches is far
more sinister than any they've faced before.

THE GRIEVING TREE
Book 2

The heroes, now in possession of the magical
Dhakaan sword, head into the monster kingdom
of Droaam. New enemies vie to control them or
kill them, and their nemesis Dah'mir returns to
wreak havoc upon them.

THE KILLING SONG
Book 3
DECEMBER 2006

For more information visit **www.wizards.com**

ENTER THE NEW WORLD OF

THE DREAMING DARK TRILOGY

By Keith Baker

A hundred years of war...

Kingdoms lie shattered, armies are broken, and an entire
country has been laid to waste. Now an uneasy
peace settles on the land.

Into Sharn come four battle-hardened soldiers. Tired of
blood, weary of killing, they only want a place to call home.

The shadowed City of Towers has other plans...

THE CITY OF TOWERS
Volume One

THE SHATTERED LAND
Volume Two

THE GATES OF NIGHT
Volume Three
NOVEMBER 2006

For more information visit **www.wizards.com**